AWAKEN

MEG CABOT

MACMILLAN

First published 2013 by Macmillan Children's Books
a division of Macmillan Publishers Limited
20 New Wharf Road, London N1 9RR
Basingstoke and Oxford
Associated companies throughout the world
www.panmacmillan.com

ISBN 978-0-330-45389-9

1 3 5 7 9 8 6 4 2

A CIP catalogue record for this book is available from
the British Library.

Printed and bound by CPI Group (UK) Ltd, Croydon CR0 4YY

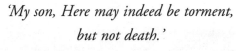

'My son, Here may indeed be torment,
but not death.'
Dante Alighieri, *Purgatorio*, Canto XXVII

In school they told us to follow the rules.

Don't talk to strangers. Safety first, they said. *Walk, don't run – unless it's from a stranger, of course.* We were supposed to run from strangers as fast as we could, the way Persephone, the girl from that old Greek myth, tried to when Hades, the lord of the dead, came after her.

Funny thing about the rules, though. Sometimes they were wrong. According to the rules, no one in our own families was ever supposed to hurt us.

Not running from my own flesh and blood was my first mistake.

My second was running from John Hayden. He was exactly the kind of stranger they were always warning us about in school. No, he didn't offer me candy or drugs. But one look into those storm-filled grey eyes and, even as a naive fifteen-year-old, I could tell what he had to offer was something way more addictive than chocolate or crystal meth.

How was I to know the reason his gaze was so storm-filled was because he, too, knew the pain of being betrayed by someone who, according to the rules, was supposed to care about him?

Maybe that's what kept thrusting the two of us back together, no matter how far we tried to run. Why else would we both have ended up on an island named for the human bones that had been found there? It turns out we have more than a few skeletons in our closets.

By now the bones that have earned this place its infamous name – Isla Huesos, Spanish for Island of Bones – are supposed to have been removed. But the tendency for cruel acts of deception to be committed on Isla Huesos's tempest-tossed shores hasn't waned.

Now it's not my family *or* John that's coming for me, but a storm. I know from the weather alerts I keep receiving on my cellphone. A large tropical cyclone, 'producing extreme winds and dangerously high flood conditions', is expected to reach landfall soon on the island where my mom was hoping she and I could make a 'new start'. According to the latest warning, I should proceed with caution (*walk, don't run*) to the nearest emergency shelter.

The problem is, I'm eighteen hundred miles *below* the earth's crust and the storm's projected path.

Still, every time my phone vibrates and I look down to see one of the alerts, my pulse speeds up a little. Not because I'm in imminent danger, but because I know people who are.

It's especially upsetting because, in a lot of ways, my family has turned out to be like the seawall Isla Huesos's community leaders built in order to protect its low-lying areas from flooding: They're not very reliable. Some of them, in fact, have turned out to be made from inferior material. They crumbled and broke apart instead of doing what they were supposed to do: keep their loved ones from drowning.

But maybe that's what I deserve for being trusting enough to believe the rules would keep me safe.

All that's changed now. This time, the only rules I'm following are my own.

And this time, when the storm comes, instead of running from it, I'm going to face it head-on.

I hope it's ready for me.

Always before him many of them stand;
They go by turns each one unto the judgment;
They speak, and hear,
and then are downward hurled.
Dante Alighieri, *Inferno*, Canto V

He Is First.

That's what it said in flowing white script on the T-shirt the girl was wearing.

'Who is *he*?' I asked her. If I hadn't been so tired, I'd have figured it out right away. Instead, I thought the shirt was referring to a new band or the title of a movie or something . . . not that I was going to get to see it any time soon.

'Oh,' the girl said, smiling, clearly happy to be asked. This was evidently why she wore the shirt, to generate questions like mine. I could tell by the cheerful, rehearsed way in which she replied, 'My personal Lord and Saviour. He always comes first.'

Don't do it. Do not *engage.* This isn't the time to have a theological conversation – or any conversation at all – beyond what's necessary. *Remember what John said*, I reminded myself: *There are hundreds of people here, maybe even a thousand. You can't help them all, only the ones who seem the worst off, or might be about to cause trouble . . .*

'Don't you think there might be *some* circumstances in which He'd want you to put yourself first?' I heard myself saying. 'What if there was a fire? Wouldn't He want you to run first and pray later?'

'Yes, of course,' the girl said with a laugh. 'But I'd still be putting Him first in my heart the way He puts me first in His heart. He's always with us, you know, keeping us safe from harm.'

I shouldn't have asked. Even the person in line behind her – a young guy who'd probably died in a jet ski accident, judging by his tropical swim shorts and lack of a shirt – gaped at her in disbelief.

'Have you taken a look at yourself in the mirror lately?' he asked her.

She dropped the smile, appearing startled. 'No. Why? Do I have something in my teeth?'

She reached to open the backpack she had slung over one shoulder, but I put out a hand to stop her. If I hadn't, I suspect she'd have found her compact mirror, then seen what the rest of us could: the crystalline shards of windshield embedded into her blonde hair like diamonds from a tiara, the angry red imprint the steering wheel had left behind on her forehead when the airbag in her car had failed to go off.

No one had kept her safe. But what would be the point in telling her so? She'd probably only start to cry, and then I'd have to waste even more time comforting her, time John had warned we couldn't afford.

'Your teeth are fine,' I said to her hastily. 'You look great. Here, drink this.' I passed her a water glass from my tray. 'You'll feel better.'

For the first time ever, it was hot in the Underworld. That's why I was holding a tray of glasses, each one filled with ice water. It was a ridiculous gesture – like handing out

5

life preservers on the *Titanic*. I couldn't change what had happened to these people. All I could do was make the journey to their final destinations a little more comfortable . . . and try to hurry them along.

The Underworld was currently suffering from overcrowding as well as overheating, to the point where conditions had grown dangerously untenable.

'Thanks,' the girl said, taking the water and sipping it gratefully. This time when she smiled, there was nothing rehearsed about the gesture. 'I'm so thirsty.' She said the latter in a voice of wonder, like out of all the things that had happened to her in the past twenty-four hours, her thirst was the most amazing.

Well, dying can be dehydrating.

'Yeah,' I said. 'Sorry about the heat. We're working on it.'

'Working on it?' the guy in the tropical shorts echoed. 'We've been waiting here for hours. How about some answers instead of water?'

'I know,' I said to Tropical Shorts. 'Sorry. The boat's on its way, I swear. We're trying to accommodate as many of you as we can as quickly as we can, but we're a little backed up at the mo—'

'Why should we believe *you*?' Tropical Shorts interrupted. 'I want to talk to whoever's in charge.'

I felt a spurt of red-hot anger shoot through me, but I fought to remain calm.

'What makes you so sure *I'm* not in charge?' I challenged him.

He burst out laughing. 'Look at you,' he said.

I couldn't help it. I looked down at myself. Whereas most of the people in line were dressed in light casual clothing, like Mr Tropical Shorts – some of them were in hospital gowns or even pyjamas, whatever they'd been wearing when death overtook them – I had on a cap-sleeved gown, the hem of which swept my feet. Even though the material was the lightest cotton, it nevertheless clung damply to my skin, and not just because the waves from the lake had grown more violent than usual and were splashing bits of foam and spray up against the side of the dock. Curls of my long dark hair had slipped from the knot into which I'd tried to tie it, sticking to the back and sides of my neck. I'd have given my cellphone or possibly even my bra for some air-conditioning or a fan.

But it turned out Tropical Shorts wasn't referring to my wardrobe.

'What are you,' he demanded, 'fifteen? Sixteen?'

'Seventeen,' I said, from between teeth I'd gritted in an effort not to throw the entire tray of water glasses at him. 'How old are *you*? Legally you have to be at least eighteen to rent a jet ski in the state of Florida.'

I knew this because my mother complained all the time that kids on personal watercrafts were always racing one another through the mangroves where she was studying her beloved roseate spoonbills. The jet skis hit dolphins and manatees (and sometimes even human snorkelers and scuba divers) just under the surface and killed them without the drivers even being aware of it.

Except for this one. Whatever Tropical Shorts had hit had hit back, hard enough to kill him.

'I'm nineteen,' he said, looking a little stunned. 'How did you know it was a—'

'It's my job to know,' I interrupted. 'You're welcome to speak to the person in charge . . . my boyfriend. That's him over there on the horse.'

I pointed across the beach to the dock opposite the one on which we stood. There, John, on his black horse, Alastor, along with two tall, muscular men clad in black leather, was struggling to hold back a much rowdier crowd. If the line I was managing was discontented, theirs was already actively rioting. No one was being offered glasses of water over there – if they had, the glasses would have been broken over someone's head, and the shards used as weapons.

'Uh, no, thanks,' Tropical Shorts said, glancing uneasily away from John as he yanked on the shirt collar of one man in an attempt to pull him from the throat of another. 'I'm good. I'll just wait here.'

'Yeah,' I said. Despite the seriousness of the situation, I couldn't help smiling to myself a little. 'That's what I thought you'd say.'

Just try to keep them calm, John had said as we'd made our way down to the beach from the castle. *One stone can cause a lot of ripples. A riot is the last thing we need right now.*

Got it, I'd said.

And no need to get physical with them yourself, John had said. *Any sign of trouble, and I'll be there.*

How will you know? I'd asked.

If there's trouble and you're involved, I'll know, he'd said, and given me a smile I'd thought might turn my legs to butter then and there.

I'd managed to avert the riot Tropical Shorts had attempted to cause with his stone, but that didn't mean everything was smooth sailing . . . especially between John and me. We were still searching for ways to smooth the ripples in our relationship. Some were appearing a little rougher to navigate than others. John hadn't wanted me to help down here at the beach. He'd wanted me to stay back at the castle with Mr Graves, tending to my cousin Alex and my best friend, Kayla, who were still recovering from the shock of being whisked from the land of the living to the realm of the dead for their own safety – never an easy adjustment, as I well knew.

But one glance at the sheer number of souls who had shown up on the beach while we'd been in Isla Huesos told me I'd be more useful there than at Alex's and Kayla's bedsides. Eventually even John had to agree.

Still, just because we were able to agree on that didn't mean there weren't going to be more stones in our path. Being in a relationship, I was learning, was hard. It was probably hard even if your boyfriend wasn't a death deity.

If he was, though, talk about issues.

The *He Is First* girl reached out to grasp my bare arm, jostling me from my thoughts.

'Excuse me,' she said. 'What's your name?'

Don't get on a first-name basis with them. This was another piece of advice John had given during my hasty emergency orientation to soul guidance. *You're here to do a job, not make friends.*

'Pierce,' I said to her. I'd appreciated John's warnings, but what was I supposed to do – lie? 'Look, I'm sorry, but I really have to go.' I motioned towards the end of the line, which was snaking down the dock and then out on to the beach, past the dunes. 'I've still got a lot of people to help—'

'Oh, right,' the girl said, nodding sympathetically. 'I know, that storm? I should have listened to the weather alerts and never tried to leave my dad's place. I didn't see that tree falling.' She giggled as if to say, *What a klutz I am for letting that tree smack into my car and kill me!* 'Anyway, I'm Chloe. I just want you to know, Pierce, He puts *you* first in His heart, too.'

At first I didn't know who she was talking about. Then I remembered.

'Uh,' I said. 'Great. Thanks. I have to—'

'No, really,' Chloe said, eager for me to believe. 'It's true; He does.'

Was it? No one had put me first in his heart the day my grandmother had murdered me. Or my ex-best friend, Hannah, when she'd killed herself. Or my guidance counsellor, Jade, the night she was killed. Or what about last night? Who'd put my cousin Alex first at any time during any part of his short, miserable life?

It turned out I wasn't the only one with doubts.

'Do you even know where you are?' Tropical Shorts asked Chloe incredulously.

'Um,' she said, looking around the dock. 'Yes. We're waiting for a boat. Right? That's what she—' Chloe pointed at me.

'*Hell*,' Tropical Shorts interrupted her. 'We're in hell.

10

Why else d'you think it's so hot? And crowded?'

The girl glanced back at me, her blue eyes wide with alarm. 'That's not true, is it? Are we in . . . ?' She couldn't bring herself to say the word.

'Of course not,' I said, shooting Tropical Shorts a dirty look. I raised my voice so that anyone else nearby who might have overheard his outburst would not miss my announcement. 'There's a boat arriving to take you to your final destination any minute now. I'm sorry it's so crowded. We're a little backed up, and the weather's not usually this hot, eith—'

I was interrupted by a thunderous rumble, loud enough to make everyone, even Tropical Shorts, cry out in surprise, then turn towards the source of the noise: a wall of fog towering nearly fifty feet high and rolling slowly but inexorably across the water in our direction.

It looked like something out of one of those mummy movies where the sandstorm spreads across the desert and swallows the brave army . . . only there was no mummy, and this was fog, not sand. And, sadly, this wasn't a movie.

'What's *that*?' Tropical Shorts asked, pointing.

'Just a little storm,' I said. 'It's normal.'

I didn't sound convincing to my own ears. Why did I think I was going to sound convincing to them? Which is probably why an old man dressed in a hospital gown echoed, 'A *little* storm? And I suppose you think those are a few little birds?' He pointed above his head.

I didn't have to look. I knew what he was talking about. A flock of black birds had been amassing and flying in tighter and tighter circles over the beach all day.

'Those are just some birds,' I said, feigning nonchalance. 'No different than this one.' I pointed to a plump white bird – the tips of her wings and tail looking as if they'd been accidentally dipped in black ink – that was sitting a few feet away from me on the dock railing. 'They're completely harmless.'

The old man in the hospital gown laughed like I'd made a joke – not a very funny one, since his laugh was bitter. 'I'm an amateur ornithologist, young lady. I know the difference between mourning doves and ravens. That' – he pointed at Hope, my pet bird – 'is a member of the Columbiformes order. They're harmless.'

He was right about that. Hope had, in fact, saved my life several times, though one wouldn't know it to look at her, especially the way she was busy preening herself as if she were at a Club Med, not a weigh station on the highway to hell (or heaven).

'*Those*,' Hospital Gown went on, pointing upwards, 'are ravens. Scavenger birds. Want to know what scavenger birds eat? Carrion . . . the dead. In other words, *us*.'

Chloe gasped, and she wasn't the only one. All up and down the line, I heard murmurs of discontent. No one likes the idea of getting their flesh eaten off them, not even people who are already dead.

It was just my luck to get an amateur ornithologist in my line.

'Hey,' I said, reaching out to give Chloe's arm a reassuring squeeze. 'Everything's under control. See this?' I showed them the heavy diamond pendant I wore on a gold chain round my neck. Normally I kept it hidden beneath my clothing, because horrible things had happened to everyone I'd shown it to in the past. But these people had already suffered the worst fate was going to offer them.

I sure hoped so, anyway.

'This diamond turns black as a warning whenever there's danger or trouble,' I explained. 'So we're all good.'

'Really? I'd say we're screwed, because that rock's about as black as you can get.' Tropical Shorts pointed to his own arm. 'And I know a little something about black.'

I glanced down. Tropical Shorts was exaggerating. But the stone had gone from its normal silver-grey to the same inky black as Hope's wings and tail tips.

Damn. I shouldn't have been surprised that the diamond had turned colours, considering what was going on all around us. Maybe, in addition to acting as a detector for Furies, the diamond also changed colours in inclement weather.

Before I could say anything, Chloe asked wonderingly, 'Is that like a mood ring? I had one of those once. It would be the prettiest purple around my mom and sisters, but whenever my dad was in the room it turned black. My dad got so mad he threw it out. He said it must have been broken.'

'Must have been,' Tropical Shorts said, raising his eyebrows at me. 'Is that why you drove away from him in the middle of a hurricane and banged up your head? You and your dad not get along so well?'

'What?' Chloe's fingers fluttered nervously to her forehead. 'What's wrong with my head?'

'Nothing,' I said, hastily burying my diamond back

beneath my dress's bodice. 'Look, everything's going to be fine. We're having a few technical difficulties right now, is all. We're doing everything we can to fix them. We appreciate your patience.'

Only I wasn't sure how you fixed fog – let alone thunder or temperatures soaring into the nineties or scavenger birds – in a skyless place housed in a vast subterranean cave where sunlight never shone. Sure, the black orchids and other flowers that bloomed in the courtyard of the castle up the hill didn't need sunlight in order to grow. They were what my mom, the environmental biologist, would call non-photosynthetic 'cheaters'.

But technically, so was I. All of the Underworld's full-time inhabitants, including my boyfriend, had cheated death in one way or another . . . though some more recently than others, so they weren't as familiar with the etiquette of the realm of the dead.

At least that's what I tried to remind myself when I heard someone running down the pier and turned around to see my cousin coming towards me at a breakneck pace.

'Pierce,' Alex said, skidding to a stop in front of me. Panting, he leaned over to rest his hands on his knees as he caught his breath. 'Thank God you're OK. I thought I'd never find you.'

I don't know which was more shocking: the sight of my cousin Alex wearing a black kerchief round his head, pirate-style, with a whip coiled in one hand, or the fact that he was showing concern for my well-being. Both were equally out of character.

'Alex,' I said when I'd recovered from my shock. 'When did you wake up?' The last time I'd seen him, he'd been back in the castle, stretched out on a cot in the kitchen, floating in and out of consciousness – a not uncommon reaction, I'd been told, to being raised from the dead, then brought to the Underworld. 'I thought Mr Graves—'

'Is that the weird old guy in the top hat?' Alex straightened and wiped some sweat from his forehead. 'Yeah, it was pretty easy to ditch him.'

'I would think so, considering he's blind,' I said hotly. 'And he isn't weird. That's how ship surgeons dressed back in the eighteen hundreds, when he first got here . . .' My voice trailed off as I realized from Alex's expression how insane I must sound.

'Right,' Alex said, sarcastically. 'That's not at all weird.'

'You didn't hurt him, did you?' I asked, eyeing the whip. Then my heart gave a nervous thump. 'Where's Kayla?'

Alex's jaw dropped. 'Oh, God. Don't tell me Kayla's here, too?'

I couldn't believe it. 'Alex, of course she is. Don't you remember? We brought her here to protect her from—'

'Never mind,' Alex said, shaking his head. 'It's too late to go back for her. The kid and that crazy-ass dog are right behind me.' He reached out to grab my wrist. 'Come on, Pierce, I heard something about a boat. We've got to find it.'

'Alex,' I said, now staring down at his hand. 'What are you talking about?'

Alex looked impatient. 'Pierce, don't you get it? I'm rescuing you.'

Each in his eyes was dark and cavernous,
Pallid in face, and so emaciate
That from the bones the skin did shape itself.
Dante Alighieri, *Purgatorio*, Canto XXIII

'Come on.' Alex tightened his grip on my arm. 'We don't have much time. I overheard that blind guy tell the kid that all hell was about to break loose—'

I winced at my cousin's choice of words as the crowd of mostly senior citizens, plus Tropical Shorts and the *He Is First* girl, began to murmur again in alarm.

'No.' Yanking my wrist from Alex's grasp, I shoved the tray of water glasses at him. He took hold of it instinctively, letting me snatch away the whip. 'You want to help keep hell from breaking loose? Give these people water. Got it? Water. Not whips.'

Then, lowering my voice so those nearby wouldn't overhear, I asked, 'What's wrong with you? We brought you here to keep you *out* of danger – to get you away from the people who were trying to hurt you back in Isla Huesos. Remember? Seth Rector? Coffin Fest? Ring a bell?'

Alex's dark eyebrows lowered into a scowl. 'Of course it rings a bell. I'm not an idiot. I finally find the evidence I need to put away those bastards for good and, the next thing I know, I get knocked out and I wake up in some—' He hesitated, his scowl turning into an expression of confusion

16

as he looked around. 'What *is* this place, anyway?'

Of course he couldn't remember. Seth Rector had purposefully locked him into a coffin in the Isla Huesos Cemetery. He'd suffocated to death.

I, on the other hand, don't think I'd ever be able to forget the memory of Alex's lifeless body tumbling out of that casket, though John and I had done everything we possibly could to find him in time. Then, after finding him dead, we'd done what some might consider the unspeakable . . . and others would consider a miracle.

'Go back to the castle, Alex,' I said to him gently. 'Find Kayla. I know I should have been there when you woke up, but you've been asleep for hours, and Mr Graves was so worried about the—'

I broke off, realizing it was probably best not to mention the word *pestilence*. But Mr Graves was convinced – and John seemed to agree – that the fog, the unbearable heat and the ever-darkening cloud of ravens above our heads were all due to one reason: the souls of the dead not being sent quickly enough to their final destinations . . . or *pestilence*, as the ship's surgeon called it.

Worse, *I* was the one who'd insisted John help me search for Alex. *I* was the one who'd made him – and Frank, and Mr Liu, and little Henry, who'd been the cabin boy on the ship on which all the men had served – spend so much time away from their world.

So if Mr Graves's dire prediction was coming true it was entirely my fault.

'Worried about the what?' Alex asked.

'Boats,' I said, instead of *pestilence*.

My cellphone buzzed. I knew why without having to check it. It was another text warning me of the storm approaching Isla Huesos. Except, of course, I already knew there was a storm approaching Isla Huesos. Frank, the *Liberty*'s second mate, had known about it without even watching the Weather Channel or receiving a text. He'd merely glanced up at the sky the morning we'd gone looking for Alex and noticed the reddish glow in the clouds.

Red sky at night, sailor's delight, Frank had said. *Red sky at morning, sailor take warning.*

If we had taken his warning more seriously, maybe none of this would be happening and I wouldn't be standing here, having to explain the situation to my cousin Alex.

Well, you see, Alex, there's good news and bad news. The good news is, even though you got killed last night by some jerks from your high school, my boyfriend, the lord of the Underworld, and I brought you back to life. So now you'll never get sick or grow old.

The bad news is you have to stay forever in the realm of the dead that exists underneath the cemetery in your hometown. No time for questions, as I have to get these people on their boat to their final destinations before this place implodes. The end.

Hmmm, that probably wouldn't work.

'Look, Alex, you're in the Underworld,' I said to him baldly. 'I'm sure you remember reading about it in school –'

He stared at me, his expression blank.

'– or maybe not. In any case, you're safe here. Or relatively safe, anyway. Everything is going to be all right.

18

You just need to be a little patient—'

'Get used to hearing that one,' Tropical Shorts advised Alex with an eye roll.

'You know, there's still plenty of room for you over on that other dock,' I said to Tropical Shorts, pointing across the way. He clamped his mouth shut. I turned back to Alex. 'Now, what's with this whip?'

Alex looked down at the tray of glasses he was holding, his expression still slightly dazed. 'I . . . I found it on my way here. It's funny 'cause I was wishing for something to use to protect myself from that freaking dog that was following me, and it . . . it kind of just appeared. Did you say the *Underworld*?'

I nodded. If there'd been time, I could have explained to him exactly why his wish had come true: it was courtesy of the Fates, who operated as sort of invisible caretakers of the Underworld and provided almost anything their full-time mortal inhabitants desired on demand. Waffles for breakfast? They appeared like magic, piping hot and swimming in butter. Dresses in your exact size that most flattered your figure? I had a closetful. A weapon with which to protect yourself from John's over-exuberant, massive hellhound, Typhon? Apparently a whip would conveniently appear.

The only thing the Fates would *not* supply was what Alex seemed to want most . . . an exit from their world.

But there was no time to explain any of this to him.

'Yes,' I said. 'The Underworld. Now go on back to the castle and find Kayla and I promise everything will be all—'

'Wait. The *Underworld*?' Alex's voice cracked. 'Where

dead people go? How stupid do you think I am? There's no *Underworld*—'

The last person I expected to come to my aid was the *He Is First* girl. But that's what happened.

'Have faith,' Chloe said, laying a gentle hand upon Alex's arm. 'If you keep Him first in your heart, He'll do the same for you.'

Tropical Shorts rolled his eyes. 'Here we go again.'

'It's true,' the *He Is First* girl said to him. To Alex, she said more gently, 'I'm Chloe. I heard her call you Alex. That's a nice name. Did you know *Alexander* means protector of men?'

'I didn't know that.' A flush had begun to creep from the neckline of Alex's T-shirt all the way to his dark hairline, I guess because Chloe was touching him. Despite the angry red wound on her forehead and blood in her hair, she really was very lovely, especially when she smiled, like she was doing now. 'Uh . . . Chloe's a nice name, too.'

'Thanks,' Chloe said. 'It's from the Bible. It means young and blooming.'

'Uh,' Alex said, looking down at her hand. 'That's nice.'

Great, I thought as I looped the whip through the sash of my dress. Alex had been in the Underworld less than twenty-four hours, and he was already attracted to a girl with whom he didn't have the slightest chance of having a relationship, because in a few minutes she'd be leaving for her final destination.

I guess I shouldn't have been surprised. The people in my family seemed to have an uncanny knack for picking exactly the worst person to fall in love with, myself included.

'I'm Reed,' Tropical Shorts leaned in to say to them. He obviously didn't like being left out. 'That's from the Bible, too.'

Chloe looked perplexed. 'I don't remember anyone in the Bible named Reed.'

'Really?' Reed folded his muscular arms. 'When the pharaoh's daughter went down to the Nile to bathe, where did she find the basket holding the baby Moses?'

Chloe's reply was automatic. 'Floating among the reeds.'

Reed smiled. 'There you go.'

Alex smiled as well. 'Cool,' he said, and fist-bumped Reed, causing Chloe's hand to slip off his arm as he did so. Alex apparently didn't notice, but Chloe did. She looked even more perplexed.

I could sympathize. Confusion over Alex's behaviour was nothing new. Also, I'd gone to an all-girls school most of my life, so boys were a mystery in general, with the exception of my boyfriend: he was a mystery wrapped in an enigma.

I was starting to suspect that was one of the things I found so appealing about John. He might have been frustrating at times, but at least he was never boring. Or, as Mr Smith, the Isla Huesos Cemetery sexton (and resident expert on the Underworld), once put it, *Eternity is a long time. So, if you have to spend it with someone, I could see wanting to spend it with someone impossible . . . but interesting.*

A horn sounded so loudly it seemed to shake the dock. Everyone jumped, even me. Hope let out a startled screech and took off. Her white wings were easily discernible,

21

however, against all the black ones above our heads.

Unfortunately, I was all too familiar with that horn – I'd just never heard it quite so close before – and I recognized the rumble that followed the ear-piercing blast. It wasn't thunder *or* my cellphone vibrating, letting me know the latest weather alert from Isla Huesos. It was a ferry engine.

'It's OK,' I said. I couldn't yet see its bow cutting through the thick wall of fog, but what else could it be? 'That's just the boat.'

'It's coming?' The *He Is First* girl gasped with excitement, looking around bright-eyed at the other passengers. None of them could summon up her same enthusiasm, maybe because they were mostly all in their eighties and nineties and were still really upset about the humidity and the remark the other old guy had made about the ravens eating their flesh. 'Oh, yay! I've been waiting for this day my whole life practically. I'm finally going home.'

Alex had brightened up. He looked about as excited as Chloe.

'Great,' he said. 'Our chance to get out of here.'

'Uh, Alex.' I watched as he looked around frantically for somewhere to set the tray of water glasses I'd handed him. 'You aren't getting out of here. Only they are.'

'What do you mean?' he asked, continuing to fumble with the tray. 'The boat's coming. You just said so.'

'Right,' I said, aware that Chloe's lovely blue eyes had gone wide and troubled as she watched our interaction. 'But we can't get on the boat. Only they can.'

Alex shoved the tray so roughly that a few of the glasses

tumbled from it, dropping into the lake. 'You said we were going home.'

'No, Chloe said that,' I pointed out. 'And she didn't mean *home* home. She meant—'

'I meant I'm finally going home to *Him*,' Chloe said, still wide-eyed. She looked at me questioningly. 'That *is* where the boat's taking us, right?'

'Absolutely,' I said to Chloe.

If they ask, John had told me earlier, *tell them the boat is taking them wherever they want to go. Heaven, their next life . . . whatever you have to say to get them moving so we can load the next batch of passengers.*

Where do *the boats take them?* I'd asked him.

He'd shrugged. *How would I know? The only ones who return to tell us are the ones who don't like where they got sent.*

Also known as Furies, I'd thought with a shudder. I'd had more experience with them than I cared to.

But they only return to earth, I'd said, just to make sure I'd got it straight, *to possess the bodies of stupid people. Right?*

Weak-willed people, he'd said with a smile. *And yes . . . usually.*

Usually? I hadn't liked the sound of that, but there hadn't been time to ask more questions.

'What about *them*?' Alex pointed at the crowded dock opposite the one on which we stood. I could no longer see John, but Frank and Mr Liu were still hard at work subduing the far more aggressive passengers waiting there.

'Those people are leaving, too,' I said. 'But they're not going back to Isla Huesos, either. And I'm definitely sure you don't want to go where they're going.'

Oh, my God, how much plainer did I have to make it? Did I actually have to say the words out loud? It seemed rude to blurt it out in front of them – *They're dead, Alex.* But it seemed like I was going to have to, since my cousin was being so obtuse.

'Well, I'm sure as hell not staying here.' Alex stood so close to me, our noses were nearly touching. 'How am I going to help prove my dad didn't kill anyone if I'm stuck in the damned Underworld?'

'As soon as we've helped these people, we can go back to the castle to discuss how we're going to help your dad.'

'Go back to the castle to discuss it? Who are you now, Principal Alvarez?'

What had happened to the old Alex, I wondered, who was so moody and withdrawn he barely said an entire sentence in a single day? Being revived from the dead affected everyone differently, I supposed. It had made Alex a real pain in the butt.

'Hey,' Reed said to Alex. 'Don't take it out on her. She's just doing her job.'

Maybe Tropical Shorts wasn't so bad after all.

'Yes, I'm sorry you won't be coming with us,' Chloe said to Alex. 'But please don't worry. I'm certain the Lord has another plan for you.' She glanced at me. 'For both of you.'

'Oh, I can assure you,' said a new, deeply masculine voice from behind me. I turned to see John sitting, tall and dark and disapproving, on the back of his horse, Alastor. 'He does.'

When I perceived, like something that is falling,
The mountain tremble, whence a chill seized on me,
As seizes him who to his death is going.
Dante Alighieri, *Purgatorio*, Canto XX

'Chloe wasn't talking about you,' I said to John, leaning my elbows against the rough wood of the dock railing. 'She meant the other lord.'

John raised a dark eyebrow. 'Oh, that one,' he said. 'My mistake.'

He should have looked intimidating – the death deity on the back of his rearing ebony stallion – and I suppose he did seem that way to everyone else, at least judging by their reactions to the sight of him. Behind me, I heard Reed let out a soft expletive of surprise, and Chloe gasped.

But he was the most gorgeous boy *I*'d ever seen, even with his mouth twisted into a slightly cynical smile at the idea of anyone referring to him as *the* Lord. He was, as no one knew better than me, far from without sin.

I'd given up trying to control my pulse, which leaped rebelliously every time I laid eyes on him. I had no more control over my heart when John was around than John evidently did over his obnoxious horse, Alastor, who was prancing around in the frothy waves as if he'd stepped on some of the water glasses Alex had dropped . . . not that it would make a difference, since they'd have been pounded to dust beneath the horse's massive hooves.

You can get away with making theatrical entrances on the back of a jet-black stallion when you're the lord of the Underworld, especially while wearing black jeans, studded wrist cuffs and tactical boots. Granted, John had abandoned the long leather coat he usually wore, but the way the strong, hot wind off the lake caused the waves to crash around Alastor's forelocks and sent John's long dark hair – 'death metal goth', I'd once overheard my mom inaccurately describe John's hair to my dad – streaming around his face and neck gave his entrance an extremely dramatic effect.

John's appearance did not, however, have the same mesmerizing effect on Alex as it did me and everyone else on the dock.

'Not *that* guy.' Alex joined me at the railing, a disgusted look on his face. 'I can't stand that guy. This is all his fault.'

Uh-oh. This was not the most opportune time for Alex's memory to be coming back . . . and not the most ideal tone for him to be taking around John.

'Alex,' John said mildly, his gaze flicking towards my cousin. 'I could tell it was you from all the way across the beach. Pierce only gets that particular tone in her voice when you're around. What are you doing here?'

He had to keep a firm hand on Alastor's reins, so the muscles in his biceps swelled a little, causing the sleeves of his T-shirt to strain.

This was extremely distracting – at least to me – but I had other things to worry about. I was pretty sure a fight was about to break out between my cousin and my boyfriend, which was bad since John and I were still searching for solid ground between ourselves, kind of like the way Alastor was searching for solid ground in the sand beneath his hooves.

'Alex thought I needed rescuing,' I explained. 'But we talked and got it all straightened out, so he's good now.'

Unfortunately, John didn't fall for this blatant lie.

'How did he get out of the castle? Typhon never would have let him past—' John broke off, his gaze going to my hip. 'Where did *that* come from?'

I looked down. 'Oh,' I said, remembering the whip. 'Alex found it, but I—'

'You're the dude from Coffin Fest,' Alex interrupted, stabbing his finger at John again. 'I remember. And you were there when I woke up in the cemetery. You brought me here.' He said the word *here* like it was the worst place in the entire universe, which isn't true, since obviously high school is. 'Well, I want to go back. *Now.*'

John raised an eyebrow . . . never a good sign.

'Don't you think every single other person here wants the exact same thing?' he asked as thunder rumbled again in the distance, louder than before. John, when emotionally perturbed, could cause inclement weather conditions with his mind, but I was fairly certain the thunder we'd been hearing all day had been meteorological, not paranormal, in origin. 'What makes you think you're more important than they are?'

'I have unfinished business back in Isla Huesos,' Alex said. '*Important* business that's a matter of life or death. You know what I'm talking about.'

'I do,' John said, reaching into the pocket of his jeans and bringing out one of the small tablets with which he and his crew stayed in touch while they worked. 'Go back to the castle, Alex. When we've gotten these people boarded, you and I can discuss your unfinished business. But now is not a good time.'

If I were Alex, I'd have done as John advised. His voice had hardened from the warm caress it had been when he'd spoken to me into something that felt more like the sand being flung by the wind around us.

Alex, however, had never been one to take a hint, much less an order, and he definitely wasn't about to now.

'Oh, I'm sorry,' Alex said, in a mock apologetic tone. 'Am I interfering with your busy cruise director activities? Far be it from me to keep the other passengers from their shuffleboard. I'm only talking about keeping my father out of jail.'

Fortunately, the marine horn gave another long, lonely blast to draw attention to the fact that the prow of an enormous ferry was bursting through the thick curtain of fog.

'Here it comes!' Chloe cried excitedly, pointing. 'The boat! I see it!'

I saw it, too. So did John, though he lifted his gaze from his tablet's screen only momentarily. The tablet also received the information telling him on to which dock to sort the dead. Lived a life of selfish debauchery and sin? Step to the right. Lived a life of moral decency? Step to the left.

Or maybe it was the other way round. It was hard to remember when the people closest to you were fighting. Who sent him this information – the Fates? The Lord from Chloe's T-shirt? Aliens? That was as big a mystery as where the tablet had come from.

'Dude,' Alex yelled at John. 'Did you hear me?'

This time John didn't bother looking up from the screen. 'As I believe I've told you before, Alex, my name is John, not Dude. Pierce, what do you know about tying off mooring lines?'

'Everything,' I said. I had no idea what he was talking about. 'I tied one off for lunch yesterday.'

I saw the skin around John's eyes crinkle as he studied the screen of his tablet, almost as if he might be trying to suppress a smile, despite the seriousness of the situation. John and I may not yet be back on solid ground with each other, but at least he was learning to lighten up a little . . . a promising sign, considering his profession – not to mention his past.

Sure enough, he was smiling as he looked up, tucking the tablet away. 'Frank and Mr Liu have their hands full at the moment over at the other dock. I'm going to need your help when that ship comes in.'

I was surprised. John had never asked for my help before, though Mr Smith had assured me that all signs pointed to my being John's chosen 'consort', which meant spouse or paramour of someone who ruled something.

John, having been born in the eighteen hundreds, would have preferred me to be his wife even though I'd explained to him that these days, people who married at our age tended to end up on reality shows on MTV.

Then John had asked what MTV was.

'Where would she have learned to tie off a mooring line?' Alex asked before I could say anything. 'She went to the most expensive private girls' school in Connecticut. All they taught her there was how to fold doilies.'

Pointedly ignoring Alex, I said to John, 'I'm sure if you show me, I'll catch on.'

'Excellent.' John's gaze on me was warm. 'Then later perhaps you could show me how to fold doilies.'

John had made a little joke!

This wouldn't have been a big deal for a normal guy, but it hadn't been very long ago that the only way John could express himself was by hurling his fists. It was astonishing how well my efforts to civilize him were paying off.

Alex didn't seem to appreciate my efforts, however.

'Are you kidding me with this?' he demanded, banging the dock railing again with his fist as he glared at John. 'She's not strong enough to handle the lines from a ship that size. And quit ignoring me. You're letting me on that boat so I can go home and help my dad.'

'Alex,' I said, turning towards him. 'I want to help your dad, too. But I already told you: that boat isn't taking anyone back to Isla Huesos, and even if it were you couldn't—'

'Was I talking to you, Pierce?' Alex whirled on me to demand. 'I don't think so. Back off.'

Behind me, Chloe let out a little scream of alarm, then grabbed both my arms and huddled behind me, using my body as a sort of shield. From what, I wasn't sure, until I looked up.

John had wheeled his horse round, urging him through the waves until he reached the end of the wooden pier. The next thing I knew, Alastor was clattering up the steps on to it. All the newly departed souls flattened themselves against the wooden railings on either side of the dock to make way for the foam-flecked animal and his rider, whose grey eyes were flashing bright as lightning.

'Oh, no,' Chloe said with a groan into my hair.

'It's all right,' I said to her soothingly. 'He promised never to hurt anyone.' Though, judging from the livid expression on John's face, it seemed as if he might have forgotten the promise he'd made so long ago that night by my mother's pool. Perhaps my efforts at civilizing him were not going as well as I had imagined.

John had pulled Alastor up short before Alex, and dismounted. The horse blew his hot breath into Alex's face.

'Was that supposed to impress me?' Alex asked John, his voice shaking a little.

'No,' John said. His own voice was surprisingly even-toned, considering how brightly his silver eyes were flashing. 'My horse doesn't like you. Sometimes I have difficulty controlling him around people he doesn't like.'

Alastor bared his teeth, each one the size of my big toe. Alex swallowed audibly.

'John,' I said, peeling Chloe's clinging fingers from my dress and slipping between the two boys. 'Alex just woke up. He didn't have time to speak with Mr Graves. He doesn't know where he is or exactly what's happened—'

'He knows you, though, doesn't he, Pierce?' John laid his

31

hands on my shoulders to move me – gently but firmly – aside. Though I dug my heels into the wooden planks of the dock, it was like trying to fight against the current of the waves below us. I found myself pressed up against Alastor's side, a position neither of us much liked.

'He knows you've never been anything but kind to him. And yet, after everything your cousin has done for you,' John continued, addressing Alex with the same kind of disdain with which Alastor regarded me, 'you show your gratitude by speaking to her rudely, and stealing a *weapon* from my home?' He pointed at the whip I'd looped through my sash. 'Particularly *that* weapon?'

I glanced down at the whip at my waist, wondering what John was talking about. True, it hadn't been very sportsmanlike of Alex to grab it – or any weapon – to use against John or any of the other residents of the Underworld, especially considering my cousin was here as a guest, even if he hadn't known it at the time.

But whips weren't particularly known for their lethality. It wasn't as if Alex had stolen a knife from the kitchen, with which he could truly have harmed or even killed someone. To have inflicted a mortal wound with a whip, he'd have had to tie his victim down, then administer multiple lashes, during which time he most likely would have been caught and stopped by one of us. It was an odd weapon for the Fates to have given him, and an even odder one for John to have been so angry about.

'What were you going to do with it?' John asked, still pointing at the whip.

'I—' Alex ducked his head to look down at his sneakers, as if realizing he'd done something not only stupid but also embarrassing. 'I . . . I don't know. I just wanted to protect myself, and Pierce, too, after I found her.'

I saw from the way John's expression softened a little that this had been the right thing to say – though Alex couldn't tell, since his head was still ducked.

Poor Alex. It wasn't completely his fault that he acted the way he did sometimes. He'd been raised by our grandmother since his father, my uncle Chris, had spent most of Alex's life in prison for transporting drugs, and he barely knew his mom. She was in the 'entertainment business', the kind you had to be over eighteen to see on the Internet.

'Apologize for the way you spoke to her,' John said to Alex, 'and perhaps I'll be able to forgive you for stealing the weapon.'

I rolled my eyes at this lordly speech. I know John noticed because the corners of his mouth twitched, even though his gaze never left Alex, whose own gaze was still fixed on his shoes.

To my surprise, Alex lifted his head and looked me straight in the eye.

'I'm sorry, Pierce,' he said, sounding as if he truly might have been. 'None of this is your fault, and I shouldn't have blamed you. I don't know what's wrong with me. Ever since I woke up, I've felt . . . strange.'

I wasn't sure it was true that none of this was my fault, actually. Maybe the stuff about Seth Rector wasn't my fault. But certainly some of the horrible stuff that had started happening since I'd come to Isla Huesos was my fault, like our guidance counsellor Jade getting murdered. That had happened because she'd been mistaken for me.

I didn't feel pointing this out would be particularly helpful that moment, however.

'It's all right,' I said soothingly. 'You're supposed to feel a little strange at first. It's normal for an NDE.'

When I saw his look of confusion, I remembered I'd never explained to him about the exclusive club to which we both belonged.

'NDE,' I repeated. 'Near death experience. That's what they call it when you die, then come back to life.'

'Oh.' Alex looked a little less confused. He knew all about the 'accident' in which I'd lost my life and become an NDE, though, unlike him, I'd been revived by natural, not supernatural, means. 'What about Kayla? You said she's here. Is she an NDE, too?'

'No, Alex. She was there when the police caught us in the Rectors' mausoleum, rescuing you. We brought her here to keep them from arresting her.'

Alex said, 'Oh,' again and looked somber.

I thought it might be appropriate to give Alex a hug, but the last time I'd tried, he'd stiffened like the corpse he'd turned into a few hours later. The Cabrero family wasn't particularly demonstrative, unless you counted murder.

'I . . . I'm sorry about the whip,' Alex said, more to John than to me. 'But . . .' He added this last part in a defensive rush. '. . . I'm still going to try to get out of here first chance I get.'

'I'd expect nothing less from someone related to Pierce,' John said. His tone had grown warm again. 'But until you do find a way to escape you might as well make yourself useful. Have *you* ever tied off a boat before?'

Alex made a contemptuous face. 'I live on a two-mile-by-four-mile island. Of course I've tied off—'

They were interrupted by another long blast from a marine horn. But this time it didn't emanate from the boat that was churning towards the pier on which we stood. It came from further out across the lake, somewhere deep inside the centre of the murky grey fog that was bearing down on us as rapidly as the ferry.

'Is something wrong?' Chloe asked anxiously. She'd noticed the same thing I had . . . a look of anxiety that suddenly appeared on John's face. Something was definitely wrong, at least judging by the way his eyes had narrowed – and his jaw tensed – as he stared out across the lake. But what was he seeing that the rest of us couldn't?

'Captain Hayden!' Another set of footsteps sounded on the wooden dock, these much lighter than Alex's had been – but louder, because their owner was wearing a pair of thick-heeled, silver-buckled shoes.

I turned to see Henry Day racing towards us, a metal object clutched in one hand. Following not far behind him – but at a much less rapid pace – was my friend Kayla, wearing a gown of flowing lavender silk, her long dark hair curling wildly about her face and bare shoulders. While Henry's face was tight with worry, Kayla's expression was one of annoyance, especially when she spotted Alex.

'Thanks a lot for ditching me, Cabrero,' she snarled at him.

'I didn't ditch you,' Alex protested. 'I didn't even know you were here.'

Kayla dismissed him with a queenly sniff, then said to Henry, 'I thought I told you to quit running. You'll fall down in those stupid shoes someday and hurt yourself.' She looked at me and shook her head. 'Seriously, chickie.' (Chickie was her nickname for me.) 'How do you put up with these people?'

I smiled, pleased – but not really surprised – to see her back to her old self so quickly, even after everything she'd been through. If I had to use one word to describe Kayla, it would be *adaptable*, which also, she'd once told me, happened to be what she'd seen written across the top of her disciplinary file. *Antagonistic towards authority figures but highly adaptable.*

'Thanks, I've had a lot of practice,' I said.

'Captain,' Henry said. He cast Kayla and me a disapproving look. He was only ten years old physically, but he'd lived for more than a hundred and fifty without any sort of female influence, so he did not have a lot of patience for girls. *'Look.'*

Henry thrust the object he'd been carrying at John.

It was a brass spyglass, one that I recognized from John's bedroom, where he kept a number of nautical tools that had been scavenged from the sunken *Liberty*, the ship he and Henry, Mr Graves, Mr Liu, and Frank had sailed from England. A storm sank it in the port of Isla Huesos.

John raised the spyglass to one eye, then stood peering

out at the approaching ship. I turned to offer Kayla one of the glasses that hadn't tumbled into the lake.

'Thirsty?'

'Oh, God, yes,' she said, taking the water gratefully. 'Do you know what the awful-smelling stuff is in the pots that old man is brewing back there in the castle?'

I nodded. 'Beer. Yes, I know, Mr Graves has been trying to get his recipe right for quite a while.'

'He made me taste some,' Kayla said between sips of water. 'I hate beer. But I've had worse, actually.' Her gaze moved past me to take in the beach, the dock and finally the gigantic horse standing next to me. She slowly lowered the now empty water glass. 'What the *hell*?'

'Oh, we're not in hell,' Chloe informed her, sprightly. 'We're here waiting for the boat that's going to take us to our final destination.'

Kayla's gaze slid towards her. 'Really,' she said, her pierced eyebrow lifting. 'How nice for you.' Then she noticed Reed. 'Well,' she said, her expression changing. 'Hello.'

He grinned. 'Hi. How are you today?'

Kayla's smile was bright enough to light up the entire Underworld. 'Doing much better now that I've met you. I'm Kayla Rivera, who—'

'Sorry, she has to go now,' I said to Reed. I took Kayla by the arm and dragged her a few feet away. 'Could you please not flirt with the dead people?' I hissed at her.

She glanced back at Reed over a bare shoulder, startled. 'No way. He's dead? That guy does *not* look dead. How'd he die?'

'What does it matter?' I asked. 'I thought you liked Frank.'

'I like Frank, but *I'm* not dead. Is that what's with Cindy Lou Who's hair over there?' Kayla nodded at Chloe. 'Is that blood? She's dead? I thought she just had a bad experience with some hair dye.'

'They're all dead,' I said. 'I thought Mr Graves explained it to you.'

'He did, in between beer tastings. But how am I supposed to tell who's dead and who's not if they don't have telltale bloodstains? You know, it's good this place gives out free gifts, because who'd want to stay if they didn't?' She patted the sparkling amethyst-tipped pins in her own voluminous hair, which matched the purple streaks she'd dyed there. 'I'd be so out of here otherwise. Dead people and giant horses and dogs and homemade beer? Yuck. FYI, if my mom doesn't hear from me by the time her shift at the hospital ends, she'll probably call out the National Guard.'

'Good luck with that,' I said. 'Remember that reward my dad was offering for my safe return from my kidnappers?'

'Oh, was this where you were?' Kayla looked surprised. 'No wonder you were in no hurry to come back. I wouldn't, either, if I was kidnapped by someone who looked like that.' She grinned a little wolfishly at John, who still stood with his back towards us, peering through the spyglass Henry had rushed down from the castle. Then she added, 'Which Frank does, of course. Where *is* Frank, anyway?'

I pointed at the dock across the beach. 'Over there.'

Next thing I knew, she'd shot over to the railing to wave

and blow kisses in Frank's direction, which didn't work out quite as well as I suspect she'd hoped, since when Frank looked up and smiled – almost as if he'd felt Kayla's kiss travel on the hot wind, then settle upon the jagged scar that ran down one side of his face – one of the men in the line behind him used Frank's momentary distraction to wrap a burly arm round his throat.

Fortunately Frank reacted quickly and decisively by thrusting the heel of his hand into the other man's nose. Kayla looked upset by the turn of events, her hands flying to her face in alarm. Concern for Frank hadn't been why she'd gasped, however.

'Guillotine,' she shouted across the beach. 'Use a guillotine chokehold on him, Frank, you idiot!'

I shook my head in wonder. It wasn't that I was surprised by what Kayla was screaming, or that I minded that she'd been checking out my boyfriend's backside – which I had to confess did look particularly well proportioned in the snug-fitting jeans he was wearing.

It was that the way she was acting reminded me of something my dad had once told me. The military had performed a study to find out what kind of equipment my dad's company could provide to help keep fighter pilots calm and levelheaded when they were flying in their F18s and being shot at by the enemy, thousands of feet above the earth at speeds exceeding a thousand miles per hour.

Pulse monitors were applied to the fighter pilots' chests and were read around the clock by scientists on the ground.

The problem, Dad said, was that the heart rates of the

fighter pilots remained perfectly steady when they were in the air, and even when they were under simulated attack.

It was only when those same pilots were back home, jockeying for a position with their shopping cart in line to buy dinner at their crowded local grocery store, for instance, that the scientists saw the readings on their heart monitors skyrocket.

It just goes to show that you can't tell how anyone is going to react in any given situation, Dad had said.

It was no surprise to me that Kayla was taking the discovery that there was an underworld beneath the island on which she lived completely in her stride. The only thing I'd ever seen really upset her was when she'd witnessed John and me revive Alex. She'd been sure we were vampires . . . Oh, and my suggestion that she join me for ice cream once after school with Seth Rector's girlfriend, Farah Endicott. I'm pretty sure Kayla thinks Farah's a vampire, too.

'Uh-oh,' Kayla said, elbowing me. She pointed at John, who was slowly lowering the spyglass Henry had passed him, his expression troubled. 'Looks like the boyfriend's not happy.'

But when I glanced in the direction in which John had been peering with the small folding telescope, I saw what could only be good news: the prow of a second ship breaking through the thick wall of fog.

The passengers over on the pier manned by Frank and Mr Liu saw it, too. They began to cheer. They thought they were being rescued from their present misery.

They didn't know they were about to board a ship to some place much, much worse.

'What's wrong?' I crossed over to John to ask. 'Haven't you had two ships come in at the same time before? You don't have to worry, you know. We'll all help.'

John handed the spyglass back to Henry. I wasn't sure if he'd even noticed me, let alone Kayla; he'd been so transfixed by whatever it was he'd viewed through the lens.

'Let Frank and Mr Liu know what's happening in case they haven't noticed yet.' John was speaking in a swift, low voice, so quietly I was certain only Henry and I could hear him. 'Tell them I'll take care of it, but they'll need to be ready just in case.'

Henry nodded crisply. 'Right away, Captain,' he said.

Henry pulled his own tablet – or magic mirror, as Henry adorably referred to it – from a coat pocket, and began to type.

'Just in case?' I stepped away from Kayla, lowering my voice to match John's so she and the others wouldn't overhear. 'In case what, John? What's going on? I said that Alex and Kayla and I can—'

'The problem's not that the boats are coming in at the same time.' John's tone was barely audible. He didn't want to broadcast his concerns to the public. But his expression was graver than I'd ever seen it. 'It's that they're coming in too fast.'

When he looked down at me, I saw something in his light grey eyes that I'd seen there only a handful of times before: it was fear.

'Pierce, those boats aren't going to stop until they hit something. And the only thing in their way is us.'

When they arrive before the precipice,
There are the shrieks, the plaints, and the laments,
There they blaspheme the puissance divine.
Dante Alighieri, *Inferno*, Canto V

'What?'

I whirled round to see for myself.

The first ship – as large as the ferryboat to Martha's Vineyard my parents and I used to take on vacation, which could easily fit hundreds of people as well as their cars – was churning straight at us through the mist, looking like a great white shark headed for its prey.

The second boat was ploughing through the water towards the dock on which Frank and Mr Liu were still toiling.

John was right. Both ships were making a direct path for the docks.

I spun back towards John. 'Can't you contact the captain and tell him to turn, or . . . or drop anchor, or whatever it is boats do?' My knowledge of nautical terms was limited to things written on raunchy-joke pirate shirts I saw the tourists wearing around Isla Huesos, such as *Give up your booty* or *Prepare to be boarded.*

'There is no captain to contact.' John's mouth was a grim, flat line.

'Then who's steering them?'

'Normally? The same forces that decided to put me in

charge,' he said, his lips now curving into a bitter smile.

'The *Fates*?' I cried, appalled.

Of course. Who else was going to ferry the souls of the dead to their final destination?

John lifted a warning finger to his lips, pointing at Kayla and the others, all of whom were watching the boats, completely unaware of the impending danger. John evidently wanted to keep it that way, since he took me by the arm and pulled me closer towards Alastor, from whom everyone always steered a wide berth, so we'd be out of their hearing range.

'I don't want to cause a panic,' John said in a low voice.

I highly doubted Kayla or Alex knew what a Fate was – at least in the context I'd used the word – but I nodded anyway.

'Of course,' I said. 'But I don't understand. After all you've done for the Fates, working like a slave down here for nearly two hundred years, *this* is how they repay you? Why would they do that? It's so unfair—'

My indignant sputtering on his behalf wrenched a smile out of him . . . a smile I recognized all too well from some special moments we'd shared in his bedroom the night before.

'So you do still care about me,' he said. He slipped an arm round my waist. 'I wasn't sure. You never answered my question.'

'What question?' I asked. What was wrong with boys? They got romantic at the weirdest times. 'What are you even talking about?'

'You know what I'm – what's *that*?' He sprang away from me as quickly as he'd pulled me towards him. I felt something reverberate at my waist.

'Oh,' I said, pulling my mobile phone from the sash of my dress. 'It's nothing. I have my cell set on vibrate. I keep getting these text alerts about the storm back in Isla Huesos.'

I turned the phone off and tucked it away again.

'What about that?' He pointed at the whip on my hip. 'Why are you still carrying *that*?'

I looked down at it. 'Oh. I don't know. To keep it out of the hands of children, I suppose.' I laughed to show him I was joking, although I wasn't really. My cousin Alex's behaviour still bordered on the childish sometimes.

John didn't laugh, however.

'That whip was my father's,' he said, his face carefully devoid of emotion. 'He used to use it on the ship when he . . .' He seemed to want to say something, but decided better of it. 'Well, he used to use it quite often. I have no idea how your cousin found it. I thought it went down with the *Liberty* along with everything else belonging to my father.'

'Oh, John,' I said softly, touching the side of his face. Now I understood why the sight of the whip had upset him so. John's relationship with his father had been what my therapists would call challenging. 'I'm sorry. I'll get rid of it.'

'No,' he said, and managed a smile, though it seemed to me one wracked with the pain of memories best forgotten. 'Everything that's ever turned up from the ship has always

44

done so for good reason, like your necklace.'

As he spoke, he'd reached out to tug my diamond from the bodice of my dress, with the confident proprietorship of a lover. But when the grape-size stone tumbled into his hand, the smile faded.

The diamond was the colour of onyx.

My heart gave a sickening lurch, the kind it gives when you hear the siren to an emergency services vehicle going down your street and you realize the reason it's so loud is because it's stopped in front of *your* house. It's *your* house that's on fire, someone *you* love who's sick or in trouble or hurt.

Normally? The same forces that decided to put me in charge, John had replied when I'd asked who was steering the boats.

Who was steering them now?

Furies.

No wonder my diamond had turned black. It had nothing to do with the weather.

'John, what's happening?' I asked, feeling as sick as if someone had punched me in the stomach. 'I thought Furies could only possess humans on earth. How could they come here, to the Underworld? We told Alex and Kayla they'd be safe here, but we may as well have left them in Isla Huesos if Furies—'

'Don't worry,' John interrupted, dropping my diamond and reaching for my shoulders to give me a little shake. 'They *are* safe here. Or at least they will be. I'm going to fix this.'

'How?' I tried not to let my doubt show, but all I could

think about was Mr Graves's warning: pestilence. If this wasn't pestilence, I didn't know what was. 'If the docks are destroyed, all these people – Chloe, Reed, everyone – their souls will never get to where they're supposed to go.'

'Yes, they will,' he said firmly. 'Because the docks aren't going to get destroyed.'

'But if the Furies have control of the boats—'

'You've got to trust me. I know I've let you down before—'

'What?' I shook my head. 'No, you haven't.'

'I have. But I'm not going to this time, I swear it.'

'John.' This was exactly like him. He always took everything on himself, convinced he had to save the world and do it single-handedly. 'No. Let me help you for once. That's what I'm here for, at least if everything Mr Smith says is true—'

'You can help me. Here.'

Surprised, I held one of my hands out to meet the one he stretched towards me. Except for the mooring lines, this was as close as I could recall to John ever requesting help from me. It wasn't his fault he was so stubbornly intent on protecting me. Back when he'd been born, women were put on pedestals and told to do nothing all day but look pretty (except for all the women who got worked to death on farms or in cotton mills or having a baby every year because there was no birth control). Even though John knew things were different now, he still tended to think of me as one of those pedestal ladies.

So it was a bit of shock when what he handed me

were the reins to his man-eating horse.

'Take Alastor,' he said in a low, urgent voice, 'and get back to the castle. Whatever happens, you'll be safe there, behind the walls.'

'Um . . . what?' I said, more out of astonishment than from any need for further information, since I had a pretty good idea of what he'd said and absolutely no intention of following his instructions.

'Alastor knows the way,' he went on. 'If you're on his back, no one will dare interfere with you. People,' he added, 'tend to be intimidated by Alastor.'

'I can't think why,' I said drily, looking up at the stallion's ink-black eyes, which at that moment happened to be rolling towards John, as if to echo my own sceptical thoughts about his plan. The horse had laid down his ears, a sure indicator that he was displeased . . . enough so that Hope, my pet dove and full-time protector, sensed it and flew down from the cavern's ceiling to scold him, fluttering around the stallion's head and trilling her disapproval.

Alastor's ears flicked forward as he eyed the bird, looking as if he'd like nothing more than to make a bite-size snack out of her.

'Alastor,' John said in a warning tone, and the horse whickered innocently.

I shook my head. 'John. That's a very nice plan, but I think I can do more than run away and hide in the castle. And what about Alex and Kayla?'

'Take them with you. And I'm not asking you to run away. I'm asking you to—'

'What about all these other people?' I interrupted, looking around the beach. It was hard to keep my temper but, remembering my job as a consort, I tried. 'There must be a thousand of them, at least, and more souls coming every minute. We can't just abandon them.'

'I have no intention of abandoning them.' He'd begun to peel off his black T-shirt, a sight which simultaneously confused and thrilled me. It also made me angrier at him, because he was using unfair weaponry against me. 'Get yourself to safety. Leave the rest to me.'

'You think I'm just going to – I'm sorry, is it too warm in here for you?'

He stared at me uncomprehendingly, his hair adorably mussed from where his shirt collar had ruffled it coming over his head. 'What?'

I didn't know whether I wanted to grab him by those wide, muscular shoulders and kiss him or shake the living daylights out of him.

'Why are you undressing?' I asked.

'Pierce, there isn't much time,' he said, sitting down at the edge of the dock. 'You're a skilled rider. You should be able to handle Alastor without any problem. He's not really as wild as he acts. He's simply not used to polite society. He only needs a little taming.' Bending over to unlace his tactical boots, he glanced up at me from beneath some of the long dark hair that had tumbled across his eyes. 'A bit like his owner, as you keep assuring me.'

I shook my head again. 'How could you know anything about my riding skills? You've never seen me on a horse. I used to ride back in Connecticut, but you couldn't possibly have seen me then, because you and I weren't—'

My voice trailed off. *Together*, was what I was going to say, until I remembered that just because we hadn't been together didn't mean he hadn't been watching me . . . or *watching over me*, as I'm sure he'd have preferred to think of it. Death deities couldn't always be counted on to follow modern social niceties, such as 'don't spy on people'.

Remembering how often I'd eavesdropped on my parents, I realized humans couldn't always be counted on to follow this rule, either, so I didn't hold it against him.

'John,' I said. 'Why are you taking your shoes off?'

He'd neatly folded and draped his shirt across his boots, lined up side by side next to the closest post.

'I don't want to get them wet,' John explained matter-of-factly, climbing to his feet. 'Here, take care of this for me while I'm gone, will you?' He passed me his tablet. 'I know you don't need it – you have your own. But maybe your cousin could use it . . . or your friend Kayla. That way she won't have to keep shouting across the beach at Frank . . .'

I assumed he was joking. I remembered a time when he never joked, just brooded, and could only attribute the change – like the fact that refreshments and blankets were now being given out along the docks – to my influence.

But I was going to have to teach him that there was a time for jokes and a time to be serious, and now was a time for the latter. The sight of his clothing stacked into such a tidy pile made my pulse stagger. After my friend Hannah had died, I'd spent a lot of time online, researching suicide.

I'd wanted to figure out how she could have done what she'd done, only realizing later that I wasn't going to find the answer on a website.

One thing I did learn, though, was that people who take their own lives by leaping off bridges and cliffs often leave small stacks of belongings next to the place from which they jumped, things they feel they won't need in the afterlife, such as their shoes, eyeglasses and wallets. The police called them suicide piles.

The sight of John's shirt and shoes piled up like that – not to mention the fact that he'd given me his precious tablet – instantly reminded me of those piles.

'Where are you going that you think *you* don't need it?' I asked John, thrusting the tablet back at him. 'And why do you think you're not coming back?'

'Of course I'm coming back.' John tucked the tablet into the tight sash of my gown, next to my cellphone. His smile was reassuring. 'I told you. I'm going to fix this.'

'How?' I demanded, my voice beginning to rise. 'By sacrificing yourself for everyone else, exactly like in my dream?' He stared down at me, confused, the smile wavering a little. 'What dream?'

'Remember that morning I woke up in your arms, crying? It's because I dreamed about how you died,' I said. 'I was on the *Liberty*. There was nothing I could do to save you. I watched you drown.'

It was the first time I'd admitted to him that I'd known every detail of the stormy night he'd been thrown overboard from the deck of the *Liberty*: how he'd been left to be tossed about on the waves as punishment for the crimes he'd committed at sea: mutiny . . . and murder. Even though he'd committed those crimes for a very good cause – to save the lives of his fellow crewmates, Henry, Frank, Mr Graves and Mr Liu – he'd still been found guilty in the eyes of the law . . . and apparently in the eyes of the Fates as well.

But knowing they hadn't felt guilty enough to let him die – they'd granted him the gift of eternal life, after all – hadn't made my dream any less horrifying . . . or the fact that, during it, it had felt as if someone had carved out my heart and thrown it, still beating, into the waves after him.

Now it appeared that nightmare was about to be reenacted while I was awake.

'Pierce,' he said.

He attempted to raise his hands – to touch my face, I suppose – but I wouldn't allow it. If he touched me, I'd shatter like glass.

'Admit it,' I said, my voice gruff with emotion. 'I'm about to watch you drown all over again. You're going to go out there and try to stop those boats from wrecking. Isn't that how you got yourself killed the last time? It's what you do.'

'No,' he said. He seemed to be having a hard time suppressing a smile. 'Because I can't die. I already did and came back, remember?'

'You can still be hurt,' I reminded him. Now I did touch him, but only to hold up one of his own hands to show him his knuckles, thick with scars.

'True,' he said. His eyes were glinting way too brightly.

'But I heal very quickly, remember? And someone has to try to stop them.'

'You said there's no way to slow them down at that speed.' Icy tendrils of dread began to squeeze my heart. 'So what good is it going to do if you try?'

'I didn't say slow them down.' I recognized the glint in his eyes. It was the same dangerous look John always got right before he was about to do something reckless. 'I said I'm going to try to stop them.'

I sank my fingernails into his hand. 'John. *No.*'

'Pierce, it's the only way,' he said. The dangerous gleam grew into another one I recognized: stubbornness. He was going whether I liked it or not. 'At least I can protect the docks.'

'But what about you?' Cold slivers of dread now arced out from my heart to travel down my spine. 'Who's going to protect *you?*' I nodded to my diamond. I didn't dare release his hand to point at it, for fear he might disappear. 'My necklace – you saw what it does to Furies. Take me with you. I can kill them.'

His fingers were already slipping away from mine, despite how tightly I'd held on to them.

'I know you can, my bloodthirsty little love,' he said, his grin wider than ever. 'The problem is that the Furies know it now, too.' Instead of moving away from me, he wrapped his arm once more round my waist, drawing me close to his bare chest. 'The last place you should be is out here in the open where they can find you. You're our weapon of last resort. We can't afford to lose you.'

I looked up at his lips, hovering just inches above mine. I hadn't realized how much I'd missed those lips until they were as close as they were now. I could feel the heat from his thighs through the thin material of my dress, the strong sinews in his arms beneath my hands.

'I'm the one who can't afford to lose *you*,' I said.

'But I can't die,' he reminded me. 'I only know what it's like to feel dead inside. That's how I felt until the moment you appeared on this beach . . . remember? You marched up to me and started telling me how unfairly you thought I was treating everyone. That's when I started feeling alive again for the first time in . . . well, a long time. That's why it hurt so much when you left—'

'Why do you have to keep bringing that up?' I asked. His close proximity was making me feel a little breathless. 'I've apologized a million times for throwing that tea in your face—'

'Because that was my fault. I didn't handle that situation, or others involving you, in the' – he searched for the word he wanted – 'gentlemanly fashion I should have. But I swore if I got a second chance I'd make it up to you. It hasn't been easy. Sometimes it's seemed as if I'd lost you. That made me feel dead again inside.'

I couldn't take my eyes off his lips. 'So then why are you in such a good mood?'

'Because,' he said. He was holding me so close I could feel his own heart beating against mine, strong and steady. 'I think I have the answer to my question.'

'What question?'

'Whether or not you've forgiven me. You must have, or you wouldn't be so concerned for my health.' He was openly grinning now, his teeth flashing even and white against skin that was almost as dark as mine due to the amount of time he spent wandering around the Isla Huesos Cemetery. 'Tell me you love me.'

'No,' I said. It was difficult to keep my voice from shaking, but I was determined not to fall apart in front of him. I figured that was what a consort would do, stay strong.

The smile faded, his face awash in sudden uncertainty. 'No? No, you don't love me? Or no, you won't tell me?'

'I mean, no, I'm not telling you that. See, this way you won't be able to do anything stupid like sacrifice yourself for the rest of us. You'll have to come back to find out how I really feel about—'

He didn't let me finish. He lowered his lips to mine, kissing me so deeply that the cold shards in my spine turned to warm tingles, rippling from the soles of my feet all the way up to the base of my neck. Even my frozen heart began to thaw. Every inch of me melted at his touch, became soft in response to his hardness, alive in a way it hadn't been the second before his mouth met mine.

It wasn't only because he had the ability to raise the dead and heal wounds (and I had a lot of wounds to heal – my scars simply didn't show on the outside, though, so no one could see them), or even because he was so incredibly attractive.

It was because of what I hadn't told him: that I loved him. I don't know how he couldn't tell from the very first second our lips touched. Every beat of my heart seemed to shout it: *I love you. I love you. I love you.*

But I knew I was right. I didn't dare say it out loud.

Then, just as abruptly as he'd started kissing me, he thrust me away, as if I were something he'd suddenly remembered he needed to resist. Which I was, at least for now. He was something I needed to resist, as well, because, like he'd said, the Furies weren't only on those boats. They were everywhere.

I love you. I love you. I love you.

'Don't worry,' he said. The smile had returned, but it wasn't quite as cocky as it had been before. 'I'll be back.'

Then he leaped over the dock railing and dived towards the dark, churning waves, vanishing from sight right before he struck the water.

If only I'd realized then that *I'll be back* were the last words I was ever going to hear him say.

Kayla appeared a moment after John vanished, keeping a wary distance from Alastor's enormous jaws.

'Did I see what I think I just saw?' she asked.

'I don't know,' I said. I'd ducked my head in the hope that what she thought she saw weren't my eyes filled with tears. 'What do you think you just saw?'

'Your boyfriend dive into, like, three feet of water. He didn't come up, either. He's probably drowned or turned into a merman. Honestly, I don't know which would be worse—'

'Did you see a splash?' I interrupted.

Kayla looked surprised. 'Now that you mention it . . . no, no splash.'

'Yeah. He's not in the water.' All the warmth that John had injected into my body with his kiss had disappeared. I felt cold again, and not only because fingers of fog had begun to creep ashore and were tingeing the formerly hot wind with ice.

'Well, where is he, then?' Kayla asked.

I exhaled. 'I can only assume he's off fighting invisible forces of evil. They're called Furies. Did Frank mention those to you? John's job is to fight the Furies and to make sure this place runs smoothly and that the souls of the dead get to their afterlives. And Frank's job is to help him.'

Kayla shook her head with enough energy to send her springy dark curls bouncing on her bare shoulders. 'The way Frank described it, it's *his* job to run this place. Your boy, John, is more like his sidekick. Frank said they get paid in pure solid gold. He said he's going to give me some.'

'Right,' I said, reaching for Alastor's bridle and then gritting my teeth in annoyance as he swung his head away from me. 'You should totally believe everything boys tell you, especially Frank. Help me grab this horse, will you?'

'Uh, no thanks,' Kayla said. 'Frank better not have been lying about the gold. I was planning to use it to pay for my surgery.' She pointed to her chest. One of the first things she'd told me the day we'd met was that she was having breast reduction surgery as soon as she turned eighteen.

'Yeah,' I said. 'Well, if we don't get out of here, you'll be able to use those as flotation devices.'

Kayla laughed. 'You really are crazy, chickie,' she said. 'You know that? I couldn't understand what you were doing in all my classes at first. I was like, 'Poor little white girl.' But now I know. No wonder they put you in D-Wing.'

'They put you in D-Wing, too,' I said defensively. 'So what does that say about you?'

'Everyone knows *I'm* crazy,' she said. 'But you go around looking like the pretty little rich girl on the outside, not a care in the world.'

Her words chilled me to the bone, more than any wind ever could. Did people really think of me that way? I wondered. *Pretty little rich girl?* Was that what I got for keeping my scars so well hidden, buried so deep?

'Well, everyone's wrong,' I said. 'I'm not just a pretty little rich girl without a care in the world. I'm the queen of the Underworld. So people better stay out of my way.'

Kayla laughed. 'You better take your hand off that whip handle when you say that. You look more like the queen of something else.'

'Sorry,' I said, dropping my hand from my waist. 'I need to get rid of this thing.'

Behind Kayla, everyone had started crowding around the area where John had disappeared.

'I'm telling you, he went in,' Reed was saying, peering down into the dark, agitated water.

'I didn't see a splash,' Chloe said. 'He disappeared right *before* he went in.'

'Right,' Reed scoffed. 'A guy disappeared into thin air. That's impossible.'

'It's impossible for there to be flocks of *Corvus corax* inside a cave,' the old man in the hospital gown said, 'but you're not going to deny they're flying above our heads, are you?'

Reed eyed him. 'I wouldn't dare.'

'There he is!' Henry had his spyglass to one eye. 'I see him!'

Everyone looked in the direction Henry was pointing, including me. There, in the wheelhouse of the ship – the one careening towards the dock on which Frank and Mr Liu were toiling – was a lone figure, barely discernible across such a far distance and with the fog closing in.

'That can't be him,' Alex said. 'No one can swim that fast.'

'It *is* him,' Henry said. 'Look.' He passed my cousin the spyglass. 'And he didn't swim. He can blink himself wherever he wants to be and, a second later, there he is.'

Alex snorted, peering through the telescope. 'Right, Shorty.'

'How do you think you got here?' Henry asked, sounding offended. 'He brought you by blinking, that's how. And my name isn't Shorty. It's Henry.'

'I don't know what you're talking about, Shorty,' Alex said. 'No one can blink anyone anywhere.' Then his voice changed as he saw something through the telescope. 'That *is* him.'

Though it was impossible to make out John's face from such a distance without the help of a magnifying lens, it wasn't hard to see that the ship on which he was standing was changing course. It had begun to turn, slowly but inexorably, towards the one headed our way.

'What's he ... That is so weird,' Alex said. 'There's no one else in the wheelhouse. There's no one steering those ships. No one but—'

Alex abruptly lowered the spyglass, staring across the water at the two boats as if he'd just realized something. The realization was evidently not a good one, since the next word out of his mouth was of the four-letter variety.

'Alexander!' Chloe cried, shocked. Her gaze went to Henry. 'There are children present.'

Henry hurried to reassure her. 'Oh, I'm used to it, miss.'

'That doesn't make it right,' Chloe said, with a pretty scowl.

Alex was ignoring them both. 'That's why he went out

there. There's no one steering them, and they're coming in too fast,' he said. He swung an accusing look at me. 'Was that what the two of you were whispering about?'

'Yes,' I said. 'He's going to try to stop them.'

Everyone had turned to stare at me, I suppose because I was sitting on top of Alastor's back, where I'd climbed before any of them, including Kayla, had noticed. I'd felt the horse stiffen with indignation beneath my legs, but I already had a firm grasp of the reins in my left hand and John's father's whip coiled in my right, just in case Alastor tried anything foolish. Of course I'd never hit him with the lash (which was too long to be of any use as a riding crop), but I might flick him with the coil if he tried to throw me.

But he must have noticed the whip, because though he tossed his head a few times he didn't rear or kick. He merely snorted, as if to express his extreme displeasure with the situation.

From the volunteer work I'd done in animal shelters in my past life – before I'd died the first time – I knew that half the battle when it came to untamed creatures like Alastor (and his master) was psychological. You had to make them think that you weren't afraid of them, and that you were the boss. You weren't going to put up with any of their nonsense.

Of course, it was a bit different when you were dealing with a nine-pound feral cat as opposed to a death lord's three-thousand-pound stallion.

Alex shook his head slowly from side to side. 'I don't

know which one of you is crazier,' he said, looking back towards John. 'You or him.'

'Yes.' Chloe sounded politely timid. 'Shouldn't you be wearing a helmet or something, Pierce? That horse is awfully big. What if you fall?'

'Under normal circumstances,' I said, 'yes, I should be wearing a helmet. But these aren't normal circumstances, are they? Look, I need all of you to listen to me . . .'

My voice trailed off as I realized no one was paying the slightest bit of attention to me. All of them were staring at the water and the spectacle of the enormous ship John was steering . . . directly into the path of the other.

Alex was right. Even with the fog swirling so densely around the two boats, I could see clearly what John was planning on doing. The gaping hole in my chest where my heart had once been – before John had ripped it out and taken it with him – seemed to widen another inch, allowing more of the suddenly chilly air to come seeping in.

'I don't understand,' Chloe said. She, too, was nervously watching the drama playing out across the lake. 'Why is he steering that boat *away* from the other dock?'

Alex lowered the spyglass. 'Because he's going to try to ram it into the one that was supposed to be picking you guys up.' There was grudging admiration in his voice.

'*Why?*' Chloe spun round to face Alex.

It was, I suppose, a bit like watching a professional car race in which one of the drivers had gone completely mad and decided to smash his car into all the others. You didn't want to watch, but you also couldn't look away.

The problem was I was in love with the mad driver, and watching him on this insane suicide mission was destroying me.

'But if he smashes his boat into that other one,' Chloe protested, 'he'll be killed!'

'Maybe not,' Reed said in a hopeful voice. 'He could rig the steering wheel and jump off at the last minute. I saw that in a movie once.'

'He'll get sucked under by the boats' propellers as they go down,' the old man in the hospital gown disagreed gloomily.

'No, he won't,' Kayla snapped at him. I saw her glance my way. 'He'll be fine. He'll be just fine.'

'Right. You don't know the captain,' Henry said to Alex in an offended tone. He snatched the spyglass away from him. 'The Haydens love to smash things up.'

Henry wasn't exaggerating. John had smashed up nearly every obstacle put in the path of his pursuit of me, including but not limited to shopkeepers, teachers and even sets of iron cemetery gates. A wooden boat would be nothing to him.

'Seems like a waste to me,' Hospital Gown said, his tone now disapproving. 'Two perfectly good boats—'

'He doesn't have any choice,' I said hotly. 'He's doing this to save the docks.'

I'd navigated Alastor until he'd moved his heavy bulk into the middle of the pier, surprised at how willingly he obeyed my commands, seeing as how all I wore on my feet were ladylike slippers, so when I dug my heels into his sides he could hardly have felt it. It wasn't particularly comfortable, riding bare-legged in a dress, but like Kayla I could adapt, too, in an emergency.

'So maybe,' I went on, when Hospital Gown and everyone else around him had looked up at me in surprise, 'you could do him the courtesy of not letting his efforts go to waste. We need to start evacuating this dock, so if you all will follow me to the castle, where you'll be safe—'

Kayla wasn't the only one to echo, 'Evacuate?' but she was the person standing closest to me, so she was the only one to whom I responded softly, so the others couldn't hear.

'We need to get back to the castle,' I said. 'John says it's the only place we'll be safe.'

Kayla blinked her exotically made-up eyes. 'Safe from what?'

'Those invisible forces of evil I mentioned earlier—'

I didn't mention that I'd been John's primary concern, or that he hadn't said anything about Chloe or Reed or the others. But how could I take Alex and Kayla and leave the rest of them all standing there? Who was to say the Furies wouldn't come after them?

Before Kayla could say anything, Hospital Gown burst out with, 'Evacuate? We've been waiting here for hours; we're at the front of the line, and now you're telling us we've got to move some place else?'

All around him, old people lifted their voices to unite with Hospital Gown's in a chorus of protests. 'He's right!' and 'We're not going anywhere!' and 'We want to speak to someone in charge!'

You try to do one nice thing for people, and look what it gets you.

'*I'm* in charge,' I shouted back at them.

I'd have been better off staring them down in cold silence, but to do that I'd have to have been more sure of what I was doing. And I hadn't the slightest idea of that.

Still, I plunged on, hoping, like a substitute teacher on the first day of school, that the volume of my voice would hide my anxiety and make up for my lack of experience.

'All I want to do is make sure none of you gets hurt,' I yelled. 'So get in line behind me and we'll all—'

It was too late. Alastor's ears pricked forward and he snorted. Then Hope let out a squawk of alarm and suddenly took off from between Alastor's ears, as if frightened by something. *But what?* I wondered. I hadn't been shouting *that* loud. Could she have sensed my own fear?

As I looked around to see what had startled her, a bolt of lightning split the air, thrusting the entire cavern into stark white daylight, instead of the perpetual pinkish dawn it nearly always seemed to be in.

Chloe wasn't the only one who screamed. I'm pretty sure Kayla and Alex – as well as Hospital Gown and most of his friends – did, too. I know my ears were ringing afterwards . . . possibly from a scream of my own.

When I lowered the arm I'd lifted to protect my dazzled gaze, I saw that the two ships were so close to the docks I could have looked into John's eyes – if his long hair wasn't partially obscuring his face – as he struggled to twist the wheel, which some unseen force was attempting to pull in the opposite direction.

Furies. Without any weak-willed human bodies to possess the way they did on earth, they couldn't be seen by the naked eye. But I should have known that they were all around us, not only by the colour of my diamond and what had happened to the boats, but also by the chill in the air, the lightning and now the almost undetectable but ever increasing shaking of the boards of the dock beneath us. The remaining water glasses on the tray Alex had left on the railing began to drop into the water one by one, until finally the empty tray itself slipped, with a plop, into the lake.

People seemed eager to take my advice to evacuate now. The problem was, they couldn't.

'W-what's happening?' Chloe cried, reaching for the closest solid thing she could grab on to, which happened to be Alex.

True to his name of protector of man – and now girl – Alex slid an arm round her just as the waves began to slap over the side of the pier, dampening everyone's legs to the knee.

'I don't know,' he said. 'But I think Pierce is right. We'd better—'

His voice was drowned out by the loudest clap of thunder I'd ever heard.

Except that it wasn't thunder. I twisted in the saddle to see if John was all right, knowing as I did that there was no possible way he was going to be able to employ that trick Reed had suggested and rig something to hold the wheel in place as he leaped to safety.

I was right. The sound we'd heard was the prow of the boat John had been steering ripping out the hull of the ship in front of it as it rammed against it, with John still aboard.

'Dost thou not hear the pity of his plaint?
Dost thou not see the death that combats him
Beside that flood, where ocean has no vaunt?'
Dante Alighieri, *Inferno*, Canto II

The sound of splintering wood and sheering metal as the two ships collided echoed so loudly through the cavern that it felt almost like a physical blow. For some of us on shore – those of us not lucky enough to have hands to fling over our ears to protect them, that is – it *was* a physical blow.

'The ravens,' the old man in the hospital gown cried.

It had begun to rain. But no ordinary rain, unless raindrops had suddenly turned into large black birds.

The ravens that had been flying in their predatory circles above, stunned by the sound of the ships imploding, began to drop, one by one, from the air, landing like grenades of blood and black feathers all around us.

'Watch it,' Reed said, pulling Alex and Chloe out of the way as one of the birds shot by them, nearly striking them both. Instead, it hit the dock railing, then ricocheted into the water, where it bobbed for a moment, until, incredibly, it recovered itself. After giving its wings a good shake, it flew away, though it got only as far as a nearby boulder before crash-landing again in confusion.

It was one of the lucky ones. Most of the other birds

plummeted into the sand or rocks, while recently departed souls screamed in horror at the piles of tiny bones and feathers all around them.

My heart already in my throat over John, I glanced about frantically to check on Hope. Though her wings had never been clipped, she surely hadn't been flying at as high an altitude as those ravens when the echo sounded, and could not have been as badly affected by it as they were. And with those blinding white feathers she should have been easy to spot – much easier than John, who could be halfway to the bottom of the lake by now . . .

I hadn't told him I loved him. *Why hadn't I told him I loved him?*

Better not to think of that now. But I had no better luck spotting Hope anywhere on the shore than I did John in the water, since Alastor, like the ravens, had been stunned by the sound of the colliding ships and panicked in response to the assault on his sensitive ears. He reared, frantic to get back to the castle and to his comfortable stable, where birds didn't plummet from the sky and people weren't screaming at the sight of the birds' mutilated corpses all around them. Though I tried to soothe him, it was like trying to calm a thrashing shark.

'Careful!' Kayla ducked as the stallion's enormous, silver-clad hooves swung dangerously close to her face.

I was holding on for dear life, but I managed to get out two words: 'I'm trying.'

There was nothing I could do but allow Alastor to go where he so badly wanted. He was too strong for me to control when he was in this agitated state, and the more he tried to resist me the more likely he was going to hurt someone . . . probably me.

Alastor wasn't the only one panicking, either. The people standing at the front of the pier, who would have been the first to board the boat if it had actually arrived, were instead the first to suffer the after-effects of the ships' collision.

In the moments following the initial impact, the boats sprang apart as lake water rushed in to fill their empty passenger holds. What I could also see from my high vantage point on Alastor's back – whenever he twisted in that direction – was that a four-foot wave filled with debris was surging outwards from the crash and heading directly towards the pier.

'Get everyone off the dock,' were the last words I was able to gasp out before Alastor wheeled round, practically whipping my head off.

Fortunately, it seemed as if Henry had heard me. He must have, since behind me I heard him bellow, 'Everyone, please, it's too dangerous to stay here. We've got to follow Miss Oliviera – she's the lady on the big black horse. Walk, don't run—'

That's all I heard before Alastor took off, thundering down the pier, his hooves flying so quickly I wondered if they were making sparks. At the speed he was going, the wind whipped my face so fiercely my eyes began to water. All I saw ahead of us were blurred shapes. I could only hope the horse wasn't knocking people down in his frantic flight to escape.

Though I couldn't see, I could hear. Once I no longer heard the hollow drumming of Alastor's hooves on the wooden boards of the dock, but the much deeper thud of his feet hitting dry sand, I began to pull his reins as hard as I could to the left, knowing that when a horse's eyes are forced to look in a direction he doesn't want to go, he has no choice but to slow down, and eventually to stop or turn in that direction. I knew, of course, that the castle was where I was supposed to be heading, but I couldn't leave the beach without turning round for one last look for my bird and the boy I hadn't told I loved.

Alastor wasn't giving up without a fight. I thought he was going to pull my arms from their sockets, but he finally slowed down – with considerable snorting – and eventually stopped, pawing ill-temperedly at the ground.

'Sorry,' I said to him. 'But you're not the only one who's suffering here.'

I twisted in the saddle to look behind me and saw that very few of the departed had listened to Henry's advice of *walk, don't run*. People at the end of the dock had already begun to shove against those in front of them, desperate to get to what they perceived as the safety of the shore before the waves of debris-filled water hit them.

I didn't blame them, but I knew it wouldn't be long before someone was crushed or pushed off the pier and into the water, where the choppy waves would sweep them up and under the dock and out of sight.

What happens to the soul of someone who goes missing in the Underworld? I wondered.

Better question: What was going to happen to these people now that the ships that were supposed to take them to their final destinations had been destroyed?

This was something I hadn't considered before inviting them all up to the castle. Would the Fates provide new boats? How could they, if the Furies had driven them off?

I had more important things to worry about at the moment, however. I scanned the surface of the water for John. Surely he'd had time to blink himself – as Henry liked to say – out of the ship's wheelhouse before the collision. Only, where had he ended up? Why had we spent so much time kissing and no time agreeing on a point to meet afterwards? Next time I was going to know better. If there was a next time . . .

There had to be. To think otherwise was to invite madness.

Instead of John, however, all I saw – besides bewildered lost souls beginning to shiver in winds that were rapidly turning freezing cold – was Frank, standing at the end of his dock, brandishing a pair of brass knuckles.

'You think dying was painful?' he was demanding of the men and women who were shuffling past him. Word had obviously spread about the evacuation. 'Try breaking out of this line. I'll show you what real pain feels like.' He noticed me and gave me a smile, along with a wink and cordial nod. 'Hello there, Miss Pierce.'

'Hello,' I said. 'Where's Mr Liu?' I had to raise my voice to be heard above the sound of the steadily rising wind.

'He's over there,' Frank said, waving at a bulky figure

further down along the pier, 'making sure all of our "guests" are headed away from, and not into, the water. Some of them seem to think this is their golden opportunity to escape what the Fates have in store for them.'

They aren't wrong, I thought a little bitterly. *The Furies have made sure of that.*

'Have you seen John?' I asked him.

'Not yet, but don't you worry about him,' Frank called back. 'He always turns up.'

I found nothing in this remark to inspire confidence, since I happened to know at least one of the places John liked to 'turn up' was the cemetery.

'OK,' I said. 'Well, if you see him before I do, would you tell him—'

One of the men in Frank's line broke ranks, darted across the beach, and fell to his knees at Alastor's feet, causing the horse to stagger backwards a few steps in alarm. The man didn't look like a lot of the people from the rest of his line. He was probably around my dad's age and was dressed pretty conservatively, in a pair of khaki pants and a collared shirt that had been neatly pressed at one time.

The effect was somewhat ruined by the large bloodstained bullet hole in the centre of it, however.

'Sweetheart,' he said, his hands clasped in supplication as he looked up at me from the sand. 'You gotta help me. There's been some kinda mistake. I'm not supposed to be here. I keep telling these guys I'm supposed to be with those other people over there' – he pointed at my dock – 'but they won't listen—'

'Sorry.' I hated it when people I didn't know called me sweetheart. How did they know whether or not my heart was sweet? 'But I have to go.'

'You don't understand,' Khaki Pants pleaded. There were tears running down his face. 'I've got a daughter about your age. She needs me. Yeah, I may not have been the most perfect father, but who is? That doesn't mean I deserve to be with these people here.'

I stared down at him, thinking of my own dad. Which line would he end up being sorted into when he died, this one, or the one with Hospital Gown, Chloe and Reed? A lot of people really hated my dad, the infamous millionaire Zack Oliviera, because his company was partly responsible for one of the largest accidental oil spills in history, which was still affecting the wildlife and economy of not only Isla Huesos but also the entire Gulf shoreline.

That didn't mean my dad was a bad person, however. He'd always been there for me when I needed him (well, with the exception of those times his mother-in-law had tried to murder me). But he hated Grandma and had done everything he could to keep me away from her. Dad was almost like a walking Fury detector, now that I thought about it.

Maybe the Fates made mistakes, just like people. Obviously they did, if they thought it was fair to punish someone like John for a crime he'd been completely justified in committing.

I was opening my mouth to tell the poor man in the khaki pants that though I sympathized with his plight there wasn't much I could do to help him at the moment – I had problems of my own – when Frank strode up and wrenched the man back to his feet.

'The lady said she has to go,' Frank snarled, dragging Khaki Pants back to the line. 'You can tell her your sad story – which I'm sure is perfectly true – later.'

'It *is* true,' Khaki Pants insisted. 'You know, I was abused as a child. Isn't anyone going to take that into account? It's not my fault—'

'If I had a piece of eight for everyone I met down here who tried to use the fact that he was abused as a child as an excuse for his behaviour, I'd be the richest man in the world,' Frank said. 'My father abused *me* as a child, but I never hurt anybody. Well,' he added thoughtfully, 'anybody who didn't deserve it, that is.'

I glanced away from Frank and his new friend, distracted by the crowd of lost souls who'd gathered around Alastor. They were keeping a careful distance from his baleful glare but looking up at me expectantly, like I had something they wanted.

It took me a second or two to realize that I did.

'Excuse me, dear,' an old woman said in a quavering voice. In her silk blouse, with a pearl necklace at her throat and a cane in her hand, she could have been a teacher from my old school in Connecticut. Maybe that's why I didn't mind so much when she called me 'dear'. 'It's getting quite cold. We saw the accident, so I know it will be a while before the next boat arrives. Is there somewhere we can go in the meantime to be out of this wind?'

73

I looked up and down the beach, though I knew very well there was no shelter of any kind for them, unlike at a normal terminal. Passengers had never had to wait that long for a boat before. Of course, never before had they faced such dangers as bird bodies plummeting from the sky and much worse, for all I knew.

There was only one thing I could say – though I knew John wasn't going to like it very much when he found out.

'Yes,' I said to the old woman. I pointed towards the castle. 'You can go there.'

'Oh,' she said, her gaze following the direction of my finger. 'I see.'

She didn't look all that excited. It took me a second or two to realize why. Every time she took a step, her cane sank into the wet sand as she leaned on it. It was many, many feet to the castle.

Worse, I could see that several of the people from Frank's line – including Khaki Pants – were eyeing her pearl necklace with a great deal of interest, even though I had no idea what they thought they were going to do with it once they'd snatched it. It's not like there were any pawnshops in the Underworld where they could make a quick buck selling it.

'Hold on a minute,' I said to the old lady with the pearls. 'I'll get you some help.'

I glanced around for Mr Liu. He was so huge he could pick her up and set her on his shoulder.

Only, Mr Liu looked busy. One of his charges really had jumped into the lake, as they'd feared would happen, and

Mr Liu had leaped in after him. Now he was towing him to shore.

It seemed like I was going to have to start offering rides to the castle on Alastor's back like he was a pony at a children's party. He ought to love that.

Then I heard Mr Liu call my name . . . my first name. Mr Liu had never called me by my first name before, only Miss Oliviera. Normally unwavering in his old-world politeness, I knew something truly horrible must have happened to make him forget it.

Alastor must have heard the urgency in Mr Liu's voice as well, since his ears turned forward, and before I had a chance to press my heels against his sides, he'd plunged into the water, splashing towards the Asian man and the body he was towing . . .

. . . a body that, as I grew closer, I began to realize looked familiar. It was male, and shirtless, in black jeans.

It was John. And he looked – there was no other way to put it – dead.

After she thus had spoken unto me,
Weeping, her shining eyes she turned away . . .
Dante Alighieri, *Inferno*, Canto II

'He said he couldn't die.'

I looked accusingly at Mr Graves from the bed where I was sitting next to John's lifeless body.

'He can't.' The ship's surgeon had a strange instrument pressed to his ear. It looked like an upside-down trumpet, only it was made of wood. He pressed it against John's naked chest, listening for the same heartbeat I'd been unable to find down on the beach. 'At least, he isn't supposed to.'

'Then I don't understand what's going on here,' I said, fighting to keep my voice steady. 'Because he seems super dead to me.'

'To me as well.' Mr Graves moved the trumpet-like instrument to a different part of John's chest and listened some more. 'This is very troubling.'

'*Troubling?*' I echoed. 'I think I could find a better word than *troubling* to describe the fact that my boyfriend, who was supposed to be immortal, is dead.'

My voice broke a little on the word *dead*. I couldn't stop replaying over and over in my head that last moment I'd spent with John on the dock.

Tell me you love me, he'd said.

Why hadn't I said yes when I'd had the chance?

How could any of this be happening?

When I'd tumbled off Alastor's back and into the rough waves to snatch John's lifeless body away from Mr Liu, he'd assured me in a voice as broken and ragged as my own that if we got him up to the castle and to Mr Graves, the surgeon would know what to do.

I'm not sure if Mr Liu had ever really believed the ship's surgeon had some magical cure for death that the rest of us didn't know about, or if he'd only said this to placate me, seeing my near-hysteria. He couldn't have thought it would keep me from doing what I'd done next, which was drag John to the beach – with Mr Liu's help, and Frank's, when he'd realized what was happening – and attempt to revive him myself.

Why wouldn't I think I could bring John back to life? I'd done it for Alex. I knew a thing or two about CPR, since it's what had saved my life the first time my grandmother had tried to kill me. I was convinced it – or my diamond pendant, or a combination of both – would work on John.

Only they didn't. Of course they didn't. This was the Underworld. This was where things came to die.

It wasn't until someone took me by the shoulders and physically pulled me away from him that I realized my own lips had grown as cold and frozen as John's from pressing my mouth – along with my heart – against his for so long.

'Pierce.' It had been Alex's voice I heard in my ear. 'We've got to go. We've got to get away from here. Look. The storm. It's getting worse.'

He was right. The thunder was growing louder, and somehow, it had begun to rain, though at first I thought that was because the fog had finally closed in on the beach.

Except that the fog had turned from white to red. It was the colour of poinciana blossoms. The mist clung with enough persistence to make it feel like a steady drizzle . . .

'Oh, God,' I'd murmured, looking down at my arms, then at John's chest. We'd each been covered in a fine spray of pink.

Red sky at night, sailor's delight. Red sky at morning, sailor take warning.

Then Alex pointed upwards. I saw that the ravens that had survived the sound of the ships' impact had regrouped and were spinning in a tight circle, waiting for a chance to do what the old man in the hospital gown had assured us they were waiting to do . . . feed on the dead. Only now, I realized with horror, it wasn't the flesh of the dead they wanted.

It was the body of my dead boyfriend.

'The castle,' I'd said, scrambling to my feet. 'We need to get him – get *everyone* – to the castle, *now*.'

Mr Liu wanted to carry John, but Alastor put up such a fuss, rearing and whinnying and thrusting his nose against John's body, as if he were trying to nudge him back to life – or at least knock him off the bigger man's shoulder – we gave up and laid him across Alastor's saddle. The horse seemed comforted by the feel of his master's weight across his back and, allowing me to hold his reins, turned to head back towards the castle without once baulking or even so much as snorting.

I wished more than once during that long, frightening walk through the red mist, with the departed souls fighting and complaining behind us that they did not understand what was happening – except, thankfully, for Reed and Chloe, who helped along Mrs Engle, which turned out to be the name of the nice old lady in the pearls – that I could be an animal and not fully understand what was happening. Then maybe I'd have been able to delude myself into thinking that John was only sleeping, or unconscious, and that I could nudge him awake, the way Alastor had tried to.

I wished it almost as much as I wished that Hope would suddenly appear, fluttering her (mostly) pure white wings and fussing about, letting me know all was not lost.

Except that Hope never put in an appearance, even when we finally reached the room John and I shared. I'd been sure I'd find her perched on the back of my dining-room chair, fastidiously grooming herself. To my utter disappointment, her perch was empty. She wasn't there, or anywhere else that I could see.

Not only that, but no fire blazed in the enormous hearth to greet us, as it had every other time I'd walked in. None of the sconces along the passageway had been lit, either. The gleaming silver bowl in the centre of the table, normally heaped to overflowing with grapes and peaches and apples and pears, was empty. Even the fountain that usually burbled so animatedly in the courtyard was silent.

All of this, I thought with foreboding, could mean only one thing: the Fates had deserted us.

Tears filled my eyes, but for once I didn't mind them because they blurred the sight of John's long-limbed body stretched out beside me, completely still and virtually the same colour as the crisp white sheets beneath him.

Thankfully, they also blurred the faces of the people gathered around John's room and the bed on which he lay, which was a small mercy. What would I want to look at Alex for, as he slouched on the couch and mindlessly (and irritatingly) flipped through the pages of a book he'd found on the nightstand? *Zzzzzpppt* went the pages. *Zzzzzpppt.*

Or Chloe as she knelt at the end of John's bed, murmuring whatever prayers she'd been taught were appropriate to say at someone's deathbed (which weren't doing any good, as far as I could tell. John's eyelids never stirred).

I definitely didn't need to see Reed, still shirtless and looking all around the room, like, *What is this weird place?*

I didn't even want to look at Kayla as she sat beside me, patting me on the shoulder and murmuring over and over again, 'Everything's going to be all right, chickie. Everything's going to be fine.'

How did that make any sense? Everything clearly *wasn't* going to be all right. Nothing was ever going to be all right again.

'Here, dear,' Mrs Engle said, removing, then replacing, a cup of tea that Henry had thrust into my hands, even though I had never touched it to my lips. She kept refilling it from a pot Henry had brought from the kitchen. Every time the pot ran low, I heard Henry's overlarge shoes clip-clop against the floor as he shuffled out to refill it.

'Try to drink it, won't you? It will help.'

What was she talking about? Tea wasn't going to help anything.

Crying helped a little. The tears kept me from seeing the expression on Frank's face as he mumbled, periodically, 'I think I'll go check on that lot out there in the courtyard,' in a voice so clogged with emotion I knew he was actually leaving the room so no one would see *his* tears.

Mr Liu, meanwhile, sat silent as a stone at the bottom of one of the double sets of curved staircases that led to a set of – locked – doorways back to earth. His brawny arms were folded over his chest, his head bowed so low. His long, single black braid had fallen over one shoulder, and his face was cast in shadow.

The fact that I knew he, too, was crying – and that the reason Henry kept slipping from the room for more tea wasn't because anyone wanted it, but so I wouldn't see *his* tears – didn't make it easier to bear.

Maybe because he was a man of science and it was his job to break bad news, Mr Graves was the only permanent resident of the Underworld not shedding any tears. His words simply caused other people to.

'When I said troubling,' the doctor went on, fumbling to slip his old-fashioned stethoscope into one of the deep pockets of his black coat, 'of course what I meant was that it's troubling in an intellectually curious manner. You see, all of us were granted eternal life, so long as we don't stray too far from the Underworld. Technically, the captain didn't do that.'

'But *technically*,' Kayla said, 'he's still dead.'

'Well, yes,' Mr Graves admitted. 'I'm afraid that's true.'

In the brief silence that followed, my personal cellphone buzzed – no doubt I had another text message from the National Weather Service in Isla Huesos – and at the same time, John's tablet, which was tucked into my sash beside the phone, let out a chime.

No one remarked on this, least of all me. John's tablet had been doing this at regular intervals – notifying me whenever a new soul had arrived and needed to be sorted.

How John hadn't been driven witless by these near constant alerts, I had no idea. I was ready to pitch the stupid thing across the room. Unfortunately, that wouldn't do anything to bring John back.

'So what gives, Doc?' Reed asked.

'I beg your pardon?' Mr Graves looked confused.

'Why'd the dude die?'

'Oh. I'm afraid I don't know.' Mr Graves sighed. 'I can't find a wound. No sign of trauma or internal injury. He doesn't appear to have drowned—'

'Why did he die this time and not before?' I asked, my voice sounding croaky from disuse. 'He's been hurt by Furies plenty of other times, badly' – I kept my gaze averted from the scars on his chest, the scars it seemed a lifetime ago that I'd run my fingers across, making him gasp – 'and he didn't die then. Why this time?'

'I honestly couldn't say. If I were to perform an autopsy, then of course—'

I dropped the teacup I'd been holding in my hand. It fell

to the stone floor, spilling its lukewarm contents, but didn't shatter.

Before anyone could move to clean the puddle up, however, it was quickly lapped away by John's massive dog, Typhon, who had stationed himself at the end of John's bed from the moment they'd lowered him on to it, refusing to move.

A part of me had wondered if the dog's hot breath might warm some life back into his master. So far, sadly, this hadn't worked.

'Perhaps,' Mrs Engle said, stooping to lift the teacup, 'it might be better to leave talk of autopsies and such things until we've all had time to grieve—'

I wasn't crying enough to miss the sidelong glance she threw me. By *we*, she meant *me*.

'Yeah, Doc,' Alex said. *Zzzzzppt* went the pages of the book in his fingers. 'No offence, but your bedside manner could use a little work.'

'Cabrero,' Kayla said, narrowing her eyes at Alex. 'If you do that one more time, I will take that book from you and hit you with it till *you're* dead. Again.'

From the wall where he leaned, Reed smirked.

'Please,' Chloe said, miserably, raising her head from her steepled fingers. 'Could you please not fight, you guys?'

'No one is fighting,' Mr Liu said from the staircase where he sat, not lifting his head. 'Any more.'

Alex's fingers stilled on the book, and he cast Kayla and Reed warning looks. 'No. Sorry. No, we're not.'

'I beg your pardon, Miss Oliviera,' Mr Graves said to me

with an apologetic smile. 'I simply meant that an autopsy is often the only way to determine the cause of death in cases like this. I certainly wouldn't perform one on the captain, nor do I recommend digging a grave for him . . . at least, not yet.'

I raised my head, a twinge – just a tiny one – of hope darting through me.

'Why?' I asked.

'Only that there's reason,' Mr Graves said, 'to suppose that the captain might wake up.'

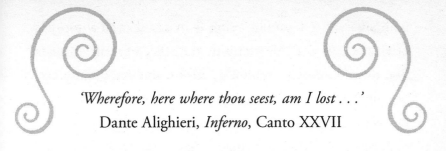

'Wherefore, here where thou seest, am I lost . . .'
Dante Alighieri, *Inferno*, Canto XXVII

The twinge of hope I'd felt turned to a spark.

I knew that was ridiculous. Dead was dead. If anyone knew that, it was me.

Still, I couldn't help noticing Mr Liu's head jerk up, as if he, too, had felt a spark of hope.

Nor could I help repeating, 'Wake up? How could John wake up from being dead?'

'Like me, you mean?' Alex asked. Now that most of my tears had dried up, I could see that the book he was holding was *A History of the Isle of Bones*, which Mr Smith had loaned to me, and which had caused John and me to have one of our biggest fights.

I couldn't remember who'd won that fight. I couldn't remember why we'd fought – why we'd ever wasted what precious little time we had fighting about anything at all – in the first place.

'Not like you,' Mr Liu growled at Alex from the darkness, his tone disapproving.

'Mr Liu is right,' Mr Graves said. 'You were granted a second chance at life by your cousin and Captain Hayden. The captain, on the other hand, was granted a second chance at life by the Fates, along with a set of extraordinary gifts, one of which was the ability to grant life himself. He then brought all of us back to life. We've all been attacked by Furies before, but none of us has ever been killed.' He turned his head back towards me. 'It was from a Fury attack that I lost my sight, you know. Though we heal much more quickly here, we're not immune to injury or pain. But this is the first time death has been the result of a Fury attack.'

I glanced involuntarily at John's supine body, taking in the long white scars that marred his otherwise perfect skin. The fact that the full-time residents of the Underworld weren't immune to injury had been plainly obvious to me for a long time.

The fact that they were immune to ageing, but apparently not death, was only just dawning on me.

'So?' Alex asked rudely. The jibe at his not deserving his second chance at life had evidently stung a little.

'So while it's not *likely*,' Mr Graves said, 'I'd say there's every reason to be hopeful that the captain will recover his heartbeat, just as I'm hopeful that with time I'll recover my sight.' He reached out to pat my knee, the part of me that was closest to him. I don't know how he'd known it was there. Maybe he felt my body heat, the way I could feel Typhon's hot breath. 'Time heals all wounds, you know, Miss Oliviera, even in this place.'

I suppose he did it to comfort me, the way Kayla had patted my shoulder. But I didn't feel comforted, neither by the gesture nor his words. The spark of hope I'd felt died as surely as if someone had doused it with a cup of tea.

This wasn't how it was supposed to go. Mr Graves was supposed to make everything better, not tell me the same kind of platitudes my own doctors had told my parents back when they'd been convinced I was crazy because I kept seeing a leather-jacketed mystery boy every time my life was in jeopardy.

Every reason to be hopeful? Time heals all wounds?

When someone in the medical field started spewing those golden oldies, it was time to give up all hope entirely.

I wanted to leap from the bed and strangle him, but I was pretty sure people who strangled blind doctors didn't get to go on the nice boat after they died.

'So we're just supposed to sit here and wait, while the Furies are out there, most likely preparing to attack again? We're supposed to *hope* John comes back from—' I shook my head, overwhelmed with confusion and, suddenly, frustration . . . though at whom or what, I wasn't sure. 'Where *is* he, anyway? His soul, I mean? Where would the soul of the lord of the Underworld go when he dies while he's *in* the Underworld?' In my imagination, John and Hope were somewhere together, enjoying a nice plate of waffles. But I highly doubted this was the case.

'Now *that*,' Mr Graves said, his unkempt grey eyebrows furrowing, 'is an interesting question, and one over which the captain and I have had some lively discussions. According to the myths – in which of course I do not believe as a man of science – there was a Greek god of death, Thanatos, and he—'

I shook my head, images of John and Hope dining on

waffles instantly dissipating. 'Thanatos? Who's Thanatos? I thought Hades was the Greek god of the dead.'

'Only of the Underworld,' Mr Graves said. 'Thanatos was a very minor god, but it was he who was in charge of bringing actual death upon mortals and then escorting them to Hades.'

'Like the angel of death?' Chloe asked, innocently, as I felt the ground seem to rock beneath me.

'Oh, he was no angel,' Mr Graves said. 'Even the gods themselves, including Hades, hated Thanatos, because he would take life indiscriminately. And, once taken, he would never surrender it. Nonsense, of course, but the Greeks weren't known for their scientific expertise . . . although, interestingly, it's from the name Thanatos that we get certain medical terms, such as eu*thana*sia, which literally translates to a *good death*—'

'You knew about this Thanatos guy all along,' I asked carefully, having recovered from the shock of his revelation, '*and you never thought to mention him before?*'

Mr Graves looked a bit startled. 'Of course I knew about him. But you can't think that means I believe him to be real. I only mentioned him because you asked me—'

'*What if he's real?*' I demanded, climbing to my feet. 'What if he's real and he has John?'

'But that's preposterous,' Mr Graves said with a humourless laugh. 'He doesn't exist.'

'We've never seen the Fates before, either, but we know for a fact they exist, don't we?'

Mr Graves blinked. 'Yes, but we've seen empirical

evidence of their existence.'

'We may be looking at empirical evidence of the existence of Thanatos right now!'

'My dear Miss Oliviera,' Mr Graves said. 'It's good not to lose hope. But keep in mind Thanatos is a *fictional* character made up by an ancient civilization in order to explain death, a natural phenomena, to a frightened populace in the absence of science.'

'Like Hades and Persephone?' I countered. 'And the Underworld? *That* kind of fictional?'

Mr Graves's mouth fell open, but he seemed at a loss for what to say. I'd stumped him.

'What if Thanatos is the one who's behind this Fury attack,' I demanded, 'and he has John? If he does exist, I want to find him, so I can do something to help John' – I flung my arm out to indicate the next room and the courtyard beyond it – 'and maybe even all those people out there, other than sit around and *hope*.'

I half expected that at the mention of her name, there'd be a flutter of white wings and Hope would show up. But she didn't. Either she was lying dead somewhere on the beach with all those other birds, or she'd fled – along with the Fates – for some place where hope actually existed.

Mr Graves cleared his throat, but it was Mrs Engle who spoke.

'You've already helped all of us a great deal, dear,' she said kindly.

'You really have,' Chloe agreed from where she sat on the floor, stroking Typhon's head. The two of them made an odd-looking pair, like something out of an illustrated version of *Beauty and the Beast* . . . if Beauty had had blood in her hair.

'Well, I'm not so sure,' Henry harrumphed as he came clomping back into the room, a newly warmed pot of tea in his hands and an apron tied round his waist that was so large on his childish body the hem trailed nearly to the floor. 'All the people you've helped can barely fit into the castle as it is. They're spilling over into the back gardens and the stable yard and into the hallways, not to mention *my* kitchen—'

For a second, the room seemed to turn as red as the flowers that grew on the tree across from John's crypt in the Isla Huesos Cemetery.

I didn't panic. It seemed like a good sign to me, the first indication that the blood was beginning to pump again in my veins. I'd been almost sure it had frozen solid when I'd first seen John's body floating in the water.

'What was I supposed to do?' I demanded. 'Furies are on the loose, birds of prey were dropping out of the sky like feather bombs, there aren't any boats coming and it's raining blood. Do you think I should have just left them there?'

'Miss Oliviera.' It was Mr Graves's voice. I couldn't see anything too well, due to the red staining everything. But I could hear perfectly well. 'Need I remind you that they're already dead?'

'*Souls* of the dead.' I pointed at John, though of course Mr Graves couldn't see my finger, and to be truthful I could see only the dimmest outline of it. '*He* could be one of them. *I* was one of them once. *She's* one of them.' I pointed in the general direction of Mrs Engle. 'So are they.' Chloe and Reed. 'No one gets left behind. *No one.*'

'I understand that,' Mr Graves said gently. I'm certain he couldn't tell what was happening with my vision – no one could but me. But he must have recognized by the tremor in my voice how upset I was. 'All of this – everything you've done – serves the dead and serves them well. But a physician's responsibility must always be what's best for the *living*. Regardless of the strength of our feelings for the dead, we must always think to ourselves, *How can I best serve the living?* For it is the living whom we serve and who matter most.'

Slowly, the red began to recede from my eyes.

'I know that,' I said, slightly ashamed of my outburst. 'I went to Coffin Fest.' With the very person for whom it had been named – whether its organizers knew it or not. 'I do understand how important it is to properly dispose of the dead –' my gaze slid towards John's body – 'when the time comes.'

'Then you know,' Mr Graves said, 'that it isn't only because of the threat of disease. It's because of the very real possibility of revenants.'

'Could you people please speak English?' Reed asked. 'What's a revenant?'

'A revenant is someone who's come back from the dead,' Mr Graves said, 'the way many in Isla Huesos believe the captain had, because they often saw him roaming the

91

cemetery. That's how Coffin Night became a tradition . . .
The people of Isla Huesos came to believe if they enacted a
yearly funeral pyre tradition the captain, whose spirit was
restless from an improper burial, would rest. But a revenant
is dead, not alive, like you and the captain.'

'Wait. You mean a zombie?' Reed's voice rose excitedly.
'Is that what those Fury things are that everyone keeps
talking about? *Zombies?*'

'Or ghosts?' Alex asked. 'If you guys say we were running
from *ghosts* back on that beach, I swear to God, I'll—'

Henry slammed the teapot down on a side table with
enough force to shut up both Alex and Reed. When he spun
round to face us, the expression on his pink-cheeked face
was as angry as I'd ever seen it.

'Ghosts? You think a ghost did *that*?' He thrust a finger
at John.

'Well, isn't that what those Fury things are?' Alex asked.
'Really badass ghosts?'

Mr Graves rolled his sightless eyes towards the ceiling.

'Ghosts want to hurt people on earth who wronged them
while they were alive.' Mr Liu's deep voice came from the
recess of the staircase. 'Furies only want to hurt the captain –
and those of us close to him – for wronging them after
death. The closest thing to a zombie is what any of you
would be if you left this world and re-entered your corpse
after it had begun rotting.'

Looking a little shame-faced, both Reed and Alex lowered
their gazes to the floor. In the silence that followed, the
sound of a scuffle could be heard breaking out in the

courtyard. Then Frank's voice, grinding out a curt warning, drifted towards us: 'Everyone keep your hands to yourself, or I guarantee you'll lose 'em.'

The warning was accompanied by a curse word or two colourful enough to make Chloe blush. Mrs Engle seemed offended, too, since she said, in a scandalized tone, 'Really, I've had as much of this as I can take. Ghosts and Furies and zombies? Could we please try to remember that a young man is dead?'

She seemed to have forgotten that she, too, was dead.

'Sorry, ma'am.' Frank appeared in one of the archways, pushing back the gauzy curtain and striding, panting and bloodied from a cut on his forehead, into the main room. 'But it's getting a bit dicey out there.' To me, he said, 'It'll be dark soon. What are we going to do about that lot?' On the words *that lot*, he tilted his head in the direction of the courtyard.

'They're hungry, but there's nothing to feed 'em or to give 'em to drink, except beer,' Henry added. 'We're already running low on tea.'

All eyes, I noticed with alarm, were on me, as if I were supposed to do something about the fact that we were running low on tea.

'What are you looking at *me* for?' I asked. The anger flowing through my veins had definitely been preferable to the despair that had been slogging through them before, but now that it had faded, along with the light outside, I felt tired and confused. '*I'm* not in charge.'

As if in direct denial of this, John's tablet began to chime again at my waist to indicate that yet another new soul had entered the land of the dead.

'Actually,' Mr Liu said, rising to his feet, 'I think you *are* in charge. The captain gave that to you.'

'Right. He chose you. You're *the one*.' Henry sounded exactly as he had the first day we'd met, when he'd been just as quick to assure me that I was not, in fact, *the one*. 'Don't you remember?'

I looked from the chiming tablet back towards their inquisitive faces.

'Well, *I* don't know what to do,' I said, though I knew this wasn't a good thing for anyone in a management-level position to admit. 'What have you guys done before when this has happened?'

Mr Graves's shaggy grey eyebrows rose to their limits as he stared at a point several feet above my head. 'Miss Oliviera,' he said. 'The Furies have never destroyed two of our boats and killed the captain before. And certainly no one has ever invited the souls of the dead up from the beach and into the castle.'

I didn't miss the unspoken accusation in his voice. *No one until* you, *you strange girl who sees red – literally – whenever you get angry.*

'True,' Frank said. 'But then the Fates have never left us before, either.'

The Fates have never left us before, either. The words caused a chill to go down my spine and the fine hair on the backs of my arms to stand up. I glanced over my shoulder at the still, waxen form of John stretched out upon the bed.

Wake up, I attempted to will him with my mind. *Don't leave me alone with this mess. Don't leave me alone, ever.*

His wide chest didn't move. His eyelids remained shut.

'What are Fates?' asked Chloe in a small voice from where she still knelt beside Typhon at John's bedside.

'The opposite of Furies,' Mr Graves explained to her. 'Spirits of good, instead of evil.'

'Well,' Reed said drily. 'There definitely aren't any of those around here.'

I saw Chloe give Reed's foot a nudge with her own. 'How can you say that?' she whispered.

'I didn't mean you.' Reed smiled at her. 'Your spirit's looking plenty good from here.'

Alex, having overheard this, curled his lip in disgust.

'Not *me*,' Chloe whispered, and nodded in my direction. '*Her*. How can you say that after everything she did to help us?'

Reed glanced towards me. 'Oh, right. Her spirit's looking pretty good, too,' he added generously.

Alex rolled his eyes and said, 'Fates aren't the kind of spirits you can see, you idiot. They're like Furies. You can only—'

'I always thought that the Fates were Greek goddesses in charge of mankind's destiny,' Mrs Engle interrupted, seeming anxious to break the sudden tension between the two boys, both of whom were clearly attracted to Chloe. When Mrs Engle saw that she had their attention, she went on, 'I worked as a school nurse for thirty years – retired now, of course. But those kinds of things do

95

tend to sink in and stay with you—'

'Who cares what the Fates are?' Alex burst out. Mrs Engle's scheme wasn't working. 'The question is, where'd they go? And how do we get them back?'

'I don't think it will be easy,' Mr Graves said. He sounded annoyed with Alex. Welcome to the club. 'I believe they've been driven away because there's an imbalance here. An imbalance is virtually always caused by pestilence—' A note of primness crept into the surgeon's voice, as it always did whenever he gave a lecture on pestilence, his favourite subject (aside from beer). 'Whenever an imbalance occurs and pestilence is able to slip into a system, it causes infection.'

'Like when I got my eyebrow pierced,' Kayla asked, 'and I didn't clean it well enough, and it got infected?'

'You pierced your *eyebrow*?' Mr Graves turned his head towards her, his expression horrified. 'Good God, young lady, *why*?'

'Never mind that now,' I said impatiently. 'What can we do to fix the imbalance . . . drive away the Furies and get back the Fates?'

'Well,' Mr Graves said, returning his attention to me. 'If we could determine what's caused the imbalance, I'm quite certain we could correct it. But until then I'm afraid we, like the captain, have only one thing to hang on to, and that's—'

I held up a single hand. 'Don't say it.'

Mr Graves looked taken aback. 'How did you know what I was going to say?'

I lowered my hand. 'Because it was going to be hope.

And I don't want to hear the word *hope* again. I don't believe in it any more.'

Hearing this was apparently more than Chloe could bear. She rose from the floor – leaving Typhon looking sad to have lost his ear scratcher – and hurried towards me.

'Pierce, you mustn't say that,' she said. 'These light momentary afflictions are preparing us for an eternal weight of glory beyond all comparison—'

I cut her off with a grim look. 'I've got bad news for you, Chloe. There's not going to be any eternal weight of glory unless we get you, and all the rest of these people, to a boat. Mr Graves, I've got some news for you, too.' I turned towards him. 'In twenty-first-century America, where I'm from, we've got better weapons against infections than hope.'

Mrs Engle coughed politely. 'Dear, if you're speaking about antibiotics, I believe the doctor was using the term *infection* as a metaphor—'

'Why, yes,' Mr Graves said to Mrs Engle, looking pleased. 'I was.'

'Well, I'm not,' I said. I lifted the diamond on the end of my necklace. 'I'm talking about this.'

'I don't know what an antibiotic is,' Henry said, reaching round his waist to untie the apron he was wearing, then tossing it to the floor. 'But, if you're talking about killing Furies, I'm ready.'

'So am I,' Frank said, drawing a knife from his belt. 'Only where do we find them?'

'The same place we can find food for our guests,' I said.

'And a couple of new boats to take them where they need to go.'

Mr Graves looked bewildered. 'And where would that be?'

'Isla Huesos,' I said.

Mr Graves's expression of bewilderment turned to a frown. 'Isla Huesos? That port of degradation and sin?' I'd forgotten he wasn't a fan. 'And how do you think you're going to get there? Only the captain possessed the ability to travel between this world and the next, and he is, to put it mildly, indisposed.'

'That isn't strictly true,' I said. 'Well, it's true John's indisposed, but it isn't true he's the only one who possessed the ability to go back and forth between this world and the next.' I glanced down the hallway at the curved double staircase I knew so well. 'Does anyone know where John keeps the keys to the doors at the top of those stairs?'

For the first time in a long time, I saw Mr Liu smile. 'No,' he said. 'But I know where there's an axe.'

The infernal hurricane that never rests
Hurtles the spirits onward in its rapine;
Whirling them round, and smiting, it molests them.
Dante Alighieri, *Inferno*, Canto V

'It will never work.'

I was at the dining table, filling my tote bag with things I thought I'd need for my journey, trying to ignore Mr Graves.

'It won't bring him back,' Mr Graves continued in a low voice, so the others wouldn't overhear. 'And, even if it would, the captain would never want you to risk your own life in order to save his.'

'Then I guess it's a good thing he isn't around to watch,' I whispered. Raising my voice, I said to my cousin Alex, 'Give me that book.'

'You think *A History of the Isle of Bones* is what's caused the imbalance that's making this place implode?' Alex read off the title in a sarcastic voice as he handed the book over. 'Yeah, Pierce, I'm sure that's probably it.'

'Things were fine around here before it showed up,' I said tersely as I put the book in my bag.

'In that case,' Alex said, 'you better take me along, too.'

'The whole reason they brought you here is because everyone back in Isla Huesos was trying kill you,' Kayla pointed out. 'Remember?'

'Actually,' Mr Graves said, 'they succeeded in killing him.' Lowering his voice again, he whispered to me, 'Just as the Furies succeeded in killing the captain. Which was always their ultimate goal. Now that they've succeeded, I can't imagine they'll continue to attack us. So you see, Miss Oliviera, there's no point in your embarking on this scheme of yours—'

'Really? What are we going to feed these people?' I asked. 'How are we going to get them to their final destinations? Are we simply going to wait for the Fates to come back? Or are we going to make our own luck, like my father always said a truly successful person does?'

Mr Graves shook his head. 'I highly doubt your father would go along with this if he knew what you were up to.'

'Well, then it's a good thing he doesn't know.'

'Not *everyone* back in Isla Huesos was trying to kill me,' Alex declared. 'Only Seth Rector and his cronies. Which goes to show that I was on to something. If I wasn't close to finding evidence implicating them instead of my father in Jade's murder, why would they have killed me?'

'Because you found their stash,' Kayla reminded him. 'Drug dealers tend not to like that.'

'That's why Pierce has got to take me with her,' Alex said. 'I can explain that to the police.'

'I thought you said the police are all in Seth Rector's father's pocket.' Kayla was sitting on top of the dining-room table, swinging her legs beneath the long skirt of her purple gown.

'Maybe not all of them.' I paused as I dropped my mobile

phone into my tote bag, thinking back to the assembly they'd had on my first day of school. 'Police Chief Santos seemed really determined to keep Coffin Night from happening.'

'Maybe because he wants to keep people out of the cemetery, the hub of Seth Rector's drug empire,' Alex said. 'The chief is probably getting kickbacks.'

'Or maybe,' Kayla said, 'you watch way too much television.'

'Oh, I'm sorry, Kayla,' Alex said, his voice dripping with sarcasm. 'Did *your* dad spend most of your life in jail for a non-violent crime he was probably tricked into committing by Seth Rector's father, or was that *my* dad?'

'Jesus,' Reed said from the chair at the dining table where he'd been quietly sitting. 'What kind of town do you people live in, anyway? Coffin Night? Drugs?' He looked at Chloe, huddled in a chair opposite his. 'Did you know about any of this stuff?'

She shook her head, her eyes wide. 'I'm homeschooled.'

'I agree with that young man,' Mr Graves said, his head turned in the direction from which he'd heard Reed's voice. 'This has all gone too far. I understand that Miss Oliviera is anxious to get revenge for the captain's tragic death –'

Or find Thanatos, I thought but didn't add aloud. *If he exists.*

'– but the welfare of these people has to be our highest priority at the moment. And the sad truth of the matter is now that they've killed the captain the Furies are no doubt gone for good—'

Thunder rumbled overhead. But it was only because of the growing storm outside, not John being witty, since when I glanced sharply towards the bed I saw that John was still gone. As it had grown darker outside – not to mention colder and wetter – it had been thundering more often.

We'd also allowed more of the souls of the dead inside. I noticed a few of them start in alarm at the ominous sound.

My spirits lower than ever, I decided I didn't want to argue any more with Mr Graves. I didn't want to *talk* any more. My eyes were hot and tired from all the crying I'd done, and my throat hurt, despite the amount of tea Mrs Engle had foisted upon me to soothe the ache.

I feared nothing would ever soothe the ache, however. Especially since I'd come to the slow realization that, with John gone, so was the bond between us. Why was I even doing any of this? I was free to go back to my old life, before I'd ever known anything about magic diamond pendants, death deities and the realm of the dead.

So there was nothing to keep me from picking up my bag, stepping back into my own world, and leaving all these people and their problems and complaints behind.

Yet, for some reason, here I was still standing in the Underworld, arguing with old Mr Graves like someone who still had a stake in this game.

'Look,' I said to the ship surgeon. 'Remember what you said? Our responsibility must always be to do what's best for the living. Right? Which means we need to get the dead to their final destinations before they start piling up down here. Otherwise, next thing we know, they'll be overflowing into the streets of Isla Huesos, and we'll have—'

Mr Graves looked pained. '*Pestilence.*' He almost spat the word.

'Exactly. But if I can find a couple of boats and figure out a way to get them here, and maybe find this Thanatos guy, too – if he exists – and get him to let go of John . . . and, while I'm at it, prove who killed Alex, and my counsellor, Jade . . . well, you said it yourself: I've got to try. It's my responsibility.'

'And how,' Mr Graves asked, his sightless eyes wide, 'do you plan on doing any *one* of those things?'

'I haven't the slightest idea,' I said flatly. 'I'll just have to figure it out as I go along.'

'That,' Mr Graves said, 'is hardly reassuring.'

Even if I did flee to my mother's house, the next time I saw my grandmother, I'd remember what she'd done. She'd never be punished for it.

I couldn't live with that. Not that it would make any difference. Without John, my life would be as bleak and meaningless as one of those boring black-and-white movies they were always showing at the cinema art house back in Connecticut.

But innocent people, like my counsellor, Jade, would still have been murdered, and someone needed to pay for that. And the people here in the Underworld still needed my help. I couldn't abandon them, no matter how hopeless I felt. They were my responsibility now, the way they used to be John's. They were the choice I'd made that night in his bed when he'd asked if I understood the consequences of what we were doing. I'd thought he'd meant the consequence of possibly creating a demon baby.

What he'd meant was *this*.

You couldn't go back to your mom's house and hide under the covers when you had a baby, pretending you couldn't hear its cries. That big, fat, demanding baby was your responsibility now. You had to take care of it, for as long as it needed you, even when it wasn't being cute and giggly, but when it was crying and hungry.

I should never have worried about having a demon baby as a result of making love with John in the Underworld: the Underworld itself is a demon baby.

I should have known there was a catch. In Greek myths, there was *always* a catch.

'Ready, Pierce?' Frank had come over, a heavy-looking sack hanging off one shoulder. Whatever was in the sack jingled faintly as he walked.

'Why does *he* get to go with you, and not me?' Kayla glared.

'Because I'm the ... what's it called? Oh, right. The muscle.' Frank had cleaned up the cut on his forehead, but he still resembled, with his long facial scar, black leather trousers, and multiple tattoos, a cross between a pirate and a biker from a motorcycle gang. In my opinion, Frank had been born in the wrong century.

Kayla whipped her head round to glare at me. 'If you guys are going to kill Farah Endicott, I want to be there.'

'Why would anyone want to kill Farah Endicott?' Alex asked. 'What'd she ever do to you? Seth Rector's the one who murdered me. If anyone's going to get popped, it's him. And I should be the one who gets to do it.'

'You guys,' I said, dropping John's tablet into the tote bag. I couldn't keep carrying things around in my sash. Not only did it look unwieldy, it was uncomfortable.

And, now that the Fates were gone, I couldn't wish for a new gown with pockets. I couldn't even bring myself to change into the only modern-day dress in my closet. That's because it was the one John had asked me to wear on our first date . . . the one that had ended up being what I'd worn the night we'd . . . well, never mind. I'd never be able to wear that dress again.

'No one is getting popped,' I said firmly.

Mr Graves agreed.

'Yes,' he said. 'Please cease this talk of, er, popping people immediately. This is exactly why I said from the start of this that the captain wouldn't approve of any of—'

'Mr Graves,' I said to him. 'I've got this.' I pulled my diamond from the bodice of my dress and showed it to Kayla. 'Look. This kills Furies when I touch it to someone who's possessed by one. It doesn't kill people. And, as far as I know, Farah Endicott is not possessed by a Fury.' Farah's boyfriend, Seth, I wasn't so sure about, so I didn't mention him, since I didn't want to rile up Alex any more than he already was.

Kayla looked down at the stone in my fingers. 'It's the exact same colour as my streaks,' she said, pulling on one of the violet strands in her voluminous curls. 'And my dress.'

'It is right now,' I said, tucking the diamond away again.

'It only turns this colour when you're close by. I don't know what that means, but that's what it does.'

Kayla looked pleased. 'It means you should take me with you. Amethyst's my birthstone. I was born in February. I'm an Aquarius. Aquarians are highly adaptable. They get along with everyone.'

Alex made a sound in his throat that suggested he didn't agree with this statement.

'Everyone,' Kayla corrected herself, 'except fake bitches like Farah Endicott. And my brother, of course.'

Frank let the sack he'd been shouldering fall to the floor. The jingling sound it made as it hit was loud enough to draw the attention of a number of people in the room. 'No. She's not going. They *saw* her. Or they will have by now, on the film from those cameras at that bloody tomb. It's too dangerous.'

'They saw all of us,' I reminded him.

'Oh, sweetie,' Kayla purred, wrapping her hands round one of Frank's heavily tattooed biceps. 'It's so sexy when you get brutish and protective. Even though it won't do any good, because I'm going. We may be in the Underworld, but I'm pretty sure this is still a free country. Or under one, anyway. You can't tell me what to do.'

Mr Graves's face had gone almost as purple as my stone. 'Frank. What is in that bag?'

Frank shrugged his arm from Kayla's grip in order to reach defensively for his sack. 'Just a few weapons we might need if we run into trouble, and some gold coins for bribes, of course—'

The surgeon threw an aggrieved look in my direction, as if to say, *This is the team you've chosen to save us?*

I didn't entirely disagree with his opinion on the matter. Taking Frank instead of Mr Liu – who was adding wood to the fire he'd started in the hearth, hoping it would help warm the shivering dead – had been a tough decision.

But what other choice could I have made? The worsening storm outside had forced us to give shelter to hundreds of discontented, hungry people, resulting in a growing storm *inside*. I needed to leave someone strong behind with this rabble, someone who could manage them but who also wasn't a hothead, someone who would keep them safe while also showing them compassion. Already we'd had to banish the man in khaki pants who'd kept insisting to me that he was on the wrong dock, because he'd sidled up to Chloe and done or said something that had caused her to scream, startling Mrs Engle so badly she'd dropped a tea tray.

She's my daughter, Khaki Pants had insisted. *I can't believe she's here. I just wanted to say hello.*

Chloe, her eyes wide and frightened, insisted she'd never seen Khaki Pants before.

I understood more than ever why the two sets of passengers had to be kept separate, and also why strong individuals of a certain temperament were needed to ensure that they stayed that way.

I was also finally able to understand how, after nearly two hundred years of dealing with this, John had lost his grip on his humanity, and why, by the time I'd met him, he'd so often behaved like a brute.

It seemed wiser to take Frank and leave Mr Liu. Kayla, however, was another matter.

Until she said, as I was shouldering my bag and turning to leave, 'You know, I left my car parked at the cemetery after I followed you guys there. If the storm's gotten as bad as everyone says, you're going to need a ride.'

I didn't want to endanger anyone's life except my own. But considering all the warnings I'd received on my phone – and the fact that John wasn't around to teleport me anywhere – the offer of free transportation that would keep me dry was too good to pass up.

'Fine,' I said to her. 'But you're staying in the car. You're the driver, that's *it.*'

Alex cried out in dismay, even as Kayla let out a happy squeal and began to leap around. Mr Graves shook his head in disapproval. Reed, still shirtless over at the dining table, raised his hand.

'Excuse me,' he said. '*I* can drive. Why does she get to be your wheelman and I don't?'

'Because Miss Rivera isn't dead,' Mr Graves snapped. 'And you are. If you were to leave the Underworld now for any reason other than to re-enter your corpse – which I have no doubt is in a mortuary somewhere, either filled with embalming fluid or cremated to ashes – you'll lose any chance whatsoever at moving on to what awaits you in the afterlife. That is your choice, of course, but you asked earlier what a revenant is. A revenant is what you'll be if you choose to walk out that door . . . doomed forevermore to abide here with us in the Underworld. Is that really what you want, young man?'

Reed put his arm down. 'Uh, no. I withdraw the question.'

I was zipping up my tote bag, ready to go, when Henry approached me.

'Miss,' he said, tugging on my skirt.

'Forget it, Henry,' I said. 'You're not coming. We need you here, and not just to bring people tea. You're the only one who knows where anything is, now that John is . . . away.'

'No,' he said. 'Not that. I have something for you.'

I turned and held out my hand, hoping he wasn't going to present me with a kiss. If he did, I knew I would completely break down. I could not – would not – fail these people.

And yet I had no idea how to save them.

Instead of rising on to his tiptoes to press his lips to my cheek, as I'd feared he might, he pressed a well-worn, smooth piece of wood into my palm.

'What's this?' I asked, surprised.

'It's my slingshot,' he said matter-of-factly. 'I modified it for you.'

I saw that he had, indeed, tied one of my hair bands between the two wooden prongs.

'Vulcanized rubber is best,' he explained, pulling on it. 'I figured since you were a girl, and your fingers aren't very strong, you'd need something quite a bit stretchier than the rope I normally use. This thing from your hair works like a peach. What you do is, you put your diamond in the pocket

109

here, see' – he demonstrated using a small stone – 'stretch it back, and then let go. If you run into anyone who's possessed by a Fury, just shoot your diamond at 'em. That way you don't have to get so near them, see? And they can't hurt you.'

Tears welled in my eyes, but I blinked quickly in order to dash them away before he could notice.

'Henry,' I said. 'It's the most ingenious thing I've ever seen.'

I didn't mention that if I went around shooting my diamond necklace at Furies, I would also have to run around trying to find where it had landed after hitting them. This apparently hadn't occurred to the boy. While he'd lived in the Underworld for more than a century, he was still mentally only ten or eleven or so.

'I thought you'd like it,' he said, looking pleased.

I tucked the slingshot into my bag, then reached down to ruffle his hair and kiss him on the forehead.

'Thank you,' I said.

Henry's round cheeks turned pink.

'It was nothing,' he said, and started to turn away, then seemed to have second thoughts and flung his arms around my waist, which was approximately as high as he stood.

'Don't die,' he said into my stomach.

'I won't,' I said, hugging him back. It was more difficult than ever to hold back my tears. 'You don't, either.'

'I can't,' he said, releasing me as abruptly as he'd flung his arms around me. He reached up to scrub angrily at his eyelids, then glanced nervously in the direction of the bed on which John's body lay. 'At least, it's not *likely*.'

I didn't follow his gaze. I still couldn't glance towards the bed without feeling the way I had when I'd fallen into that swimming pool the day I'd died . . . like icy cold water was filling my lungs.

'Keep it that way,' I said to Henry, and turned towards the bottom of the double staircase, where Frank and Kayla already stood, waiting for me.

'Pierce,' Frank said. 'Tell her she isn't coming.'

'She's coming,' I said. 'We need her car and her driving skills. I don't have a licence. I'm not a very good driver.'

'*I* can drive the bloody car,' Frank said.

'No, you can't,' Kayla said. 'You died before cars were invented.'

'If I can navigate a two-hundred-foot clipper ship through the Florida Straits during a hurricane, I'm fairly certain I can drive an automobile.'

'I am the only one who drives my car,' Kayla said.

Mr Liu stood alone on the opposite staircase. I could tell from his expression that he wanted to speak to me privately. I crossed the flagstone floor until I reached him. He looked down at me, his expression sombre.

'When you first came here,' he said quietly, 'you were like a kite flying high in the wind, with no one holding its strings. Only the wind that fuelled you was your anger.'

I shook my head. 'I wasn't angry. I was frightened.'

'Maybe a little,' he said. 'But mostly you were angry, like the captain. That isn't a bad thing. That's why he chose you. You're very alike. You both feel angry – at what was

111

done to you, and at what you see being done to others. You both need someone holding on to your strings, to keep your anger from taking you so high into the sky you're lost forever.'

Tears filled my eyes. This time, I couldn't stop them. All I could do was hope that if I didn't speak they might go away on their own.

'Now that the captain is gone,' Mr Liu said, 'there's no one to hold on to your strings. You're going to go wherever the wind – your anger – blows you. You might even blow away from us altogether. The thought has crossed your mind.'

'No.' The word burst from me unbidden, along with a sob. I choked both back. 'No,' I said in a calmer voice. 'That isn't true.'

How had he read my mind? And what was this nonsense about my being a kite?

'It is true,' he said. 'Until you get control of your own strings, you can help no one. Not the captain. Not us. Not even yourself.'

I reached up to swipe at my tears.

'Mr Liu,' I said. 'Thank you for that. Now I really need to get going—'

'I know you don't believe me, but I'm not the first to say it to you. Someone else has said it to you before, I think, only in a different way.'

'Mr Liu,' I said, laughing in disbelief through my tears. 'I can guarantee that no one else has ever accused me of being a kite fuelled by anger with no one to hold on to my strings.'

'No. But a person who needs to discover herself?'

Children who fail to do well in school can often still be successful in life – my school counsellor's assurance to my parents, back in Connecticut, suddenly popped into my head – *if they discover something else in which to engage.*

Mr Liu must have read the dawning recognition in my face, since he held out his massive hand. 'Here,' he said.

I looked down. 'Oh, no,' I said, instantly recognizing what he was giving me. 'I can't take that. John said—'

'You must take it.' Mr Liu's voice was unyielding. 'It is the string for you to hold on to.'

It was the whip, neatly coiled and attached to one of Mr Liu's wide leather belts, through which Mr Liu had poked a few extra holes so it would accommodate my slimmer waist.

I took the belt from him, shaking my head even as I reached up to put my arms round his burly neck to hug him. 'Thank you,' I whispered in his ear, which had multiple silver hoops pierced through it.

He patted me awkwardly on the shoulder. 'Remember,' he said. 'Don't let go of your strings.'

My eyes so filled with tears I could hardly see, I nodded, then wrapped the belt round my waist. The last hole fit, but barely. The end of the belt trailed down almost to my knees, so I tucked it back through. I suspected the effect wasn't going to win me any teen magazine fashion awards.

Then Mr Graves was back, saying how there was absolutely no reason for us to go to Isla Huesos, as he was fairly certain he had enough yeast left over from his attempts at beer brewing to bake some bread, and if we could only *wait* –

Thunder clapped again, loudly enough to cause even

113

the thick castle walls to tremble.

'No more waiting.' Mr Liu took me by the arm and began to sweep me up the stairs, saying, in a low voice, 'Go now. We'll hold them off as long as we can—'

'Hold *who* off?' Kayla asked, alarmed, lifting her long skirts as she hurried up the stairs after us. 'The Furies? I thought all they wanted was to kill Pierce's boyfriend.'

Thunder boomed so long the metal sconces on the walls rattled.

'Clearly that isn't all they want,' Mr Liu said. At the top of the stairs, he gave Frank a stern look. 'Don't be late getting back. For your sake, as well as ours.'

Frank adjusted his bag, which tinkled suggestively. 'I know what I'm doing.'

'I very much doubt that,' said Mr Liu.

We reached the open doorway. Standing in front of it was my cousin.

'What if *I'm* the one causing the pestilence?' Alex asked. 'Wouldn't it be better if I came with you? It might draw the Furies away from here.'

'Alex,' I said hotly. 'As you once pointed out to me, the whole world doesn't revolve around you. And I'm pretty sure that's true of the Underworld, too. But if it's so important to you to come with us, please, be my guest.'

Mr Liu might not have been so far off base about me being fuelled by anger after all. Because as I said the words *be my guest*, I shoved Alex into the doorway, then followed him through it, figuring whatever happened next, he'd thoroughly deserve.

'Thou wouldst conduct me there where thou hast said,
That I may see the portal of Saint Peter,
And those thou makest so disconsolate.'
Dante Alighieri, *Inferno*, Canto I

'What the—'

As he stumbled through the doorway, Alex let out a stream of expletives so colourful I was glad Chloe wasn't around to overhear it.

Frank seemed to agree. 'Kiss your mother with that mouth, mate?' he whispered, lifting a finger to his lips.

It was so dark, however, the gesture was barely visible. Outside, I could hear the steady pounding of rain. The scent of moist earth was heavy in the air.

'I don't have a mother,' Alex said irritably to Frank. 'What *is* this place? Why are you whispering? And what's this I'm stepping in?' He lifted his shoes in disgust as they made crunching sounds against the material carpeting the stone floor. 'Sick, it's everywhere.'

'Dried poinciana petals,' I whispered. 'There's a huge tree outside.'

I realized I might have overreacted when I shoved him through the door. I hadn't given him or Kayla much prepping as to what to expect. As a team leader, I kind of sucked.

On the other hand, experience was on my side. The first

time I'd passed through this door, the journey had ended with my own body on a gurney in an emergency room.

This time, because none of us was dead, we ended up somewhere else entirely . . . somewhere I'd also been before. Only that time I'd had John as my guide.

As my eyes adjusted to the dim lighting – Mr Liu had closed the door on his side, blocking off any glow from the Underworld – I could make out Frank's silhouette as he went towards the ornate metal gate at the front of the tomb and checked to see if there was anyone around who might notice us creeping forth.

But who'd be out for a stroll in a cemetery in the middle of a hurricane?

Through the small, cross-shaped slits that had been built into the brick walls, I could see that the dark sky was tinged with pink. Frank's words echoed, once more, through my head.

Red sky at night, sailor's delight. Red sky at morning, sailor take warning.

The digital numbers on Alex's waterproof wristwatch read 11.00 p.m. I could see no sign of streetlights on any of the roads surrounding the cemetery.

'The hurricane must have caused a power outage,' I murmured.

Alex was looking around, as was Kayla, but Alex was the more vocal in his complaints.

'What is this place?' he asked again. 'A church?' He nearly struck his head on the low ceiling and winced. 'For midgets?'

'It's not a church,' Frank said, before I could figure out a diplomatic response. 'But you still might want to show a little respect.'

'Why?' Alex asked. 'Did someone die in here? It sure smells like it.'

'You might say that,' Frank replied. 'It's a crypt.'

Kayla said, 'No way.' Alex's response was less polite.

'Yes, it's a crypt,' I said quickly. No point in glossing over it. 'It acts as a portal through which the souls of the departed can enter the land of the dead . . .'

That's how John had explained it to me once, anyway.

'Unless you aren't dead, of course,' I went on rapidly. 'Which we aren't, so don't worry. Then the portal opens to the Isla Huesos Cemetery.'

My explanation must not have sounded all that reassuring, since Alex started swearing again.

'Crap,' he said, looking panicky. 'You didn't say this is where we're going. You didn't say anything about a cemetery.' He dived to wrap his fingers around the wrought iron gate that barred the way out, poinciana blossoms crunching madly beneath his feet. 'Get me out of here.' He shook the bars when they didn't budge. *Get me out!'*

'Alex,' I said, in what I hoped sounded like a soothing voice. 'Come on. There's nothing here that can hurt you. Truly evil spirits are everywhere *but* graveyards.' This was a conclusion I'd come to through experience . . . the experience of having been murdered in my own backyard.

Alex threw me a disbelieving look over his shoulder. 'Are you kidding me? I got killed in a cemetery, remember?'

'Oh, right,' I said. I'd forgotten Alex's own experience

was quite dissimilar to my own. 'Never mind.'

Frank rested a heavy hand on Alex's shoulder. 'Easy, son,' he said, though he probably wasn't more than a couple of years older – at least in looks – than Alex. 'We need to make sure no one's out there.'

'Of course no one's out there,' Alex cried. 'Look at it. It's a hurricane! But I'd rather be out there in the rain than standing around in some phantom tollbooth, waiting for the dead to pass through me in order to get to the Underworld . . . or for someone to kill me *again*. So get me *out*—'

Frank looked at me, his eyebrows raised.

'Alex,' Kayla said, sounding amused. Despite what she'd seen the last time she'd been in the Isla Huesos Cemetery, she was apparently unbothered at being in it again. 'That's not what *The Phantom Tollbooth* is about.'

'Frank,' I said, feeling sorry for Alex. 'Help him.'

Frank leaned over to help Alex open the gate.

'Anyway,' Kayla went on. 'You were just in the Underworld, surrounded by the undead. What's the difference?'

'The difference is,' Alex said in a tightly controlled voice, 'now I'm back in the cemetery where I died, and I would prefer to exit it as soon as possible, thanks.'

A second later, the gate was open, and Alex burst out of John's tomb. Once he reached the poinciana tree, he turned to stand beneath it, but even its enormous branches didn't offer much shelter from the pouring rain.

'If you think about it,' Kayla said, the first to break the

silence that followed, 'it's kind of normal for him to have post-traumatic stress, considering what happened last time he was in one of these.' She raised her hand to indicate the crypt. 'Except there's no coffin here. Why is that?'

'There was never a body to put in a coffin,' I said to Kayla. 'Up until now. This is John's tomb.'

Kayla's eyes widened, then she quickly looked away.

'Oh,' she said in a small voice. 'I'm sorry.'

'It's OK,' I said. My voice sounded equally small.

I couldn't blame her. It had been hoped that building the crypt would help put John's spirit to rest. Mr Smith – the most recently appointed cemetery sexton – had even had a name carved over the door to the tomb: HAYDEN.

These things had done nothing to quell its owner's indomitable spirit, however, which had remained restless . . . until now.

'You all right?' Frank asked me. I barely heard his voice above the howling of the wind it was so soft, softer than I'd ever heard it. Soft with concern. Concern for me, a girl he'd hated the day he met me.

'I'm fine,' I said quickly, and adjusted my bag so it sat more squarely on my shoulder. 'We need to find something to wedge that door open.'

The door either hadn't been there or hadn't been particularly noticeable any of the other times I'd been inside the tomb . . . No big surprise since it was made of rotting wood and hidden in shadow. I was worried if it didn't stay open we'd be locked forever from the Underworld (unless I *really* messed things up and wound up dying again). I didn't have John's gift of teleportation. If I did manage to get help for these people, I was going to need a way to deliver it to them (although how I was going to fit a boat through such a small door was a problem I was going to have to deal with later).

'Hang on,' Frank said. 'I have just the thing.'

Frank reached down, then pulled a long object from the dead blossoms on the crypt floor. In the darkness I couldn't tell what it was until I heard the sound of breaking glass as he smashed it against the wall.

'Captain Rob's Rum,' I said with a sad smile. The brand had been named after John's abusive, alcoholic father. 'How appropriate.'

'Finally, a use for it that won't give a man a splitting hangover.' Frank wedged the broken neck in the door.

'Are you coming or not?' Alex shouted at us from beneath the poinciana tree.

'We're coming,' I assured him, and stepped out into the rain.

I swooned away as if I had been dying,
And fell, even as a dead body falls.
Dante Alighieri, *Inferno*, Canto V

Kayla found four soggy parking tickets beneath her wipers.

'Isla Huesos cops really *are* evil,' she declared.

She'd unlocked the doors, and we were all inside her messy subcompact.

'You think they'd suspend alternate-side-of-the-street parking regulations during a hurricane,' Alex said. 'I can't believe you didn't get towed.'

'I can't believe your automobile didn't get stolen,' Frank said. 'Is it normal to keep the keys in a little case in the wheel well?'

'It is for me. That way I can't lose them.' Kayla stuffed the parking tickets into her glove compartment, where I couldn't help noticing there appeared to be half a dozen other unpaid tickets. 'Besides, no one ever looks there for them.'

'I'm shocked you ever have trouble finding anything,' Frank commented sarcastically, peeling away an Island Queen napkin that had become stuck to the bottom of his boot. 'It's so tidy in here. What's this?'

Kayla snatched the ruby-coloured bra he'd dug out from behind his back. 'You should know, you're the one who got it off me,' she said.

Alex, seated behind them, hooted. Now that he was safely out of the cemetery, he seemed to be in a better mood.

'Shut up, Cabrero,' Kayla said, chucking the bra at him. Alex laughingly deflected it as Kayla checked her reflection in the light-up compact mirror she'd fished from the side panel of her door. 'Oh, great, my eyeliner is running. I look like a drowned hoochie mama.'

'You look fine,' I said. 'Can we please go before someone sees us?'

'Who's going to see us?' Kayla reached for a spare make-up bag she also kept in the side panel. 'It's pitch-black on this street.'

It was true. All up and down the narrow streets along the cemetery, the windows of every quaintly painted beach cottage were dark, even though, according to Alex's watch, it was now only a little after eleven o'clock at night.

'For all we know,' Kayla went on as she carefully repainted the black lines around her eyes, 'there isn't a single soul left alive in this town except for us. Well, and the cops who gave me these tickets.'

'Thanks, Kayla.' It was Alex's turn to sound sarcastic. 'That's a really pleasant thought. Some of us have family members we're worried about, you know.'

'I'm sure your dad is fine, Alex,' I said as comfortingly as I could. 'The power is out in this part of town, is all.'

'And you're not the only one with family,' Kayla reminded him as she painted. 'I'm worried about my mom. Well, not really, because she's required to be on duty at the hospital for as long as this storm lasts, and the hospital was built to withstand category-five hurricane-force winds. But she's probably freaked I haven't called. Which reminds me, do you think if there's any Furies around they'll find us if I turn on the AC and charge my phone? Because my battery is dead and the windows are too fogged up for me to see out of to drive. Could you all breathe less?'

She switched on the engine, and a second later, a powerful blast of lukewarm air was blowing at Alex and me from the front seat. Kayla immediately pulled her phone from the bodice of her dress and plugged it into the charger on her console. 'OK, Pierce,' she asked, 'where are we going?'

'Richard Smith's house,' I said at the same time Alex said, 'My house.'

Alex glared at me. 'Who's Richard Smith?'

'He's the cemetery sexton. Remember, you met him at school the day we had that assembly about Coffin Night. He's an old friend of Grandpa's. I think he might be able to help us figure out where the Fates went, and if there really is a Thanatos—'

Alex's expression, in the dim glow from Kayla's dashboard, was twisted with outrage. 'Pierce, my dad probably thinks I'm dead—'

'You *are* dead, mate,' Frank said. 'To everyone who ever mattered to you, anyway. Get used to it.'

'But I'm *not* dead,' Alex said. 'I'm an NDE, like Pierce. And the last thing I want to do right now is go visit some old friend of Grandpa's—'

'Alex, Mr Smith is the only person I can think of who

123

might know of a way to help your dad *and* all those people we left behind in the Underworld—'

'Meaning your boyfriend,' Alex interrupted with a scowl.

I prickled. 'I didn't say that.'

'But it's obvious *he's* your biggest priority,' Alex snapped. '*Thanatos?* That was practically the first word out of your mouth. And you never even mentioned going to see your mom. Ever since you met him, *he's* all you care about. The rest of us were worried sick the whole time you were gone, but you didn't care. Now *he's* dead, but he and his world are *still* all you're worried about.'

'Oh, my God, Alex,' I said. 'That isn't true. I worried about you and Uncle Chris and my mom and dad the entire time I was gone.'

Frank tilted the rearview mirror so he could see Alex.

'It's true, mate,' he said. 'First time I ever met her, you were all she talked about, how she had to go back and fetch you out of that coffin. Nearly drove the captain mad.'

I gave Frank a disapproving look in the mirror to show him that I didn't need his help. When I looked back at Alex, I could see that his expression remained defiant, but his eyes had a sheen to them, reflecting the light . . . or maybe some unshed tears.

'I did worry a lot about you,' I said to Alex. 'And your dad, too. But if we don't fix what's happening in the Underworld your dad's problems aren't going to matter, nor are anyone else's who lives in Isla Huesos, because Isla Huesos itself isn't going to be around for much longer.'

Then it occurred to me. *Alex's eyes were reflecting the light.*

What light? All the streetlamps were out, and the dashboard console was glowing green.

'Someone's coming,' I said, glancing away from Alex and down at the diamond at the end of my necklace. Sure enough, it was no longer the comforting purple it always was in Kayla's presence but a deep black.

'What's that?' Kayla asked, pointing.

Through the streams of rain battering the windshield, I could see a single white arc of light swinging along the sidewalk.

'A lantern,' Frank said.

'No,' I said, my skin growing cold, and not because of my damp clothes or because Kayla had the AC set so high. 'It's a flashlight.'

'A flashlight?' Kayla echoed in disbelief. 'Who'd be out in weather like this?'

'No one we want to run into,' I said. 'Start driving.'

'Where?' Kayla asked, beginning to back out from her parking space.

'Anywhere,' I said, reaching into my bag, at the same time that Alex said, 'Except my house.'

Whoever was holding the flashlight noticed the lights on Kayla's car and began to approach at a more rapid clip. I heard a male voice shouting. It was impossible to distinguish exactly what he said with all the wind and rain. But his voice sounded disturbingly familiar.

'Faster, Kayla,' I said tensely.

'I'm trying,' Kayla said. 'But I was never good at parallel parking.'

'For Christ's sake,' Frank said. 'You should have let me drive—'

'You weren't even born in this century,' Kayla snapped.

'He's crossing the street,' Alex said as the shadowy figure loomed closer.

Suddenly the man was in front of the car, seemingly half blown there by the wind. The headlights from Kayla's car threw his features into strong definition. I couldn't help giving a gasp.

'Do you know him?' Frank asked, glancing back at me.

'From a long time ago,' I said, my voice barely audible above the pounding of the rain on the roof of the car and the rhythmic tempo of the windshield wipers. 'But . . . it can't be him. There's no way he'd be here. There's no way he'd—'

Though he couldn't possibly have been able to see me through the windshield – especially with me in the back seat and the glare of the high beams in his face – it seemed to me as if our gazes locked. I could have sworn a little smile of triumph played upon his face.

'Pierce.' Now there was no way to mistake what he was saying. He raised his flashlight and pointed the beam directly at me, through the windshield. 'Come out of the car, and I won't have to hurt the others.'

I didn't feel afraid, exactly. It was more a sense of inevitability, like I'd always known this moment was going to come. I wasn't at all surprised that it came outside the cemetery gates John had kicked open in frustration when we'd last discussed this particular individual.

'Shit,' Kayla said. 'He's in front of us, and I can't back up. We're trapped.'

'Who is he?' Alex demanded. 'What does he want with you?'

'Mr Mueller, my teacher from my old school,' I said calmly. 'See how he keeps one hand in his pocket?'

Everyone looked. Mr Mueller did, indeed, have one hand clutched tightly round his long, heavy metallic flashlight, while the other he kept hidden away in the pocket of his long black rain slicker.

'John crushed that hand to pieces,' I explained, 'when Mr Mueller touched me inappropriately with it.'

I didn't figure they needed to know the part about how, at the time, I'd been trying to entrap Mr Mueller to prove he'd caused the suicide of my best friend, with whom he'd been having an affair.

'Great,' Alex said. 'That's just great, Pierce. So what's he want now, the rest of his hand back?'

'Can't you tell him we don't have it?' Kayla asked with mounting hysteria.

'Don't worry,' Frank said. 'The captain took care of one hand. I'll take care of the other.' He started to get out of the car.

'Frank,' I cried. Now I wasn't feeling so calm. 'Don't—'

Mr Mueller didn't like Frank getting out of the car instead of me. He raised the flashlight high in the air, then brought the end of it down so hard on the windshield, it left a perfect imprint in the shape of the instrument. Crystalline lines spread out from the indentation, all the way towards Kayla, who screamed.

'No one gets out but the girl,' Mr Mueller rasped, right before his mouth turned into a yawning chasm of blood and razor-sharp teeth, hundreds of them in multiple rows, like a shark.

Now it wasn't only Kayla screaming in terror. Frank swiftly shut the door and locked it, even as the entity into which Mr Mueller had turned scrambled for the handle.

'Drive,' I said, my heart slamming against the back of my ribs.

'There's nowhere I can go,' Kayla said.

'Go forward,' I said as Mr Mueller darted round the front of the car, clearly intending to reach her door.

'But we'll hit him,' she cried.

'Exactly,' I said.

'I can't kill someone!'

'You hit your brother in the head with a fire extinguisher.'

'But that was family! And I didn't kill him.'

When she still didn't move, frozen in terror behind the wheel, I dived between her seat and Frank's to hit the gas pedal at her feet with my hands.

I couldn't see where the car went. My gaze was on the gas pedal and Kayla's purple silken slippers. But I felt the lurch as the small compact rocketed forward. The top of my head slammed into the dashboard as the car impacted something large and heavy, something that let out an unearthly scream before landing hard against the hood. Kayla, shrieking, steered wildly, seemingly to shake off the assailant, stepping on my fingers as she tried to brake, crying, 'Pierce, Pierce, what are you doing? We hit him, oh, my God, Pierce, we hit him, it's over, let go!'

Finally Frank wrapped strong hands round my arms and thrust me back into my seat, saying, 'It's all right. He's gone.'

When I pushed my hair from my eyes and looked behind us, my heart still thumping like a drum, I saw that Frank was only partially correct. In the red glow of Kayla's tail lights lay a large misshapen lump of Mueller, rain pouring all around him.

Not too far from where he stretched across the middle of the road lay the heavy flashlight, its beam pointing haphazardly at his feet. That's how I happened to notice his shoes.

'Tassels,' I said in disgust.

Alex, too, was turned in his seat.

'You guys,' he said. 'He's still moving.'

Disappointed, I said, 'Kayla, back up over him.'

Kayla cried, 'No! We should call an ambulance.'

He was going to kill us.

'He's a Fury,' Frank said. 'Let's go. He'll be all right.'

No sooner were the words out of his mouth than a bolt of lightning shot down from the sky, striking a massive sapodilla tree in the yard of a nearby home. The ensuing fireball caused us all to duck and shield our eyes.

When we turned to look back, most of the sapodilla was gone. What was left of its trunk lay twisted and in flames in the middle of the road on top of Mr Mueller's remains, which steamed gently in the rain.

'Well,' Frank said, after a moment's stunned silence. 'He probably won't be all right now.'

'Oh, my God, oh, my God,' Kayla cried, gripping the steering wheel. 'I just murdered someone! Someone not even related to me. A teacher!'

'You didn't murder a teacher,' I said calmly. 'I did. And I should have done it a long time ago. He was a perv who caused my best friend to kill herself. For all we know, he could be Thanatos.'

'The lightning is what actually killed him,' Frank pointed out. 'Not us.'

'Still,' Kayla said as she gazed tearfully at her windshield. 'Look what he did to my car. No way will my insurance cover this.'

'Do you want to save the Underworld,' I asked her. 'Or not?'

Kayla shook her head, her aurora of bouncy curls restored, thanks to the AC.

'I just want to go home,' she said.

'Well, you won't have a home any more if these guys have their way. So how about you drive us to Mr Smith's house instead, and we find out what's going on around here?' I glanced at Alex. 'Is that OK?'

He was looking back at the massive branch covering Mr Mueller's corpse.

'What?' he asked. 'Oh, yeah. Sorry. I was just thinking . . . maybe you did do a few things back at your old school in Connecticut other than sit around and make doilies.'

'Thanks for finally noticing,' I said.

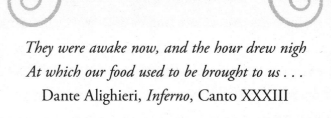

They were awake now, and the hour drew nigh
At which our food used to be brought to us . . .
Dante Alighieri, *Inferno*, Canto XXXIII

'Pierce?' Mr Smith said, looking from me to Frank to Alex to Kayla and then back again as we stood, bedraggled from the rain we'd dashed through in order to get to his front porch. 'What on earth—?'

His voice was nearly drowned out by the loud rock music booming in the background. It was a song my parents used to listen to a lot back when they were happily married.

Mr Smith didn't live too far from the cemetery, but his house was in a new condo village (designed to look like old Victorian town houses) off a pretty popular road in Isla Huesos known for its bars and restaurants. While everywhere else we'd driven was in total darkness – and some places half underwater, deserted except for TV vans and news journalists standing in the water in hip waders, reporting earnestly on the 'life-threatening conditions' wrought by Hurricane Cassandra (Cassandra apparently being the name given to the 'monstrous' hurricane bearing down on South Florida) – Mr Smith's town house was brightly lit. He'd closed all his dark green storm shutters, but light still streamed out behind them, on to the porch.

'How come you have power?' Alex asked Mr Smith. 'And

is that *Queen* playing on the stereo?'

'Oh,' Mr Smith said, looking a little embarrassed. 'Patrick and I have a generator. We usually ask the neighbours over for a little hurricane party whenever there's a storm. That way they can watch the forecast and we get to enjoy the lobster from their freezers that would otherwise spoil.'

Kayla stared at him. 'We just killed a man with my car,' she said.

Frank quickly put his arm round her. 'Please excuse my girlfriend,' he said to Mr Smith. 'She's had a bit of a shock. May we use your water closet?'

Mr Smith's eyes widened to their limits behind his gold-rimmed spectacles.

'You mean my bathroom? Yes, of course, come in,' he said. 'Where are my manners? I'm so sorry. Patrick?'

As he called for his partner, we filed, dripping, into Mr Smith's foyer, which was painted a tasteful pale blue with white trim. There was a wooden staircase, also trimmed in white, leading to a second floor, a doorway to a manly looking study walled with ceiling-to-floor bookcases, and, not surprisingly, an old-fashioned hat rack, covered with Mr Smith's many straw hats and fedoras. On the wall were framed vintage art posters of the Jazz Age burlesque dancer Josephine Baker.

This was not the kind of art I'd expected to see in Mr Smith's house.

'More refugees from the storm?' A man carrying a red drink cup and dressed in a white shirt and khaki shorts came strolling down the hallway along the side of the stairs. 'The more, the merrier—'

He dropped the cup when he saw us. Red liquid spilled on to the expensive Persian hallway runner. Neither man seemed to notice.

'Patrick,' Mr Smith said. 'You remember Pierce, don't you? You met her at Coffin Fest the other night.'

'Oh, my God, of course!' Patrick cried, rushing over to give me a big hug.

Patrick had been a self-proclaimed fan of mine since the media firestorm over my alleged kidnapping had catapulted the photo of John snatching me – and the reward my father had offered for my safe return – into the media. Patrick was a sucker for stories about thwarted young love. He thought my parents didn't approve of John because he was older and lived out of town.

Patrick didn't know how *much* older than me John was, and how *far* out of town John lived.

Correction: *had* lived.

'What are you doing here?' Patrick asked, his face wreathed in smiles. 'Rich, why didn't you tell me they were coming? It's all right. There's plenty of lobster tacos.'

I couldn't bring myself to hug him back. I was in too much shock over everything that had happened, in addition to having heard Patrick call Mr Smith *Rich*. I couldn't think of Mr Smith as anything but Mr Smith.

'I didn't know they were coming, Patrick,' Mr Smith said in a voice that suggested he didn't approve of his partner's effusiveness. 'Could you please get them some towels and maybe some warm drinks? As you can see, they ran into a bit of trouble on the way over.'

'Car trouble?' Patrick asked sympathetically, finally letting me go. 'Did you have trouble finding a parking place? I know there aren't many left; everyone from down island comes up here to park during storms so their engines won't flood. There's still room in the above-ground parking garage behind our building if you want to move your car. That's where we keep ours—'

'Patrick,' Mr Smith said, taking me by the arm. 'The drinks and towels?'

'Oh, right,' Patrick said, laughing at himself. 'Sorry. I just get so excited during storms! I love how everyone comes together to help everyone else out. I wish there could be that feeling of community every day. Anyway, drinks and towels – not to mention tacos – are back here in the kitchen. Follow me, everyone.' He seemed to notice what we were wearing for the first time and looked us up and down with delight. 'Oh, my gosh, costumes! Is someone throwing a fancy-dress hurricane party? Why didn't we think of that, Rich?' To me, he asked, with a grin, 'Where's that hot boyfriend of yours? Oh, my gosh, I love your belt.'

Tears filled my eyes, but not because his question had reminded me that John was gone. It was because, in the background, the song had ended, and I could hear the laughter of Mr Smith's neighbours as they shared their food and his lovely home. I realized we'd entered a true shelter from the storm, filled with life and love. There was no sign of the death and pestilence we'd been dealing with for so many hours.

The tears were because I felt horrible for spoiling this little oasis, for bringing that death and pestilence along with us. That's what I was now, I supposed: a harbinger of doom, queen of the Underworld.

I saw Frank closing Mr Smith's front door and locking it, after first having peered outside to make sure we hadn't been followed. I knew both from his relieved expression and the pale grey my diamond pendant had turned that we'd brought with us no Furies. We were safe . . . for the moment.

I managed to control my tears and didn't think anyone had noticed them until I felt an arm round my shoulders. Startled, I looked up and saw my cousin standing beside me.

'John's gonna meet up with us later,' Alex said to Patrick. 'He's got some stuff to do now. I'm Alex, by the way, Pierce's cousin.'

'Oh,' Patrick said, shaking the hand Alex had extended. 'Nice to meet you. I've got a shirt that would probably fit you if you want to change out of that wet one.' He eyed Frank, who stood a head and a half taller than everyone else in the room. 'You, we probably can't accommodate. What are you supposed to be, anyway, a Hell's Angel?'

Frank shrugged his enormous shoulders. 'Yes,' he said simply.

As Patrick led the others down the hall towards the laughter and music, Mr Smith steered me by the arm into the book-filled library, closing the white-panelled French doors behind him.

'What in heaven's name is going on?' he asked, thrusting a fluffy blue-and-white towel at me from a basket that sat on the floor by another set of French doors. I supposed they led out to a pool area, which would explain the towels, but since they were covered by storm shutters, it was impossible for me to tell. 'What was that girl talking about? Did you really kill a man? And where is John?'

I sank down into a brown leather armchair and pressed the towel against my damp hair.

'Yes, we did kill someone,' I said, the words coming almost robotically from my lips. It was surprising – but then again, not surprising at all – how little I cared about having killed Mr Mueller. Maybe emotion would come later. Or maybe not. 'He tried to kill us first, though.'

'Good God,' Mr Smith said. He sank into the mate of the leather chair in which I sat, his brown skin suddenly looking almost as grey as his short-cropped hair. 'Who was he?'

'A teacher from my old school in Connecticut.'

'What on earth was he doing *here*?' Mr Smith asked, slipping off his spectacles in order to polish them, something he often did in times of great distress.

'I was hoping you'd be able to tell me. Did we awaken the ancients, or create an imbalance, or some mumbo jumbo like that? That's what Mr Graves thinks.'

Mr Smith shook his head before slipping his glasses back on. 'I don't know who Mr Graves is, nor did I understand a single word you just said. Go back to where your teacher tried to kill you.'

'He was pretty specific that if I didn't get out of the car he'd kill everyone else inside it to get at me,' I said. 'So we ran him over. Then lightning hit a tree, and it fell on him.'

Mr Smith stared at me.

'Oh, dear,' he said. 'John still hasn't learned to control his temper, I see.'

I stared back, confused. 'Why would you say that?'

He blinked at me through his spectacles. 'Didn't you tell me that when John gets angry, he causes it to thunder and lightning?'

'Yes,' I said. 'He does. I mean, he did. But John wasn't there.'

'He wasn't?' Mr Smith knitted his grey eyebrows with concern. 'Where is he?'

Tears filled my eyes once again, only this time, it wasn't because of how touched I was by the shelter Mr Smith was providing us – and others – from the storm.

'John's dead,' I said, my voice breaking.

This time, I didn't try to stop my tears, not even when I saw the look of incredulous shock – and sorrow – that spread across Mr Smith's face. My tears came spilling out of me as quickly and as hotly as my story. I found myself telling him everything that had happened, from bringing Alex back to life that horrible morning in the cemetery, to the awful moment I'd seen John's lifeless body in the waves. I left out nothing . . .

Well, almost nothing. I saw no reason to let Mr Smith know that my relationship with John had reached a more intimate level. Some things are private, after all. And I didn't think that could have anything to do with all the unfortunate events that had been going on in the Underworld.

I did tell him other things, though, even things that might have seemed inconsequential, like Hope being lost. I don't know why, except that the words Mr Liu had spoken to me right before I'd left the Underworld kept running through my head: I really *was* a kite fuelled by anger, with no one to hold my strings now that John was gone. I had killed a man and felt no remorse whatsoever about it.

Mr Smith, though, was one of the most grounded, compassionate people I'd ever met . . . despite his somewhat morbid interest in death deities. If anyone could help figure out a way to save us – to save John, and perhaps, through saving John, save me – it was him.

He listened intently as I spoke, ignoring the muted sound of the laughter and music coming from down the hall, his expression troubled, tears glittering in his own eyes, as dark brown as the leather on which we sat. When I was finished, he lowered his hands, which he'd kept pressed to his cheeks from the time I'd said John was dead until I finished with, 'And . . . well, then we got here. That's it, I guess.'

To my surprise, he said none of the things an ordinary person might say, like, *Oh, Pierce, I'm so sorry for your loss*, or *You have my deepest sympathies*.

Instead, he said, his dark eyes still glittering compassionately behind the lenses of his glasses, 'My dear. You're wrong. So, so wrong.'

I stared at him. For the first time all evening, I actually felt something. What I felt was probably what Mr Mueller must have felt when I'd rammed Kayla's car into him.

'Wrong?' I echoed. 'About what? There's no such person as Thanatos?'

'Oh, no,' he said dismissively. 'Not about that. About hope. Hope is not lost.'

I took a deep, disappointed breath.

'I told you,' I said. Why had I thought coming here was such a good idea? Alex was right. We ought to have gone straight to Uncle Chris – although, of course, Uncle Chris lived with my grandmother, so this would have been risky, considering she was possessed by a Fury. But Mr Smith was usually so on top of things. Not any more, I guess. 'Hope is gone. I haven't seen her since all of the ravens fell to the ground after the boats collided—'

Mr Smith was using one of his old-school handkerchiefs to scrub at his moist eyes.

'I'm sorry, I don't mean your bird,' he said. 'Although I don't believe she's lost, either, at least, not forever. She'll come back, as pets often do after the storm, when the worst is over and the sun has come out again. She knows her way home.'

I sat and stared at him. What was he talking about?

'What I meant,' he went on, after tucking the handkerchief away, 'was *hope*. You said you feel as if all hope is lost, and that the Fates have deserted us. But I don't believe that's true, not for a second, any more than I believe John is dead.'

Suddenly the pleasant white walls of his library became pink-tinged. Uh-oh.

'Mr Smith, I'm sorry, I know this is difficult for you,' I said, keeping my voice controlled with an effort. There were a number of knick-knacks on his shelves, little glass ornaments shaped like boats and shells. I didn't want to snatch up any of them and throw them. But the part of me fuelled by anger felt like doing so. 'Believe me, it's difficult for me to accept, too. But I listened to John's chest myself. There's no heartbeat. I performed mouth-to-mouth on him. He never started breathing again. I even pressed my necklace against him, the way we did with Alex. It didn't work. Nothing worked. Trust me, he's dead. There wasn't anything anyone could do—'

Mr Smith waved his hand in front of his face, as if my words were a bothersome gnat. This didn't help alleviate the red glow in my eyes. If anything, it intensified.

'Oh, I know. I believe his *body* is dead right now. But John's spirit isn't. Why else do you think that bolt of lightning came out of the blue and struck that tree, causing it to fall on that teacher of yours? That was pure, vintage John. He was trying to help you, in that overly dramatic way of his.'

The minute he mentioned the lightning, the red pulled back from my vision the way an ocean wave receded from a shoreline. What he was suggesting was crazy . . .

. . . crazy enough to be true.

The lightning *had* been an odd coincidence, considering the fact that my boyfriend had always been able to control the weather with his mind and the way he'd always showed up whenever someone was threatening me.

Except that John was dead.

'Thunder and lightning *were* a signature trick of John's,'

I heard myself murmur, despite the fact that I refused to allow myself to hope.

'So you told me,' Mr Smith said, rising from his chair and going to his bookshelves. 'It makes sense that he'd try to protect you in the afterlife as he did in life . . . whatever afterlife he's experiencing right now, that is.'

'But,' I said. No. I wasn't going to hope. 'That's impossible. Unless . . .'

'It's no more impossible, I should think, than anything else you've experienced so far, such as finding yourself in an underworld that exists beneath our world, and discovering that you, a fairly below-average student, are the co-regent of it. Now, where did I put that book?'

'You mean . . .' I was starting to feel something other than anger. It felt, dangerously, like optimism. '. . . you think John is around somewhere? Like in spirit form?'

'More than in spirit form,' Mr Smith said. 'I think your friend Mr Graves is right about there being an imbalance in the Underworld. I have my suspicions about what caused it, but more important, I do believe it caused an opportunity for the death god, Thanatos, to capture John's soul. The question is, how are we going to save him?'

The Guide and I into that hidden road
Now entered, to return to the bright world . . .
Dante Alighieri, *Inferno*, Canto XXXIV

'There are other questions, of course,' Mr Smith was saying as he stood with his back to me, scanning his floor-to-ceiling bookshelves. 'And other pressing concerns. How are we going to help all those poor souls you left behind in the Underworld? And how are we going to defeat the Furies and return the Fates, and thus restore the balance so that this fair isle doesn't turn into a flaming ball of magma? But,' he added lightly, 'I believe once we've located and recovered John, those other things will be a bit easier to manage. I hope so, anyway. All of the bridges are shut down due to the storm, so it's far too late to evacuate.'

I was barely listening to him. Instead, I was glancing around the room, my mind spinning. Mr Graves, the man of science, had been *right*? There *was* a Thanatos keeping John's soul from re-entering his body, holding him captive between life and death?

Had John really caused that lightning bolt to strike that tree and kill Mr Mueller? If he had, that meant he'd been with me the whole time. Was he here with me now? If so, why couldn't I feel him? All I could hear was the insistent howl of the wind outside, sucking and banging the shutters against the windows, a strange contrast to the cheerful music playing down the hall.

What if it was true, and John had become some kind of guardian angel to me? In a way, the thought was oddly comforting. But I didn't want a guardian angel. What good would that do me? Guardian angels couldn't hold you in their strong arms and tell you everything was going to be all right. They couldn't eat breakfast with you, or tease you, or tell you that you looked beautiful even when your hair was piled on top of your head because you'd just washed your face and you knew you didn't look beautiful at all.

I wanted John the boy, not John the angel. I wanted him whole, back the way he was, not some stupid angel . . .

John? I asked with my mind, looking cautiously around the room. *Are you here? If you're here, give me a sign.*

'Ah,' Mr Smith said, stepping down from a small library ladder he'd used to find the tome he'd apparently been looking for. 'Here it is.'

He walked over to a wide mahogany desk and opened the book to the appropriate page. I rose from my chair to take a look.

On the page before me was a photo of an ancient Greek statue. It showed a winged boy mounted on a galloping horse, swinging a sword over his head.

Well, some of the legs of the horse were galloping. The others had fallen off in an earthquake or something. So had the boy's face, and most of his wings.

'Thanatos,' Mr Smith said. 'The Greek personification of death.'

I looked down at the photo. 'He's just a kid.'

'I suppose you could say that. The Romans did view him as a child of the dark night. It was said even the sun was afraid to shine upon him. But that *kid*, as you refer to him, destroyed whole armies with a single swipe of that sword. He killed without a thought to his victims. He was said to be without mercy, without repentance, and without a soul.'

'So in other words,' I said, 'a typical teen boy.'

Mr Smith frowned at me, then read aloud from the inscription beneath the photo. 'Here's what the poet Hesiod wrote in *Theogony* about Thanatos: 'His spirit within him is pitiless as bronze: whomsoever of men he has once seized he holds fast. He is hateful even to the deathless gods.''

'Because he was shut up in his room all day,' I said, 'sexting and playing video games.'

Mr Smith frowned. 'They didn't have video games in the years before Christ—'

'You know what I mean,' I said. Something about the statue bothered me. It reminded me of something or someone, but I couldn't figure out who, especially since the form had no face. 'If the gods were deathless, then how did he manage to kill John?'

Mr Smith raised an eyebrow. 'Miss Oliviera, I told you upon one of our very first meetings, John isn't a god. He's simply an unfortunate young man who was thrust into a position of great responsibility at a very young age—'

'How come there's nothing about this Thanatos guy in the Hades and Persephone myth?' I interrupted. I already knew how great John was. I didn't need to hear it.

'Because he doesn't figure in it. He's a minor player in Greek mythological literature, considered more a spirit than a deity. The father of psychoanalysis, Sigmund Freud, believed we all have a little Thanatos within us. He called it the death drive and claimed it's what makes us engage in risky behaviours from time to time.'

I raised an eyebrow, remembering the way John had clung to the wheel of the ill-fated ship until the last minute. 'That sounds like John. So how do I get him away from this Thanatos, once I figure out who he is? I'm guessing he wasn't Mr Mueller, or John would already be back.'

Mr Smith shook his head and closed the book.

'I ought to have known, given our past conversations,' he said tiredly, 'that you wouldn't understand. You can't *literally* engage Death in a fight to the death for the life of your boyfriend, Pierce.'

'Whatever, I get it that this Thanatos freak is probably a metaphor,' I said, beginning to pace the room. 'But in case he's not, I've already killed one guy tonight. What's to keep me from killing another?'

Mr Smith regarded me helplessly from behind his desk. 'Because that is not who you are. I understand that with your teacher you were acting in self-defence. But the entire reason John was so drawn to you is because you are the spring to his winter. You are the water to his fire. He is the storm. You are the sun that appears after the storm.'

I stopped pacing to stare at him. 'Are you purposefully trying to make me throw up?'

'Miss Oliviera, please,' Mr Smith said, opening his arms

wide as if to say, *Why are you blaming me for stating the obvious?* 'I know that to you I must seem sometimes like the silly old man who loves to talk about death deities, but give me some credit for having lived a bit longer than you and having seen a few more things. Yes, storms are damaging, but we need them because they clear away the bracken that prevents new flowers from having a chance to grow. And of course we need the sun to shine on those new flowers that without the storm might never have had a chance to bloom.'

Tears formed again in my eyes. '*Stop it.*'

'Now you're the one who's being silly,' Mr Smith said. 'It's good to be the storm and be able to defend yourself and others when you have to, but it's just as good to be the sun . . . maybe better.'

'I'm not the sun,' I said, reaching up to wipe my tears. 'Or springtime, or water, or any of those things. I've been told on pretty good authority that I'm a kite with no strings, fuelled by anger.'

'Of course you are,' Mr Smith said, 'when John isn't around. I believe I mentioned that he wasn't particularly enjoyable company before you came into his life. That's why it would be nice to get the two of you back together. You really only function well as a pair.'

'Right,' I said in a not very steady voice. 'So maybe we should concentrate on figuring out what's happening in the Underworld.'

'What's happening in the Underworld is fairly obvious,' Mr Smith said, peeking inside my tote. My cellphone had begun to ring. 'The goal of the Furies has always been to destroy the Underworld. And now that they've killed John – or believe they've done so, anyway – and crippled the transportation of souls, the only thing that stands in the way of their goal is you. Once you're gone, there'll be nothing left of the Isla Huesos Underworld, and your friend Mr Graves's prediction will come true: pestilence will reign here on our once fair isle.'

'So I was right,' I said. 'There really is a Fury convention going on out there.' I nodded towards the shuttered windows. 'Except the only activity on the agenda is killing me.'

'I would imagine so,' Mr Smith said, reaching inside my bag. 'Unless, of course, we can throw a spanner in the works.'

'What does that mean?'

'Throw a—' He heaved a sigh as he drew out my cell. 'Good God, do they teach children nothing in school these days? In olden times, the only way workers in factories could get breaks was if one of them threw a tool into the machinery, causing it to break down. A spanner is a type of tool. The only way we're going to stop the Furies is if we—'

'I already know,' I said. 'Kill Thanatos, bring back John, then find boats to replace the ones we've lost.'

'You do understand Thanatos is only a *symbol* of death, much in the way a white dove is a symbol of hope, or a pomegranate is a symbol for fertili—'

'Someday you and I are going to have a long talk about pomegranates, but not now.' I extended my hand, palm out, towards him. 'Give me my phone.'

'Someone named Farah Endicott seems to need you quite urgently,' he said drily, having glanced at my screen. 'Apparently there is a party and you are missing it. She's attached a very rude photo. Pardon me for having looked, but she uses a font that is extremely large, and quite a lot of what I believe your generation calls emoticons and what my generation calls an inability to conduct face-to-face conversation.'

'Yeah,' I said, taking my phone as he passed it to me. 'There's a Coffin Night party at Seth Rector's dad's place in Reef Key. I thought it would be cancelled due to Hurricane Cassandra. I guess not.'

'Oh, no,' Mr Smith said. He was still poking through my bag. 'Master Rector's party appears to be quite the rager, as you people call it. I won't, of course, mention to you that it seems a bit coincidental to me that you received an invitation to his party *after* you dispatched a Fury, and that I'm quite certain you're being lured into a trap so that you can be killed. You'll have figured that out yourself.' He pulled out my copy of *A History of the Isle of Bones*. 'I didn't *give* this to you, you know,' he griped. 'I only *loaned* it to you. It's out of print. It's not like you can download copies on the Internet.' He flipped through his precious book like I might have hurt it. 'Did you actually read it?'

'Of course I read it,' I said, glancing up from my phone. I was looking at the photo Farah had sent. It was of her and Seth and their friends. They were all giving the camera the finger. Classy. 'Well, the parts about John, anyway.' I paused, looking around nervously for signs, like flickering lights, that John might be eavesdropping. 'It was good,' I continued. 'I promise to give it back later. And of course I know this party is a trap. I'm not stupid. And quit going through my stuff.'

'So sorry,' Mr Smith said, closing my bag. 'I've never been privy before to the personal effects of a co-regent of the afterworld.'

I barely heard him. I was staring at the photo Farah had sent. *Where u at, girl?* she'd written at the bottom of the photo. *We miss u! Get on over here!* Mr Smith had been right about Farah's generous use of emoticons, many of which were smiley faces wearing devil horns.

That wasn't what I found so fascinating about her message. It wasn't even the garishly painted wooden coffin in the background, on which our class's year had been scrawled in gold, or the fact that a girl I didn't know was riding the coffin like a horse.

It was Seth, with his tousled blond hair and easy smile, straight white teeth and an all-over surfer tan. He looked so wholesome in his polo shirt and board shorts – well, except for the obscene gesture he was making to the camera. The shirt he had on in the photo was black, probably in honour of the occasion, Coffin Night.

I couldn't quite put my finger on what bothered me about him.

Oh, yeah. He'd killed my cousin.

'You're not going,' Mr Smith said. 'Are you?'

'Of course we're going,' I said, lowering the phone. 'They

actually invited me the other day, before I killed Mr Mueller.'

Mr Smith sighed. 'The police will be looking for you.'

'They've been looking for me all along,' I said.

'But you hadn't killed anyone then.'

'We'll have to be extra careful,' I said. 'Thanks for everything.'

He sighed again, then looked heavenward. 'At least use Patrick's car. The police won't be looking for that.'

'Why Patrick's car?' I asked curiously. 'Why not yours?'

'You'll see,' Mr Smith said.

A few minutes later, I did.

'But of this water it behooves thee drink
Before so great a thirst in thee be slaked.'
Dante Alighieri, *Paradiso*, Canto XXX

There were only two ways to reach Reef Key, the remote island located a mile or two off the coast of Isla Huesos where Seth Rector was throwing his Coffin Night party. One of them was by boat. But with coastal advisories warning of tidal surges of as much as four feet due to the massive power of Hurricane Cassandra, getting to Reef Key by boat was out of the question.

That same surge made the narrow two-lane highway that led to Reef Key almost impassable.

Almost. Unless you were driving a specially equipped recreational vehicle.

'Is that a snorkel?' Alex asked after Patrick threw the cover off the tricked-out hardtop Jeep he had parked in the above-ground parking garage we'd already heard so much about.

'Of course,' Patrick said, looking pleased. 'This baby can cross through depths of up to six, seven feet, easy. I installed the filtration system myself – along with the roof rack, fog lights, winch and CB radio.'

'Wow,' Alex said, widening his eyes at Kayla and Frank and me as if to ask, *Where'd this nutcase come from, anyway?*

Which wasn't very nice, considering Mr Smith was standing right there, too, and Patrick was his special friend. 'A CB? How forward thinking of you.'

'Hey,' Patrick said, looking serious. 'You think this is a joke? Climate change is real. They've got these buoys out in the ocean between Cuba and Isla Huesos, measuring the sea level, and every year the level goes up another inch thanks to all those melting glaciers. At that rate, everyone on this island who owns property on the waterfront will be underwater within our lifetimes . . . maybe sooner. That's why Rich and I bought a place eighteen feet above sea level . . . Not that that does anyone much good in a storm this size – and storms this size are becoming more and more frequent. That's why we've got this baby' – he patted the side of the Jeep Wagoneer fondly – 'so we can get out fast if we need to. But she's only for extreme emergencies. No one should be out on a night like this.'

'Yeah,' I said, apologizing for all four of us. 'We know. But we really need to get to this party to, uh . . .'

'Pick up her sweetheart,' Frank rushed in. 'He's stranded and needs a ride. And the coppers are still looking for him, you know.'

Mr Smith had buried his face in one hand, as if embarrassed for us.

I didn't blame him. I was embarrassed for us, too.

But Frank's lie – which wasn't entirely untrue – did the trick. Patrick handed over the keys, which had a fob depicting Napoleon Dynamite with the motto SKILLS!

'Go,' Patrick whispered to me. I had to lean in to

152

hear him. 'Go and get your boy.'

Outside the above-ground parking garage, open on four sides, lightning had flashed, followed a few seconds later by a boom of thunder so loud it seemed to shake the cement floor beneath our feet. I hadn't been sure at the time if it had been John or the storm.

Now, sitting snug and dry in Patrick's car as it approached Reef Key, I was fairly certain I knew. The waves crashing on either side of the road didn't quite wash all the way across it, so we hadn't had to use the snorkel feature. But every time lightning streaked the night sky I could see the clouds overhead, dark and violently colliding with one another, moving even more quickly than we were. It did almost seem as if a part of John was alive and being held somewhere against his will, and was taking out his wrath about it by churning up the sea and sky.

'Guess I don't have to ask which one it is,' Alex said as we approached Seth Rector's father's multimillion-dollar development. Only one of the units was finished, and I could see it lit up like a beacon through the rapidly beating windshield wipers.

'I still can't believe we're doing this,' Kayla said from the back seat beside me. 'This is the stupidest thing I've ever done, except possibly for that time I did all those lemon drop shots on my birthday.'

'It's going to be fine,' I said in what I hoped sounded like a convincing voice. 'We won't be staying long.'

'What are lemon drop shots?' Frank asked from the front seat. He'd reluctantly allowed Alex to drive, but only because the latter had actually driven a car before and had a licence. The two of them were equally in love with Patrick's tricked-out Jeep.

'Never mind,' I said. 'Just don't drink if someone offers you one at the party. Don't drink anything anyone offers you, in fact.'

'Why are we even doing this?' Kayla asked. I recognized the anxiety in her voice from the day Farah Endicott had asked us to sit at her table at Island Queen – now undoubtedly underwater – and Kayla had refused. 'How is going to a stupid party given by the guy who killed Alex possibly going to help the Underworld?'

'It's going to help me,' Alex said, 'when I walk up and kick him in the nuts.'

'We're here to look for Furies and evidence that Seth and those guys murdered Jade,' I said. 'That's all. We are not killing anyone, kicking people in any part of their anatomy or bribing anyone with pieces of eight.' I smacked Frank in the shoulder as I said this last part. 'Is that understood?'

'What if they try to kill us first?' Frank asked, clearly disappointed.

'Then,' I said, 'you may maim them. But only a little, and only in self-defence.'

Frank looked more cheerful.

Alex found a place to park along the road leading to the spec house. It was impossible to park any closer due to the waves, which were sweeping well into the development's construction site, swamping its half-poured tennis courts. The private swimming lagoon, of which Mr Rector had been so proud, had been swallowed up by the sea, its recirculating waterfall now clogged with sea grass.

The driveway of the demo home was just as clogged, only with expensive sports cars and F-150s, the vehicle of choice for most students at Isla Huesos High School. They had clearly got to Reef Key well before the weather had turned.

'They'll have been drinking since way before the storm started, too,' Kayla informed us grimly.

'How nice,' I said, before we left the safety of Patrick's car to run the considerable distance through the rain to get to the front door.

In order to take advantage of Reef Key's natural beauty – water views on three sides, mangroves in which my mom's favourite bird, the roseate spoonbill, had once nested (before construction and the oil spill caused by my dad's company disturbed them) – without compromising the multimillion-dollar homes' integrity during storms like Cassandra, all of the houses on Reef Key were being built on ten-foot-high stone pilings.

The space beneath the pilings – at least according to the presentation Mr Rector had shown me the time he and Farah's dad had taken me for an impromptu tour – could be filled with a three-car garage, or a storage room, or even a stylish in-law apartment (which would technically be illegal since, according to recently passed legislation, this violated flood-zone regulations. But who was going to tell?).

It was a haul climbing up the majestically curved steps to the front door, especially under the assault of the rain, and I could only imagine it would be worse when carrying bags of groceries or, in the case of Seth and his friends, kegs of beer. I heard the heavy beat of the music coming from the house before we'd hit the first step. By the time we reached the gaudy stained-glass door – double dolphins cavorting in sea foam – it was so loud I could make out the lyrics.

Alex didn't bother knocking or ringing the bell since no one would have heard anyway. He let himself in, hoping, I expected, that the sight of him alive and well would send everyone running and screaming in shock.

'Surprise!' he shouted.

Not a single person noticed. The people dancing – and there were a lot of them – went right on dancing. The people sunk down on the white leather couches, smoking, went right on smoking. The people gathered around the sliding glass doors, looking out over the water, pointing at something and laughing, went right on pointing and laughing.

'Better luck next time, mate,' Frank said to Alex sympathetically, and slapped him on the shoulder.

'Move,' Kayla said, shoving Alex a little so she could get inside from the rain. She and I stood on the white tile floor of the threshold, dripping and looking around. There was a DJ in one corner – or rather a guy who looked like he attended IHHS but had his own portable equipment and probably a large van. But he seemed to be doing an adequate job of keeping everyone in the mood . . . him and the keg in the corner opposite him.

'Beer,' Frank said appreciatively. 'Real beer!' He immediately began moving towards the line for the keg.

'Great,' Kayla said with a sigh. 'Ditched for beer. Story of my life.'

'I can't believe this,' Alex said. 'No one recognizes me.' He looked down at himself. 'Is it the shirt?'

'Oh, my God,' Kayla said irritably. 'I liked you better before you died, when you were the silent, moody type. Ever since they revived you, you never shut up.'

'Maybe that's it,' Alex said. 'Maybe instead of an NDE, I'm a whadduyacallit? Oh, right, a revenant, and no one but you guys can see me.'

'Everyone can see you,' I assured him, closing the door behind us. 'It's just that it's a party. Everyone's too busy having a good time to care about anyone else.'

'This sucks,' Alex said sullenly. 'If someone murders you and you get revived and come back to wreak vengeance on your killers, they could at least have the decency to notice you.'

I patted him on the shoulder in a manner I hoped he'd find comforting.

'Mr Rector has a business office downstairs,' I said. 'Since no one is paying attention to you anyway, why don't you go break into his computer and look for proof of his dirty dealings?'

Alex stared at me blankly. 'Like what?'

'I don't know,' I said. 'Like that he set up your dad to take the fall for his drug dealing back when they were in high school together. Or maybe that he uses his current business for money laundering. Something like that would be good.'

Alex brightened. 'That's an excellent idea,' he said. 'I can't believe I didn't think of it myself.' He began to mill through the crowd, barking, 'Move it,' in a deep voice that sounded to me like an imitation of Frank when anyone got in his way. Everyone was so drunk that they actually followed his command.

'Ladies.' Frank returned, carefully balancing three red drink cups in his hands. 'Elixir of the gods, one for each of you.'

Kayla made a face. 'Is that beer?'

Frank made the same face right back at her. 'No, it isn't. I know how you feel about beer, my fair young lass. I got the two of you punch, from right over there.' He nodded at a crystal bowl set up on a long narrow table along the lone wall that wasn't made up of sliding glass doors. Beside the punch bowl were bags of chips and deli trays that might once have contained meat and crudités, but which now looked as if they'd been ravaged by hungry raccoons.

Kayla, who'd taken a sip of the punch, quickly spat the mouthful back into the cup.

'Don't drink it,' she said to me, and dashed the cup in my hands to the floor.

'Kayla,' I said, looking worriedly down at the pale pink stain on the floor (pale pink because the rainwater from our dripping clothes had diluted it). 'What's wrong?'

I'd never been to a high school party before. After becoming an NDE, I hadn't exactly been a social butterfly, and no one had invited me anywhere once they heard about the mess I'd got into with Mr Mueller. He'd been incredibly popular, and I'd been incredibly not so.

Still, I was pretty sure it wasn't socially acceptable to go around dumping your drinks out on the floor, no matter how wild the party or how huge the hurricane was raging outside it.

'It's mystery drink,' Kayla said in a tone that suggested I should know what that was. When I looked blank, she explained, 'Everybody brings whatever pills they find in their parents' medicine cabinet and dumps them into a bowl of vodka mixed with Kool-Aid.'

She pointed at the empty prescription bottles scattered amidst the crumpled potato chip bags.

'Oh,' I said, thinking of all the warning labels written along the sides of the drugs I'd been prescribed after my accident: *May cause drowsiness. May impair the ability to drive or operate machinery.* I'd actually heard of this kind of thing before, but they'd been referred to as pharma parties. 'I thought parties like this were a myth created by the media.'

'Like the Underworld is a myth created by the Greeks?' Frank asked.

'Good point,' I admitted.

'In Isla Huesos, nothing is a myth. Look.' Kayla pointed grimly at my chest. My diamond was as black as the night sky outside the wraparound sliding glass doors.

'Oh, my God!' The voice was so shrill it was easy to hear above the pulsating thump of the music.

A second later, Farah Endicott was in front of us, all stick-straight hair and cherry-red lip gloss.

'You came,' she cried, woozily waving a party cup as she spoke. 'I was just saying to Seth that I didn't think you were going to make it; the storm's gotten way too bad.'

'Well,' I said to her with a watery smile. 'We made it.'

'You sure did,' she said. 'I'm so glad. And you brought your friends.' She said the word *friends* so it came out sounding like *friendsh*, then leered drunkenly up at Frank. 'I've never met you before. I can guarantee I'd have remembered *that*.'

'And I you, fair madam,' Frank said, leaning forward to lift the hand in which she wasn't holding a cup, then lightly kissing it on the knuckles.

'Oh, my,' Farah said, giggling, while Kayla rolled her eyes at Frank's courtliness. 'This party is getting better and better! And I see you came in costumes.' She glanced down at my belt. 'I love your whip! It's cool you respect the occasion. It's Coffin Night, you know. You guys totally rock . . . not like *some* people.'

She glanced darkly in the direction of the coffin. There were several girls dancing on top of it, a risky proposition in their stiletto heels, especially considering the coffin was hollow and made only of plywood, sagging under their combined weight.

'We told them to guard it from juniors,' Farah said mournfully, 'not *trash* it. Even though it's not full-size, it took me 'n' Serena all day to paint it.' She looked back at us. 'You're supposed to write your name on it with these gold pens.' She pulled a metallic marker from the back pocket of her denim mini. 'We're trying to get the signature of everyone in the class. But it hardly matters now. You can't even see them.'

'Would you like me to go over there and knock those

girls' heads together?' Kayla offered, apparently finding Farah less offensive when she was three sheets to the wind.

'Aw, that's so sweet of you,' Farah said, touched. Then her gaze seemed to focus and she really looked at Kayla for the first time. 'Hey, you're that girl with the big boobs Serena is so mean to online.' Farah's eyes became misty with tears. 'I don't know why I'm friends with Serena. You're super nice, and you look really beautiful in that dress. Oh, my God. Have you seen what the storm is doing to this place? Seth and those guys are over there making fun of it.' She gestured towards the group gathered in front of the floor-to-ceiling windows at the far side of the room. 'But it isn't funny. My dad is going to lose all the money he invested in this development, and then he's never going to be able to pay for me to go to college, and I'm not smart or athletic enough to get a scholarship anywhere.'

Farah surprised everyone by throwing her arms around Kayla and beginning to sob into her hair.

'Uh,' Kayla said, startled. 'There, there.' She patted Farah on the shoulder. 'It can't be that bad.'

'Yes, it is,' Farah wailed, still clutching Kayla. 'I'm going to have to go to Isla Huesos Community College. Then I'll have to live on this stupid island forever, like my dad. And there isn't even a Gap, let alone a Sephora.'

After uttering the word *Sephora*, Farah sagged in Kayla's arms, her eyes closed.

'Farah?' Kayla cried, giving the girl a shake. 'Farah? Aw, dammit. Someone let this girl have way too much mystery drink.'

'What do we do?' I asked worriedly as Frank hurried over to take Farah's limp body from Kayla. Perhaps not surprisingly, no one seemed to notice that the girlfriend of the party's host was unconscious.

'I'll call nine-one-one,' Kayla said, sounding dubious. 'But I'm pretty sure an ambulance won't be able to get out here with that storm surge. Besides, there's a standing evacuation order for all low-lying areas. Category Two hurricane or higher, it's considered "remain at your own risk". First responders aren't supposed to put themselves in harm's way for these areas until storm waters recede due to the risk of debris. At least, that's what my mom told me.'

'Guess it's a nice cold bucket of water in the face for you then, missy,' Frank said, throwing Farah, fireman-style, over his shoulder.

'Uh,' Kayla said. She had her phone out and was dialling. 'That's not how we do it in this century, Frank. We put overdose victims in recovery position on the floor so they don't choke on their own vomit, then check their pulse and breathing until the ambulance arrives.'

'What fun is that?' Frank asked, disappointed.

'The bedrooms are that way,' I said, pointing down the hall. 'See if you can find an empty one to put her in.'

Frank nodded and stalked off, Farah's head bobbing along behind him, her bright copper-coloured hair swinging like a horse's tail.

'Busy,' Kayla said, indicating her phone. 'If they won't come, and she doesn't come around soon, we might have to take her to the hospital ourselves in Patrick's car. Not that I care about her,' she added hastily. 'But, unlike the rest of these losers, I don't consider death a reason to party.'

I looked in the direction she was staring, at the girls who were shimmying on top of the coffin. Suddenly, I realized I recognized two of them. One of them was Farah's best friend, Serena . . . SerenaSweetie, she called herself online. The other was a girl named Nicole, who'd complained about the Rector Wreckers – Seth and his friends – vandalizing the house next door to hers during last year's Coffin Night. She and Serena had begun to dance suggestively with each other, drawing a crowd of excited male admirers.

This was one reason no one had noticed their friend Farah passing out and being carried off to a back bedroom by a six-and-a-half-foot-tall stranger with a six-inch scar down one side of his face. Lucky for Farah, that stranger had nothing but good intentions.

'Yeah,' I said to Kayla. 'I know what you mean. Keep trying to reach nine-one-one. I'll go get Alex and then find you guys so we can get out of here. Coming here may not have been the best idea after all.'

Kayla nodded, then walked swiftly – her phone still pressed to her ear – down the hall in the direction Frank and Farah had disappeared while I turned to go in search of Alex. Who knows? Maybe he'd found something, and the perilous journey out to Reef Key wouldn't have been a complete waste of time—

'Pierce? Pierce Oliviera?' bellowed an all-too-familiar voice.

I say, that when the spirit evil-born
Cometh before him, wholly it confesses;
And this discriminator of transgressions
Seeth what place in Hell is meet for it . . .
Dante Alighieri, *Inferno*, Canto V

'Pierce!' Bryce, Seth's not-very-bright football-playing friend, was really happy to see me. 'Pierce Oliviera!'

He pronounced my last name wrong, but since most people did unless I corrected them, I let it go. With Bryce around, no one could kill me. Bryce had a neck thicker than an ordinary person's thigh and an IQ about as high as the temperature, but he was a fan of my dad's, and I was pretty sure he'd object if anyone tried to murder me in front of him.

'Hey, you guys,' Bryce said excitedly, as he dragged me towards the rear of the room. 'Look who I found! Zack Oliviera's daughter. You know, Zack Oliviera, that guy who runs the big oil company?'

'The one that sells all the stuff to the military?' a guy I didn't know asked.

Seth and his friends had pulled some of the deck furniture inside. Now they were sitting on it so they could watch Cassandra in all her fierce glory, as if the sun loungers and chaises were seats in a theatre, and the storm was something being shown on a screen in front of them, in IMAX.

'That's the one,' Seth said to his friend, with a lazy grin.

Bryce hadn't been weird or creepy about demanding that I come to the back of the room to say hi to Seth. He'd simply seized my hand and refused to release it, the way an excited puppy would grab the pant leg of a new visitor.

'Come on,' he'd said, when I'd insisted I was leaving. 'You can't come all this way and not even say hi to Seth. He's gonna be so disappointed. Besides, you hafta come look at the storm. It's so cool!'

It was at that moment I saw Alex appear at the top of the stairs leading down to the basement. Our gazes met, and he froze, recognizing Bryce.

I had no idea whether or not Bryce was one of the people who'd been present when Alex had been murdered, but I saw my cousin shrink back into the shadows of the stairwell, attempting to conceal the file folder he was holding in his hands. He'd found something in Seth's dad's business office . . . something he didn't want anyone to see him leaving with.

That's why I said, in a voice I hoped was loud enough for Alex to hear, 'Sure, Bryce. I'll go say hello to Seth.'

'Great,' Bryce said happily, and he dragged me across the room to where Seth and his friends were sitting.

'How are you doing, Pierce?' Seth asked, rising from the chaise longue on which he'd been sitting. 'Glad you could make it. What's that thing you've got on? A whip? Kinky.'

He leaned down to give me a kiss hello . . . a kiss hello that didn't feel any different from any other kiss hello I'd ever received, except that Seth was standing so close that I could smell his scent: freshly applied deodorant and expensive body spray and whatever detergent his mom – or, more likely, housekeeper – used to launder his clothes. It was so different from the way John smelled – of the wood smoke from the fireplace in his room and something else, something distinctly John – that for a second I felt such a wave of longing for John wash over me I could hardly speak.

Then Seth leaned away, and I couldn't smell him any more, and the wave of longing for John was gone. It was strange.

When I glanced behind me, I could see that Alex was gone, as well. I wasn't sure if he'd made it out of the stairwell and out of the front door, or if he'd slunk back down into the basement. Whichever it was, he appeared to have escaped.

'Sorry,' I said to Seth. 'I didn't see you over here.' It was a small lie, but one I hoped he would buy. 'But I did talk to Farah. She doesn't seem to be feeling too well.'

Seth looked puzzled. 'What?'

'She's passed out,' I explained. 'My friend had to carry her into one of the other rooms. We're trying to call an ambulance, but you might want to—'

One of Seth's friends, and another fellow football player, Cody, burst out laughing.

'An ambulance?' Cody echoed in a scornful tone. 'An ambulance'll never be able to get out here in this weather. Neither will the cops. Why do you think we're holding the coffin party out here, anyway? Not just so none of those goddamned juniors can find us and jack it. Am I right?'

He turned towards Bryce, and the two of them

166

bumped chests, yelling, *'Wreckers rule!'*

Wreckers was not only the name of the Isla Huesos High School mascot, but how Seth referred to his personal crew. His ancestors had been employed as wreckers back when the *Liberty* had sunk.

'Look, don't worry about Farah,' Seth said to me, while smiling amusedly at his friends' antics. 'She's a lightweight who's never been able to hold her liquor. She does this every time we party. She'll wake up and barf and be out here dancing again in no time. Hey, c'mere, I want to show you something.'

That's when he took my hand and tried pulling me down on to the chaise beside him.

'Seth,' I said, resisting. 'I can't. We were just leaving—'

'Who's we?' he asked with a grin. 'You and that boyfriend of yours?' He glanced around the room. 'I don't see him anywhere. He's not *actually* keeping you locked up like your grandma is going around saying, is he?'

'No,' I said, struggling to think of some excuse to get away. 'But someone really should keep an eye on Farah.'

'Yeah, if you want a lapful of spew. Believe me, I've been there, and it's not pretty.' With alarming force, he managed to wrestle me on to the lounger. For someone who'd joked about my boyfriend holding me prisoner, he seemed pretty intent on keeping me that way. 'Take a look at that. What do you think?'

I had to admit that in front of us stretched a truly amazing scene. It wasn't only the angrily heaving waves of the usually serene Florida 'flats' – water normally so still and calm that paddleboarders could navigate it while standing upright with a six-pack and a dog sitting at their feet.

It was the spectacular breadth of sky visible on three sides from inside the house, clouds towering so high they resembled New York City skyscrapers and were occasionally lit as brightly when lightning crackled through them.

Then there was the spec home's backyard stretched out beneath us, a raised deck built of sandstone tiles that would have been the colour of the beach had Mr Rector not bulldozed all the beaches in order to build over them. Enclosed by three-foot glass walls so the ocean view wouldn't be impeded, the spec house's deck came complete with an outdoor kitchen that included a barbecue, mini-fridge, sink and built-in picnic table.

The crown jewel of the deck, however, was a kidney-shaped aquamarine swimming pool, with an attached hot tub that featured a waterfall that overflowed into the pool. Unlike the lagoon we'd seen while driving in, the waterfall was still working. Though, according to my mother's maintenance company, the number one rule when preparing your pool for a hurricane was to switch off its power source, the generator was still operating it, along with the pool's pump.

There appeared to be something at the bottom of Mr Rector's pool. It could have been a double dolphin tile design, to match the one in stained glass on the front door, but it was raining too hard to tell.

'Check it out,' Seth said to me with a grin, pointing at the pool. The generator had kept the pool lights bright, so it was easy to see what happened next . . .

. . . which was that a powerful wave crashed against the glass wall around the backyard, surged over it and then across the sandstone, then dumped itself into the pool, filling it with dark, brackish salt water.

I realized then what was at the bottom of the pool: seaweed. Not just seaweed but debris of all kinds, including what looked like pieces of driftwood, coolers from fishing boats that had come loose from their moors, possibly even fish. The entire backyard was flooded. I saw a lobster buoy that had detached from its trap bobbing next to the barbecue. A deck chair floated by. How the lights were even still on with so much salt water corroding the circuits, I didn't know. But I knew it wouldn't last long.

All the guys seated around the sliding glass doors hooted appreciatively at the wave, then knocked cups as an impromptu toast to Mother Nature's wrath.

'That one was *superior*,' Bryce shouted excitedly. 'Was that one superior or what, Seth?'

Seth's gaze remained fastened on the pool, but his smile grew devilish.

'That one was superior,' he said. Then his gaze swung towards me. 'What did you think, Pierce? Did you think that one was superior?'

Startled to find myself under such a bright, searching gaze, I struggled to find a reply. *His eyes*, was all I could think. *His eyes look so familiar . . .*

But I didn't know anyone with eyes that colour. John's eyes weren't blue. They were grey, as grey as the diamond hanging round my neck. Or as grey as it normally was, I realized after a quick glance down, when it wasn't swirling as black as that ocean out there.

No, Seth's eyes were the same aquamarine as the pool. Or, at least, the same aquamarine as the pool used to be.

His eye colour wasn't what I found familiar. It was something else.

'Yeah,' I said, unable to tear my gaze from his. 'That one was superior.' Then I licked my lips. I was thirsty, but after what had happened to Farah, there was nothing I dared to drink. 'Do you guys think maybe you should turn off the power down there?'

'Why?' Seth asked, his tone slightly mocking. 'You aren't worried someone might get hurt, are you?'

I felt a private storm surge of my own. What was with this guy? How could so many people have liked him enough to have voted for him for class president? Of course, I had some inside knowledge about him they didn't have.

Reminding myself of Mr Liu's warning to hold on to my own kite strings, I tried to keep my tone even.

'People have already gotten hurt,' I said. I was flirting on the edge of danger, I knew, but I had Bryce to protect me if things got tricky. My diamond wasn't going to be much use. I didn't think Seth was a Fury, though someone close by obviously was. No, Seth was just an old-fashioned killer.

Seth raised a blond eyebrow at me. 'Really? Who?'

'Farah,' I said. I could tell it wasn't the answer he'd expected when the other eyebrow lifted to join the first. 'She says this storm has cost her dad a lot of money. She probably won't be able to go to college now.'

Seth tucked his lips into a mock pout. 'Aw,' he said. 'Poor Farah.'

'She's not the only one who's gotten hurt,' I said. I said it softly enough that he had to lean forward to hear me. The music was loud, and another wave had struck, causing the guys around us to cheer. 'There's also Alex.'

He'd glanced away to look at the wave, but when I mentioned Alex, his head whipped back towards me.

'Alex?' He raised his cup to his mouth and took a sip of beer. He wasn't having anything to do with the punch bowl of mystery drink. 'Alex Cabrero? He's a sweet kid. How'd he get hurt?'

The fact that he was pretending like he didn't know set off another surge inside me. But I knew I had to keep myself in check.

'You know perfectly well,' I said with a smile. 'You and the other Rector Wreckers stuffed him into a coffin the other night, then left him there to die.'

Another one, who had his throat pierced through,
And nose cut off close underneath the brows,
And had no longer but a single ear . . .
Dante Alighieri, *Inferno*, Canto XXVIII

Seth lowered the cup from which he'd just sipped, his face never changing expression. But I saw a few drops of beer spill out on to his black polo shirt.

'I don't know what you're talking about,' he said. 'But you better remember who I am, little girl. No one messes with a Rector and gets away with it.'

I had to laugh. What had he thought, exactly, encouraging me to sit down with him? That I'd be too intimidated by his good looks and social position to mention it? Or had he planned on raising the subject himself and making some kind of threat, and I'd beaten him to it?

If so, it had been a dumb miscalculation on his part.

'You do know what I'm talking about, Seth,' I said. 'I'm sure your father's shown you the security tape by now, so you know my friends and I got Alex out. He's alive, and he'll be testifying against you . . . for all of it, not only your trying to kill him.'

Anyone looking at us would have thought we were having a perfectly friendly conversation. We were leaning close together. Even though there were so many people in the room, laughing and screaming and dancing, and the music was playing so loudly, it was almost as if the two of us were alone in our own romantic little bubble.

Except there was nothing romantic about what we were discussing.

'You know what's going to happen now,' I went on. 'You'll be arrested for attempted murder. You're eighteen, so you'll be tried as an adult, like my uncle Chris was twenty years ago, when he took the blame for that drug run your dad sent him on. It's nice we're keeping it all in the family, isn't it?' I smiled at him pleasantly. 'So I guess instead of saying, "Aw, poor Farah," we should be saying, "Aw, poor Seth." Right?'

I had to hand it to him: he covered pretty well. He didn't even blink when a streak of lightning lit up the sky outside so brilliantly it looked bright as noon.

'Seriously,' he said. 'I don't know what you're talking about. But I do know if you ever repeat any of what you just said my family's attorneys will slap a slander suit against you so fast you won't know what hit you. I don't care how much money your father has.'

'Really?' I couldn't have sounded less impressed. 'Did you ever consider that if there's a tape of us getting Alex out of that coffin, there's also a tape of you putting him *in* there, Seth?'

He did blink, then. But only once.

'Listen, you crazy whip-carrying bitch. Your cousin is dead, so he's not testifying about shit,' he said. 'And, even if you did have a copy of that tape, there's nothing on it. We checked. Lightning must have fritzed out the cameras or something . . .'

I laughed again as his voice trailed off, and he realized his mistake.

'I thought you didn't know what I was talking about,' I said.

The thunder outside was nowhere near as menacing as the expression on Seth's face as he demanded, 'What makes you think anyone would even believe you? Everyone knows why you moved here in the first place. You killed your teacher back east.'

'I did kill my teacher,' I said. 'But it wasn't back east.'

'You stupid slut,' Seth said. He was angry now . . . really angry. Enough so that his blue eyes looked more like ice than pool water, and I glanced in Bryce's direction to make sure that if those tanned hands, hardened from so much football practice and windsurfing, happened to wrap round my throat I'd have backup. 'You really think anyone would believe you? You punched your own grandmother in the face, then ran off with that long-haired freak. You're mentally unstable, your boyfriend's got a million-dollar bounty on his head and, if you come anywhere near me, I'll make sure every news outlet in the country hears how you stalked me exactly the way you stalked that teacher of yours—'

I was still staring at the front of his shirt. My mind seized on the detail that had been bothering me since I'd noticed it in the photo Farah had sent me earlier in the evening: those polo shirts Seth habitually wore – like the one he was wearing tonight – all had little men stitched over the left breast.

Little men riding a galloping horse.

The boy in the photo Mr Smith had showed me of Thanatos, the Greek personification of death, had also been riding a galloping horse.

Only instead of swinging a sword high in the air with one arm, the man on the front of Seth's shirt was swinging a polo mallet. He lacked wings, but then so did the statue, now that time and natural disasters had worn them away.

He destroyed whole armies with a single swipe of that sword, Mr Smith had said. *He killed without a thought to his victims. He was said to be without mercy, without repentance and without a soul.*

So in other words, I'd joked, *a typical teen boy.*

Just like Seth Rector, whose parents, in the middle of their family mausoleum, had erected a statue of Hades and Persephone.

The goal of the Furies has always been to destroy the Underworld, Mr Smith had said.

'Are you even listening to me?' Seth hissed. 'I don't think you know who you're messing with.'

I raised my gaze to lock with his. 'Oh,' I said, 'I know *exactly* who I'm messing with. The guy who killed me – not to mention my best friend, my guidance counsellor, my cousin and now my boyfriend. Am I right?'

Something in my tone caused his eyes to widen, not so much with alarm as with incredulity.

'You're crazy,' he said. 'As crazy as everyone says.'

'Oh, I know you didn't *literally* kill me,' I said, plucking my necklace from the bodice of my gown, then beginning to twirl the diamond round my finger on the end of its chain. 'You just pluck people's souls from their bodies. You *literally* killed Alex, though. And Jade, too, I think. You know what Jade told me once, before she died? That there's no such thing as crazy. There's no such thing as normal, either. Those aren't therapeutically beneficial words. I don't know if that's really true. But I do know one thing: if you don't let go of my boyfriend's soul in the next five seconds, you're going to find out just how crazy I can get.'

'You can't do anything to me, you crazy bitch,' he said, glancing back towards his friends. 'Not in front of all these people.'

'Oh, yeah?' I dropped my diamond and leaned forward, planting one hand on either side of his chest, trapping him inside my arms. He leaned back as far as he could, until his spine was stopped by the raised end of the chaise longue. 'Watch me.'

He could easily have got away. He could have knocked me aside and stood up. But he didn't. He simply lay there, breathing hard, wondering what I was going to do.

What I did was lower myself slowly against him, then reach up to cup his cheeks between my hands. When he still didn't protest, I pressed my mouth to his, my hair forming a dark, fragrant tent around our faces.

He didn't knock me aside then, either. It wasn't because he was too much of a gentleman to hurt a lady. Look what he'd done to Jade. He didn't knock me aside because he *liked* it . . . at least at first. He opened his lips beneath mine, let out a faint moaning sound and lifted his hands to grip

176

my waist, which just showed that all boys – even ones possessed by Greek personifications of death – could be shockingly stupid sometimes.

Seth closed his eyes, but I didn't. That's how I saw the diamond dangling from my pendant fall against the curve of his bicep as he clutched me to him.

It's also how I saw the diamond begin to burn his flesh.

He evidently didn't notice the pain or the smoke. But plenty of other people did.

'Woohoo,' I heard Cody hoot. 'Rector, you dog. You two are smoking!'

Seth was too busy trying to ram his tongue into my mouth to pay attention . . . an attempt I thwarted by moving my face away from his and kissing him on the cheek instead.

Unfortunately, he kept moving his head so that my lips met his open mouth. This was very unwelcome, but didn't last long, since the smell of his charring skin – and the sensation of it – soon caught his attention.

He ripped his mouth from mine, then looked down at his arm. 'What the—?'

It was too late. The blue smoke from the wound in his arm was circling in a slow arc towards the ceiling.

'Uh, Seth, Coach said no smoking until end of season, remember?' Bryce did not understand what was happening.

Seth released me, shaking his arm until the diamond rolled harmlessly away, on to his shirtfront. Then, as the stone began to seer through the cotton jersey, he thrust me roughly away from him, towards the far end of the chaise.

'Stop it,' he said in a voice that sounded nothing like

Seth's. It was deep and wild, and as angry as the ocean outside the glass doors. 'Stop it now.'

'I'm not doing anything,' I said. I glanced towards Seth's friends, my eyes wide and innocent. 'You guys, you saw it. Seth and I were kissing, and now he's having some kind of fit or something. Maybe you should call his dad.'

'Seth?' Bryce looked down at us, his expression troubled. 'Hey, bro, what's going on?'

Seth gritted his teeth as he clutched at his arm. The wisps of smoke that escaped from between his fingers turned thicker . . . and blacker. Black as my diamond. Black as his pupils, which seemed to fill the entirety of his eyes.

'I'll kill you,' he snarled, saliva bubbling out of the sides of his mouth. 'I'll kill you for this.'

'Dude,' Cody said, slapping a hand to Seth's back. 'Are you OK?'

'*Don't touch me.*' Seth whipped his head around to rage at him. Cody instantly pulled his hand away.

'Um,' I said. 'I don't think he's OK.'

Outside, there was a flash of such brilliance that I thought at first it was a nuclear explosion. It lit up the sky, the sea and the entire room . . . which was immediately after plunged into total darkness when the generator ground to a halt. Girls screamed – a particularly shrill sound, since the speakers had also failed – and I heard glass breaking. Then thunder crashed with such violence that the entire house shook.

When the lights flickered back on a second later, causing us all to blink, I saw that there was a tall figure standing behind Seth who hadn't been there before.

'Hey,' Cody said, noticing the figure as well. 'Who are—?'

Who are you? That's what he was probably going to ask. But before Cody could finish his sentence the figure grabbed a handful of Seth's shirt, then dragged him from the chaise longue to his feet.

'It's one thing to kill me,' John said to him. 'But kiss my girlfriend? I don't think so.'

Then he pulled back one of his powerful fists and planted it squarely into the centre of Seth's face.

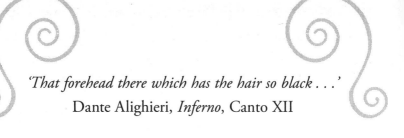

'That forehead there which has the hair so black . . .'
Dante Alighieri, *Inferno*, Canto XII

John put a pretty solid end to the coffin party when he broke the host's nose.

At that exact moment, the sea broke through the glass wall around the spec home's deck and came gushing through the backyard, around the side of the house, and towards the driveway full of cars.

The party guests who weren't screaming about all the blood coursing down Seth's face suddenly began screaming about their vehicles, and they streamed from the house in a futile effort to save them . . . everyone except those helping Seth, who was cradling his own head and moaning, and Bryce, who immediately came to his QB's defence.

Dropping his head, Bryce came at John like a bull, his face red with rage. John sidestepped him, then slammed a fist into the younger boy's stomach. As a ball player, it couldn't have been the first time Bryce had ever been struck in the gut, but it might have been the first time he'd ever been struck with such force, judging by the look of injured surprise that spread across his face. While Bryce was still doubled over in pain, trying to catch his breath, John plunged another fist into his kidneys. Bryce grunted, then sank to his knees, all the fight clearly knocked out of him.

'John,' I said urgently, since he was still breathing hard and pacing back and forth in front of Bryce, looking not unlike the 'wild thing' I used to accuse him of being. He seemed ready to hit Bryce again – or anyone else in the room – at the least provocation.

None of the few remaining males looked as if they cared to engage, however. The DJ, Anton, was pointedly minding his own business as he swiftly packed up his equipment, and a few stoners were watching the fight with wide, astonished gazes from a nearby couch.

'John,' I said again, reaching for him as he swung by me with no sign of recognition. Wherever Thanatos had been keeping him, the conditions had evidently not been pleasant. 'It's me, Pierce. It's all right.'

He threw me a sceptical look from beneath a lock of dark hair that had fallen over one eye. 'Is it?' he asked as he paced, opening and closing the hand he'd used to punch Seth and then Bryce. 'Funny, because it doesn't feel all right. How could you have let him kiss you like that?'

Oddly, it was that irritable snarl, more than any loving greeting, that made me realize John was fine. He had really and truly come back, just as he'd assured me he would on that dock back in the Underworld, and he was entirely himself.

'John,' I said, my eyes filling with tears. Tears of joy.

'How could you even have let him *touch* you?' he asked. 'Didn't you know who he was?'

'Of course I knew who he was,' I said. Waves of love and

relief were washing over me with as much force as the waves of seawater that were washing over – and destroying – Reef Key. 'Thanatos, the Greek personification of death. He was holding you captive—'

'Yes,' John said. 'Exactly. And you kissed him!'

'Well, all of Seth's friends were standing around. How else was I supposed to get my necklace close enough to him long enough to burn him without making it look suspicious?'

John's scowl deepened. 'You could have had Frank hold him down,' he said.

I couldn't help grinning up at him. I was so happy he was back and arguing with me. 'Next time,' I said, 'I will definitely have Frank hold him down.'

'It isn't funny,' John said. 'You kissed him on purpose just to annoy me. So do you know what I get to do now?' He stopped pacing and pointed at himself. '*I* get to kiss someone – whoever I want – just to annoy *you*.'

I reached out and took hold of the hand he'd used to point at himself, which also happened to be his punching hand. He'd skinned his knuckles on something sharp – possibly Seth's teeth – and they looked tender. I raised the bruised, battered hand to my lips.

I was standing close enough to him that I could see how quickly his pulse was leaping in his neck, and how, at my gentle touch, his pulse began to slow. His expression softened. Somehow he'd managed to acquire a shirt – a white one, loose around the collar, but close-fitting everywhere else, like his jeans – and a pair of boots not unlike the ones he'd left on the dock back in the Underworld.

I wondered where he'd found them. Although his long dark hair was a tangled mess, and he needed a shave, he looked good. Death suited him.

'All right,' I whispered, rubbing his hand across my cheek. 'You get one free kiss . . . whoever you want.'

Although I could see him struggling, he couldn't maintain his scowl. A smile broke across his face. It was like the sun breaking out across a tempest-tossed sea.

'What if who I want to kiss is you?' he asked.

'I think that can be arranged,' I said.

Wrapping his hand round the back of my neck, he drew me to the hard wall of his chest. His arms weren't the only thing that enveloped me. The smell of him enveloped me as well – that comforting smell of wood smoke and autumn and something distinctly John that I realized, as his lips came down over mine, now meant only one thing to me: *home*.

'There's something you promised you'd tell me when I got back,' he murmured after finally letting me up for air.

At first I was too dazzled by his kiss to remember what he was referring to. Then I blushed.

'Not *now*,' I said, looking down at Seth, who sat on the floor a few feet away being fussed over by Farah's friends Nicole and Serena. Bryce was still recuperating nearby, too, though Seth didn't seem all that sympathetic.

'Did you not hear me?' Seth demanded of Bryce, swatting away the blood-soaked napkins the girls kept pressing to his face. 'I said get up and *take him out*.' He shot a deadly look in John's direction.

'Bro, I'm not feeling so good.' Bryce clutched his stomach. 'Maybe if Cody and those guys hadn't left. But that guy is pretty big.' Looking up at John, Bryce whispered, as if Seth wouldn't be able to hear him, 'Dude, I think you'd better go. My friend here is really mad at you.'

John glared at Seth. 'Tell your *friend* the feeling is mutual. He's lucky I didn't kill him. In fact—'

John began to move with murderous purpose towards Seth, but I caught him by the wrist.

'John, no,' I said. 'Don't waste your energy on him. We have more important things to do—'

Right then, one of them came stumbling from the back bedroom into which Frank had carried her.

'Seth,' Farah cried. 'Where are you?'

She wasn't exactly fully recovered, as Seth had assured me she'd be. Kayla and Frank stood on either side of her, each with an arm round her waist. Their support appeared to be all that was keeping Farah on her feet. The only reason she'd stopped moving was because they'd both stumbled to a halt when they saw John. A pleased smile spread over Frank's face.

'Well,' he said. 'Look who's back from the dead.'

Farah, however, only had eyes for Seth.

'I turn my back on you for one minute,' Farah cried, weaving unsteadily on her high heels, despite her human crutches, but nevertheless able to focus a laser-like glare of wrath at Seth, 'and I find out you've been hooking up with *Pierce Oliviera?*'

Seth wasn't paying any attention to Farah, however. He

was staring at someone who stood behind her. Not Kayla or Frank, though. It was someone who'd popped his dark shaggy head up from the basement stairwell.

'Hey, Seth,' Alex said, waving a file folder he had tucked in one hand. 'Bad news. Your dad's office is completely flooded. So's your truck. But there's some good news. I managed to print out all this stuff from your dad's computer before it got ruined. Some kind of geographic reports on Reef Key and how it shouldn't ever have been made into a housing development on account of – well, your dad probably told you why, didn't he, Seth?' Alex winked at him. 'I'm sure some nerds who know more about this stuff than I do are going to find it very interesting when I send it to them.'

Seth went white as a ghost beneath the blood that was smeared all over his face.

'No,' I heard him mutter. 'It's not possible. *You're dead.*'

'No, he's not,' I said. 'I told you.'

'Listen,' Kayla said, ignoring everyone. The usual sparkle was gone from her eyes, and not because she was missing the rhinestones she often pasted at the corner of each of her eyelids. She looked at John and me. 'I'm glad you're back,' she said to John. 'But I don't want to be responsible for adding another inhabitant to your world. Princess here has had way more than just too much to drink—'

Farah's head had been lolling, but it jerked up at the word *princess*. 'Don't call me that,' she slurred. 'Can't you call me *chiquita* like you do your friends?'

'Yeah,' Kayla said unsmilingly. 'Not gonna happen. I

think we need to get her to the hospital. Nine-one-one says the ambulance can't make it through with the tidal surge this high, but I know Patrick's Jeep can—'

'Take her and go,' John said. 'Pierce and I will settle things here.'

Outside, the wind was howling so loudly the sliding glass doors had begun to shake. I questioned once again Seth's wisdom in not boarding them up. My diamond had gone from ink black to a midnight blue, indicating that while no Furies were immediately present, we weren't entirely clear of danger.

Seth climbed to his feet as Kayla and Frank began to drag an unresisting Farah towards the front door. 'Bryce,' he said, in a tightly controlled voice. 'Don't let those freaks go another step farther.'

Bryce was distracted, however. 'Hey,' he said, gazing at the sliding glass doors. 'Maybe we should go with them. It's getting kind of bad out there.'

Seth whirled on Bryce to demand, 'Are you kidding me? Have you seen who's *with* them?'

The DJ, who himself was on his way out, looked up in alarm at hearing Seth's tone, and even a couple of the stoners raised their heads from the leather couches and blinked at him.

'Cabrero,' Seth shouted, when Bryce only looked at him blankly. 'The file, you idiot! Get that file from Cabrero!'

Bryce shook his head, then turned his attention back towards the storm. 'I'm sorry, dude,' he said. 'It's like what they were saying on the news. The bad side of the hurricane is starting to pass over, you know?'

Alex had hurried forward to open the front door for Frank and Kayla. Now, after the two of them had safely passed the stained-glass double dolphins, Alex turned to wave the file folder suggestively at Seth, along with both his middle fingers.

'Better luck killing me next time,' he called. 'Oh, and great party, thanks.'

He disappeared into the storm, slamming the double doors behind him.

'You idiot,' Seth yelled, throwing an empty red party cup at Bryce. The floor was littered with them, everyone having dropped them where they stood as they'd fled the party. They lined the floor the way red poinciana blossoms lined John's crypt, surrounding the cracked, empty coffin Farah and Serena had decorated.

'Hey, man. Not cool,' the DJ said disapprovingly to Seth. He threw on a rain poncho. 'I'm out of here.'

'Can we get a ride?' Nicole asked, grabbing her sequinned clutch. 'I'm pretty sure my Audi's not gonna start.'

'If you help carry my equipment,' the DJ said. He strode over to lift each of the remaining stoners from the couch by their shirt collars, like a shepherd tending to his flock. 'Blue van parked over by the bulldozers. It's a hike. My speakers get wet, you're paying for them.'

Serena grabbed a turntable. 'Bye, Seth,' she called over her shoulder. 'Great party.' The gaze she sent in my direction – or, more accurately, John's direction – indicated that she hadn't actually thought it was such a great party at all. 'See you later.'

'Yeah, bye,' Nicole said. She grabbed a box of cables and headed out of the door, not seeming to care that her carefully straightened hair was about to be ruined.

'I'll take the speakers,' Bryce said as he ambled forward. 'You coming, Seth?'

Seth shot Bryce a look of pure contempt. 'No, I'm not coming. I'm not going anywhere.'

'But . . .' Bryce looked confused. 'He said he'd give us a ride. And your truck's underwater, bro.'

'I'm staying right here.' Seth was staring at John, who was staring right back at him, aquamarine-eyed gaze meeting grey-eyed gaze. 'Until I've finished up my business.'

Bryce shrugged. 'OK, bro. But I don't think Anton's gonna wait.' He shuffled out of the door.

'Really, Seth?' I couldn't believe it. 'I think your business with us is finished, for the time being.'

'Yeah? Well, I don't think so. Who is your cousin going to give those papers to?'

'How am I supposed to know?' I asked. 'I don't even know what they say.'

'Doesn't your mom work for the Isla Huesos Marine Institute?'

'How'd you know *that*?' I demanded, shocked.

'Because while this guy was allegedly kidnapping you,' Seth said, with a sneer in John's direction, 'my dad and I went to comfort your mom in her grief, and she told us.'

John took a threatening step towards Seth, but I put out a hand to stop him. I'd forgotten how Seth and his father had been inside my house.

'You weren't comforting her,' I said. 'You went there to get the coffin materials back.'

'If your cousin rats my family out,' Seth said, 'all of you might find yourselves in coffins – real ones.'

'And you,' John said, taking a forceful step, one I was powerless to stop, 'might find yourself thrown out of those windows over there.'

'John,' I said, grasping his arms with both hands. To Seth, I said, 'If building this place is in violation of some kind of environmental regulation, I'm sure someone would have already noticed by now, don't you think? Unless,' I added, my voice dripping with sarcasm, 'your dad bribed a bunch of people to look the other way, which I can't imagine he'd have done, because he's always been such an upstanding, law-abiding citizen, hasn't he?'

Only Seth, John and I remained in the house. I don't know who Seth was trying to impress when he said, 'Reef Key has been in my family for years. My great-great-great – whatever – grandfather William Rector bought it from Isla Huesos County in 1845 when it was nothing but a sandbar covered in shrubs. No one else has ever given two shits about it. We should be able to do whatever we want with it.'

To John's credit, he didn't move a muscle. He didn't show any indication at all that he'd known Seth's *great-great-great* – whatever – *grandfather William*, nor that he had despised him for the thieving pirate he'd been, colluding with ship captains to wreck their own boats on purpose so that Rector could swoop in and 'save' their cargo for one half its value. John's own father hadn't been much better, having been one of those captains willing to risk the lives of his crew for a percentage of the profit from that cargo.

'It appears to me,' John said with admirable calm, 'that your family – and you in particular – does whatever it wants, regardless.'

'Damn right,' Seth said. 'And we've gotten rich because of it. Maybe not Oliviera rich, but—'

Something struck one of the sliding glass doors overlooking the backyard. Not with enough force to break it, but hard enough to make a startlingly loud sound. I threw both arms in front of my face, and John quickly thrust me behind him, placing himself between me and the still rattling glass.

'Oh, crap,' Seth said with a shaky laugh. 'That scared me. But look. It was just a bird.'

'A bird?'

Horrified, I lowered my arms and started for the windows, but not before John had a chance to grab and stop me.

'Not that bird,' he said. 'Hope is safe.'

'How do you know?' I asked. 'Was she with you?'

'No,' he said. 'But, trust me, she has enough sense not to be out in a storm like this.'

'Well, that bird didn't,' I said. 'Why would Hope? What if she's trying to find me?'

'Hey, you should see this,' Seth said, from in front of the sliding glass doors, where he'd gone to look out over the balcony. 'It's some kind of black bird. There's hundreds of them. They're all over the place. They're raining down from the sky. I've got to get a shot of this.' He dug into his jean pocket for his cellphone. 'No one will ever believe it.'

'Seth,' I said anxiously. 'I wouldn't do that if I were you.'

I knew he'd tried to kill my cousin. I knew he'd probably killed Jade. I knew he – or at least a death god who'd possessed him – had ordered my boyfriend to be killed by the Furies, then held him captive. He'd threatened to kill me, multiple times, and even threatened my mother. But I couldn't stand there and watch him kill himself.

Seth laughed. 'God, would you relax? I'm not stupid, all right? These doors are made from the same kind of glass they use in windshields, impact resistant.'

Remembering Chloe, and the tiny shards of glass she'd had embedded in her hair like diamonds from a tiara, I said, '*Impact resistant* doesn't mean if something hits them hard enough they won't shatter.'

Seth had his mobile out and was snapping away eagerly as, outside, the wind raged and ravens rained from the sky.

'Yeah, well,' he said. 'You guys can run if you want, but I'm staying here. These babies can withstand gusts of up to two hundred miles per hour—'

Another raven struck one of the doors, almost as if it had hurled itself at it in an effort to get inside. No, to get at *someone* inside. Not Seth. It hadn't chosen the sliding glass door nearest Seth. It had chosen the one nearest us.

John and I exchanged looks. We were under attack.

The second door didn't hold. The entire panel shattered into a spiderweb configuration, then the glass fell from the

191

metal frame and splintered against the tiled floor at our feet.

John yanked me into his arms.

'We're going,' John shouted to be heard above the wind and rain.

I knew what was going to happen next. When I opened my eyes again, I'd be somewhere else – most likely the Underworld. John didn't know that in the Underworld ravens were also raining from the sky . . . or maybe he did. There wasn't time to ask, nor was there time to tell him. There was time to say only one thing.

'Seth.'

John's hold on me tightened. He knew precisely what I was saying. *Save Seth, too.*

'No,' he said.

And, as I heard another glass door explode, the room disappeared.

When I opened my eyes again, we were in darkness.

Love, that exempts no one beloved from loving,
Seized me with pleasure of this man so strongly,
That, as thou seest, it doth not yet desert me . . .
Dante Alighieri, *Inferno*, Canto V

At first I couldn't tell where we were. All I knew was that it was quiet, and dry, and so dark that John's face was indistinguishable to me, though it was merely inches from mine.

Then lightning flashed, and I was able to recognize, through a few patterns thrown across the floor, that we were on the landing on the stairs of my mother's house.

'John,' I cried, releasing the deathlike grip I'd been keeping on his neck. *'Here?'*

'Shhh.' He pointed up the stairs. Down the hallway, dimly lit by a single battery-operated LED candle, I could see that the door to my mother's bedroom was closed. 'It was the only place I could think of.'

'But—' A million questions flickered through my mind, dancing as wildly as the fake candle flame.

Then thunder rumbled . . . not so loud as it had out on Reef Key. We were inland – well, as inland as anyone could be on a two-mile-by-four-mile island – and on as high ground as Mr Smith's house. The storm wasn't nearly as bad here as it had been out by Mr Rector's spec house. Besides, Uncle Chris had boarded up every single one of my

193

mother's windows as tight as a drum.

The thunder was still loud enough, however, that I was worried it might wake my mother, and the last thing I needed at the moment was a barrage of parental questions.

'Follow me,' I said, taking John's hand. Creeping up the rest of the stairs, I snagged the LED candle from its table in the hallway, then led him into the room across the hall from my mom's, gently closing the door behind us once we were both inside.

'Is this your room?' John asked with a grin, looking around at the lavender walls and curtains my mom's decorator had chosen.

'Yes.' I set the LED candle on my desk and looked around. Nothing had changed since the last time I'd been there, except that the goodbye letter I'd left for my mother was gone. Seeing the room for the first time from John's perspective, however, I felt mortified. It seemed so devoid of personality. No surprise, since I'd had no say whatsoever in its decor . . . no interest, either. 'Can we not talk about it?'

'Why?' he asked, surprised. He was so tall and broad-shouldered he resembled a rhinoceros in a tea shop as he moved about, inspecting things. 'I like it. Is this yours?'

He picked up a stuffed unicorn Hannah Chang had given to me for my birthday and that I'd kept on my bookshelf as a matter of habit for so long I'd forgotten I owned it.

'Yes,' I said.

'I didn't know you liked unicorns,' he said.

'I don't,' I said, blushing. 'I mean, I do, but not the rainbow kind. Someone gave that to me as a gift. I—'

Bringing him here had been a huge mistake. Although I hadn't brought him here, I remembered. He'd brought me. I was actually a little surprised he'd never been in my room before. But John had odd, old-fashioned standards, and I was quite sure that while he'd considered it perfectly acceptable – even his moral duty – to spy on me at school, the Isla Huesos Cemetery, airports, city streets, jewellery shops and every other public venue, my bedroom would be completely off-limits.

'John, we can't leave him out there,' I said, deciding it was time to change the subject. 'He could be hurt.'

John picked up a bottle of black nail polish I'd left on a shelf, sniffed it curiously, then made a face and put it down again.

'Who could be hurt?' he asked.

'Seth,' I said. 'He could be dying. I know how you feel about him, but that wasn't him. That was Thanatos. Well, OK, yes, some of it was him. But the part about you, that was Thanatos. I know you probably have post-traumatic stress from whatever he did to you, and I totally understand that, he completely deserves to be punished, but that's not our call to make. You're better than he is – you still have your humanity, and he doesn't. We can't—'

'What's *The Lord of the Flies*?' he asked, reading from the title of a book on my bookshelf.

'It's a really boring book with no girls in it. I don't even know why I still have that; they made us read it for school.'

'Do you like *anything* in your room?' he asked.

You, I wanted to say. *I like you. I love you.*

195

I don't know why I couldn't say it. I don't know why everything was suddenly so awkward. Maybe because we'd left Seth Rector to die. Maybe because we still needed to save the Underworld and, through saving the Underworld, Isla Huesos. Maybe because my mother was asleep in the next room.

'Everything I like I already took to the Underworld.' I indicated my tote bag, which I'd lugged from Mr Smith's house to the party, and from the party to my house. I wasn't the sort of girl who forgot her purse, although I had a tendency to forget most everything else. 'I packed it in there when you brought me here the last time, to say goodbye to my mom. Just like I packed everything I needed to come here to rescue you. Like your tablet. I have it, in case you want to check to see whether or not Seth is still alive.'

He put the book back where he'd found it.

'It won't make any difference,' he said. 'I happen to agree with Mr Darwin's theory of natural selection. That's from a book Mr Smith loaned to me, *On the Origin of Species*. Perhaps you read that in school, as well as the one about the lord of the flies.'

'No,' I said flatly. 'But I've heard of it.'

'Then you'll agree that if it's Seth Rector's time to die it's because he's less suited to his environment than the rest of us.' I opened my mouth to disagree, but John held up a finger to stop me. 'Not because we might have rescued him, but because he does extraordinarily stupid – even wicked – things. So isn't it better that he doesn't live to reproduce and make little Rectors who'll most likely also do extraordinarily stupid, wicked things? Doesn't Seth Rector's father also do stupid, wicked things? And his father before him? Do you think it was an accident that Thanatos happened to choose to possess Seth Rector? No. He chose Seth Rector because Seth Rector's was the mind most easy for him to access and corrupt. It was the mind most like his, of anyone on this island. I suspect Thanatos has been possessing the minds of the Rector men for many, many years, because they've all been as stupid, yet wicked, as Seth.'

'Gee,' I said, walking over to my bag, pulling out John's tablet and then my own phone. 'And I only figured it out because of his shirt.'

'I meant to ask you about that,' John said. 'How *did* you figure it out? What about a shirt?'

'The little polo player on the shirts Seth always – never mind,' I said, when I saw John's blank expression. Not only was he the kind of boy who never noticed what other boys wore, but he was a boy who'd been born more than a century and half ago and had no idea what designer labels were. 'Look, I'll grant you that natural selection is a good argument for not helping Seth. But I know someone else who had a father who did a lot of stupid, wicked things. You. Aren't you glad someone gave *you* a second chance?'

John scowled. 'I only did one wicked thing, and I did it to save the lives of my crew.'

'*One* wicked thing? I could name a half dozen wicked things you've done today alone. You killed a man!'

'He was a Fury, and you tried to kill him first. I only finished what you started,' he said.

'You've been wanting to kill Mr Mueller for years,' I said.

'And Darwin would agree with me that the species is better off without him.' His brow wrinkled as he looked at me. 'Why are you wearing my father's whip on a belt around your waist?'

I had forgotten all about it. 'Oh . . . Mr Liu gave it to me. For protection, I think.' Another white lie, but less embarrassing, I felt, than telling him what Mr Liu had really said, about my needing it because I was a kite with no strings.

'My father's *whip*?' Now his eyebrows went way, way up.

I realized the subject needed immediate changing.

'Oh, look,' I said, casually handing him his tablet. As usual, I'd been able to make nothing out on it, since the symbols it displayed were completely foreign to me. But there were several messages on my own phone, and I began to read them aloud to him. 'Kayla says they're at the hospital, and everything is fine. Well, Farah's probably going to have to have her stomach pumped, so that's not so good. And they've closed all the roads, so they're going to have to stay there a while. Maybe all night, until the storm ends. Unless you want to go get them, of course.'

'If they're not in any danger, why would I leave here?' John asked, sinking down on to my bed. He was staring at the screen of his tablet, as I'd known he would. It had been a long time since he'd seen it, and he was a workaholic. I was sure it was telling him all sorts of dire things about the state of the Underworld, not to mention the status of people who were in peril of dying and travelling there soon.

'Oh,' I said. 'Well, that's OK. Frank really likes the cafeteria food. But Kayla isn't sure her mom is so wild about Frank.'

John let out a sarcastic laugh, still staring down at his screen.

'You might want to laugh more quietly,' I said, loosening the belt Mr Liu had given me, and allowing it to fall to the floor, 'unless you want my mom to come in here and not feel so wild about you.'

John sobered instantly. 'What about Alex?'

'There's no word from him,' I said. 'Alex only calls or texts me when he's dying. Is he?'

John glanced back down at his screen. 'No.'

'Well, that's a nice change. What about Seth?'

'He's on the brink, but I think he'll live,' he said. 'Unfortunately.' I sank down beside him on the bed, and he showed me his screen. On it, Seth was huddled in a closet, his face bathed in the light of his cellphone as he shouted frantically, 'What do you mean, the roads are closed? Someone has to come get me, the generator failed, I don't have any electricity. There's no air-conditioning. Do you have any idea what the humidity is like out here?'

Seth's image disappeared as John turned off the tablet and placed it on my bedside table.

'It appears,' John said, 'that he's going to be fine, if a little uncomfortable.'

'Any word from Mr Graves on how he and the others are doing?'

'As well as can be expected, under the circumstances,'

John said. 'At least they were when I saw them a little while ago.'

I stared at him. 'You saw them? *When?*'

'On my way back to life,' he said. 'I had to stop and pick up a few things, you know, such as my body, before I could rip you away from the arms of Thanatos.'

'So *that's* how you got this,' I said, leaning forward to pluck at his shirt. 'And the boots. I wondered. I wish I could have been there to see everyone's faces when you went from being stone-cold dead to sitting up and talking.'

'There were some screams,' John said. 'Particularly from one old woman—'

'Mrs Engle,' I said. 'She's a school nurse. She was very attentive to you when you were dead. You know, I think she and Mr Graves may have a little thing going on.'

John looked at me in astonishment. 'A *thing*? What exactly happened while I was gone? Conditions were *not* as I left them. I told you to go back to the castle, not take everyone on the beach back with you.'

I slipped off my shoes and tucked my feet beneath me, not easy when wearing such a long skirt. 'I had to make some tough executive decisions,' I said. 'Running that place is not easy. I don't know how you've done it all these years. We had problems with kamikaze ravens as well. I thought that with Thanatos gone, maybe the Fates would come back, but I guess not if Mrs Engle is still around.' Then something occurred to me, and I gasped. 'Oh, John!'

He looked at me in alarm. 'What is it?'

'I've killed Thanatos. How is anyone's spirit going to be

escorted to the Underworld? Isn't that what Thanatos does? Mr Smith said the word once. A *psycho . . . psychopomp.* One who escorts the souls of the newly dead.'

I could tell from John's expression that this was the first time the thought had occurred to him, too.

'Is the soul of everyone who dies from now on going to be trapped between this world and the Underworld, like you were?' I asked. 'Have I made things worse? Oh, no. I've got to call Mr Smith and ask him—'

John's fingers wrapped round mine before they could reach the phone.

'No,' he said. 'Don't. You haven't made things worse.' His grey-eyed gaze was imploring. 'How could you? Pierce, what you did – I know I wasn't happy about the way you did it, but what you did . . . when I was . . . *where* I was . . . it was the worst place I've ever been in my life. I thought the Underworld was the worst place I've ever been when I first got there, and I was all alone, but where he kept me – I can't even put into words how horrible it was.'

The fingers around mine were like ice. In the dim light from the electric candle, I could see that his forehead was dewy with sweat, even though the house was still cool with air-conditioning. The power hadn't been out for that long.

'It was like a cellar,' he said, 'dark and cold, and I didn't know when or even if I'd ever be let out. I could see a crack of daylight streaming through, but the door to get to it was just beyond my reach, no matter how hard I strained against the ropes that were keeping me bound. What was worse was that I knew the light wasn't light at all . . . it was you. I could see you, hear you, smell you, even. But I couldn't reach you.'

'Oh, John,' I said, my heart welling for him. 'I'm so sorry. I didn't know.'

'How could you?'

In the flickering light from the fake candle, I could see a muscle leaping in his jaw. He was hunched forward on the side of my bed, his elbows on his knees. I had never seen him look more miserable, except maybe for when he was telling me about his father. I laid a hand on his back. It felt hard as a boulder.

'The closer you came to finding me,' he whispered, 'the wider the shaft of light became. I could see more and more of what you were doing. But I still couldn't reach you, and I couldn't get you to understand that I was there, to see me or hear me, the whole time. It nearly drove me mad.'

'I did know that you were there,' I said, lifting my hand to stroke some of his tangled hair. 'At least I began to suspect you were once you sent that tree crashing down on Mr Mueller. That was quite subtle, not at all your usual style.'

John chuckled grimly at my sarcasm. He captured my hand in one of his own.

'You've always been able to make me laugh,' he said. 'Even when things are at their worst. How do you do that?'

'According to Mr Smith, it's because I'm the sunshine,' I said, unable to keep a note of self-deprecation from creeping into my voice, 'and you're the storm.'

'That sounds like something he would say.' Grinning, he

pressed my fingertips to his lips. 'I think he's probably right.'

'Oh, John, no!' His lips felt as icy to the touch as his hands. 'Why are you so cold?' I slipped my free hand around his shoulders while I tried to think what a responsible adult, like my mom or Mrs Engle, would do in this situation. 'Do you want me to make you some soup? I could go downstairs and make you some soup – it's a gas stove, so it should still be working – and bring it back up—'

'I don't need soup,' he said. 'All I need is you.'

He dropped my hand to snake his arm round my waist, burying his face in the curve between my neck and my shoulder – a favourite place of his – then sending me sinking slowly back against the voluminous pile of soft 'accent' pillows my mom's decorator had insisted on stacking against my headboard.

You don't sleep on them, the decorator had explained to me. *They're called throw pillows because you 'throw' them off the bed right before you go to sleep.*

I don't know why anyone would bother throwing those pillows off the bed when they made such a deep, comfortable nest for two people who'd been through as much as John and I had recently. I liked the way they towered around us, forming a safe cocoon against the world as John clung to me in the semi-darkness, his heart pounding hard against mine, listening to the rain as it continued to pour down outside my shuttered windows.

At least, I thought, he was able to speak about what he'd been through. That had to be a good sign. On television, doctors were always saying how it was healing for soldiers and other victims of violent assault to talk about their traumatic experiences.

'What else?' I asked, as thunder rumbled off in the distance and his lips roamed sleepily along the curve of my collarbone.

'What do you mean, what else?'

'I mean, what else about when you were with Thanatos?'

He lifted his head to stare down at me as if I were a madwoman. 'Why would I want to talk about Thanatos *now*?'

'Because,' I said, 'talking about it might be therapeutic. Whether you admit it or not, you've had a lot of distressing experiences in your life.'

He leaned up on one of the accent pillows to look me in the eye. 'So have you.'

'That's true,' I said. 'But my parents have also paid for me to have a lot of therapy, so the chances of my suffering from any long-term neurosis is minimal.'

'*This* is all the therapy I need,' he said, raising his hand from my waist to another part of my anatomy, nearer my heart.

I sucked in my breath. 'I'm pretty sure in therapy, that would be called a diversionary tactic.'

'Then I need a lot more diversionary tactics,' John said, his fingers moving to tug on the string that kept the bodice of my dress closed in the front. 'Also, there's something you promised to tell me that you *still* haven't said—'

I don't know if it was the intoxicating mixture of his closeness; his kisses; the comforting cocoon of pillows; the romantic, constant drumming of the rain outside; or the fact that, after so long, we finally seemed to have found somewhere we could safely be together. But it wasn't long before I found myself murmuring, '*I love you, I love you, I love you,*' exactly as I'd longed to the entire time he was gone.

He expressed his love for me, as well, as emphatically as ever . . . so much so that I was relieved for the booming thunder outside, since I knew it would cover any sounds we might make that could wake up my mom – though at times I wasn't certain whether the thunder was being generated by John or the storm itself.

Later, lying lazily in his arms beneath my white down comforter, I said, 'We can't fall asleep. There's too much we still have to do.'

'I know.' His chest was rising and falling beneath my cheek in a slow, rhythmic movement as he breathed. 'But I think it's all right for now.' He held up my diamond, the only thing I was wearing. 'It's silver. There's no danger. We deserve to rest for a few minutes.'

'No,' I said firmly. 'If we fall asleep and my mom finds us in here, she'll kill you all over again.'

'If you'd just marry me,' he said, 'the way I asked you to, everything would be fine.'

'You don't know my parents,' I said. 'Believe me, everything wouldn't be fine if we got married.'

'I would rather be open with them,' John said. 'I can provide for you.'

'Yeah,' I said. 'That's not really the issue. And, besides,

you live in an underground cave.'

'In a *castle* in an underground cave.'

'That is currently overrun with the souls of the dead.'

John thought about this. 'With a bit of luck, that's something we'll soon resolve.'

'Luck,' I said, gazing sleepily at the still flickering LED candle. 'That's something neither of us has ever had much of.'

He stroked a lock of my hair. 'We found each other, didn't we?'

'That was my grandmother, not luck. She made sure we met so she could kill me later and break your heart because she hates your guts.'

His hand stilled on my hair. 'Oh. That's right.'

'Don't let me fall asleep.'

'I won't,' he said.

The last thing I remember was lightning as it made a bright white stripe against my wall when it flashed between the slats of the shutters. I never heard the thunder that followed, however.

And light I saw in fashion of a river
Fulvid with its effulgence, 'twixt two banks
Depicted with an admirable Spring.
Dante Alighieri, *Paradiso*, Canto XXX

Sunlight streamed through the slats in the storm shutters, making cheerful patterns across my walls.

I heard birdsong outside, as well. I hadn't heard birds singing while the hurricane was blowing. I could also hear the steady hum of the air-conditioner. That meant the power was back on. My room was cold enough that I needed to pull the down comforter up over my bare shoulders and snuggle closer to John for warmth.

The storm was over. It was morning. And I was in my own room, in my own bed, next to John.

Then a coldness that had nothing to do with the air-conditioning gripped me.

The storm was over. It was morning. *And I was in my room, next to John.*

We'd fallen asleep. After I'd told him not to let me fall asleep, he'd not only let me fall asleep, he'd fallen asleep himself. He lay beside me in a chaotic scatter of throw pillows, the comforter half on, half off him – but mostly off – his bare chest rising and falling deeply, dead to the world.

Probably not the best choice of words.

But I had the feeling he was going to wish he was dead to

the world when he woke up and saw who stood in the open doorway a few feet away, holding a steaming cup of coffee and staring at the two of us in complete and utter shock.

'Mom,' I said, sitting bolt upright in bed. 'This is not what it looks like.'

'Isn't it?' my mother asked in an icy cold voice. She was wearing the fluffy bathrobe I'd given her for Mother's Day. 'Because I have the feeling it's exactly what it looks like.'

I threw the comforter over John, as if, were he hidden from view, he would no longer exist. Perhaps he'd get the clue, wake up, and blink himself somewhere else. It would be the best thing that could happen.

Unfortunately, the lumps beneath the comforter stayed exactly where they were, except that they began to move slightly.

'Actually,' I said, 'it's kind of a funny story.'

'Is it?' Mom asked. 'Your letter to me was far from humorous.'

John threw the comforter from his head and chest and stood up. Thankfully, he was wearing his jeans, although I didn't know how or when he'd pulled them back on.

'I'm very sorry we had to meet under these circumstances, ma'am,' he said, extending his right hand. 'My name is John Hayden. I'm very much in love with your daughter.'

I don't know why John didn't simply grab my hand and blink us somewhere else, the way he had the last time we'd encountered my mother. I supposed it had something to do with what he'd said the night before, about wanting to be open with my parents, and also probably something to do with the fact that no one was actually trying to kill us.

He didn't know my mom very well.

Her dark eyes widened to their limits. She did not shake John's hand.

'Pierce, I'd like you and your *friend*,' she said, stressing the word *friend* as if it tasted unpleasant in her mouth, 'to get fully dressed and then come downstairs so your father and I can discuss a few things with him.'

Now it was my turn to widen my eyes. 'Dad? He's here?'

'He's in the kitchen,' my mother said, 'making waffles. Or at least he was. Right now he's on the phone with his lawyers, since I just received a somewhat disturbing phone call from Seth Rector's father, complaining that you and – John, is it?' She gave John a sceptical look, as if she doubted that was his real name. 'That you and John assaulted his son last night at some party. What you were even doing at a party in the middle of a Category Three hurricane, I don't care to know, let alone why you assaulted him. But Mr Rector fully intends to press charges.' She sighed. 'Another name to add to the long list of people you've struck in the face, including your own grandmother.'

My jaw dropped.

'You've got to believe me, Mom,' I said. 'Those are all lies. Everything Seth is saying is a lie, and everything Grandma said is a lie, too. Like I said in the letter I left you, I wasn't kidnapped. Grandma tried to kill me. Twice. John is the one who saved me—'

My mother had already started shaking her head.

'Pierce,' she said. 'Please. I'm so tired of all this. I don't know what your father and I ever did to make you so unhappy. Maybe we weren't the best role models, and Lord knows we went through a rough patch. But it isn't fair of you to take it out on innocent people like Seth and your grandmother—'

'Innocent?' I burst out. 'You've got it all wrong, Mom. John saved me from them. He saved me from Mr Mueller, too. I can prove it. Remember the shadow on the security tape from my school in Westport? That was *him*. That was John. He saved me from Mr Mueller again last night.'

Mom's expression changed. Her mouth, which had tightened into a thin, disapproving line – she usually wore lipstick but obviously wasn't wearing any this early in the morning – fell open. I saw the hand she'd kept wrapped around the coffee mug tremble slightly, and she reached out to clutch the doorknob to my room, as if to steady herself.

'Mr Mueller?' she echoed faintly, her gaze flicking from me to John. 'They just said something on the news about how there was only a single fatality in the area from last night's storm . . . a Mark Mueller of Connecticut who was struck by a falling tree. But surely . . . that couldn't be the *same* Mark Mueller as—'

'It was, ma'am,' John said gravely. 'You can ask Mr Richard Smith. He'll tell you that it's true. I believe he's an acquaintance of your father's—'

'That crazy old cemetery sexton who was so rude to me that first day of school?' My mom looked at me like I was the one she thought was crazy. 'What's *he* got to do with any of this?'

'You can just ask Alex, Mom,' I said. 'He was there, too.'

'Alex?' My mother's hand shook some more. 'You know where Alex is? He hasn't been answering his cell. His father's frantic—'

'I do know where he is.' John stepped forward and neatly rescued the drooping mug from her hand, before she'd spilled a single drop. 'Not to worry, Alex has been with us.' John didn't add the part about Alex being murdered, then revived. 'Why don't we go downstairs so we can talk about this with your husband—'

'Ex-husband,' Mom said like someone in a daze, as John took her by the elbow. 'Pierce's father and I are divorced. But we're reconciling—'

'*What?*' I'd shuffled from the bed, wrapped in my comforter, to rifle through my closet in search of something to wear. Hearing the bombshell Mom had just dropped, however, I nearly lost my hold on the comforter.

'We still have a lot of things to work through. Obviously.' Mom shot me another disapproving look, no doubt because she'd seen what I had on beneath the comforter, which wasn't much. 'And the last thing we need right now is to become grandparents, so I hope the two of you are at least using protection.'

I blanched. I'd forgotten all about that particular detail during the storm, what with all the love talk, and the thunder, and the nearly having got killed a few hours earlier. What had I been thinking? Or, more accurately, *not* thinking? Mr Smith had said he'd never heard of a death deity capable of siring children . . . but what if that was only because the Underworld was so inhospitable to new life? He'd said nothing of what might happen *outside* the Underworld.

Fortunately John could not know what she was talking about. They didn't have protection – at least the reliable kind my mom was referring to – back when he'd been alive.

'It's all right, Dr Cabrero,' he said soothingly. The *doctor* was a nice touch. It made up for all the *ma'am*s. Mom hated it when boys *ma'am*ed her. 'We're going to be married, just as soon as your daughter will have me.'

Oh, my God.

'Zack!' my mother began to shout hoarsely. She turned and ran from the bedroom. *'Zachary!'*

Furious, I let the comforter drop and from the closet ripped the first dress I touched.

'Are you crazy?' I hissed at John, pulling the dress over my head, then searching for a pair of sandals. 'Do you have a death wish or something?'

'They're your parents,' John said. He'd found his shirt and was tugging it on. 'They deserve to know the truth.'

'The truth? That I have to live eighteen hundred miles below the earth, with a bunch of dead people, for the rest of eternity? How well do you think *that's* going to go over?'

'They love you,' he said, following me as I darted into the hallway and started down the stairs. 'They'll understand.'

'You don't know my parents,' I said. 'I've been trying to tell them the truth about you since the day I died and met you, and all it's gotten me is a lot of appointments with a bunch of shrinks. They are *not* going to believe the truth about you, and they are *not* going to let me be with you.'

On the landing, John caught hold of my arm, then turned me round to face him.

'Pierce,' he said, looking down into my eyes and smiling as he smoothed a dark curl of hair from my forehead. 'They can't stop us from being together. And they *will* believe you. Because I'm here with you. You're not alone any more.'

Though my heart was hammering with fear – a worse kind of fear, in a way, than I'd felt when it was Mr Mueller who'd stepped into Kayla's car headlights, or when I'd realized Seth was Thanatos – I smiled tentatively back at him.

John was right. My parents couldn't stop us from being together. So many people had tried – Furies included. But none of them had succeeded.

'Could someone please explain to me what in the hell is going on here?' I heard a familiar voice bellow from the bottom of the stairs.

I looked down and saw my father standing there wearing a short-sleeved undershirt, a pair of dress slacks, and no shoes.

A significant amount of my fear dissipated as I realized I wasn't the only female member of the household who'd entertained an overnight guest.

'Wow,' I said as I slipped my hand into John's and began walking down the stairs with him. 'Did you forget the rest of your suit when you came over for breakfast this morning, Dad? And your shoes? And your belt?'

My mom, who was standing next to my dad, began to

blush, but her voice was strong as she said, 'I wouldn't crack jokes right now if I were you, young lady. You're in very big trouble.'

John squeezed my hand, and when I glanced up at him he frowned. He didn't approve of my joke, either. I guess my kite strings were getting pulled.

'Sorry,' I said. When we reached the ground floor and stood before my parents, I said, in what I hoped was a suitably chastened tone, pointing to John, 'Dad, this is John Hayden. I'm sure you remember him from various security tapes. John, this is my father, Zack Oliviera.'

'Hello, sir.' John extended his hand towards my dad. 'I know you haven't heard very good things about me, but I can assure you I'm very much in love with your daughter.'

Like Mom, Dad ignored John's hand. He simply stood staring up at him, John being a few inches taller than he was (something I knew Dad wasn't going to like, if he hadn't disliked John enough already).

'I don't care how much you claim to love my daughter,' Dad said evenly. 'I have a nine-shot .22 Magnum upstairs in my briefcase. Give me one good reason why I shouldn't go get it and shoot out both your knees so you'll never walk again.'

'Dad!' I cried, horrified, wrapping both my hands protectively round John's arm.

'Oh, God,' my mother said, looking sick. 'Zack, no – this isn't what I wanted. I'm calling the police.' She moved towards the kitchen to pick up the portable phone.

'You call the police,' John said, never dropping his gaze

from my dad's, 'and the Furies will know your daughter is here. They're the ones who've been trying to kill her.'

My dad's dark eyebrows lowered into an even deeper scowl. 'Oh, sure,' he said scornfully. 'The Furies. What are they, part of your druggie gang?'

Only then did John break my father's stare to glance down at me. 'Druggie?' he asked uncertainly.

'Dad,' I cried. Now, instead of clinging to John, I threw myself against my father. I thought my body weight would slow him down if he tried to go for the gun. 'You have to listen to me. John didn't kidnap me. He saved me, because Grandma was trying to kill me. You were right about Grandma all along. She's a Fury.'

Mom laid down the phone in exasperation. 'Now I've heard everything. You're trying to say your *grandmother* is in a gang?'

'No,' I said desperately. 'Well, yes. The Furies aren't a gang . . . at least, not the kind you're thinking of. John isn't in a gang, either. And he's not a drug dealer or a death metal goth head.' I sent my mother a narrow-eyed glance, but she appeared to have no memory of ever using that term to describe him. She, along with my father, was listening to me intently. 'I've been trying to tell you guys for two years what he is, but you wouldn't listen. Maybe that's because I didn't want to believe it myself, but I'm ready now. He's a death deity. I met him when I died and went to his world . . . the Underworld.'

Mom pressed a trembling hand to her mouth. 'Oh, Pierce,' she said, her eyes filling with tears.

I didn't think they were tears of happiness. In fact, I was sure she thought I was losing my mind.

'It's true,' I said. 'He sorts the souls of the recently deceased and sends them to their final destinations. Here, see, he gave me this necklace.' I pulled my diamond from the bodice of my sundress and showed it to my father. 'Mom, you've seen it before, remember? You asked me where I got it right after I had my surgery. I said it was a gift. Well, it *was* a gift. John gave it to me when I met him in the Underworld. It protects me. The diamond turns colours when there's a Fury around and, when I touch a Fury with it, it kills it. It was originally mined by Hades to give to Persephone—'

'That's enough,' my dad said sharply. He swung round to glare at John, his expression angrier than I'd ever seen it . . . and Zack Oliviera was famous for his ill temper. 'I don't know what you think you're going to get out of this – money, celebrity, whatever – but you've been taking advantage of a mentally ill young woman. That may not be a prosecutable offence, but, trust me, by the time I'm through with you, not only will you never walk again, you'll also never work in this country, or any other—'

Thunder rumbled. It was soft at first, like the sound of an unmuffled motorcycle engine on a neighbouring block. But as John's impatience with my parents grew, so did the sound, until every bit of glassware in my mother's house was tinkling from the vibration.

'What is that?' she cried. In a panic, she'd thrown her hands over her ears.

216

'Earthquake?' my dad asked. He tried to steer me from beneath the elaborate wrought iron and crystal chandelier Mom had hanging in the foyer, but I stepped from his reach.

'No,' I said. 'It's him.' I pointed at John. 'John, stop it. You've made your point.'

My parents hadn't seemed to have got it, however.

'That's impossible,' my dad said.

'He's ruler of the Underworld.' I shook my head. Why had I thought reasoning with them would work? 'You think he can't control the weather? John, stop it, please. It's too much.'

The thunder ceased. But a bolt of bright white lightning cracked from the centre of my mother's living room ceiling to the floor, causing one of her expensive imported carpets to burst into flame.

'I love your daughter,' John said to my stunned parents. 'And no one is going to keep us apart. I hope you understand now.'

'Now you're just showing off,' I said drily to John as I went to the garage to get the fire extinguisher.

''Tis true that in the early centuries,
With innocence, to work out their salvation
Sufficient was the faith of parents only.'
Dante Alighieri, *Paradiso*, Canto XXXII

My parents' attitude towards John improved significantly after he set my mom's living-room carpet on fire with a lightning bolt.

Improved might be too strong a word. I think they were actually a little bit afraid of him.

Fear isn't such a bad thing if it causes people to be more careful about the things they do and say. But it's upsetting to see people you love acting fearful around someone else you love, even when it's preferable to the way they were acting before. I had to help my mom into one of the chairs at the kitchen counter and make her another coffee with extra sugar before she could begin to process the whole thing. It seemed too much for her ultra-organized scientist's brain to take.

'It's not possible,' she kept repeating. 'It's simply not possible. An underworld? Beneath Isla Huesos? And that's where you've been this whole time?'

'Yes, Mom,' I said, sliding a plate of waffles in front of her. 'Here, eat these. You'll feel better, I promise.'

Maybe because his brain was more entrepreneurial, my dad was able to take the whole thing more in stride.

'So do you think you could do that trick with the lightning on a larger scale?' he asked John. 'Turn it up ten thousand or so megawatts – whatever they call them – and focus all that energy on a target about the size of, say, a military base?'

'Dad,' I said with a warning tone in my voice.

'I suppose I could.' John was eating bacon from a plate my dad had put in front of him. 'But I won't.'

'That's fair,' Dad said. 'That's fair. I like a man with principles. Would it change the way you feel if I told you this military base had fired on American soldiers?'

'John, don't listen to him. Dad, I told you, John already has a job.'

'Right, right, he sorts souls of the dead. How much does one earn in a job like that, if you don't mind my asking? Ballpark figure, of course.'

'Dad!'

'I'm just saying, if the boy came to work for me, I could pay him double or triple what he's earning now—'

'It's not that kind of job, Dad. But I do think there might be a way you could help us.'

John scowled at me over the forkful of eggs he was scooping into his mouth. We'd foregone the waffles, the memory of our great waffle fight still being a little too fresh in our minds for comfort. Fortunately, there were also scrambled eggs.

I could understand how John might not be eager to accept help from a man who'd threatened to shoot him in the knees, but the truth was that my dad had access to

219

considerable resources. And I figured if there was anything the two of us – not to mention the Underworld – could use right now, it was resources.

'My dad owns a really big company, John,' I explained.

Now John scowled into the cup of coffee he was drinking. 'You might have mentioned it one or two hundred times since I met you.'

'It's a company that makes things for the military.' I raised my eyebrows meaningfully.

John's scowl deepened as he set down the coffee cup. 'Weapons don't work on Furies. You know that.'

'Not Furies again,' my mom said. 'All this talk of Fates and Furies . . . none of it makes any *sense*.'

'Grandma being possessed by a murderous demon from hell makes perfect sense to me,' Dad said. 'It's about the only thing I've heard this morning that does.'

My mother dropped her head down on to her folded arms. 'You told Christopher it was drugs,' she said to the kitchen counter. 'Why couldn't it be drugs?'

I stared at her. 'You'd *rather* this whole thing was about drugs?'

Mom lifted her head. 'Than demons? Yes, Pierce, I would. Drugs I can understand. Drugs make sense. With drugs you can go to rehab or call the police and have someone arrested. What are we supposed to do about a demon possessing my mother?'

Dad lifted his coffee. 'You're entitled to your own opinion, of course, but if she really did try to kill Pierce—'

Mom dropped her head into her arms and groaned.

'— well, then I say John here should just hit her with one of his lightning bolts.'

'It doesn't work that way, Dad,' I said.

'I need an aspirin,' pleaded my mom.

'And I'm not talking about weapons,' I said to John. 'I'm talking about boats. Really big boats.'

My dad glanced from me to John and then back again. 'A division of my company does make boats. What kind of boat are you talking about? Tanker? Frac? Lift?'

'Passenger,' I said quickly. 'I was thinking of a passenger ship. Something along the lines of a ferry.'

'Pierce,' John said warily.

'We make ships specializing in oil services,' Dad said, pulling his cellphone from his pocket. 'But I know a guy who . . . well, let's just say I know a guy.'

'We'd need two,' I said. 'And we'd need them right away.'

'For how long?' Dad scrolled through his contact list.

'Forever.'

My father's finger froze on the screen of his phone as he glanced at me in surprise. 'I'm sorry. What?'

'Pierce.' John pushed away from the kitchen counter and stood up. 'May I have a word with you outside?'

I knew how much he hated asking my father for help, but I couldn't see any alternative.

'John, it's all right. After everything we've been through, I think we can talk in front of my parents.' I crossed the room to take one of his hands. He was so tense he was holding them both clenched in fists. I had to prise his fingers open in order to slip mine through his. 'If you've thought of

221

some other way to get the ships, tell me what it is.'

Even with me standing right there beside him holding his hand, John looked extremely uncomfortable. He wore an expression similar to the one he'd had on when my uncle Chris had confronted him (in this very same room) about kidnapping me. His dark eyebrows were furrowed deeply, his silver eyes glowing defiantly, his free hand clenching and unclenching at his side as if he was going to punch the world.

'The ships will be provided, as they always have,' he said in a low voice, 'by the Fates.'

'John, the Fates are gone. They left before you died. And I don't see any sign of their speedy return. You're here, the storm's over, the sun is shining, but Hope's not back.' Saying it aloud made my throat feel sore. But I couldn't pretend it wasn't true. 'She knows where I live. She's been here before. But she isn't here.'

'Hope will be back,' John assured me. 'And so will the Fates. I know they will.'

Before I had a chance to point out that Mr Smith had never believed the Fates were distinct entities – he believed they were the spirits of human kindness, which made it sort of understandable how they'd be few and far between on Isla Huesos – my father began shaking his head.

'Son,' he said to John, 'maybe it's time you realized that these Fates of yours don't exist.'

'Dad,' I said, my throat tighter than ever. 'You're not helping.'

'Most of us have been making our own fates for a long

time,' Dad went on, ignoring me. 'Some of us didn't grow up getting everything we wanted handed to us on gold platters by invisible fairies—'

'Neither did I,' John interrupted, his eyes flashing dangerously.

'Where I grew up,' my father went on, as if John hadn't spoken, 'there was no such thing as fate, or luck, or wishing on a lucky star. There was only hard work and being ready to seize whatever opportunity presented itself. Now, I'm not criticizing you. I appreciate what you did, looking out for my daughter when things weren't going so well for her. I wish I'd been a better listener when she came to me with her problems. I'm glad you were there for her. To me, that's fate . . . being there to give other people a hand when they need it, not being a stubborn ass—'

'Zachary,' my mother said in a warning voice, her eyes wide.

'No,' Dad said. 'It's all right, Debbie. He knows what I'm talking about. He's not going to set the carpet on fire again. Are you, son?'

John regarded my father with a narrow-eyed stare from the centre of the room. I did not share Dad's faith that John wasn't about to do something reckless. His breathing was shallow, and his fingers holding mine were clenched so tightly I half expected that the next time I blinked I'd open my eyes to find myself back in the Underworld.

It was difficult for John to trust strangers when he'd lived for so long in one place amongst a handful of people he knew so well. It had to be especially difficult for him to trust a man who was in so many ways like Seth's wrecker great-great-great grandfather.

But my father hadn't meant for anyone to be hurt in the oil spill that caused so much damage to the shoreline. My father had been trying to help. William Rector, in contrast, hadn't been trying to help. He hadn't cared how many lives he ruined in the wrecks he caused.

I squeezed John's hand. *I love you, I love you, I love you*, I thought, gazing up at him.

I don't know if he heard me, but something in either my father's words or my grip seemed to get through to him, since he said, his voice carefully controlled, 'Please call me John, not son. I won't be your son until your daughter agrees to marry me, which she says she won't do for now because her mother would want her to graduate from high school first. Pierce says no one our age gets married any more.'

A high-pitched sound between a scream and a sob escaped my mother. When we all turned to look at her, she'd slapped a hand across her mouth.

'Deborah,' my father said curiously. 'Are you all right?'

She nodded, her hand still riveted in place, and made a motion with her other hand for us to go on with the conversation. I noticed her eyes were wide and unnaturally bright.

'I'm not sure you're right about the Fates, Mr Oliviera,' John said. 'But I'll welcome any help you're willing to give us.' He held out his right hand.

This time, my father walked across the room and shook it.

'Great, great. But Mr Oliviera is my father. Call me Zack. I'm right about those fate things, though,' he said. 'You'll see.' He dropped John's hand, then pressed the name on his contact list. 'Gary? Hey, Gary, it's me, Zack Oliviera, how are you? Yeah, I know, me, too, that was some storm, huh? How'd you make it through? Any of those ferries of yours left?'

John sent me a long-suffering look as my father wandered into the dining room, his cellphone pressed to his ear.

'Thanks,' I said, slipping an arm round his waist. 'I know he can be a challenge.'

'A challenge?' John echoed in disbelief. 'That's not how I tend to describe someone threatening to shoot me.'

'I know.' I flinched. 'Sorry about that. But you see how amazing he can be when he tries.'

'Perhaps,' John said, sliding one of his own arms round my waist. 'But, Pierce, even if your allegedly amazing father is able to acquire those ships, how am I supposed to get them to the Underworld?'

'Can't you just blink them there?'

He raised a dark eyebrow. 'You do know that the heaviest thing I've ever transported to the Underworld is Frank, right?'

I toyed with the diamond at the end of my necklace. 'I'm the one who has to get rid of all the Furies somehow. Talk about challenges. You concentrate on yours, and I'll concentrate on mine.'

John shook his head, pulling me closer. 'No. We'll work on our challenges together.' He glanced at the kitchen counter. 'What are we going to do about her?'

I gazed with concern at my mom, who had her head buried in her arms again. 'She can be amazing, too,' I whispered, 'but I think I'm going to need to spend a little quality time with her in order to help her adjust, especially now that you dropped the *M* word in front of her.'

John looked puzzled. 'The *M* word?'

'Marriage. Between that and the revelation that this is about demons and not drugs, I'm pretty sure she's having a nervous breakdown.'

John's expression went from puzzled to as concerned as mine, but not, I soon learned, for the same reasons.

'I wish we had that kind of time, but we don't.' He released me to dig into his pocket for the tablet he'd retrieved at the same time I'd snuck back upstairs to brush my teeth, wash my face and run a brush through my hair. 'Mr Liu says the number of newly arriving souls has slowed down since the storm moved out to sea, but the situation is still beyond critical.'

'I'm not the one causing the imbalance, then,' I said, still fingering my necklace. 'I'm not there. It wasn't Thanatos, either, since I destroyed him. Something else is. Only what?'

There was a loud rattling sound on the other side of the French doors, all of which my mom and dad had unshuttered and thrown open to let in the beautiful morning sunshine. It sounded as if someone was letting himself in by the side gate where my mom and I kept our bikes and the trash cans.

My heart gave a sudden swoop inside my chest.

'John,' I whispered. 'What if it's the police, come to arrest us?'

John reached out and took my hand. 'They'll never lay a finger on you,' he said.

I knew what he meant. We'd be gone before the police ever got inside the room.

It wasn't the police, however. It was Alex, who loped inside, a backpack slung over one shoulder. He'd changed clothes since the last time I'd seen him. His dark hair was still damp on the ends, and he smelled newly showered.

'There you are,' he said casually, not noticing the tense looks John and I wore. 'I've been calling you for ages. I don't know why I bothered; you never answer your phone anyway.'

I'd remembered to slip my phone into the pocket of my dress. I'd forgotten, however, to turn it on.

'We, uh, just woke up a little while ago,' I said, sheepishly dropping John's hand to hit the power button on my phone. 'Where are Frank and Kayla?'

'They went to Kayla's place to change, then to your friend Mr Smith's,' he said with a meaningful glance at my mom. It was clear he didn't think we should be talking about any of this in front of her. 'They wanted to give Patrick his, er, car back. Then they said they'd meet us' – he lowered his voice, mumbling the next few words so only I could hear them – 'at the cemetery.' His tone returned to normal. 'Hi, Aunt Deb. Are you OK? You look like you've got a headache or something.'

Mom lifted her head. 'I've been better,' she said. 'Would you like some waffles?'

'That's OK, I just took my dad to breakfast at Denny's to get him out of the house.' Another meaningful glance at me. 'Away from Grandma.'

Mom looked surprised. 'Your dad? Oh, Alex, that's great. How is he doing?'

'Still charged with murder, thanks, Aunt Deb. But I appreciate your bailing him out. Dad? Hey, Dad?'

To my surprise, Uncle Chris poked his head through one of the open sets of French doors. In one hand he was holding an enormous black plastic trash can. In the other, he was dragging a five-foot-long palm frond that had been knocked down by the storm.

'Oh, hey, Deb,' he said with a grin when he saw my mother. 'Alex said he wanted to come over and I thought it wouldn't be such a bad idea to get started on your clean-up. Cassandra was a mean one, huh? Lot of poinciana blossoms in your pool, which is weird, since I didn't think there was one of those trees around here . . .'

His voice trailed off as his gaze landed on me. Then his eyes lit up . . . until he noticed John. Then he frowned a little. 'Piercey! And . . . you.'

John stepped up to him, his right hand extended. 'John,' he said. 'Remember? It's nice to see you again, Mr Cabrero.'

Uncle Chris didn't look as if he thought it was so nice to see John again, but he stuffed the palm frond into the garbage can, then shook John's hand.

'How you doing?' he asked. Then he took a deep breath

228

and said, 'Well, I'm going to get back to work. Lots to do if we're going to get this place cleaned up.' He wrinkled his nose slightly. 'Hey, uh, no offence, Deb, but it smells like burnt toast in here.'

'Oh, no,' Mom said with a semi-hysterical laugh. 'That was just Pierce's boyfriend. He set the carpet on fire with his brain.'

Uncle Chris looked at her as if she'd lost her mind – which I think she had, sort of – and nodded.

'OK,' Uncle Chris said. 'Just checking.' Then he quickly wheeled the trash can away into the backyard.

Alex, who'd slid on to one of the kitchen counter stools, froze. Only his eyes moved as he cut his gaze towards my mother. 'Wait . . . you *know*?'

'Of course we know,' Mom said. 'Why haven't you told your father yet, Alex? This involves him. After all, Grandma is his mother, too.'

Alex glanced from me to my mother like we were both crazy. 'I know. Why do you think I haven't let him out of my sight since I got here? I'm keeping him as far away from her as I possibly can. But I can't tell him about any of this. He wouldn't be able to handle it.'

Mom's glance came into focus. She frowned with disapproval. I didn't exactly blame her – Uncle Chris was a lot cooler than many people gave him credit for – but considering her own reaction when she'd heard the news, I didn't think she had much room to talk.

'Your father isn't a child, Alexander,' she said. 'He doesn't need your protection.'

'You're right that he isn't a child,' Alex said, unzipping his backpack and reaching into it. 'But you're wrong that he doesn't need protection. My dad needs a lot of protecting, because it doesn't seem to me as if anyone's ever bothered to protect him before in his life.'

Alex pulled a file from the backpack – a very similar file to the one he'd taken from Mr Rector's office in the spec house on Reef Key – and slapped it on to the kitchen counter. A photo slid out . . . a photo of my mom with my uncle Chris – both of them looking years younger, twenty years younger at least – and someone who could only be Seth Rector's father.

When my mother saw the photograph, the colour drained from her face. She reached out quickly to snatch it away, but Alex was too fast for her.

'No,' he said, his hand landing over it. 'Let Pierce see. She has the right to know.'

'Know what?' I asked, moving towards the counter.

'Pierce,' Mom said. She looked as if she were going to be sick. 'I can explain . . .'

'I'm interested to hear that explanation,' Alex said. 'I'm sure Pierce and John will be, too.' He passed the photo to me.

In the picture, my mom, Uncle Chris and Mr Rector were in swimsuits, standing on a sandy beach in front of some mangroves, the bushy kind of tropical tree my mom had always said roseate spoonbills liked to nest in. The three of them were laughing and holding something up for the camera as they mugged for the lens. The things they were holding were yellowish and long, and appeared to have been pulled from the sand. I could see the holes – not very large or very shallow – on the beach behind them, along with a lot of seaweed and driftwood.

There were more things like the ones they were holding sticking up out of the sand all around them. There were also more than a few empty beer bottles, and even an overturned bottle of Captain Rob's Rum.

'That's Reef Key, isn't it?' Alex asked. 'Before Mr Rector and Farah's dad developed it? Is Farah's dad the person taking the picture?'

'Yes,' Mom said in a faint voice.

That's when I took a closer look at what she and Uncle Chris and Mr Rector were holding up as they laughed into the camera, and finally realized what they were: bones.

Not fish bones, or animal bones.

Human bones.

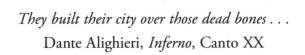

They built their city over those dead bones . . .
Dante Alighieri, *Inferno*, Canto XX

'Mom,' I said, confused, squinting down at the photo. 'I don't understand. Why are you holding up fake bones and laughing? Was it Halloween? Were you guys pretending to be pirates?'

John took the photo away from me.

'Those are not fake,' he said. He put the photo back in the file Alex had laid across the counter and closed the cover.

I glanced from John to my mother. John's expression was grim. My mother's was mortified.

I was starting to feel mortified, too, now that I understood.

'We were so young,' Mom murmured.

'You looked like you were my age when that was taken,' I said.

I didn't mean to sound judgmental. It's just that no matter how old I was I don't think I would ever have picked up real human remains and waved them around, laughing, in front of a camera.

I couldn't meet John's gaze. His skeleton could easily have been one of those on that beach, if his body hadn't ended up in the Underworld instead. The idea of anyone picking up his remains while drunk on a beach and waving

232

them around was causing my blood to boil. A faint pink hue began to tinge the edges of my vision . . . but not enough to block out the fact that my mother had buried her face in her hands yet again.

'You're right,' she said. 'I was a senior in high school. I should have known better. The four of us – Seth's father, Nate; and Farah's father, Bill; and your uncle Chris – we used to go out to that island all the time. I loved it so much . . . not only because of the birds, which were so beautiful, but because I could get away from your grandmother. She was . . . well, she was so pushy. She didn't understand why I loved nature so much. She was always trying to get me to walk with her in the cemetery for some reason.'

I knew exactly why Grandma had always been trying to get my mother to walk with her in the cemetery. She'd been trying to hook her up with John, so she could kill him. Even then, my grandmother had been possessed by a Fury. Mom clearly hadn't had a very happy childhood.

Still, that didn't excuse her behaviour.

'Gee,' I heard myself saying. 'I can't imagine why you wouldn't enjoy a nice stroll around the graveyard, considering your affinity for human skeletons.'

John shot me a disapproving look that clearly said, *Now is not the time to be sarcastic to your mother.*

'I deserve that,' Mom said miserably. 'I know. But the truth is, as much as I protest when your father complains about my mother, I couldn't stand being around her, either. Nate had a boat. So did a lot of our friends. We'd have little parties out at Reef Key. We truly had some wonderful times.'

'Sure,' Alex said. 'Of course you did.' He pulled a sheet of paper from the file in front of him. It was a photocopy of a very ancient-looking legal document. 'The Rectors own Reef Key. Here's the deed.'

Alex passed the photocopy to me. It had a lot of *aforesaid*s and *upon their oath*s in spidery handwriting, but ultimately declared that on the fifth of June AD 1845, William Joseph Rector personally appeared before the judge and was awarded a certain piece of unoccupied land belonging to the government of the United States of America situated in the township of Isla Huesos. That piece of property would heretofore be known forever after as Reef Key.

Before that, it had been known as Caja de Muertos.

'Caja de Muertos?' I looked up. Though my mom's side of the family was Spanish, the only words in their native language I knew were dirty words I'd been taught by the housekeeper we'd had when I was kid. I was pretty sure *muertos* meant dead, though.

'Coffin Island,' Alex translated for me as he plucked the deed from my fingers. 'Embrace your heritage.' To my mom, he said, 'Those Spanish explorers who discovered Isla Huesos in the fifteen hundreds. They called it Isle of Bones because the beach was covered in skeletons. What'd they do with all the skeletons? They didn't just leave them there, did they?'

Mom didn't say anything else. She simply looked down at her hands.

The pink tinge deepened until the words were swimming before my eyes. It was difficult to make out anything – or anyone – in the room. Where John was standing, I saw only a vague dark shadow.

I felt an overwhelming urge to reach out to grasp his hand, but at that moment a strong gust of wind blew through my mother's wide-open French doors. Even though the rain outside was gone, the wind that had fuelled the storm raged on.

You were like a kite flying high in the wind, with no one holding its strings. Mr Liu's words popped, unbidden, into my head. *Only the wind that fuelled you was your anger.*

No wonder I'd felt such a strong urge to reach for John. Mr Liu was right. I really did need to get control of my own strings, or I'd blow away.

I reached for the handle of the whip Mr Liu had given to me. I'd slung the belt round my waist on my way back downstairs after brushing my teeth. I wasn't sure why.

Now I knew. The minute my fingers closed round the handle, the pink began to fade.

'Wait,' I said. 'Those explorers buried the remains they found, didn't they? On Coffin Island? Is that why it's called that? Is that why you found all those bones there? A storm or something uncovered them?'

Mom brought her hands from her face. Unlike me, she hadn't noticed the wind. 'Bones aren't all we found there,' she said.

'What else, Dr Cabrero?' John asked gently as he returned from closing the French doors.

'Gold?' I asked. My mind was spinning, trying to think why she could look so pale.

Alex shook his head. 'Square grouper.'

Confused, I looked from my mother to my cousin. 'Is that some species native to this area, like the roseate spoonbill?'

Alex burst out laughing. 'No, you idiot. It's when a drug runner dumps his load in the ocean in order to avoid being charged. When you find a floating bale of marijuana, it's called a square grouper.'

My eyes widened. 'Wait. Drugs? So this *is* about drugs?'

'Don't call her an idiot,' John said, frowning at Alex.

'Sorry.' Alex even looked as if he felt a little sorry. To my mom, he said, 'So that's how this all started? A bale washed up while you guys were partying on Reef Key?'

She nodded again, her eyes shining with tears. 'Nate got the idea to dry it out and break it up and sell it to tourists. Back then, there was no such thing as Homeland Security, and no one was paying very much attention to what went on on an island so much closer to Cuba than to Miami, where all the hard drugs were. And certainly no one would ever suspect a bunch of straight-A high-school kids. It all seemed so innocent and even a little bit fun . . .'

'Until someone got caught,' Alex said.

Tears had begun to trickle down Mom's face. I handed her a napkin. She thanked me and wiped her eyes, glancing furtively towards the dining room, where Dad was still yelling into his cellphone at Gary, the guy who had the ferries.

'Exactly,' Mom said. 'Then someone had to take the fall. Nate convinced Chris to take the blame, insisting that as a minor he'd go to juvie and then serve only a year or two. Nate promised Chris that if he took the rap, when he got out, he'd have a job and a small fortune waiting for him.'

'But that wasn't true,' Alex said.

'Of course it wasn't true,' Mom said, her voice clogged with emotion. 'None of it was true. There isn't a Rector alive or dead who hasn't broken every single promise he or she ever gave. It turned out Nate wasn't even dealing marijuana any more. Unbeknownst to us, he'd cut a deal with some guys from Miami and moved on to much harder stuff. That's why Chris got charged as an adult instead of a juvenile. The police knew and wanted Chris to reveal who he was working with.'

Alex's gaze was on his father, who was across the yard, busily picking up palm fronds and other flotsam from the storm and stuffing them into the garbage can. 'But my dad wouldn't say.'

'Of course not,' Mom said. 'You know how he is, loyal to the core. I was horrified when I found out about all of it – the hard drugs, Chris being encouraged to take the blame for what Nate started, the fact that Nate never intended to keep his promise to preserve Reef Key as a spoonbill nesting ground. I was so ashamed of not having had the guts to turn in Nate myself. I wanted to, but he threatened me, saying if I went to the police with what I knew, he'd see to it that Chris had an "accident" in jail.' She began to cry again, raising the napkin to her eyes. 'He said he had friends who could arrange it. I was so frightened, I broke off our relationship and left for college and never came back to Isla Huesos, except for my father's funeral.'

'Oh, Mom,' I said, and went to her side to put an arm round her shoulders, glancing over at John. It was at my grandfather's funeral that he and I had met. Granted, I'd been only seven, and we'd bonded over a dead bird he'd brought back to life – Hope's twin. But it had still been a meaningful moment in our relationship. 'I'm so sorry all of that happened to you.'

'Don't be,' Mom said, patting my hand. 'It was my fault. I never should have gotten involved with Nate in the first place. I was the older one and set a terrible example for Chris. He was only following my lead. I thought by coming back now that he's out of jail, I could help him, but things have turned out worse than ever.'

'Well,' I said. 'You didn't know there was a hellmouth under Isla Huesos, or that Grandma was a Fury.'

John narrowed his eyes at me. 'It's not a hellmouth.'

'Oh, right,' I said. 'It's our home. An entrance to the Underworld, then.'

The sound Mom let out was halfway between a sob and a laugh. 'No. That's not something I ever suspected, although perhaps I should have. But I wasn't particularly surprised to hear Nate Rector parlayed all his illegal drug earnings into the real estate market and has converted Reef Key into a high-scale luxury resort. That seems exactly like the kind of thing the Rector Wreckers would do.'

'I agree.' I dropped my arm from round my mother's

shoulders and moved to tap the file in front of Alex. He'd kept close hold on it when the wind burst in. 'What I want to know is what it says in here about those bones they found on the beach.'

Alex grinned devilishly as he reopened the file. 'You mean, are Seth's and Farah's dads building their fancy new subdivision on top of an *ancient Indian burial ground*?'

'I believe the politically correct term would be *ancient Native American burial ground*,' I said. Alex began to crack up, which caused me to crack up, but neither my mother nor John smiled.

'It isn't funny,' Mom said. 'I know what I was doing in the photo was wrong, but I had an excuse: I was young, in love and maybe a little bit drunk.'

I widened my eyes. Mom said, quickly, 'I didn't say it was a good excuse. And, Pierce, if you ever do anything remotely similar, I will ground you for the rest of your life.'

Trying not to smile, I met John's gaze and found that he, too, was grinning. Mom still didn't seem to get it: I was *already* grounded for the rest of my life . . . in the most delicious way possible, in the Underworld, with John.

'The Calusa Indians were fierce warriors and expert sailors,' Mom, not having noticed my smile, was saying. 'And they managed to eke out an existence on these islands hundreds of years before comforts like purified drinking water, mosquito repellant or air-conditioning were invented. They stayed true to their own religion and own way of life, refusing to capitulate to invading foreigners, even as their families were being slaughtered for doing so. It's hard not to admire them for that.'

'No one here is saying they don't admire them,' Alex said, pulling another sheet of paper from his file. 'We're saying the exact opposite of that . . . that we think somewhere along the line someone dropped the ball. Because while there is this photo of you and my dad playing pirates on the beach – and of course that reference to Coffin Island in the deed – nowhere in any of the paperwork for the Rector and Endicott Reef Key Luxury Homes and Real Estate Development is there one mention of human bones being removed and properly reinterred elsewhere.'

Mom looked troubled. 'Well,' she said, rubbing at a spot of maple syrup that had spilled on to the counter, 'I suppose it's possible that Nate had them removed sometime after he and I broke up—'

'Really, Mom?' I said to her. 'If he did it right, don't you think there'd be a marker or a plaque wherever he had them laid to rest?'

She stared at the counter. 'It's been twenty years. There've been a lot of storms. It's possible they simply washed out to sea.'

'It's also possible they're sitting in some Dumpster somewhere on the construction site. He's probably already thrown them under a bulldozer and crushed them into powder, but, in case he hasn't, we need to go back and look.' I glanced at John. 'This could be what's causing the imbalance. One of the first things Mr Smith ever said to me was that no life, if it was led by a decent person, should go unremembered. He was talking about you, and Coffin

240

Night, but I think maybe we've just found out about a whole lot more bodies that were never properly buried.'

John nodded. 'We'll go back.'

Mom reached out to snatch my hand, her face draining once more of colour.

'Pierce, no,' she cried. 'You can't. Didn't you hear what your father and I said? Mr Rector has filed charges against you for attacking Seth –' She looked up at John. 'Both of you. You can't go anywhere near that place.'

'Mom.' I squeezed her fingers. 'Don't you get it? Mr Rector can't hurt you any more. He can't hurt Uncle Chris, either. You have us.'

'You have me, too.'

We turned to see my father standing in the entrance to the dining room, his cellphone dangling from one hand, his expression bemused as he stared at my mom and me.

'But then you've always had me.' He took the step down from the dining room into the living area, and crossed the room to put his arm round my mother. 'I'm not entirely certain why you ever thought you didn't. And if I overheard correctly, and it involves that Rector clown, then you not only have me, but you also have my .22 Magnum.'

'You see,' Mom said. 'This is *exactly* why I never wanted to involve your father. He always overreacts.'

'I don't think Dad's overreacting in this particular case,' I said. I glanced up at my father. 'How'd you do on the boats?'

'Gary can get them here in six hours,' Dad said, looking pleased at himself. His gaze fell on Alex. 'Who the hell are you?' he demanded gruffly.

'Zack,' Mom said. 'That's Alex.' When Dad continued to look blank, she added, frustrated, 'My brother's son? Your *nephew?*'

'Oh,' Dad said. His manner softened somewhat. 'How you doing?'

Alex looked at my father with something like wonder, taking in his business suit slacks, T-shirt and unshaven face. 'I'm fine. Nice to finally meet you, Uncle Zachary.'

It was only then that I realized why Alex seemed so astonished. It wasn't my father's peculiar state of dress. It was that this was the first time my father had ever visited Isla Huesos. Alex had never seen my father in person before, due to Dad's extreme prejudice against his in-laws . . . which was somewhat understandable, when you factored Grandma into the equation.

'Call me Zack,' Dad said to Alex. 'You know about all this Underworld business?'

'I do,' Alex said with a nod. 'I've been there. These two –' he nodded first at me, then John – 'brought me back to life after Seth Rector stuffed me in a coffin and I suffocated to death.'

'*What?*' Mom cried.

Dad, however, didn't skip a beat. 'No kidding. I'd love to hear more about that if we've got the time.'

'We don't,' John growled. 'Six hours isn't fast enough, either. We need those ships now.'

My father eyed him. 'Six hours is as fast as a two-hundred-twenty-five-foot-long ship built to accommodate twelve hundred passengers can travel . . . especially in rough seas, when they've only got two diesel engines with a top speed of' – he glanced down at his phone – 'sixteen knots.'

John looked at me. 'It isn't going to be soon enough. Mr Liu says some of the passengers have already begun to riot outside the castle.'

'Then take my dad's advice,' I said, 'and make your own fate. Do you know what I'm saying?'

He gazed down into my eyes, his expression filled with love, but also with uncertainty. 'I already told you, the heaviest thing I've ever lifted is Frank.'

'I know,' I said, reaching for his hand. 'But if you don't do this more people are going to die. People like Uncle Chris out there, and my mom.'

Dad looked up, alarmed. 'What are you two talking about?'

I crossed the room to take my father's hand. 'Nothing,' I said. 'We need a little favour from you, that's all. It's only going to take a second.'

'What is?' Dad protested as I steered him closer to where John was standing.

'Pierce,' Mom said. 'What are you doing?'

'Nothing, Mom,' I said. 'John just has to take Dad somewhere for a minute. They'll be right back.'

'What do you mean, we'll be right back?' Dad asked. 'Where are we going? I don't have my car, it's with my driver back at the hotel. I'll call him if you need to take a car somewhere, but—'

'John doesn't need a car,' Alex said, with a smirk from

where he was sitting at the kitchen counter. 'He *is* the car.'

'Wait a minute,' Dad said as I plucked his cellphone from his fingers and scrolled back to his last communication. 'Here,' I said to John, showing him the attached photo. 'Is that clear enough?'

John shrugged. 'It better be,' he said, laying his hand on my father's shoulder. 'Hopefully we won't end up on a dock in Hong Kong.' Then he laid a hand upon my shoulder, as well.

My father wasn't the only one who instantly attempted to twist away from John's grasp. Dad was the only one who wasn't successful, though.

'No, John,' I said. 'What if Grandma or some of her cronies show up while you're gone? Someone has to stay to protect them.' I gestured towards my mother and Uncle Chris, now busily skimming the pool.

'What do I look like, a helpless kitten?' Alex complained. 'I'm not going to let anything happen to them.'

John glowered at Alex. 'How are *you* going to fight a Fury?'

Alex picked up a butter knife from the kitchen counter and began to dance around, jabbing the knife into the air.

'Like this,' Alex said. 'See? I've got moves.'

Rolling my eyes, I took the whip from my waist, uncoiled it, then cracked it once, neatly striking the knife from Alex's hand, disarming him.

'Ow!' Alex cried in indignation, grasping his wrist. 'That really hurt. What did you do that for?'

'I've got moves, too,' I said, recoiling the whip.

'She always did have good aim,' my father said with admiration. 'Remember the throwing stars, Debbie?'

'How could I forget?' Mom murmured. She was staring in shock at the butter knife, which had landed with a clinking sound at her feet. 'You had to keep them locked up away from her.'

'That doesn't prove anything,' John said. But I could see the grudging admiration in his face.

'It proves you should probably let go of me now,' my father said, referring to the iron grip John still had on his shoulder. 'I don't think it's a good idea to make her angry, any more than it is you.'

John held on to my father more tightly. 'No,' he said. 'Sorry. We're still going.' To me, he said, 'If you're going to stay here, lock the door and don't answer it. Don't let *anyone* inside, no matter who it is. And don't go anywhere until I get back. Not anywhere, especially Reef Key. Do you understand, Pierce?'

I made a face. 'No. Could you explain it again? Because I was thinking about going to Reef Key without you, and also letting any Fury who knocks inside.'

John ignored my sarcasm. 'I don't know how long this is going to take,' he said. 'But I promise this time I'll be back soon, Pierce.'

I crossed the room to stand beside him, laying a hand upon his arm. 'You'd better be.'

His grey eyes seemed to burn through me. 'If anything should go wrong—'

'It won't,' I said firmly.

'Which it won't,' he said. 'But if it should, you know where to meet me, don't you? Where we met the first night I saw you back in Isla Huesos—'

'In the cemetery.' *In the cemetery* sounded better than saying *Next to your tomb.*

He nodded. 'Under our tree—'

Before he could utter another word, I rose up on to my toes to press my lips to his. He seemed surprised – surprised enough to release his hold on my father – but not unpleasantly so.

I hoped he could feel through the emotion of my kiss the words I was too embarrassed to say in front of my parents . . . words I felt I could never say enough: *I love you, I love you, I love you.*

He not only seemed to get the message, he didn't seem at all embarrassed, since, as soon as our lips parted, he whispered, 'I love you, too.'

I looked up at him and smiled, my heart so full of happiness, I was certain it was about to burst. My joy made no sense, of course. What did I have to feel joyful about? There was no future for us in this world, and the only one in which we could live was being pulled apart.

But he loved me, and that, at least, no one could destroy.

'Hello. Remember me? The dad. The dad is standing right here. Could the two of you please not do that in front of me?' My father sounded even crankier than usual. 'Also, would someone mind explaining to me exactly what's going on here?'

'Sorry, sir.' John dropped his hands from my waist and

reached to grasp my father's arm as I walked away from them. 'Don't worry. In a moment it will all become clear. Just close your eyes.'

Another burst of wind swept in from outside, causing the French door John had closed to crash open again with a bang. Flower petals and leaves Uncle Chris had yet to sweep up came swirling inside in mini vortexes. My mother yelped in alarm.

'What's happening?' she asked anxiously. 'What are they doing?'

'Don't worry, Aunt Deb,' Alex said, reaching for a waffle. 'You'll get used to it.'

'I'll be damned if I'm going to close my eyes,' my father said.

'We're all going to be damned anyway,' John said, 'if this doesn't work out.'

One. Two. Three.

Blink.

They were gone.

> *'What avarice does is here made manifest*
> *In the purgation of these souls converted,*
> *And no more bitter pain the Mountain has.'*
> Dante Alighieri, *Purgatorio*, Canto XIX

'Everything all right in here?' Uncle Chris stepped inside to ask. 'I thought I heard you scream, Deb. There a palmetto bug in the trash compactor again?'

Mom was clutching the collar of her robe closed at her neck. All the colour had drained from her face. She stood there shaking her head, staring at the spot where John and my father had been standing a second before.

'I . . . I don't understand. Where did they go?'

'To get the boats, Mom,' I said.

'But how did they . . . they were standing right there. And then they . . .'

'It's called teleportation,' I said gently. 'If John pictures a person or thing in his head, he can go to where that person or thing is. And if he's touching someone, he can take that person with him. But he can't stay away from Isla Huesos or the Underworld for too long. If he does, he'll begin to age and die.'

Uncle Chris looked at us. 'Are you talking about *World of Warcraft*? Alex loves that game. Don't you, Alex? How many points do you have? A billion?'

'That's right, Dad,' Alex said. 'A billion.'

I glared at Alex. This was stupid. He should tell his father the truth already. He'd suffered more than anyone because of it all – well, almost anyone. Uncle Chris hadn't died.

Alex seemed to read my thoughts almost as easily as John had. Or maybe he was only reading my disapproving expression.

'Hey, Pierce,' Alex said, getting up from his counter stool and going to the refrigerator. 'Remember when we played *World of Warcraft* and we hit the level where the guy was just an innocent pawn being used by all the much more evil characters?'

'I do not remember that level,' I said.

'Yeah, well, I do.' Alex opened the refrigerator, took out a carton of milk and drank from it. 'You insisted we tell him the truth, and he couldn't handle it, and did something dumbly noble, and died. Don't do that in this level.'

'Alex,' my mother said. 'Please don't drink milk straight from the carton.'

Uncle Chris saw the file Alex had stolen from Mr Rector's office sitting on the counter. 'What's this?' he said curiously, reaching for it.

'*Don't!*' Alex and I both cried at the exact same time.

'It's nothing,' Mom said. She quickly lifted the file. 'It's something of mine . . . for work.'

'Work?' Uncle Chris squinted down at the file in her arms. 'It says *Rector Realty* on it. You work at the Marine Institute. What has the Marine Institute got to do with Rector Realty?'

'I'm, um, doing some research,' Mom said. 'On Reef Key. Just a little private research of my own. In fact, I was about to head upstairs and get dressed and start my research right now on the computer.'

'That's a good idea, Aunt Deb,' Alex said. 'Want me to come help you?'

'No, thank you, Alex,' Mom said with some of her old acerbic dryness. 'I'm quite capable of getting dressed and doing research on my own.'

'Really, Aunt Deb,' Alex said, following my mom as she backed out of the kitchen and down the hallway, towards the stairs. 'I want to help.'

What Alex wanted, I knew, was not to let that file out of his sight. He wasn't used to trusting adults – it wasn't as if any had ever been there for him in the past – and it didn't look as if he was ready to start now.

'Really, Alex,' I heard my mother say from the hallway. 'I'm not going to do anything without your permission, and I'll give it back when I'm done with it.'

Uncle Chris, looking a little anxious, watched them go.

'Piercey,' he said in a low voice, so they wouldn't overhear. 'Does Alex seem . . . different to you?'

'Different?' I asked. 'In what way?'

'I don't know,' Uncle Chris said. 'He seems a little more . . . mature, or something. Almost overnight.'

Being murdered by your peers, then brought back from the dead, could certainly have that effect on you.

I didn't mention this to Uncle Chris, however. All I said was, 'I don't know. I haven't really noticed.'

I didn't like lying to him. But he was Alex's father and Alex didn't want him knowing the truth, so I felt

250

like I had to respect that.

'Well, I've noticed,' Uncle Chris said, reaching up to scratch his head beneath his Isla Huesos Bait and Tackle baseball cap. 'I think it's a good thing. Maybe that New Pathways programme you two are in at school is working on him. Or maybe it's you, being a good influence on him, Piercey. But I'm finally starting to get the feeling I don't have to worry about him as much. You know?'

I swallowed. I couldn't believe Uncle Chris and I were having this conversation.

'Uh,' I said. 'I'm pretty sure it doesn't have anything to do with me.'

'I wouldn't be so sure of that,' Uncle Chris said, grinning at me. 'I was kind of suspicious of that boyfriend of yours at first, but I think maybe he's a positive role model for Alexander.'

I tried not to glance at the burnt spot in the living room carpet. 'Maybe. Or maybe Alex straightened up because he's so worried about you, Uncle Chris, and that murder charge against you.'

'Oh, that,' Uncle Chris said with a shrug. 'I didn't do it, so I'm sure it will all get straightened out soon. It was nice of your mom to post my bail.'

His naive belief that the charges would be dropped and everything would work out because he was innocent was sort of astonishing for a man who'd spent so many years in prison. Granted, he'd spent those years in prison for a crime he truly had committed (although the penalty had been far too severe, especially for possession of a drug that was now legal in many states), but surely he must have met a lot of people in there who'd been convinced they were innocent. How could he have so much faith he'd be exonerated?

I guess that was just Uncle Chris. He was a truly positive person. No wonder my mom felt so bad about not coming forward and telling the truth about Mr Rector. He was a slimebag who preyed on those who weren't able to defend themselves.

Like the dead.

'Hey, what boats did your dad and that boyfriend of yours go to get?' Uncle Chris asked.

'Oh,' I said. 'For, uh, John's business. His boats got destroyed in the, er, storm, and my dad says he knows a guy who has some other boats John can use.'

'That's nice,' Uncle Chris said. 'I hope your mom and dad get back together. He makes Deb really happy. And I think that John fella makes you happy, too, am I right?' His eyes glinted at me teasingly.

I smiled back at him. 'What would make *you* happy, Uncle Chris?' I asked.

He grinned in that sweet, slightly childish way of his that never failed to tug on my heartstrings.

'If everyone I loved was happy, of course,' he said, as if it should have been obvious.

It was kind of funny that, right as he said this, the doorbell rang.

I uttered a curse word I'd picked up from spending way too much time in the company of Frank and Kayla. Uncle Chris looked at me in surprise. 'Piercey!' he said, shocked.

'Sorry.' My heart began to drum inside my chest. I

heard rapid footsteps in the hallway.

'It's Chief of Police Santos,' my mother said, her face a mask of concern. 'I saw him on the front porch from the window.'

'There are cop cars all up and down the street,' Alex said, skidding into the kitchen right behind her. 'Po-pos here to take us to the big house.'

'You don't know that,' Mom said to him.

'Oh, yeah? Why else do you think they're here, Aunt Deb? To help you clean up your lawn after the big storm?' Alex's voice dripped with sarcasm. 'Yeah, that's a special service the Isla Huesos police chief offers to all the attractive new divorcées on the island.'

'Mom,' I said, my heart in my throat. 'I think we need to borrow your car.'

'How's that going to work?' Alex demanded. 'Chief Santos parked in her driveway. And don't think he didn't do it on purpose to block us from getting her car out of the garage. Are we supposed to ram him?'

'Oh,' I said, disappointed. I looked at Alex. 'How did you guys get here? In your car?'

'We walked,' Alex said. 'Your genius boyfriend had Frank slash all my tyres to keep me from going out after Coffin Fest, remember?'

'Oh, right,' I said. That had worked really well, since Alex had gone out anyway and got himself killed.

'This is crazy,' Mom said as the doorbell rang again, this time accompanied by a knock and a deep voice saying, 'Dr Cabrero? We know you're home. We need to ask you a few questions about your daughter.'

'I'm going to open the door and invite him in and explain the whole situation—'

Both Alex and I had glanced down at the diamond at the end of my necklace. It was the colour of onyx. 'No!' we cried simultaneously.

'Go out the back,' Uncle Chris said.

I looked at him, startled. I had almost forgotten he was in the room, he'd grown so quiet. *Go out the back* were the first words he'd said since my mom and Alex had said it was the police at the door.

'What?' I asked him, confused not so much by the words, but that he, my sweet, beloved uncle, was the one saying them.

'The two of you,' he said, pointing first at Alex and me, then at the backyard. 'Go out the back way. The wall's too high to climb, but I saw some bikes by the gate back there. You could get on them, then pedal towards the cemetery. The cops won't be able to follow you. There's a big tree down across the middle of the road. They're still trying to find guys with enough chain saws to cut it apart since it's too big to lift.'

I stared at him. He meant the tree that had fallen on top of Mr Mueller.

Alex shook his head at his father pityingly. 'Dad, you of all people should know you can't run from the po-po. Besides, I told you, the driveway is blocked by their squad cars.'

'But we can still get bikes around them,' I said.

'Sure,' Alex said. 'But they'll see us.'

'Not if I create a diversion and distract them,' Chris said. 'In prison, we had a name for when we did that.'

Alex and I widened our eyes at him. 'What was it?'

'Well, prison riot,' Uncle Chris said with a shrug. 'That was the most accurate term for it, although we did try to think of a better one.'

'No,' my mother said, looking outraged. 'This is wrong. Christopher, you are not going to—'

'You'd better go,' Uncle Chris said, lifting my tote bag – which I'd left sitting at the bottom of the stairs – and handing it to me.

The thumping on the door had become more fevered. Now I heard the chief of police say, 'Dr Cabrero, I have a search warrant. I don't want to break down your door, but if you don't open it, I will.'

'*Go*,' Uncle Chris said, and pushed us towards the backyard.

Alex faced his father, flabbergasted, but finally grabbed his backpack from the chair over which he'd slung it. 'Don't do anything stupid to get yourself thrown back in jail, Dad,' he said.

'Why would I do that?' Uncle Chris asked, looking genuinely puzzled.

Alex shook his head, wearing an expression that clearly read, *This is going to be a disaster*.

'Christopher, wait,' I heard my mom call as she raced after her brother, who'd gone striding towards the front door.

I didn't stick around to see what was going to happen after that. I grabbed the front of Alex's shirt and dragged him through the French doors and across the back porch, down the steps and round the side of the house, towards the back gate and the bicycles Uncle Chris had said he'd seen.

'This is never going to work,' Alex was muttering. 'They're going to see us. And what about your necklace? There's obviously a Fury out there. For all we know, it could be Chief Santos.'

'It isn't him,' I said. I was surprised to see my bicycle sitting beside my mother's. Somehow she'd retrieved it from the cemetery, where I'd left it locked up, or the police had returned it after I'd gone missing. 'My necklace never turned black around Chief Santos before.'

'Well, maybe he's a Fury now. Maybe they've possessed everyone on the entire island except us, like some kind of plague. Oh, hell no.' Alex looked down at the two bikes, mine and my mother's. 'I'm not riding a *girl's* bike.'

'Fine,' I said, yanking mine from its kickstand. 'Stay here and get arrested. You deserve it for being such a sexist snob. I'm leaving.'

'Get arrested?' Alex grabbed my mom's bike – which was a red single speed with a simple wire basket – and hurried after me. 'I didn't do anything. *You're* the one who—'

'Shhh,' I said. We'd reached the gate that led from the backyard to the driveway. I held up a hand to silence Alex as I listened to what was happening on the front porch.

'I already served my time,' I could hear Uncle Chris shouting. 'Don't I have any rights?'

'Of course you have rights, Mr Cabrero,' Chief of Police Santos was saying in a patient tone. 'We're not here for you.

We're here to talk to your niece. We understand that she and this fellow we all were so worried had kidnapped her – but who we now come to find out is actually her boyfriend – were at a Coffin Night party last night out on Reef Key and caused a considerable amount of damage—'

'Persecution!' Uncle Chris shouted. 'You people are persecuting me and my family!'

'Now, hold on there, Christopher,' Chief Santos said. 'Let's not get excited.'

I heard a crash, then my mother cry, 'Oh, Christopher!'

'Come on,' I whispered to Alex, and opened the gate.

Uncle Chris had been right, I saw, as Alex and I quietly steered our bikes from the backyard, keeping our heads ducked well below the Isla Huesos squad cars parked along my mother's driveway. Riots really did cause a distraction.

Especially since Uncle Chris had lifted one of the heavy flower planters on my mother's front porch and thrown it as hard as he could at the stone walkway below, causing the planter to explode into a million tiny pieces of dirt, plaster and petunias.

Not only were quite a few of my mother's neighbours (who'd been outside in their yards cleaning up after Hurricane Cassandra) staring, but every single one of the officers accompanying Chief Santos had drawn their firearm and had it trained on Uncle Chris.

This had to be the most exciting thing ever to happen in my mother's wealthy suburban community, which was guarded twenty-four hours a day by a gated security station. The whole reason Seth Rector and his friends had befriended me my first day of school was because they knew I lived in Dolphin Key, and they believed if they stashed the senior class coffin in my garage it would be safe from the juniors.

How long ago that day seemed.

The police chief stood next to my mother on the porch, his hands on his hips, slowly shaking his head.

'Christopher,' he was saying. 'Why'd you have to go and do that? Now I'm going to have to take you in and waste my afternoon writing up a report, when I have a thousand more important things to do today. Do you have any idea how many downed power lines and flooded homes I have to deal with? There are people who lost everything they owned in Cassandra last night. The electricity is still out on half the island. Half the high school is underwater. And you're going around acting like this? Give me a break, will you?'

My heart began to beat a little faster with excitement. Half the high school was underwater?

Then I remembered I lived in the Underworld now. I didn't have to go to school any more. What a relief.

'What precisely are you going to charge him with, Chief?' my mother asked drily. 'Assaulting my front walk with a planter?'

'Let's go,' I whispered to Alex. I was aware that, though Uncle Chris had the undivided attention of the police officers, my mom's neighbours could still see us, and some of them were beginning to nudge one another and look in our direction. 'This is our chance.'

Alex remained glued where he was, however.

'No,' he whispered back. 'I don't like the look of this.'

'What are you talking about? Your dad will be fine. They're not going to arrest him. He didn't do anything. Well, anything illegal. It's not against the law to smash up your sister's flower planters.'

'Your necklace, though,' Alex said, nodding to it. 'It's still black.'

I looked down. He was right about that.

'There's a Fury around,' he said. 'Does the combination of guns and Furies sound like a good one to you?'

I looked back at the police officers gathered in Mom's yard. 'No, it doesn't,' I said. 'But it could be any one of these people. It could be *her*, for all we know.' I pointed at a three- or four-year-old girl standing on the sidewalk a few yards away, staring at us with her finger in her mouth. She was wearing a shirt that said *Daddy's Little Princess* on it.

The police chief was rubbing his chin. I could tell from his stubble that the past few days had been as difficult for him as they had been for me. He hadn't even had time to spare on personal grooming.

As the chief rubbed his chin, he finally noticed his men – and a single female officer – had their pistols drawn.

'Hey,' Chief Santos said to them in a surprised voice. 'Saddle up the pieces, people. There's no need for that.'

All but one officer obediently slipped their guns back into their holsters. The one who did not was a husky guy with a lot of dark hair. He kept his firearm pointed steadily at Uncle Chris.

Chief of Police Santos didn't notice. He turned back to my mother to say something in a low voice that Alex

259

and I were too far away to hear.

But I was sure none of my mother's neighbours missed what the dark-haired officer shouted a second later.

'Send the girl out!'

Police Chief Santos spun round.

'Poling,' he said, making a disgusted face as his gaze fell on the officer still holding the gun. 'Are you nuts?'

Poling? Where had I heard that name before?

'Not nuts, sir,' Officer Poling said. 'Just here to do my job. We came to get the Oliviera girl, and that's what I intend to do.'

'Not like this, you numbskull. We came here to question her, not shoot her. Put your firearm away, before I shoot you myself.'

I noticed a number of my mother's neighbours beginning to hurry indoors, sensing that the scene had taken a sudden turn for the worse. No one came to get Daddy's Little Princess, however. She stayed where she was, still staring at us and sucking on her finger.

'Sorry, sir,' Officer Poling said, his pistol not wavering. 'Pierce Oliviera killed a friend of mine. We have to bring her in.'

I felt the blood in my veins grow cold. He knew. But *how*?

'What in the hell are you talking about, Shawn?' Chief Santos demanded.

'My friend Mark,' Officer Poling said. 'She killed him. She's going to have to pay for that. I have my orders.'

Mr Mueller's first name was Mark.

'Orders?' the police chief echoed. 'Orders from who, Shawn? Not me. And who the hell is Mark?'

The dark-haired man looked up. It was almost impossible

not to follow the direction of his gaze, even though a part of me wanted to keep my eye on his gun.

When I raised my head, however, I knew it would be impossible to look away.

The sky above our heads was filled with ravens – the same kind that had been circling the ceiling of the cave in the Underworld just before the Furies had caused the ships to sink. There were hundreds – maybe thousands – of the scavenger birds, their black wings spread out against the cloudless blue sky, flying in circles above Isla Huesos, some of them letting out their odd, almost human-sounding cries.

I had seen ravens on the island before, but always over the cemetery, and of course at Reef Key, not my mother's house. It had made sense to see them in a graveyard and a development that had been built over a burial site. They were carrion birds, after all. They ate the dead.

So what was with the flybys over the nice gated subdivison?

The ravens clearly knew something the rest of us were just beginning to suspect . . . like that maybe there were about to be some dead bodies for them to feast on.

Daddy's Little Princess pointed to the sky with the finger she'd been sucking. 'Bad birdies,' she said. She was speaking to Alex and me conversationally, imparting information she seemed to think we needed to know. '*Bad.*'

'Yeah, kid,' Alex said. 'I think we figured that part out already.'

Only Chief of Police Santos seemed unfazed at the sight of the silently wheeling ravens.

'Don't tell me you're taking orders from a bunch of damned birds, Shawn,' he growled. 'I don't have time for that kind of thing today.'

Officer Poling did not appear to care what his chief had time for.

'Either the girl comes out,' the young officer said, taking careful aim, 'or I shoot her mother in the head.'

The bottom of my world dropped out as I saw Officer Poling swing the mouth of his gun directly at my mother.

Suddenly I remembered where I'd heard his name before. Officer Poling had been one of the two officers helping Jade to patrol the cemetery the night she died.

Helping Jade? Or helping to *murder* Jade in order to cover up for a crime some other Furies had committed?

What happened next seemed to occur in slow motion, although in reality it must have taken only a couple of seconds.

Uncle Chris stepped in front of my mother to shield her from Officer Poling's bullets with his own body. Chief of Police Santos did the same thing, only he stepped in front of both Uncle Chris and my mom, attempting to push them back inside the house and to safety.

Meanwhile, every cop standing around Officer Poling struggled to draw his or her weapon in order to point it at their colleague, sensing their chief was under attack, shouting, 'Stand down! Stand down!'

In a few seconds more, the wealthy community of Dolphin Key was going to become a shooting gallery.

'We've got to stop this!' Alex whirled round to

shout at me. 'They'll kill each other.'

Daddy's Little Princess had another opinion. 'Run,' she said in the same matter-of-fact voice she'd used before about the *bad birdies*, shaking her head until her blond ringlets quivered. 'Run away.'

Something struck me about the little girl's eyes. I didn't have time to analyse it, but I knew it reminded me of someone.

'Alex,' I said. 'Grab her.'

He looked down at me uncomprehendingly. 'What?'

'Grab the kid,' I said, pointing at Daddy's Little Princess. 'Figure out where she lives and take her inside so she doesn't get hurt if anyone starts shooting. Then meet me at the cemetery.'

Alex did as I asked, grabbing the little girl by her elbows. She laughed, thinking we were playing a game. 'What are *you* going to do?' Alex asked.

'This,' I said. Keeping one hand on my handlebars, I raised the other and began to wave. 'Hey! Officer Poling?' I shouted. 'Looking for me? I'm over here.'

Officer Poling's face wasn't the only one who swung in my direction. Every single officer who'd had a gun trained on him looked my way, too. So did my mom and Uncle Chris. So did Chief of Police Santos. So did Daddy's Little Princess. So did Alex.

Besides my mom's and Officer Poling's, Alex's expression might have been the one that was most shocked.

'Are you crazy?' Alex demanded. 'He's going to come after *you* now.'

'That's the idea,' I said, and stepped hard on my pedal.

Then saw I people hot in fire of wrath,
With stones a young man slaying, clamorously
Still crying to each other, 'Kill him! kill him!'
Dante Alighieri, *Purgatorio*, Canto XV

THANK YOU FOR VISITING DOLPHIN KEY, A GATED LUXURY
COMMUNITY IN ISLA HUESOS. PLEASE COME AGAIN!

That's what the sign in the gatehouse read. Funny how
I'd never really noticed it until I was sweeping past it as a
psychopathic cop was trying to kill me.

I had a pretty strong feeling no one in Dolphin Key
wanted me to come again, ever. Especially as I neared the
gatehouse and saw the guard inside it waving madly at
me . . . possibly because of what she saw directly behind me:
a line of police cruisers, each with their lights and sirens
blazing.

I was sure she was waving at me to stop. She certainly
hadn't raised the garishly coloured swing-arm barricade that
was supposed to keep the residents of Dolphin Key safe
inside, and undesirable non-residents out.

Then I saw that the guard was pointing at the end of the
barricade, where there was just enough room for a single
bicyclist to pass by, whether the arm was lifted or not.

I couldn't understand it. Was she trying to *help* me? She
worked for law enforcement. I was clearly a wayward
degenerate.

Yet she was urgently waving me through, while keeping the barricade firmly locked down to thwart the authorities following me.

Of course I didn't have time to ask her intentions as I swept by. I could only glance over my shoulder . . .

. . . then wish I hadn't as I glimpsed Officer Poling's face through the windshield of the car a few dozen yards behind me and felt my throat constrict with fear as I saw it contort with hatred and rage.

I don't know why he hadn't shot me instead of leaping into the nearest police cruiser and giving chase. Maybe the ravens – or whoever was controlling the Furies – told him not to.

I suppose it was better for me that he hadn't. I wasn't dead, and neither was he, as he surely would have been had he pulled the trigger . . . His fellow officers would have put him down like the mad dog he now resembled, and would probably have inadvertently taken the lives of a few innocent bystanders along with him.

But now he was hot on my trail, with Chief of Police Santos and his fellow officers hot on Officer Poling's trail. I was leading a parade of cop cars down the narrow streets of Isla Huesos.

Worse, it turned out Officer Poling found lowered gatehouse barricade arms no impediment to his pursuit of me. He simply rammed his vehicle through them, sending splinters of wood flying everywhere and causing the gatehouse guard to fling her arms over her face protectively, then reach for her radio to report him.

265

I told myself I had the advantage, since I was speeding along the same path I'd taken dozens – maybe hundreds – of times since my mother and I had moved to Isla Huesos . . . including the night she'd thrown her *Welcome to Isla Huesos, Pierce* party, which I'd fled in a similar fashion . . . only then a demon-possessed cop hadn't been pursuing me.

My feet were pedalling just as fast as they had that night, though, towards the cemetery . . . and to John. I was on a bike on well-known territory, able to traverse terrain automobiles couldn't, such as sidewalks and lawns.

At least that's what I kept telling myself.

I could only hope Alex was following along behind the trail of squad cars somewhere. I had yet to see him. I couldn't risk glancing over my shoulder again, since the sight of Officer Poling's twisted face behind the wheel frightened me so much I almost lost my footing on the bike. I had to concentrate on the road in front of me. Every crack in the pavement was as recognizable to me as the veins on my own hands, but the storm had left a ton of detritus in the road in the form of fallen branches, overturned garbage cans and the odd lawn chair. If I looked away for a second, I was afraid I'd lose my balance, then fall prey to a madman with revenge on his mind.

I told myself the feel of the wind in my hair as I sailed down the hill to the cemetery was exhilarating, not terrifying. The sirens' screaming in my ears was exciting, not earsplitting. My heart was slamming hard against my ribs not with fear, but with anticipation of seeing John. He was going to be waiting for me at his crypt, exactly where he'd said he'd be. He'd take me in his arms and assure me he'd got the ships delivered safely to the Underworld.

Oh, God, I didn't sound convincing even to myself. I could barely see where I was going thanks to the tears streaming down my face. Now Officer Poling was using the loudspeaker on his squad car: 'Pierce Oliviera. Stop. You are under arrest for the murder of Mark Mueller. Stop, or I'll shoot.'

People were coming out on to their front porches in order to see the person they thought was a real-life murderer whizzing past them on a bike. It was a good thing I lived underneath this town and not in it, because my reputation was ruined.

But what about Kayla? I regretted my decision to ever let her leave the safety of the Underworld. Certainly she was going to have to go back to her old life someday. She wasn't bound by death (like Alex) or eternal love (like me) to stay forever in the Underworld.

Why had I allowed her tough talk to sway me into believing she'd be fine? Fine against Furies carrying guns?

I prayed Kayla would be waiting safely at the cemetery (where Alex had said she and Frank would meet us), and that John and I wouldn't be too late to keep this whole thing from turning into the disaster Mr Graves had warned me about.

Maybe it already had. Maybe the pestilence was leaking from the Underworld. It certainly seemed so. The storm was over, but so far the new life Mr Smith had promised the sun would reveal in its wake wasn't good at all. The sun seemed to be revealing horrible, creepy things, things like Officer Poling, things that would have been better off left in the dark . . .

I slammed on the brakes. An enormous sapodilla tree lay in the middle of the road in front of me.

It was the one John had struck with lightning and sent crashing down on Mr Mueller's body after we'd hit him with Kayla's car.

There was a single maintenance worker wearing a fluorescent-yellow vest standing in front of the tree, smoking a cigarette. He looked surprised to see a girl wearing a whip on a belt pull up on a bike . . . or maybe it was all the cop cars screaming behind me that surprised him.

'Well,' Yellow Vest said. 'Hello there.'

The city hadn't had time yet to put up orange CAUTION signs. There must have been too many other downed trees – and worse – across the island.

Mr Mueller was gone. They had been able to remove his body by cutting away the section of the tree that had trapped it. The maintenance worker held a chain saw. The rest of the sapodilla still lay sprawled across the road. The maintenance worker appeared to have been getting ready to cut the trunk into pieces and throw the pieces into a large wood chipper sitting nearby before he'd stopped for his smoking break.

'Please,' I said, panting. 'I need to get to the cemetery.'

'This road,' Yellow Vest said, 'is closed.'

Too late, I remembered Uncle Chris had mentioned that it would be . . . to vehicular traffic, anyway.

'I know,' I said. I didn't look behind me. There was no

need to. I could hear the brakes of Officer Poling's squad car squealing to a halt a few yards away. 'But I really, really, really need to get to the cemetery.'

The maintenance worker took a long puff on his cigarette. Then he took one step to the left, revealing the space in the tree where Mr Mueller's body had lain. It was the same size as the space between the guardhouse and the swing-arm barricade at Dolphin Key, perfect for a single bicyclist.

'So go on already,' the maintenance worker said.

'Oh,' I said gratefully. 'Thank you very much.'

'Stop,' I heard Officer Poling shout. 'That girl is under arrest!'

I hesitated.

'What are you waiting for?' Yellow Vest asked me.

'I . . .' I glanced back at Officer Poling, who was getting out of the car. 'He's not right in the head.'

Yellow Vest grinned. 'Don't you worry about me,' he said, and raised his chain saw. 'I can take care of myself. You scoot now.'

He pulled the chain saw's cord. The motor roared to life, the sharp, tiny blades beginning to spin madly.

I didn't wait a second longer. I hurried through the space between the sapodilla's enormous trunk. Only when I was through, and putting my feet back on my pedals, did I look back. The worker had returned to where he'd been standing, in front of the empty space, but he must have decided his break was over, since he'd stamped out the cigarette and was staring in Officer Poling's direction.

'Well, hey there,' he said, as pleasantly as he'd spoken to

me, albeit a bit more loudly in order to be heard above the noise of the chain saw.

I didn't hear the rest of their conversation because I didn't stick around. I saw that Chief of Police Santos's cruiser had pulled up just behind Officer Poling's. Yellow Vest was right. He could take care of himself.

I couldn't understand it. Why hadn't the maintenance worker tried to stop me when the police were clearly in pursuit of me? I was obviously a criminal.

I didn't have time to ponder it. I could only pedal, so close to the cemetery now that I could see the black wrought iron fence looming in front of me. Even if he got past the guy with the chain saw and Chief Santos – which seemed extremely unlikely – there'd be no way Shawn Poling could follow me into the cemetery, because the gate would be closed and locked. Mr Smith had assured all of us that day in the school assembly that the gate would be locked all through Coffin Week.

And Officer Poling wouldn't be agile enough to climb that high, spiked fence. He'd never catch up to me now. Or, by the time he did, I'd be safely back in the Underworld, where John and I would try to return everything to normal . . . or as close to normal as things could get in the Underworld.

Except there was no possibility of 'normal' any more. Though the day was turning out to be one of the most beautiful I'd ever seen on Isla Huesos – the sky was a pure, cloudless blue, the temperature perfectly warm, the wind a little too strong for boating – what I saw in front of me as I grew closer to the cemetery filled me with horror.

Not foliage green, but of a dusky colour,
Not branches smooth, but gnarled and intertangled,
Not apple-trees were there, but thorns with poison.
Dante Alighieri, *Inferno*, Canto XIII

The ravens that had been circling my mother's house were now swooping low in the sky above the graveyard. And the storm that had raged past Isla Huesos the night before hadn't spared one inch of Isla Huesos's burial ground.

Branches torn from trees lay thrown across the top of tombs like drunken sailors on shore leave, and nearly every decorative stone angel or cherub was missing a wing. Coconuts had been fired like missiles by the gale-force winds through any mausoleum containing a stained-glass window, shattering it, and the formerly neat pathways through the crypts were carpeted with fallen palm fronds.

The place looked like a battle zone.

There was no need for me to climb the fence, since the thick black gates that Mr Smith had assured us all would be so securely bolted now swayed obscenely ajar, looking as if something – or someone – had battered them from the outside until they'd simply given way.

The cemetery sexton's office hadn't escaped unscathed, either. The windows of the small cottage where Mr Smith kept his office had been safely shuttered in preparation for the storm, but that hadn't spared the house's roof from

271

being crushed in half beneath the weight of the large Spanish lime tree that had fallen on top of it . . . the Spanish lime tree that used to litter its fruit all over the cottage's backyard, and in the branches of which Hope had once huddled in fear of Mike, the cemetery's (now former) handyman, when he'd tried to kill me.

Worse, everywhere I looked, I saw people . . . people who'd wandered into the cemetery through the wide-open gates, carrying rakes and hoes and other pieces of gardening equipment, probably to clean up their loved ones' graves.

'Oh, no,' I couldn't help murmuring with a groan. 'No, no, no . . .'

A sickening sense of foreboding grew in the pit of my stomach. If winds could twist solid metal the way they had the cemetery gates, and blow over a tree as thick and sturdy as that Spanish lime, how could a structure as old as John's tomb escape without damage? It was so old – the red bricks that made up its walls so decrepit – would it even be standing? And what about our tree – the poinciana under which we'd met and kissed, its blossoms forming a scarlet umbrella above our heads?

I pedalled more quickly, my heart booming so loudly in my chest I could no longer hear the sound of the chain saw, or even the sirens. I couldn't even hear the crunching of sea grass and palm fronds beneath my bicycle's wheels as they passed over them. My only thought was that I had to see how badly John's crypt had been affected by the storm, if the poinciana tree was even still there . . .

. . . And then I rounded the corner and saw that it was.

Well, most of it was.

Every single blossom was gone from the tree. They lay upon the ground like an undulating carpet of scarlet silk.

The tree had also lost a large limb. It had fallen across the roof of the crypt, causing part of it to cave in.

I was relieved to see that was the only damage. The redbrick structure still stood, the word *Hayden* bold as ever in block lettering above the entrance to the vault.

Standing in the middle of the carpet of red poinciana blossoms was a man. His back was to me. The sun was so high in the air and shining so brightly that, since I wasn't wearing sunglasses, it was difficult for me to determine his identity.

For a second my heart lifted, because I was certain it was John, returned from his journey to fetch the boats my father had found for him. Even now, the passengers in the Underworld were probably being boarded, order was being returned to the realm of the dead, and my father was back at my mom's house.

Of course John was waiting for me on a carpet of red poinciana blossoms. It only made sense that this would be where I'd find him. Later we'd have to deal with my grandmother, and the fact that I'd killed Thanatos, not to mention Mark Mueller. But, for now, John and I would reunite in the place where, so long ago, we'd first met.

Then, as I got closer, I realized the man standing on the carpet of poinciana blossoms wasn't John after all. He was too small and too thin to be John, and was wearing a hat. John would never wear a hat.

Besides, this man was sweeping the poinciana blossoms *away* from the front of John's tomb with a broom. John would *never* do this . . . except, of course, to sweep them up to spread them in front of my mom's house.

Then, as I got even closer, I recognized who the man was. I felt silly for not doing so before. It must have been wishful thinking on my part to ever imagine he was John.

'Mr Smith,' I said, a myriad emotions washing over me – relief, happiness, confusion and, yes, a twinge of disappointment that he wasn't John. I leaped from my bicycle, letting it fall to the ground, and rushed towards him.

'Mr Smith, what are you doing here? I'm glad to see you, but, still, there's a Fury after me. They know I killed Mr Mueller – or that John and I did, anyway. John's alive, by the way. I saved him. Anyway, it's complicated, and Chief Santos is trying to stop the guy who's after me, but you should really get out of here if you don't want to get shot or have to stick around answering questions forever, or whatever.'

The cemetery sexton turned round. He'd been standing with his back to me. I guess he hadn't heard me coming.

Funny, this had always been a bit of a bone of contention between us (until he got to know me better, of course). Mr Smith had never liked the way I'd used 'his cemetery' as a public thoroughfare, whipping around it on my bike, 'endangering' mourners, and showing 'no respect for the dead'.

That's what he'd used to say until he found out the *real* reason I'd always been hanging out in 'his cemetery' . . . John.

'Pierce,' Mr Smith said, looking down at me. The brim of his straw fedora shaded his face a bit, but I could see I'd startled him. 'Where did you come—' Then he noticed my bike lying on the ground. 'Oh, I see. What were you saying about Chief Santos?'

'He's right behind me. They're going to have trouble getting through, though, because of this guy with a chain saw . . . oh, whatever, it's a long story. It's really weird, all day total strangers have been going out of their way to—'

I broke off, realizing with a start why the eyes of the young girl in the *Daddy's Little Princess* shirt had looked familiar to me. She had eyes like Mr Smith's . . . even though hers had been blue, and Mr Smith's eyes were brown. Still, they both had a strange sort of knowingness to them and were filled with kindness.

Now that I thought of it, the guard's eyes at the gatehouse at Dolphin Key had looked the same way. So had the eyes of Yellow Vest, back at the dead sapodilla.

'Mr Smith,' I said, squinting in the sun. 'Something weird is going on. Do you have any idea why a bunch of total strangers would risk their lives or jobs to help another total stranger?'

The cemetery sexton's kind eyes narrowed beneath his hat brim. I saw him glance towards the ravens whirling around above our heads. He whispered something.

'What?' I wasn't sure I'd heard him correctly, but I almost thought he said the word *fates*.

He glanced back down at me. 'Nothing. Only that there might be hope after all,' he said.

275

'Hope?' I shaded my eyes to look up at the sky, excited, thinking he meant my bird. 'Where?'

'Not that kind of hope,' he said with a tiny smile. 'Only that all might not yet be lost.'

I lowered my head to look back at him. 'Mr Smith,' I said, 'I think maybe you should sit down and have some water. You've been standing out in the heat for too long.'

He nodded. 'Maybe I have. I see you're not wearing a bicycle helmet.' But he pointed at my chest, not my head. 'As usual.'

'Yeah,' I said. 'Maybe you didn't hear me before, but I had more important things to worry about, such as running from the cops and not being shot. Mr Smith, why are you sweeping all these poinciana blossoms from the front of John's tomb? He likes them. And don't you have more important things to do? A tree crashed through the roof of your office, in case you didn't notice.'

'I noticed,' he said. 'I'm extremely observant, unlike some people I might mention.'

'Nice,' I said. 'Nice way to talk to me considering everything I've been through, saving John's life and this island and all of that. No need to thank me, even though it turned out Thanatos was Seth Rector, and I killed him. Not that that matters to you, evidently. But whatever.'

Mr Smith looked slightly paler under his brown skin. 'You killed him?'

'Thanatos,' I assured him. 'Not Seth. He's still alive and well and pressing charges against me – and John – for assault. Why? What's the matter?'

'Nothing,' Mr Smith said. 'Only . . . it explains a lot.'

'A lot about what? Was I not supposed to kill him? I wondered about that, but I couldn't help it – he was such a jerk.'

'Thanatos takes on the personality traits of the person he possesses,' Mr Smith said. There was something a bit mournful in his tone. 'If he was possessing Seth Rector, he would, I suppose, seem like a jerk.'

I couldn't help noticing that Mr Smith's gaze was all over the place, on me one second, the ravens the next, the poinciana blossoms beneath his feet the next. What was he looking for? That reminded me of something.

'Have you seen Frank and Kayla?' I asked, glancing around, but still seeing only family members carrying gardening tools with which to tidy up their loved ones' vaults. 'They were supposed to be stopping by your place to drop the car off, then meet us here.'

'Yes,' Mr Smith said shortly. 'I've seen them.'

'You have?' I glanced back at him, surprised. 'Where are they?'

There was definitely something off about Mr Smith, besides the weird things he was saying. I couldn't put my finger on what it was, precisely. He looked as well put together as ever, in a pressed white shirt, sporty green bow tie and trim khakis, his gold-rimmed spectacles sparkling in the sun.

But I saw that he was clutching the broom handle much more tightly than necessary.

'Oh,' he said. 'They'll be here soon.'

'Mr Smith,' I said, beginning to feel less relieved at seeing him and more disturbed. It was hard to explain, but in the stillness of the cemetery – the police sirens had been cut off, and all I could hear was the occasional distant cackle of a raven – I'd begun to feel almost as if someone was watching us . . . someone besides the birds overhead. 'What is it? Did something happen to Kayla? To John?' My pulse sped up a little. 'Has John been here? Because I'm supposed to meet up with him here, too. Did he say something to you? Did something go wrong with the—'

'No,' Mr Smith cut me off, a little rudely, I thought. He slipped a hand into his trouser pocket and pulled out one of his ubiquitous handkerchiefs. 'No, no, John hasn't been here. Everything's wonderful. Why wouldn't it be?'

Everything was *not* wonderful.

I knew that because not only would Mr Smith never use a word like *wonderful* – I was pretty certain he'd consider *wonderful* the equivalent of *awesome*, a word he'd once said was overused by my generation – but he lifted the handkerchief to mop some sweat from his forehead.

No matter what the weather, I'd never seen Mr Smith sweat . . . not unless he was *extremely* uncomfortable, like if I was asking him about the possibility of getting pregnant in the Underworld.

But if he was so uncomfortable, why wasn't the cemetery sexton telling me what the matter was?

I saw his gaze dart again to my chest, the way it had when he'd mentioned my helmet.

Only then did I know what was wrong, and I didn't

have to follow his gaze to see what it was.

My diamond was black. There was a Fury around . . . maybe more than one. Mr Smith knew it, but hadn't said anything to warn me.

There could be only one explanation as to why. I saw it in the way his hand trembled as he put the handkerchief back into his pocket. The truth hit me like a slap in the face.

Mr Smith was afraid. And for Mr Smith to be afraid something had to be seriously wrong. Both the cemetery sexton and myself were NDEs. We knew what it was like to die, so death didn't frighten either of us terribly much. I wouldn't say Mr Smith had *enjoyed* dying, but I knew for certain he longed to go to the Underworld again, because he didn't remember his journey there. He'd always been a little jealous of the fact that I did, even though I hadn't liked it.

No, Richard Smith didn't fear death . . . not for himself.

But he was definitely afraid of death – or possibly something worse – now. What was it?

Without changing my tone or looking around, I slowly began to unhook the whip that still sat on my belt.

'So you know what John and I did last night after I rescued him?' I asked him conversationally.

'I cannot even begin to imagine,' the cemetery sexton said, looking extremely uncomfortable.

'We went back to my mom's house,' I said, 'snuck into my room, and made sweet love all night.'

'That's simply wonderful,' Mr Smith said. His head looked like it was about to explode not only from the effort he was making not to chastise me for my irresponsible behaviour, but because of his fear. Trickles of perspiration were flowing down the sides of his face, and there was a smile frozen on his lips. 'Simply wonderful.'

Bingo. I'd been right. Something was definitely going on. There was *no way* the cemetery sexton would ever say that John and I sneaking up to my room to 'make sweet love all night' was 'wonderful' – not unless he'd been given a complete lobotomy.

The Mr Smith *I* knew would have given me a lecture about how I should have used protection because when making love *outside* the Underworld, death deities were notorious for their ability to make little death deities . . . or something along those lines.

Whatever it was that was going on, Mr Smith was deathly afraid. So afraid, he was ignoring his basic principles in order to warn me about it. But what could it be? What could possibly be so awful to two people who'd already experienced the worst possible thing there was – death – and lived to tell of it?

'Yeah,' I said, careful not to look around, since I didn't want whoever it was that was threatening Mr Smith to know that I was on to them. 'I wonder what we'll call the baby, if there is one. Maybe, if it's a boy, we'll name him Richard, after you, Mr Smith—'

'That is *enough*.'

The sharp-toned voice came from behind me, but I knew exactly who it belonged to. I'd have recognized it anywhere.

It was the voice of the woman who'd killed me.

And lo! at one who was upon our side
There darted forth a serpent, which transfixed him
There where the neck is knotted to the shoulders.
Dante Alighieri, *Inferno*, Canto XXIV

Really? It was my *grandmother* Mr Smith was so afraid of?

I wanted to laugh.

I didn't, of course. It would have been rude. But, honestly, my grandmother wasn't that frightening. True, she'd killed me once – and tried to kill me a few other times. And when she got her Fury face on she was ugly as sin, which I could understand for Mr Smith – who wasn't as experienced with Furies as I was – was probably quite frightening.

But she was still only my grandmother.

Granted, she'd bested me once or twice – OK, three times – before.

This time, however, things were going to be different. This time, I wasn't some scared, lonely high-school girl. This time, I was armed with John's father's whip, which I knew how to use. This time, I was on my own turf, the Isla Huesos Cemetery, which I'd tromped through so many times I knew it like the back of my hand. This time, I had friends – not to mention the police – who were about to show up any minute to support me.

This time, *I* had the power. This time, I was queen of the Underworld.

Most important, this time, I was ready for her.

What I wasn't ready for, I realized the second I spun round to face her, was the fact that my grandmother had an arm round my best friend Kayla Rivera's waist and was holding a knife to her throat.

'Hey, Gran—' The words died on my lips.

'You've always thought you were so amusing.' My grandmother's voice was scornful. 'There goes Pierce, with another one of her little jokes. But you aren't amusing. You know what you are? An abomination, just like *him*.'

My pulse stuttered, then quit altogether.

Now I knew exactly why Mr Smith had been so frightened and had kept repeating the word *wonderful*. It's hard to think of anything witty to say when there's an innocent girl with a knife stuck to her carotid artery, a girl who'd been dragged into a battle between good and evil simply because I happened to sit next to her at school one day during an assembly.

All ability to think rationally fled my brain. *Not Kayla.* Those were the only words my mind could summon up. *Not Kayla.*

Then, *No wonder my diamond had always turned purple around her. Not because it was her birthstone.* It was a warning . . . a warning that I needed to save her from dying at the hands of a Fury.

At the hands of my grandmother.

'If you hurt one hair on her head, I swear . . .' My fingers tightened on the handle of my whip.

My grandmother only laughed. It sounded like the

cackle from one of the ravens.

'Or what?' she asked. 'You'll hit me with that dirty old rope? That's exactly what an abomination like you would do, strike her own grandmother.'

I wasn't surprised Grandma didn't recognize a whip when she saw one. She wasn't the sharpest knife in the drawer . . . not like the knife she was holding to Kayla's neck. It was a knife I recognized, a knife from a very expensive gourmet knife set. I knew that for a fact, because it was a knife from my mother's own kitchen. I'd used it many, many times to slice apples and sandwiches.

Now it appeared my grandmother had stolen it and intended to use it to slice open my best friend's throat.

'Pierce,' Kayla said.

The word slipped out of her without her seeming to have meant it to. As soon as it did, she bit her plump lower lip as if to remind herself to keep still, or the razor-sharp knife that had already, I saw, caused a ruby-red drop of blood to slide down the side of the silver blade would cut even more deeply. All of the dark lipstick Kayla normally wore had been chewed off due to the effort she was making to keep still, and her eye make-up was smudged from the tears she'd shed, though I could tell she'd been trying to hold them back.

Kayla was no longer wearing her flowy lavender Underworld-issued gown – I could imagine her hanging it back up in her closet, thinking, *I'm going to save this to wear later, maybe for Prom* – but a black belted shirtdress covered in kicking zebras, with black platform wedges.

Obviously, when she'd chosen this outfit, it had never occurred to her she'd be wearing it in a hostage situation.

'It's all right, Kayla,' I said, though she and I both knew this was a lie. 'Where's Frank?'

This was the wrong thing to ask.

'Dead,' my grandmother said with delight. Her cackle was echoed eerily by the ravens. 'Dead for good, this time, the way all of you walking abominations should be.'

'I don't know what you're talking about,' I said, though the tear tracks on Kayla's face seemed like explanation enough.

My grandmother sneered. 'Look for yourself,' she said, and nodded towards a nearby crypt.

Made of white marble, very old and weathered, the crypt bore an epitaph dedicated to My beloved wife, Martha Simonton, 1820–1846.

At first I saw nothing but a fat green iguana lounging in the sun on top of the tomb. Then I noticed a pair of familiar-looking black leather boots. They were attached to a pair of legs sticking out from behind the vault. Flung into the weeds not far from the boots lay a heavily tattooed, muscular arm.

I recognized the tattoos. They were rings of thorns, the same tattoos I'd seen around Frank's biceps the first time I'd met him in Mr Graves's kitchen.

'They were waiting for us at Mr Smith's house,' Kayla said. Her voice was a barely audible whisper. I had only seen her looking as frightened and sad once before, and that had been in this very same cemetery, the night we'd whisked her to the Underworld, assuring her she'd be safe there. How wrong we'd been. 'We tried to fight them, Pierce, we did. But there were too many of them.' Tears streamed freely down her face. 'I think they killed Patrick, too.'

I swung my head to stare at Mr Smith.

'*No,*' I said, feeling as if I'd been punched in the chest.

He was staring up at the sky again, scanning it, I guess for that glimpse of hope – or Hope – he'd mentioned before. He didn't meet my gaze.

'Yes,' my grandmother said with a smile, still holding the knife to Kayla's throat. 'Did you think you could go around flouting the laws of nature and never have to pay? Did you think you could kill one of ours, and there'd be no repercussions? Now we're even.'

Now we're even. Her words echoed again and again in my head, like the cries of the ravens. *Now we're even.*

Even? She thought we were *even* for what she'd done to Frank, to Patrick, to Kayla, to Jade, to me, to my family, to my friends and to John?

The red blanket of poinciana blossoms beneath Mr Smith's feet seemed to spread and grow before my eyes until it covered the ground not only beneath my own feet but my grandmother's as well. The soil beneath Frank's prone body turned as red as the drop of blood slowly trickling down the knife blade my grandmother was holding to Kayla's neck. The path that curved through the cemetery went scarlet, looking like a twisted play on the children's song 'Follow the Yellow Brick Road'. Only now it was the Murder Brick Road.

Had the poinciana blossoms really moved, blown by one of those strong winds left over from the hurricane, or was my vision playing tricks on me again, because I couldn't control the red-hot wind that Mr Liu had said fuels my anger?

I didn't know. I didn't care. For once, I had no interest in controlling my anger. I let it sweep over me the way the poinciana blossoms swept across my feet.

I slipped the whip Mr Liu had given me from my belt. It was the string he'd told me to hold on to when I felt the wind might blow me too far away.

But it was also a string I knew from experience could steer the direction of that wind.

'We're not even,' I said to my grandmother. 'Because this isn't a game. This is war. And I'm going to win.'

Despite the red swimming before my gaze, my aim was unerring, just as it had been in my mother's kitchen that morning. This situation wasn't so different, really, than when Alex had taunted me with the butter knife. All I had to do was remove the blade my grandmother was holding, the same way I'd removed the blade from Alex's hand.

The only difference was, I had to do it without hurting Kayla. I didn't care if I hurt my grandmother.

It happened so quickly she didn't even realize what had occurred. One millisecond, the knife was in my grandmother's grip, and the next, the shining blade was lying harmless at Mr Smith's feet, and Kayla was free.

'Snake!' my grandmother screamed, clutching her wrist and looking around, stunned, for the serpent she thought had leaped from the ground and bitten her. It was many moments before it dawned on her that that serpent was the granddaughter she had, for so many years, considered a useless, dim-witted fool.

'Go to Mr Smith,' I said to Kayla, because she looked equally stunned, not certain she was entirely free.

Her face crumpled, and she ran to the cemetery sexton, who dropped the broom and took her in his free arm, the other holding the knife in a ridiculous defensive stance he must have seen in an Isla Huesos Community Theatre production of *West Side Story*.

'It's not over, Pierce,' he warned, as Kayla clung to him. 'There are others.'

'Of course there are others,' I said, taking off my necklace and walking towards my grandmother, who was staring at me with her tiny, dead eyes narrowed in hatred and disbelief, cradling what appeared to be a broken arm. 'There will *always* be others. I'll have to spend the rest of my life fighting evil Furies. With great power comes great responsibility. I know, I saw the movie.'

I wasn't really listening to Mr Smith. I was trying to figure out how John and I were going to revive Frank. Patrick wasn't going to be a problem, if he actually was dead. He hadn't been dead to begin with. But Frank?

Frank was going to be a problem. *His* soul wasn't being held hostage by Thanatos. Because there was no Thanatos any more. So how could Frank be dead?

'No, Pierce, you don't understand,' Mr Smith said, his voice rising with something that sounded a little like hysteria. 'There are many, many others. And they're coming this way. *Right now.*'

I turned round to see what he was talking about. Then I froze.

Every single one of the people who'd been in the cemetery tidying up their loved ones' tombs was now moving steadily in my direction, their rakes and shovels held high in the air, like villagers intent on driving a monster from their princess's castle.

The problem was these people had mistaken the princess for the monster. I could tell by the direction of their flat, dead-eyed gazes, and the name their slack-jawed mouths kept murmuring over and over, the same name Officer Poling had been shouting through his squad car's loudspeaker.

Pierce Oliviera.

It wasn't my grandmother they were coming after.

It was me.

And I beheld therein a terrible throng
Of serpents, and of such a monstrous kind,
That the remembrance still congeals my blood . . .
Dante Alighieri, *Inferno*, Canto XXIV

I rushed to stand in front of Kayla and Mr Smith, my whip ready. I wouldn't be able to hold off the amassing hordes of Furies for long, but I was determined to go down trying.

'What's wrong with your grandma?' Kayla demanded. Her 'high adaptability' had apparently returned. 'Grandmas are supposed to be sweet and bake you brownies and love you unconditionally. Why is yours such a bitch?'

Mr Smith cleared his throat disapprovingly at Kayla's strong language. 'Mrs Cabrero can't help it; she's possessed by a demonic—'

'Screw that,' Kayla said. 'I'm tired of that excuse. She's possessed by a Fury, she had a bad childhood. You know who had a bad childhood? *Me.* But I don't take it out on innocent people.'

Kayla's rant was reminding me of someone else's. Then I remembered whose. Frank's, when that guy in the khaki pants back in the Underworld had insisted he'd been put in the wrong line.

Better not to think of Frank right now.

'Come on,' I said. 'If we hurry we can make it to the—'

— door to the Underworld in John's crypt, where it's safe,
I'd been about to say.

But when we turned around, I found our path to the
crypt blocked by Mike, the cemetery's former handyman.

I hadn't seen Mike since I'd given him a concussion in
the yard behind Mr Smith's office some time ago, but he
looked as if he'd healed up pretty nicely from that. Despite
the fact that he'd resigned from his position, he was still in
his sleeveless handyman overalls, all his lewd tattoos showing.
He grinned at us while tapping the heavy end of a shovel
into the palm of his hand, as if in eager expectation of
tapping it against the side of one of our heads.

'Going somewhere?' Mike asked. A decidedly salacious
grin lit up his otherwise dead eyes.

'He's the one who killed Frank,' Kayla murmured. Beneath
what little make-up remained on her face, her skin had taken
on a deathly pallor. I'd never seen her look more frightened.

'Killing that scum was my pleasure,' Mike said, his grin
growing broader.

'Please, Pierce,' Kayla whispered. 'The flicky thing, with
your whip. Do it.'

'Yes,' Mr Smith said. 'Although I don't, in general,
approve of violence, I think now would be a splendid time
to do the, er, flicky thing Kayla suggests.'

I looked around. We were trapped. Even if I managed to
get the shovel out of Mike's hands – and a shovel was a lot
heavier and harder to manage with a whip than a knife –
there was no way all three of us would be able to pass him to
get to the safety of the crypt. Mr Smith was an academic

and an old man, and not a very athletic one, at that. He'd never be able to outrun the Furies that were closing in on all sides. My grandmother was still behind us, too, laughing, despite the pain in her arm.

'Not so high-and-mighty are you now, eh, Miss Queen of the Underworld?' she cackled.

'We're not going to make it,' I said to Mr Smith and Kayla. 'At least, not all three of us. We're going to have to stay here and fight them.'

'I like the sound of that,' Mike said, licking his lips crudely at Kayla.

I expected her to collapse right then and there, given her ashen hue. But she seemed to have some last reserves of fire in her.

'You know what?' Kayla turned to snatch the knife from Mr Smith – which was probably a good thing, since the cemetery sexton obviously had no idea what to do with it – and said, 'Killing this scum will be *my* pleasure.'

Mike laughed when he saw the knife, then held up his shovel. 'You seem to be forgetting something, girlie. Size matters.'

Kayla curled her lip. 'I didn't forget. The size of my hatred for you is so big it can't be measured by any instrument known to man.'

'Whoa,' I said. 'Nice one, Kayla.'

'Girls.' Mr Smith looked from me to Kayla in distress. 'Please. Please don't do this. Save yourselves.'

'Save yourselves,' Kayla said with a giggle. It was semi-hysterical, but it was still a giggle. Talking smack had given her some self-confidence. 'After we get out of all this and I have my surgery and open my high-end beauty salon, that's what I'm going to call it. Save Yourselves.'

'I love that idea,' I said. 'I'll be your first customer.'

'Thanks,' Kayla said. 'I've been meaning to tell you that I think you could use some highlights. Just a few, to frame your face.'

'Girls,' Mr Smith said. 'Please. Don't worry about me. You know I don't mind dying. And now with Patrick—'

I held up a hand, palm out, to stem the flow of his words, and repeated what I'd said that horrible night in the castle, when we'd all been gathered around John's body.

'No one gets left behind,' I said.

'*No one.*' Kayla narrowed her eyes at Mike as he began to circle us, holding the shovel above his head as if it were a baseball bat.

Mr Smith blinked rapidly behind his spectacles. It was hard to tell in the bright sunlight, but I suspected he was blinking back tears. 'Miss Oliviera, despite all our differences and everything that's happened, I just want you to know that our acquaintance has been one of the greatest pleasures – and privileges – of my life.'

'Thanks, Mr Smith,' I said, cracking my whip at a woman wearing a T-shirt that said *I Survived Coffin Fest* who'd come a little too close with her rake. The woman snarled and recoiled. 'Same here.'

'I suppose,' Mr Smith said, 'now would be the appropriate time to say, er, see you in the next world?'

'Now would,' I said.

Suddenly Mike lunged at Kayla with a roar, holding his shovel high in the air. Kayla screamed and swung her knife at his midsection, but he easily dodged the blade, and she missed. A lascivious leer spread over Mike's face. I'd have snapped my whip at him, but I was occupied by a large man carrying a stone cherub, which he was about to throw at my face. Mr Smith, unfortunately, had my grandmother to contend with. She flung herself at him, hissing like a snake . . . a snake who owned a shop called Knuts for Knitting and wore orthopaedic sneakers.

I was certain in the next second I was going to see Mike's shovel connect with my best friend's head, then have to hear her screams of pain.

Instead, I saw a familiar black tactical boot connect with Mike's groin and heard *his* screams of pain.

'If you'd let me kill this man when I had the chance, Pierce,' John said calmly, 'none of this would be happening.'

The only time I'd ever been happier to see him was the moment he'd come back to life.

John seemed to come from out of nowhere, a blaze of fists and glory. Mike had sunk to the ground, weeping in pain, red poinciana blossoms staining the knees of his overalls. My grandmother was so surprised she backed away from Mr Smith, shouting, 'Get up! Get up, you fool!' in Mike's direction. But it seemed unlikely Mike would be getting up any time soon.

A moment later, the man who'd been about to throw the stone cherub at me joined Mike on the ground. Mr Liu, who'd followed John from the half-collapsed crypt, had torn the cherub from his hands and struck him with it. The cherub crumbled to pieces.

My grandmother howled in rage, and above our heads the ravens let out similar cries of wrath.

'Hello,' Mr Liu said to me in his usual laconic fashion. 'I see you're using my gift.'

He nodded at the whip. I wanted to throw my arms round him, but this hardly seemed the time or place, since Furies were still coming at us from all sides.

'Not that I'm not happy to see you both,' I said, taking my whip to a third man who was rushing at us with a wickedly pointed garden hoe. 'But what took you guys so long?'

'We were slightly preoccupied,' John said. He seized the hoe and broke it over his knee, then threw the non-pointed end forcefully at the man, hitting him in the solar plexus. 'I had a couple of ships to deliver.'

'And passengers to board,' Mr Liu added. He flung a piece of the stone cherub at a fifth Fury.

'Couldn't that have waited?' I asked. 'It's a mess out here.'

'It was an even bigger mess back there,' John said. 'But Mr Graves finally got things under control, thanks to your father—'

'My *father*?'

'He got us the boats,' John said, looking at me in some surprise, as if to say, *You were there. How could you not remember?* He went on to explain patiently, 'I was able to get them to the Underworld, and Mr Graves was able to start boarding the passengers . . . with a little help.'

'From who?' I asked.

'Them,' John said, and nodded towards the wrought iron gate to his crypt.

I saw a familiar figure – one that was considerably smaller than anyone else in the cemetery – slip through the gate, then turn to gesture eagerly to someone still inside the vault.

Henry, of course, I expected – though I didn't approve. A Fury battlefield was no place for a child, even one who'd lived a century and a half in the Underworld and had grown used to life without a mother.

But Reed, who'd found a shirt and a pair of long pants somewhere, and also armed himself with an ancient harpoon gun? Chloe, her hand wrapped tightly round Typhon's collar, against which the enormous dog was lunging in excitement? Mrs Engle *and* Mr Graves, both with their hands wrapped round the bridle of a snorting Alastor, who barely fit through the tiny opening? When the horse finally managed to squeeze through it, he kicked the first Fury who was foolish enough to come close to him, square in the chest.

'John,' I said in horror. '*No.*'

John shrugged. 'They volunteered to stay behind. Not only volunteered, they *insisted.*'

'John, Mr Graves told them that if they came out that door, they'd lose any chance whatsoever at moving on to what awaits them in the afterlife. Now they'll never be able to—'

'Pierce,' John said in a patient voice. 'They know that. I explained it all again to them. None of them cared. I don't know what went on down there while I was dead, but you developed some loyal subjects. No way were they going to leave you behind.'

I shook my head, tears filling my eyes. This was all too much. 'John, I can't let them do this for me. They're *revenants* now.'

John looked me straight in the eye, a small smile playing on his lips, even as a man with a pair of pruning shears came charging at us.

'Pierce, a revenant is someone who's returned from the dead,' John said, snatching away the shears. '*You're* a revenant. So am I. We're all revenants. Did you ever think we were anything else?'

Stunned, I stared at him. Why hadn't it occurred to me before? No wonder my grandmother hated me so much and kept calling me an abomination. An NDE was simply another, more pleasant name for a revenant. Both Mr Smith and I had actually died and come back to life, exactly like Reed and Chloe and Mrs Engle . . . and Alex and John and Mr Liu and Henry and Mr Graves.

John was right. *We were all revenants.*

John gave the man who'd been holding the pruning shears a jab in the jaw that sent him spinning. Across the way, I heard Reed whoop admiringly. 'Dead boy can punch!'

John turned to give a little bow of acknowledgment in Reed's direction. Reed saluted, then sent the butt end of his harpoon gun into the sizable stomach of a nearby Fury.

I was still trying to puzzle out the intricacies of male camaraderie when I felt a hand on my arm and spun around, my whip flying, only to see Henry's face peering up at me.

'Miss,' he cried, ducking beneath my lash. 'It's only me, miss.'

'Henry,' I said, relieved. 'Don't do that. You shouldn't be here – it isn't safe.' My point was illustrated as my bicycle went flying past us both, hurled by an outraged Fury. 'What is it?'

'My slingshot,' he said. 'The one I made you. Do you still have it? You should use it. Put your diamond in it, and shoot it at them, and then once they're hit they won't be Furies any more.'

Again with the slingshot.

'Henry,' I said, pulling him to the side of a nearby crypt, out of the range of flying bicycles, since Mr Liu had picked up the shattered remains of mine, and was hurling it back at the original thrower. 'Your slingshot is in my tote bag, which I left over there—'

I pointed across the blossom-strewn path, to where Mr Smith was engaged in what looked like a fight to the death with my grandmother, something I'd only just noticed.

'Oh, no,' I said, my heart sinking.

'I'll get it,' Henry cried, misunderstanding my disappointment, and darted towards the bag.

'Henry, don't!' I raced to stop him, nearly colliding with a woman who seemed to come from out of nowhere, swinging a pickaxe at the little boy. I kneed her in the stomach, then struck her hard on the back of the neck with the butt of my whip. As I did so, the diamond at the end of my necklace brushed her skin. A puff of smoke trickled up from the small burn.

I didn't have time to stick around to watch what happened next. Mr Smith – and Henry – needed me.

Besides, no sooner had the woman collapsed than she was replaced by a man who came running up with a machete. They just kept coming, and coming, and coming. Every time one of us managed to disarm or knock a Fury down, another one seemed to rise up in his or her place, while, overhead, ravens screamed so raucously my ears had begun to ring.

Maybe we *were* revenants, I thought dimly. But this could be the day we all died, as my grandmother put it, 'for good'.

Considering her broken arm, she and Mr Smith were almost evenly matched, but she was still a Fury and so possessed inhuman strength. Also inhuman emotions.

'Sinners,' she hissed at Mr Smith as her hands closed around his throat. 'Abominators.'

Henry had landed, unscathed, beside my tote bag and was rooting through it.

'Hold on, miss,' he shouted at me. 'I've almost found it. You've got a lot of things in here.'

Mr Smith was incapable of making anything but a gurgling sound, but I believe he was saying something else. His eyes, behind his spectacles, which were askew, seemed to be saying, *Do it.*

I was happy to oblige.

I cracked my whip, sending it wrapping round my grandmother's throat multiple times, enfolding her as tightly as a warm, hand-knitted scarf . . . one that a loving grandmother might send to her granddaughter in the mail for her birthday. Then I yanked on it as hard as I could, so it was more like the grip of a boa constrictor than a muffler.

Grandma's hands instantly left Mr Smith's neck and flew to her own throat. Now she was the one who was gurgling.

I pulled even harder on the whip, bringing my grandmother to her knees, and went to crouch beside her.

'How do you like the scarf I made you, Grandma?' I hissed in her ear.

Her dead eyes rolled towards me, showing no sign of fear, only hatred and contempt. She was unable to speak, because she was unable to draw in air to breathe. I knew the sensation. It was the one I'd felt when I'd been sitting at the bottom of the pool, after I'd tripped over the scarf she'd made me and drowned.

'Pierce.' Mr Smith coughed out my name. He was finally able to speak. 'Don't.'

I barely heard him. All I could see was red, and all I could hear was the cawing of the ravens.

'So I'm an abomination, am I?' I whispered to Grandma. 'You did all this so I would destroy John, and the Underworld? Kind of like Eve in the Garden of Eden, huh?'

Grandma nodded, an evil smile spreading across her face, even as she gulped for air.

'Pierce, no,' Mr Smith said. 'You mustn't. I know it seems like it, but it isn't her. It's the demon inside her . . .'

Dimly I became aware of footsteps striding up behind

me. I heard Chloe's voice saying my name, then John calling, *Pierce. Pierce, don't.*

But I didn't release my grandmother. If anything, I held on to her more tightly.

'Well, nice try, Grandma,' I said, reaching out to hold her close to me, so close I could feel her pulse beating next to mine. 'You just made one mistake. I'm not Eve. I'm smarter than that. I'm the snake.'

Then I lifted the Persephone Diamond and crushed it to her heart.

'Thine arrogance, thou punished art the more;
Not any torment, saving thine own rage,
Would be unto thy fury pain complete.'
Dante Alighieri, *Inferno*, Canto XIV

I loosened the cord round my grandmother's neck. She slumped to the ground with a moan. A wisp of black smoke rose from her chest and drifted harmlessly into the air.

'Say goodnight, Grandma,' Reed said.

'She isn't dead,' Henry explained to him. 'That's how they get when they've had the evil driven from them.' He held out his slingshot, which he'd finally found at the bottom of my bag. 'But why didn't you use this? It would have been excellent if you'd hit her in the head at a distance with the diamond. Not the eye, of course, but maybe the centre of the forehead. That would smart.'

'You're a little boy who's been without a mother for far too long,' Chloe said in disapproval, still holding on to Typhon's collar as the dog drooled on my grandmother's *Cat Lover* sweatshirt. 'And, anyway, how's she supposed to get the diamond back afterwards?'

'Oh,' Henry said mournfully. 'I never thought of that.'

I looked down at the whip I'd unwound from my grandmother's neck. The answer had been staring at me all along. No wonder I'd felt such affinity for John's father's whip, even before Mr Liu had told me it was the string grounding me to earth.

'Are you all right?' John knelt beside me to ask, laying a strong arm across my shoulders.

'Better than I've been in a long time,' I said.

I'd slipped the chain that held my diamond from round my neck and was holding it in one hand, while holding the tip of his father's whip in the other.

'I hate to leave her like this,' John said, looking down at my grandmother, who seemed to be only half conscious. She was murmuring something about having to get back to the shop to do inventory. 'But we've got a lot more Furies to get rid of.'

'We're on it,' Reed said with a wicked grin, shouldering his harpoon gun. Chloe had to drag Typhon away, but he found plenty of sport chasing Furies through the cemetery. To him it seemed like a game – much as it did to Henry, who rushed off with his slingshot, with which he'd found many rocks to fill. The dog was so large and frightening-looking that many of the Furies simply dropped their weapons and ran off at the sight of him.

'We'll stay with her,' Mrs Engle volunteered, kneeling at my grandmother's side. 'Won't we, dear?'

She held out a hand for Mr Graves, who took it and knelt down beside her. 'We will,' he said. 'You lot go on. I know you have much to do.'

I was too busy with the task I was performing in my lap to realize at first what I'd seen. Then I lifted my head and said in disbelief, 'Mr Graves. You took Mrs Engle's hand. You *saw her hand.*'

John had risen to go back to the task of fighting Furies, as well. But he froze when he heard these words and spun round.

Mr Graves looked sheepish. 'Now, now,' he said, waving a hand dismissively. 'Don't get too excited. I've been seeing shadows for some time. I didn't want to tell you and get everyone too hopeful—'

'But that's amazing!' I exclaimed, jumping to my feet.

'They're only shadows,' he said. 'Maybe my sight will improve over time, maybe it won't.' Then he lifted his head to peer in my direction. 'But I will say you're quite a bit smaller than I thought you'd be, considering the volume of your voice. Wherever you were in the castle, I could always seem to hear you. It's remarkable. I thought you'd be a much larger girl.'

I wasn't certain this was a compliment.

My grandmother groaned and reached out to take Mr Smith's hand.

'Oh, dear,' he said. 'Perhaps I'd better stay, as well.'

I turned my disbelieving eyes to him. 'After what she did to Patrick?'

He looked uncomfortable. 'She wasn't herself. And I owe it to your grandfather. We were friends, and . . . I should have looked after her a little more closely after his death.' He squeezed my grandmother's hands. 'As a religious but not very intellectually curious woman, the discovery that there exists a world beyond ours that isn't the traditionally taught heaven and hell must have been deeply disturbing to her. Of course, to her, that world would have seemed very threatening, and so that world would have needed destroying, along with John. Oh, she's waking up. How are you, Mrs Cabrero?'

My grandmother blinked at him and said vaguely, 'What? Oh, hello, Richard. How are you today?' like they'd run into one another at the grocery store. Her gaze flicked right past Mr Graves and Mrs Engle, since she didn't know them, but when she noticed John and me her mouth flattened into a thin line of disapproval.

'You two,' she said. She looked – and sounded – angry, but more like a prissy grandmother than someone possessed by an evil spirit. 'When I get you home, young lady, we are going to have a thing or two to discuss with your mother. Having boys over all night long! I never heard of such thing. Why, in my day—'

I glanced at John in alarm. His eyes were wide.

'Hmmm,' Mr Smith said, gently setting down my grandmother's hand and giving her shoulder a pat. 'I see that without a demon controlling her mind, Mrs Cabrero's reverted back to her, er, more conservative, religious roots. Perhaps taunting her about your sexual relationship with John wasn't the best way to handle that situation earlier.'

'You did *what*?' John had stood to hit a Fury who'd come storming up. He was way more shocked over what Mr Smith had said than the fact that the Fury had been carrying a pitchfork.

'I didn't know she was there!' I protested.

'Oh, dear,' Mrs Engle said, and turned pink. Mr Graves

put his arm round her and looked rightfully outraged.

'I suppose your mother will think it's all right,' Grandma went on in a critical tone. 'She's always had modern ideas. But this is a small town, and people talk. I won't have my only granddaughter behaving like a slattern.'

'I won't have her behaving like a slattern, either, Mrs Cabrero,' John said earnestly. 'I keep asking her to marry me, but she won't.'

'*John*,' I cried. Now I was the one who was outraged.

'Well, that's more like it,' my grandmother said, seeming pleased. 'A young man with proper Christian morals, in this day and age? That's what I like to see. Though he'll have to get a haircut, Pierce, whoever he is. He looks like one of those dirty hippies that ride their motorcycles around downtown, making all that racket.'

'Oh, my *God*, no,' I said with a groan, as John looked confused and asked, 'What's a hippie?'

With all this drama, it was almost easy to forget there was a Fury war going on . . . at least until Kayla walked up to us, dragging behind her the shovel Mike had dropped.

'Here,' she said, handing it unceremoniously to Mr Smith. 'You're an undertaker, right? You should be good with this.'

'Cemetery sexton,' Mr Smith said, looking nervous. 'I'm a cemetery sexton, actually. Undertakers and cemetery sextons are two different things.'

'Whatever,' Kayla said. She had a dazed look on her face. 'Start digging.'

'And, uh, why should I do that?' Mr Smith asked.

'Because I'm about to murder someone, so we're gonna need a grave.'

She walked over to Mike's prone body, then raised the knife I'd confiscated from my grandmother, ready to plunge it into the back of the handyman's neck.

'He killed Frank,' Kayla said simply. 'He should pay.'

The knife was on a downward swing when I went rushing towards her, crying, 'Kayla, no!'

It was John who stopped her. He flung an arm round her waist and swung her bodily off her feet, pulling her from Mike's side and startling her so badly she screamed and dropped the knife. It fell to the ground below, landing in the poincianas that lay in such a thick cushion that the metal blade didn't even make a sound against the paved path.

'Kayla,' John said, keeping a gentle but restraining hold on her as she struggled to escape him and retrieve the knife. 'I understand how you feel, but that's not the way.'

'Why not?' Kayla asked, looking furious as she squirmed in his grip. 'Frank's dead. He killed him.'

John's face went slack with shock at the news.

I thought he'd known, but it was clear from his expression that he hadn't. Kayla's words seemed to have been almost a physical blow to him. Unfortunately, much as I wanted to put my arms around him to comfort him in his grief, this was not the time for that.

'We'll fix it,' John said to Kayla, taking her by both arms and giving her a little shake, since holding her had done no good. His heartache and desperation were obvious both in his tone and the tightness of his grip on her. 'I swear, Kayla. I'll find a way to fix it.'

'John.' I laid a hand upon his shoulder. I didn't want him to make promises he couldn't keep, especially not to someone I cared about as much as Kayla. 'I killed Thanatos. Remember?'

John's gaze met mine and held it. Around us was chaos – the shrieking of the increasingly agitated birds overhead, coupled with the shrieks of the Furies as they battled, Typhon's ferocious barking, the mad whinnies of Alastor, the rushing of the steadily growing wind in the few palm fronds that remained in the trees and Kayla's sobs.

But there was a stillness within John and myself that, now that we were truly back together, no amount of external mayhem could disturb.

I love you. I love you. I love you.

There was no need to say it out loud any more. We could read it in each other's tear-filled eyes.

'*We'll* find a way to fix it,' he said, correcting himself as he looked back down at Kayla. 'I swear we will.'

The fight had gone out of Kayla. She was staring down at her feet, her riotous mane of multicoloured curls falling over her face. 'I don't know how you're going to do it and have him be . . . the same.'

'We'll find a way,' John assured her. 'Kayla, you have to believe me. But killing this piece of trash . . . that isn't going to help anything.'

They were so intent on their discussion neither of them saw the piece of trash they were discussing sit up and look around, notice the knife lying next him, then reach for it.

But I did.

'Not this time,' I said, and struck Mike in the chest with the tip of my whip.

Mike cursed and dropped the knife to clutch his heart with both hands. His face twisted in pain as smoke began to pour from his chest.

John and Kayla stared down at Mike as he lay curled at their feet, moaning. John knelt to lift up the knife.

'What did you do?' he asked me in wonder.

I'd jerked the end of my whip back to me. Now I held it up so the sunlight caught the winking, shining object on its tip: the Persephone Diamond John had given me.

'This works much better,' I said. Then I noticed another Fury behind them. 'Hold still.'

Crack. The Fury, who appeared to be around our own age, dropped the switchblade he'd been holding and ran away, grabbing his arm, from which a thin trickle of black smoke began to stream.

John turned to grin at me. 'Well done.'

'It was Henry's idea, really,' I said. 'I modified it a little. I can't take all the credit.'

John glanced around at all the many Furies who were still roaming the cemetery. I could practically see the plan forming in his head. 'We'll be able to reach more of them more quickly on horseback.'

I wasn't sure I liked this plan. Alastor and I had formed a détente, but it was still an uneasy one, based mainly on mutual sadness over John's death. Now John was alive and well. I swallowed.

'Great idea,' I lied.

John whistled, and Alastor came thundering up, a Fury clutched in his jaws by the neck of his shirt. John shook his head in disapproval, and the horse reluctantly dropped the man, who fell panting in front of the massive silver hooves. I quickly flicked him with the end of my whip, and he cried out in pain, rolling into a ball, though the diamond had barely scratched him. A puff of smoke floated into the air from the back of the man's head. Alastor whinnied approvingly, enjoying the sight of another's pain. That's the kind of horse he was.

'Nicely done,' John said admiringly to me.

'It was nothing,' I said.

'Mr Liu?' John called.

The gentle giant came lumbering forward, dragging two Furies by their heads. 'Yes?'

John handed a still-shaken Kayla over to Mr Liu while I quickly touched the tip of my whip to his two captives. 'We're going to put an end to this. Would you look out for her?'

Mr Liu dropped his dazed Fury friends and nodded at Kayla, his expression, as always, implacable. 'My pleasure.'

Kayla looked up at him with tear-swollen eyes. 'Let's go kill someone.'

'Kill?' Mr Liu shook his head. 'Maim is better.'

Kayla shrugged. 'OK.'

John mounted Alastor, then reached a hand down from the saddle. 'Step on my boot,' he said as I grasped his fingers, 'and swing yourself up . . .'

I gave Alastor the evil eye, which he returned, but he allowed me to swing myself up into the saddle in front of John . . . undoubtedly because John was right there, watching.

If I'd known I'd be riding a death lord's horse around the Isla Huesos Cemetery, swinging a whip at people possessed by Furies, I probably wouldn't have chosen to wear a dress. But things never seemed to work out as I planned.

I'm not going to lie and say there weren't parts of it that were fun. It was hard work and required a lot of concentration. Swinging a whip from the back of a moving animal isn't as easy as they make it look in Westerns. But I wasn't trying to rope cattle – all I was trying to do was touch Furies . . . who, granted, made pretty challenging targets, since they were running away from a thundering hell horse. Several times I missed when they dodged and was certain I got them in the face. Not that I didn't think they deserved it, but I had to keep in mind what Mr Smith kept saying, that they were humans possessed by demons and didn't know what they were doing.

Maybe.

Reed and Chloe and the others soon caught on, and then it was a matter of them herding the Furies into areas where Alastor could reach them. And all I had to do was flick them.

'You know, Pierce,' John said in my ear, his arm tight around my waist as we chased down a woman in an Outback Steakhouse uniform who was running from us without fear, her gaze as dead-eyed and glazed as every Fury before her, 'I think we're winning.'

'Against the human Furies, maybe,' I said. I caught the woman, sending her sprawling, moaning, into a pile of decorative funeral wreaths, smoke funnelling up from her right shoulder. 'But not *them*.'

I raised my gaze. The ravens were still gathered overhead, squawking angrily.

'Wait,' John said, pulling Alastor to a stop. 'Look. Do you see that?'

'What?' I shaded my eyes with one hand and looked.

At first I didn't see anything. The sun was so bright, and the sky so achingly blue it was difficult to see anything but the black vees the ravens made against it. But then I saw what John was talking about. A flash of white, fluttering amidst the black specks.

'John,' I said, sinking my fingers into his arm. 'Is that . . .'

A fat mourning dove, pure white except for a few inky black feather tips on her wings and tail, suddenly swooped down to land between Alastor's ears. The horse, startled, reared up a little, snorting.

'Hope!' I cried, reaching for her. The bird allowed me to snuggle her against my cheek, cooing happily. 'Oh, Hope, where have you been?'

Hope only cooed some more, rubbing her face against mine, then began to search my hair, obviously looking for food.

'I don't know where she's been,' John said. 'But, wherever it is, she found some friends.'

He pointed upwards. There were now white vees visible

311

amongst the black ones. First only a few, then more white birds than black ones, and the white ones seemed to be *battling* the black ones. The ravens, under attack by a larger and superior force, quickly gave up, disappearing from the sky at a rapid rate.

Only the white birds weren't completely white, I noticed, when one swooped close enough for me to get a better look at it. They were —

'Pigeons!' I cried in surprise.

'Mourning doves,' John corrected me. 'I told you. Hope's a mourning dove. They vary in coloration.'

The one that had swooped close to me was much larger than Hope, and grey . . . as silver-grey as my diamond when there weren't any Furies around. As silver as John's eyes. It was black, however, on its wingtips and tail. It landed, exactly as Hope had, between Alastor's ears, but since it weighed so much more than Hope, its landing was nowhere near as graceful.

Alastor gave an angry whinny and shook his head, attempting to fling the bird from it, but the mourning dove was determined to cling to its roost and hung on, cooing loudly, in what I considered a decidedly masculine manner.

'Hope,' I cried. 'Is that your husband? Is that where you were this whole time? Did you fly off to find your family and then bring them home to help us fight those nasty ravens?'

'OK,' John said, his grip tightening on me. 'Now you're talking to the birds. I think you've killed enough Furies for one day. Let's go round up the others and head home—'

'Of course I talk to Hope,' I said. 'You talk to Alastor. And why wouldn't that be Hope's husband? You're the one who told me mourning doves mate for life. I think we should name him. What do you think would be a good name for—?'

'Excuse me,' said a deep, masculine voice behind us. 'But would you two mind getting down off that horse? We'd like to have a word with you if we may.'

I turned my head and looked down. It was Chief of Police Santos. Standing next to him was my father and my cousin Alex.

And, he to me: 'Thou'lt mark, when they shall be
Nearer to us; and then do thou implore them
By love which leadeth them, and they will come.'
Dante Alighieri, *Inferno*, Canto V

'Patrick Reynolds,' Chief of Police Santos said, looking at the notepad he'd drawn from his belt. 'Says here he's in stable condition after surgery for blunt-force trauma to the head. Neighbour found him and called an ambulance.'

Mr Smith buried his face in his hands. 'Oh, thank God.'

I laid a hand on Mr Smith's back. We were all gathered on the front porch of the cemetery sexton's office. Even though the roof of the back of the cottage had been smashed in by the Spanish lime tree, the front of the house seemed sturdy enough, and the porch offered a rare bit of shade. Though it was late afternoon, the sun was still beating down like it was . . . well, an island in the subtropics.

'It was Mike,' Kayla said, her voice as cold as the bottle of water we'd each been handed by one of the emergency medical services technicians who'd shown up shortly after Chief Santos and his officers. 'Mike did it.'

Chief Santos didn't have to check his notepad. 'I got that, young lady,' he said. 'The last five times you said it.'

'I just want to make sure.'

Kayla hadn't said anything about Mike having killed Frank, because John had assured her that he was going to

314

'fix' Frank. Mr Liu had hidden Frank's body in John's crypt so the police wouldn't find it. We'd all agreed privately that it was better not to admit to Kayla that John had no idea how he was going to 'fix' Frank.

The thought of Frank lying dead in that cold, dank crypt made me shudder. I could only imagine how it made Kayla feel.

'His prints are all over Mr Smith's house,' Chief Santos said. 'We have them on file from a B and E he committed a few years back. Mike actually has quite an extensive record.'

'I thought he was doing better,' Mr Smith said mournfully.

Chief Santos made a sarcastic sound, like a hard-bitten cop who didn't have much faith left in humanity. Of course, he didn't know the island he worked on had literally been overrun by demons from hell, though he might have wondered about the odd migratory patterns of the birds here.

'You might want to see if his DNA matches up to any found at the scene of Jade Ortega's murder,' I said. 'Also Officer Poling's.'

Chief Santos sent me a sharp look. 'What do *you* know about Officer Poling?'

'My daughter's not going to offer up any more information,' my dad said casually, from the porch railing against which he was leaning, 'without a lawyer present.'

'A lawyer shouldn't be necessary,' Chief Santos said with practiced ease, turning a page in his notepad. 'She isn't being charged with anything. I'm just curious. Officer Poling is dead.'

My eyes widened. 'He *is*? What happened?'

'He drew his weapon on a civilian,' Chief Santos said. He kept his gaze on his own handwriting. 'We were forced to fire.'

Now I knew why it had taken the police so long to get to the cemetery. It hadn't just been the tree that had been blocking the road.

'Was the civilian the man with the chain saw?' I asked worriedly, though I was fairly certain I knew the answer. 'Was he hurt?'

'Yes, he did have a saw and, no, he was unharmed,' the chief said, looking up at me. 'Why? Did you know him?'

I shook my head. John, seeing my discomfit, put his arm round me, and Hope, still sitting perched on my shoulder, trilled a few notes. Her mate, perched in the rafters of the porch, trilled back.

Why had the man with the chain saw, I wondered yet again, risked his life to save me, a total stranger? None of it made any sense.

'What kind of dog did you say that was again?' Chief Santos said, pointing at Typhon, who lay in the dirt at the bottom of the porch steps, panting heavily, though he'd been offered a large bowl of water by the EMTs.

'He's a bullmastiff,' Mrs Engle said cheerfully as Chloe gave the dog a pat on the head, which he showed his appreciation for by licking her on the leg.

Chief Santos eyed the dog sceptically. 'Yeah,' he said. 'I've seen those kinds of dogs before, and they didn't look like that. I've seen you before, too,' he added, jabbing his pen in Chloe's direction. 'You look a lot like that girl that's been all over the news, the homeschooled, Christian one from Homestead, who they say gut shot her father because he was physically abusing her mom.'

I stared at Chloe in horror, remembering the man in khaki pants with the huge bloodstain on the front of his shirt, the one who'd kept insisting he was in the wrong line – the one to hell – and that he knew Chloe.

He *had* known Chloe. She was the one who'd put him in that line.

'Oh,' Chloe said to Chief Santos, a dazzling smile on her face. 'That couldn't be me. That girl died in the storm in a horrible car accident.'

'Yeah,' Chief Santos said, lowering his pen. 'I heard that.'

I noticed the shards of glass were gone from Chloe's hair, and she'd washed away the blood, too.

'Oh, the poor dear,' Mrs Engle said, laying a hand on Mr Graves's shoulder. 'How perfectly awful for that girl.'

'Sounds like a bad situation all around,' Mr Graves agreed.

'But I'm happy that her mom is finally free,' Chloe said.

'I'm happy for that girl's mom, too,' Reed said, reaching out to take Chloe's hand.

On my shoulder, Hope cooed happily, but I was thinking of a different girl, the one from my mom's neighbourhood who'd worn the *Daddy's Little Princess* T-shirt. I wondered what had happened to her. I looked around for Alex in order to ask him. He had been with my father and the chief of police earlier, but now he seemed to have disappeared.

'What are *you* two supposed to be?' Chief Santos demanded, his gaze falling on Mr Liu and Henry, Mr Liu in his leather and tattoos, and Henry in his silver-buckled shoes and long, nineteenth-century jacket.

On cue, Henry flung his arms around Mr Liu and began to weep crocodile tears. 'Daddy,' he cried. 'Don't let the policeman take me away!'

Mr Liu laid a massive hand upon Henry's head and patted his not-particularly clean hair. 'He's adopted,' he said to Chief Santos in his usual laconic fashion.

'I see,' Chief of Police Santos said, not falling for the act for a second. 'OK. Here's the situation. I got a problem with all of this. And all of you, too.' He made a circle in the air with his pen that seemed to incorporate the whole of the cemetery and everyone sitting on the porch, as well.

All except for Alex, I noticed, who was still gone. I hoped he wasn't off sulking somewhere over Reed and Chloe clearly being together now.

'My people and I come in here because we hear screaming and we understand from you, Mr Oliviera, that your daughter is in danger, and what do we find?' Chief Santos went on. 'We find your daughter on a horse with the boy who just yesterday you were insisting had kidnapped her, but now we discover you're dropping that charge—'

'It was all a misunderstanding,' Dad said with a smile and a wave of his hand. 'Love the boy like a son.'

John and my father exchanged smiles that wouldn't have persuaded even the newest rookie on the force that they cared for each other. I knew they were only making a go of it for my sake. Chief Santos looked completely unconvinced but continued.

'And we find folks on the ground all over the place with superficial wounds – some way more serious than that – and no memory whatsoever of what they were doing in the cemetery in the first place.'

'Well, *I* can tell you that,' Mr Smith said. 'They were here cleaning up after the storm, doing a lovely and much-needed job of keeping our cemetery looking well tended, when the sun became too much for them, and they simply succumbed to heatstroke.'

'That,' Chief Santos said, looking the cemetery sexton dead in the eye, 'is a load of bull, and you know it. Heatstroke? Fifty to sixty people? All in the course of a few hours? Some of those people have concussions. Some of them are suffering from blunt-force head trauma. Some of them have dog bites. Two of them have *horse* bites. A couple of them were bitten by humans. *All* of them have small, oddly shaped burn wounds that are reminiscent of one that a female officer of mine received a few nights ago at Coffin Fest. Now, I want the truth. None of these people is what I would call an upstanding citizen – begging your pardon, Mr Oliviera, since I know one of them is your mother-in-law. But with the exception of that scumbag, Mike, none of them is a murder suspect, either. So I want you to be straight with me. What happened here?'

Mr Smith folded his hands in a position I recognized. He was about to give a lecture.

'I'll tell you what happened, Chief Santos,' the cemetery

sexton said. 'What happened today was a victory of the Fates over the Furies.'

'*What?*' Chief Santos said.

I wasn't sure I understood, either.

'It's very simple,' Mr Smith said. 'In everyday life, we're given a choice. Do the right thing, do nothing or do the wrong thing. All too often, people choose to do nothing. And that's all right. It's easier. Sometimes it's difficult to know what's right and what's wrong. But every so often a few people choose to go out of their way to do the right thing . . . like your gentleman with the chain saw, Pierce.'

I felt as if a burden had been lifted from my heart. Suddenly, I understood.

'He was a Fate,' I said. 'All those people trying to help me today . . . the man with the chain saw, the woman at the gate – even the little girl. They were Fates.'

'Yes,' Mr Smith said. 'Exactly. Fates are anyone who chooses to be on the side of good. If enough people go out of their way to help someone else, the spirit of kindness eventually breaks through the darkness, the way sunshine breaks through clouds after a storm and allows even more kind acts to follow. My hope has always been that some day kindness will prevail, and there won't be any Furies for us to fight.'

John stared at Mr Smith in disbelief, looking, in his own way, as jaded as Chief Santos. These two had more in common than either of them probably knew, each having seen his fair share of hardship; John having lived it, and Chief Santos having arrested it.

'I hope that, too,' I said, because I wanted to believe in Mr Smith's version of the Fates, whether or not it was true.

Chloe sighed happily, dropping her head to Reed's shoulder. 'Me, too. That story reminds me of angels. I wish he'd tell it again.'

'Do *not* tell it again,' Chief Santos said testily. 'Something went on today in this cemetery. Something goes on in this cemetery all the time, doesn't it? Not only during Coffin Week, but all the time. It doesn't matter if we keep the gates locked; something's always going on in here. Something no one ever talks about. Something's wrong with this *island*, and no one will tell me what it is. Well, I'm going to tell you people, whatever it is' – he jabbed his finger at the ground for emphasis – 'it stops right *here*.'

'Chief Santos.' My father rose from the porch railing, his cellphone in his hand. 'I've got my wife on the line. She wants to speak to you.'

I'm sure I was the only one who noticed he said *wife* and not *ex-wife*, and the only one whose heart gave a happy flip over it.

Chief Santos looked at my father as if he were crazy. '*What?*'

'My wife,' Dad said, holding his phone towards the police chief. 'She has something she wants to tell you. It's about what's wrong with this island. It has to do with Nate Rector and the luxury homes he's building out at Reef Key. Something to do with some bones.'

I sucked in my breath and looked around for Alex. But Alex was still nowhere to be seen.

'Bones?' Chief Santos was beginning to look like he was developing an ulcer. 'Could you please tell your wife I'll call her back? I don't have time to talk about bones right now.'

'Actually, Chief,' my father said in a voice as cold as ice, 'I think you do. My wife is an expert. She has a PhD' – if he said *wife* again, I was pretty sure my heart was going to fly out of my chest and flutter up to sit next to Hope's husband – 'and knows some pretty important people. They're flying down from the Smithsonian up in Washington, DC, to look at these bones. I guess they're pretty old, and Nate Rector's built his houses right on top of them, and the people in Washington are pretty ticked off—'

Chief Santos took the phone from my dad, holding it as if he expected it to give him an electric shock.

'Sure,' he said. 'I'll be happy to take the call.' His expression said he'd be anything but.

He began following my dad from the porch as they walked to Chief Santos's car. The last thing Chief Santos said, before raising the phone to his ear, was to John.

'You.' He pointed from John to Alastor, whose reins had been tied to the porch railing. 'It's a violation to keep or ride a horse within city limits, unless of course you're an officer with the mounted police unit.' He glared at John. 'Which you ain't, kid.'

John nodded. 'I know, sir. It will never happen again.'

'It better not,' he said. Then he lifted the phone to his ear. 'Dr Cabrero? Hello, yes, it's me, Chief Santos. Yes, I was just with your daughter. She's fine. Your mother? Well, ma'am, she was taken to the hospital for observation, along with a few dozen other people. No, no, she's going to be fine, superficial injuries to her throat, broken arm, burn mark, seemed a bit disoriented. Well, best I can figure out, ma'am, it's all from' – he turned as he approached the cemetery gates to shoot Mr Smith a murderous look – 'heatstroke. Now what's this your husband is telling me about some bones? Is that so? I'll be very interested to speak to Mr Rector about that. Tell you what, we'll swing by his house and pick him up right now.'

As soon as he was out of earshot, Chloe exploded with laughter.

'Oh, my goodness,' she said. 'I was sure I was caught that time!'

'You *murdered your dad*?' Kayla said. She'd been silent almost the entire time on the porch . . . understandably. The Fates may have won this round, but it was hard to call it winning when we'd lost Frank, though none of us as yet had had the courage to admit this to Kayla. Perhaps, in a way, she was beginning to sense it.

Chloe's laughter quickly died. 'I know it's a sin,' she said. 'The Bible says he who strikes his father or mother shall surely be put to death. But I *did* die because of what I did. So maybe someday the Lord will forgive me.'

Kayla and I exchanged glances. I supposed this logic made a certain sense to Chloe, although I didn't think it was fair for her to have died for defending her mother.

'I thought you'd been waiting your whole life to go to heaven,' I said to her gently.

'How are you so sure this isn't heaven?' Chloe said, looking very serious.

'Because innocent people like Frank get killed here,' Kayla said. 'I highly doubt that happens in heaven.'

I nodded. 'Seriously,' I said. I didn't want to cause Chloe to second-guess her decision, especially since there was nothing she could do about it now, but I wanted her to understand the consequences . . . which made me feel a bit like John. 'The Underworld is not heaven.'

'I know that,' Chloe said. 'But maybe I feel the way that old man said . . . like I want to do things to help people. I don't think you get to do that in heaven.'

'Old man?' Mr Smith was on his phone, presumably with the hospital, checking on Patrick, but he paused his call to cast a scandalized glance at Chloe. 'Did that young woman just call me an old man?'

'Oh, no. She was talking about Mr Graves,' I lied to him.

He nodded and returned to his phone call, though I wasn't certain he believed me.

'In the Underworld, I'll get to help people, and to me that seems like heaven,' Chloe was going on, oblivious.

Kayla stared at her. 'You know,' she said. 'I kind of get what she's saying. Only I want to help people have better hair.'

'Well,' I said to Chloe. 'Great. Because the Underworld is where you're going to have to live now. It's where we all live now, at least seventy per cent of the time.'

'One hundred per cent of the time,' John said.

'There are so many of us now,' I said. 'I was thinking we

324

could probably time-share all the soul-sorting down there.'

'I don't know what time-share means,' John said.

'A time-share in the Isla Huesos Underworld,' Reed said. 'That sounds like heaven to me. "The parched ground shall become a pool,"' Reed quoted, '"and the thirsty land springs of water: in the habitation of jackals, where each lay, shall be grass with *reeds* and rushes."'

Mrs Engle, impressed, began to applaud. 'Oh, lovely,' she said. 'And very apt. Isaiah?'

'Exactly,' Reed said, and winked. Chloe sighed again and clung to his arm. To me, he mouthed over her head, 'My dad's a pastor.'

I rolled my eyes, realizing Alex had never stood a chance with Chloe.

Funny how, as I was thinking this, I heard Alex call my name and turned to see him walking up to the porch.

'Where's Kayla?' he asked.

'She's right here,' I said. Kayla, who'd been sitting beside me, stood up. 'Where have you been all this time?'

'Busy,' Alex said. He jerked a thumb over his shoulder. 'Got a package for her.'

Frank was walking behind Alex, looking unhappy as he brushed the dust from his trousers.

'Does anyone have a drink?' he asked. 'Dying's thirsty business.'

O joy! O gladness inexpressible!
O perfect life of love and peacefulness!
Dante Alighieri, *Paradiso*, Canto XXVII

Anything can happen in the blink of an eye.

One. Two. Three.

Blink.

A girl meets a boy, full of sadness and longing. The boy takes that girl to another world, a dark world from which he tells the girl there is no escape.

You don't have to worry about that girl, though, because she knows there *is* a way to escape, a way to break the curse, let sunlight into the world . . .

. . . or at least let the boy out for a vacation every now and then.

Mr Graves had been right. There *was* a pestilence causing an imbalance in the Underworld. What he'd been wrong about was the cause. He'd suspected the pestilence was caused by John or one of the permanent inhabitants spending too much time away from the realm of the dead.

And while certainly the Underworld could not function smoothly without anyone to attend to the needs of the dead, leaving it for too long was not the cause of the imbalance.

The cause of the imbalance was Alex. None of us realized it – least of all Alex – until I released Thanatos from his prison inside Seth Rector's body, and he found a new home inside Alex.

'He really seems to like me,' Alex informed us cheerfully, as we watched Kayla's tearful reunion with Frank in front of Mr Smith's cottage. 'Watch what I can do now.'

Alex picked up a coconut and kicked it. It disappeared, seemingly into the stratosphere. If Alex had any interest in continuing high school – which he did not – he would now have been extremely welcome on the Isla Huesos football team, instead of an object of ridicule to them.

'I can do that,' John said, unimpressed.

'Well,' Alex said. 'I could kill you with a single touch. Should I do that, instead?'

'Please don't,' I said, wrapping hands protectively round John's arm.

'And how did you discover that you had this remarkable grasp over life and death?' Mr Graves asked.

'Well,' Alex said. 'After I got that little girl back to her mom – who thanked me profusely, by the way – and was following all the cops who were tailing Pierce on her bike, I saw them stop, because that crazy cop had pulled out his gun and was going to shoot this guy with a chain saw. And I felt this crazy urge come over me to go over and yank out the cop's soul. I honestly can't explain it any other way.' He took a swig from the water bottle he held. 'So I did it.'

'You yanked a man's soul from his body?' I asked slowly.

'Yeah,' Alex said with a shrug. 'It was easy. That's when I knew I had that death dude living inside me. And, honestly, you guys, I've never felt better in my life.'

I think all of us were astonished except for Chloe, who said, 'Well, it makes sense. After all, your name does mean protector of men. And who is a greater protector of men than someone who brings them the sweet relief of death?'

Frank and John and Mr Liu and I all gave her sour looks, and Chloe hastily added, 'Except of course someone who escorts their souls to their final resting place. That's a really important job, too. And obviously anyone who dies before their time won't consider you very protective, Alex.'

'Yeah,' Alex said with a nod. 'I'm going to have to work on that. But I think it's a handy skill to have, you know, in emergencies. I really can't believe Thanatos spent so long in Seth's body. I think even *he* thought Seth was a drag. But it was a Rector tradition to have Thanatos dwelling within the youngest male, so—'

My eyes widened. 'So the Rectors knew?'

'They had to have,' Alex said with another shrug. 'How else do you explain that hideous mausoleum and the statue of Hades and Persephone?'

'Extremely poor taste?' Kayla suggested.

'No,' I said, shaking my head as I thought of Seth's shirts. 'It was more than that. They knew *something*. They were proud of it. But they didn't understand who Thanatos was, exactly. And they couldn't control him. That's what led to their downfall.'

'Exactly,' Alex said. 'I think Thanatos really appreciated it when you released him, Pierce . . . you know, *later*, after he thought about it. Being a Rector wasn't good for him. It put him in a bad mood. That's why he chose me.

I'm a lot more easygoing than Seth.'

'And more modest,' I pointed out wryly. 'So where is Officer Poling's soul now?'

'Oh,' Alex said with a shrug. 'He's down in the Underworld. He's your responsibility now. I don't want anything to do with him. That guy's a real douche, even without the Fury in him. You know he killed Jade, right? He and that Mike guy mistook her for you, Pierce. I choked the truth out of him – his soul, I mean. I even got him to cough up where he hid the murder weapon. It's a wrench, part of a set Mike owns.'

'You mean the cemetery owns,' Mr Smith piped up. 'Mike keeps his tools in the shed behind my office.'

'Poling said Mike threw the wrench into the harbour.'

'If I report it missing,' Mr Smith said, 'and suggest the police question Mike again, I'm sure it won't be long before he strikes some kind of deal.'

Alex looked relieved. 'That will clear my dad, then. Anyway, after I figured out I'm Thanatos, and then I dealt with your dad and the cops and stuff, and I heard Frank was dead, I just went over to the crypt and revived him. It seemed kind of natural, in a way, like I always knew how to do it . . . or was destined to do it, or something.'

I knew what he meant. It was the way I'd felt when I'd finally realized how the Persephone necklace and the whip Mr Liu had given me fitted together. As if I'd found my place in the world at last, and what I was destined to do, odd as it sounded.

Alex looked around. 'Is there anything to eat? I'm *starving.*'

Mr Smith was right. We do need storms sometimes, because they clear away the bracken so that the sun can shine on flowers that might never otherwise have had a chance to bloom.

Chief of Police Santos did eventually arrest Mike both for the murder of Jade Ortega and the attempted murder of Patrick Reynolds. After the missing wrench was dredged from the bottom of the harbour, Mike struck a plea bargain and took a sentence of life in prison in order to avoid the death penalty. All charges against Uncle Chris were dropped.

Seth Rector, who'd successfully murdered Alex, was a little more fortunate. There was no proof he'd murdered Alex, since there was no body . . . Alex was still alive. So Seth couldn't be prosecuted for *that* crime.

Oddly enough, however, Chief of Police Santos happened to find more than a dozen gold doubloons dating back to the seventeen hundreds (and worth more than ten thousand dollars each) in a black velvet bag in Seth's locker during a random locker sweep at Isla Huesos High School one afternoon.

Seth, completely shocked, claimed he'd never seen the coins before and had no idea where they'd come from. As he was led down the breezeway in handcuffs, he saw John Hayden leaning casually against one of the outdoor cafeteria tables, his arms folded across his chest. As Seth passed by, John narrowed his eyes at him, then wagged a single index finger. *Shame on you.*

Seth began to shout that he'd been 'set up by Pierce Oliviera and that freak boyfriend of hers'.

Chief Santos advised Seth to save it for his father's lawyers.

Mr Rector's lawyers, however, were quite busy, as Nate Rector was facing prosecution for numerous felonies, including wilful and wanton destruction of a known indigenous burial site, improper disposal of human remains, desecration of a cemetery, disturbance of a historically significant archaeological discovery and wilfully misleading the Reef Key Luxury Resort investors through purposeful obfuscation, lack of disclosure and lack of fiduciary responsibility.

Which meant that not only were the Rectors broke, but Reef Key was also very likely going to be reverted back to the roseate spoonbill sanctuary and mangrove habitat my mother had always remembered so fondly.

Since Mr Rector had misled not simply his investors, but also his business partner, Farah's father, Mr Endicott was spared the many charges against the Reef Key developers. This was good, since I'd grown fond of Farah. After Kayla returned to school, she reported that Farah continued to be friendly, no longer hanging out with Serena and Nicole and the Rector Wreckers (which more or less fell apart as a group after Seth went to jail for felony theft, anyway). Farah ate lunch every day with Kayla – who was determined to graduate a semester early and get her cosmetology degree, in order to open Save Yourselves – and had decided the local community college might not be so bad after all. It turned out Bryce was going to go there, and Bryce's father owned most of the bars downtown, as well as a private plane.

'I can go to Miami whenever I want to go shopping,'

Farah said. 'Bryce has his own platinum American Express card. Seth didn't even have that.'

I was pleased to hear that things were turning out so well. Maybe Mr Smith was right . . . not just about storms sometimes being a good thing, but about Fates really being small acts of kindness by random people. Certainly that seemed to have improved the quality of life in the Underworld.

Being John's consort – and cousin to the personification of death – had its challenges. People can be resistant to change, even positive change. I could understand that when you've spent more than a century and a half living in an underground castle sorting dead people on to boats all day, spending a few months or weeks or even days above ground with live people could be a scary concept.

When you're a flower that's suddenly had all its protective bracken swept away, facing the sunshine for the first time could be frightening.

Maybe that's why – after things had settled down and it became clear that, while we'd never be *entirely* free of the threat of a Fury attack, we might not be in *imminent* danger of one – when I suggested the idea of going on a vacation to John, he completely freaked out.

I explained to John about work sharing and how vital it can be to a successful and happy place of employment, and how much healthier everyone would be – and how much better they would get along – if we took a day off from the Underworld *every once in a while*. Frank was always asking for time off to meet Kayla for dinner – and sometimes even entire weekends – in Isla Huesos, and John was happy to allow it. Why couldn't we do the same?

'It's different,' John said.

'Why?' I asked.

'Because of your grandmother.'

I was ready for this argument.

'You know my dad won't allow her in the house because of what she did,' I said, 'even though she doesn't remember it. And Mom won't have anything to do with her, either. It turns out Grandma's personality without a Fury possessing her isn't that great. All she wants to do is go to church and criticize people. I have no idea why my grandfather married her,' I added with a sigh, 'except that she must have been pretty, once.'

'She's weak-minded and negative,' John said. 'That's why it was so easy for a Fury to possess her. And also why there's no reason a Fury wouldn't be able to take possession of her again. And your uncle, who doesn't know about any of this, still lives with her.'

'Not for long,' I said defensively. 'Uncle Chris is moving out.'

'He is?'

'Yes, he is, remember, I told you? My dad bought him that boat, and he started a fishing charter business, and now he's saved up all that money and he's getting his own place, since he can't stand Grandma, either. Also because Alex went to boarding school—'

The excuse Alex gave to his father for why he wasn't living at home any more was that he'd got a scholarship to a very prestigious boarding school . . . the same boarding school in Switzerland, in fact, that my dad had always been threatening to ship me off to.

Alex now saw his father only when he came home from 'boarding school' during holidays and breaks. But when he did, they spent almost the entire time working together on Uncle Chris's boat. I'd never seen the two of them happier.

My father was only too pleased to facilitate Alex's lie. He'd found the entire adventure with John – teleporting to get the boats, visiting the Underworld, even discovering that his daughter had a boyfriend with supernatural powers – extremely exciting.

The only problem was, now every time he saw John, Dad wanted to be teleported somewhere, such as Paris, even just for a few seconds, as a joke. He didn't understand why John wouldn't participate with him in a joint-teleporting – or corpse-reviving – venture.

'Even if you only revived people's dead pets,' he'd insist, 'we could make billions.'

This might perhaps have been another reason John wasn't particularly eager to leave the Underworld often, especially to visit my parents, though he was too polite to tell me so to my face. He cited fear of lingering Furies as the main reason, and the fact that we had so many responsibilities in our roles as lord and queen of the Underworld to simply dash off whenever we wanted to.

Mr Graves didn't approve of any of us leaving at all, at first, for any reason, but as time went by and nothing bad happened – the realm of the dead returned to normal; hot, delicious meals began appearing again on the dining table three times a day, courtesy of the Fates; and new rooms and wings showed up in the castle as if by magic . . . a chapel for Chloe, a gym for Reed, a library for Mrs Engle, and a 'sick' game room for Alex, complete with every console imaginable – there was really no protest he could give. Nothing except – as Mr Graves stood outside the game room one night, watching, with his fully restored sight, Alex and Reed patiently explaining to Henry, Mr Liu and Frank the finer points of *Call of Duty* – 'We're doomed.'

'Cheer up,' Mrs Engle said to him. 'It's better than Furies.'

'Is it?' Mr Graves didn't seem certain.

Mrs Engle laughed and hugged him. Flowers were blooming everywhere after the storm, even in the most unexpected places.

We may have had to listen to the sound of video game explosions ringing through the rest of the castle, but John and I couldn't hear them from the privacy of our bedroom, which we did not, thankfully, have to share any more with anyone else, as the Fates generously supplied everyone with a room of their own.

Still, as the days after the storm stretched into weeks, and the weeks stretched into months, I found that, though I had more happiness than I'd ever dreamed possible, living with John in the Underworld and doing work I actually enjoyed and found meaningful, I was missing . . . something.

Not school, of course, since unlike Kayla, I didn't have a goal outside the realm of the dead towards which I'd been striving (Frank had become Kayla's primary investor in Save

Yourselves, though I knew that, when the time came, I'd invest, as well).

And not the sunshine, either, since any time I wanted I could slip out the door at the top of the double staircases through which I'd once bolted so madly, and take a stroll through the Isla Huesos Cemetery (though I rarely mentioned doing so to John, who would definitely not have approved, even though I always kept my whip at my side).

It seemed ungrateful of me to complain, since I had so much happiness, and there were so many people in the world who would have been happy with a mere sliver of my portion of it. But I couldn't help wishing that, now that they were finally back together again, I could spend more time with my parents.

Yet it always seemed as if just when my parents and I began to relax in one another's company, it was time to go back to the Underworld.

I understood why John didn't feel comfortable hanging out in Dolphin Key. More than once, Chief Santos dropped by my parents' house for an impromptu 'visit' that happened to coincide with one that John and I were making. Was he watching the house . . . or John? The chief of police was no dummy. He hadn't believed a word we'd told him in the cemetery. He knew something was wrong and was still determined to get to the bottom of it . . . someday.

He wasn't wrong, either. Ever since I'd met John, our lives had been in perpetual danger, and a lot of that danger had come from a member of my family, one who didn't seem particularly anxious to make amends. I'd heard that the burn my diamond had singed into my grandmother's skin had left a permanent scar.

But Grandma couldn't remember – or, at least, pretended not to – how she'd got it. She seemed to remember very little about what had happened during the time she'd been possessed. She even turned out not to have much of a work ethic, since Knuts for Knitting began to fail financially. This was only partly because Mr Smith's partner, Patrick, had stopped buying his knitting supplies there.

Grandma began to complain that if things didn't look up she was going to have to close the shop and move away.

'Good riddance,' said my father. Apparently his motto of forgiving and forgetting didn't apply to people who'd tried to kill his daughter.

The only person who offered to help was a distant cousin in Tampa, who sent Grandma a brochure on an assisted living community founded by her church. Grandma became enchanted with the idea, sold both her house and Knuts for Knitting and left Isla Huesos, another piece of bracken the storm had swept away.

This suited everyone fine except for John, who still didn't believe we'd seen the last of her.

'Even after she's dead and we've sent her on,' he said, 'I still won't trust her evil spirit not to show up and try to hurt you again.'

Patrick, on the other hand, made a full recovery. Mr Smith would tell me about it when I'd happen upon him in the cemetery, which I visited even more often as the days grew colder, now that winter was upon us (though winter on Isla Huesos meant that the temperature occasionally dipped below seventy degrees).

'I'd think you'd have bad memories of this place,' Mr Smith said, falling into step beside me one evening as the sun was setting.

'I don't,' I said, amused. 'It seems peaceful and beautiful to me.' We were near John's crypt, the roof of which had been repaired. The branches of the poinciana tree were bare of blossoms, but that was all right. I'd been assured it would bloom again in the spring. 'Maybe because it's where I met John.'

'Strange,' Mr Smith said. 'I can remember a time when you didn't think quite so fondly of him as you do now.'

'I can remember a time when he didn't think so fondly of me, either,' I said wryly.

'No such time existed,' Mr Smith said. 'I know another person who thinks fondly of you. Patrick. He often asks about you. He wants me to invite you and John over for dinner. He doesn't understand, of course—'

Mr Smith delicately avoided mentioning what it was that Patrick didn't understand, that John and I were Underworld royalty and couldn't go out to eat like normal people. Also that Patrick had been struck from behind, and so unable to identify his attackers, one of whom might very well have been my grandma. There'd been a second set of fingerprints found at the scene that the police had never been able to identify.

'Patrick keeps reminding me that you never tried his lobster tacos,' Mr Smith said.

This struck me to the heart. I longed to go back to their

house and enjoy their festive hospitality and have the lobster tacos I'd missed. *Why couldn't we?* I wondered. The storm was over. The sun was shining. Why were we still hiding?

I put the question to John later that evening as we lay in bed together in front of a roaring fire in the hearth.

'Obviously it wouldn't be a good idea, I know, to run off and leave the Underworld for months and months at a time,' I said, 'because then you'll turn into a hundred-and-sixty-year-old man—'

He ignored my attempt at humour.

'But a few days or nights here and there . . . what would be the harm? Mr Liu and Mr Graves, now that he can see, can certainly handle things for a night or two. I'm not saying it would ever be a good idea to leave Chloe and Reed in charge, or – God forbid – Frank or Henry, but Mrs Engle has turned out to have a nice soothing influence on everyone. Even Alex . . . well, I wouldn't trust Alex to bird-sit, and Alastor would eat him alive, but surely he could be kept from burning the place down. And we, in turn, could look after things for everyone else if *they* wanted to go away for a bit, like we do whenever Frank wants to go visit Kayla. Speaking of Kayla, surely there must be some reason my necklace still turns purple around her even though she's not in danger any more. Maybe she's supposed to be my queen-in-waiting. Maybe we could get her to come here and queen-sit a few nights a month.'

John lowered the book he'd been reading. 'I'm sorry,' he said. 'Were you speaking to me?'

'I know you were listening,' I said in disgust, taking the

339

book from him and tossing it over the side of the bed. 'You couldn't possibly have been reading that. You were holding it upside down.'

He laughed and put his arms round me. 'How can I read when you're next to me? Your beauty is too much of a distraction for any man to concentrate.'

'Don't try to flatter your way out of this,' I said. 'Even Persephone got six months' vacation away from the Underworld every year.'

'Is that what you want?' he asked, drawing away a little, looking hurt. 'Six months' vacation away from me every year?'

'No,' I cried, instantly regretting my choice of words. It was hard to remember sometimes that, even though he was very much the lord of this castle, a part of him was also still very much the wounded beast it had taken me so long to tame. I doubted the wounds the Furies – and I, though inadvertently – had inflicted upon him in the past would ever fully heal. 'Of course not.'

'Well, what am I supposed to think?' he asked. 'You won't marry me, and all you ever talk about is how you want to go away. Don't think I'm not aware of your rambles in the cemetery—'

'Not away *from* you. Away *with* you. So we can live a normal life in the sunshine, just for a little while.'

'Normal people get married,' he said, lifting a dark eyebrow.

'Normal people have their own houses under the sky,' I said. 'They don't live in castles in the Underworld.'

He thought about this for a moment.

'We could do both,' he suggested finally.

I caught my breath. 'Do you mean it?'

He nodded. 'I don't see why not. We could have a little house and stay in it sometimes. *Not near your mother's house,*' he added sternly, when he saw my face light up. 'I don't want to live anywhere close to your father. And you must know, Pierce, your grandmother will never enter our doorway.'

'No, of course not. Oh, John, I know the perfect place.' I sat up so abruptly that Hope, who was perched on the end of the bed, gave a flutter, startling her mate, whom we'd settled upon calling Courage, so we had both Hope and Courage with us at all times. 'Mr Smith lives in a cute little Victorian condo downtown. They all look out on to this pool in the back, with the sweetest garden. It's on the highest point on the island, and when there's a storm, they have hurricane parties, and Patrick makes lobster tacos. We could get a place there. Since we'd only be staying there every once in a while, it wouldn't have to be very big. And we'd have neighbours we knew right away.'

John smiled at me, then reached over to smooth a strand of my dark hair away from my face. 'Is that what you want?'

'I think it would be nice,' I said, reluctant to reveal to him how very much I wanted it, in case it didn't work out. I knew there was nothing he wouldn't do for me – except allow me to be hurt – and it would be complicated, if not downright impossible, for a young man with no credit whatsoever to buy a condominium. 'My father could lend us the money.'

I knew John would never take a handout from my father. He'd insisted on paying Dad back for the boats. I'd wisely stayed out of that conversation, but I'd seen the way it had irritated my father. Dad loved throwing his money around.

What he did not love was having money thrown back at him.

John knew this, so it wasn't a surprise to me when his smile broadened. 'Frank's not the only one who's been saving his gold coins, you know.'

'Really?' I eyed him. 'I thought you planted them all in Seth Rector's locker.'

'There are a lot more where those came from,' John said. Then he grew serious. 'But remember, Pierce, if we do this, the Underworld must always be our first and only priority. We can never neglect the dead.'

'Of course we can't neglect the dead,' I said, leaning down to hug him again. 'I owe everything I hold most precious to the dead: you.' Then I added, 'But I couldn't help thinking it might be a good idea for us to get a place outside the Underworld because maybe, after we're married, we could—'

'Wait,' he interrupted, surprised. '*After* we're married? Now you *want* to get married?'

'No, of course not *now*,' I said. 'We have to wait until after Kayla has her business up and running and has had her surgery, because she wants to be my bridesmaid, and she says she doesn't want her boobs to look humongous in the photos. Well, the photos of her and me, since you'll probably show up as a big blur in them, like you always do on film.'

John was silent for a moment. Then he said, 'I love you,

but approximately half the time I don't understand what you're saying.'

'The feeling is mutual,' I assured him. There was a pause, and then I took a deep breath and said, all in a rush, 'What I was trying to say before was that another reason it would be good for us to have our own place outside the Underworld is that maybe, after we get married, we could have a baby.'

He lifted his head from the pillow, then rolled over suddenly, trapping me beneath his arms and staring down at me very intently. '*What?*'

'Well,' I said, embarrassed. My cheeks were burning, but I plunged on anyway. 'I was doing some reading, and Mr Smith is wrong – not for the first time, but whatever. Hades and Persephone *did* have children. They're largely forgotten in Greek mythology, but they do exist. I figure they must have been conceived during the months Persephone wasn't in the Underworld, since, as you know, no life can grow here. So I don't see why we can't do the same thing.' I felt as if I were going to be roasted alive by the heat of his gaze. 'You do *want* a baby someday, don't you? I never even asked what you thought about the idea—'

He showed me, very enthusiastically, what he thought about it by kissing me hard, on the lips . . . then kissing me in other places as well.

He seemed to like the idea very, very much.

Which just goes to show that anything can happen. Anything at all.

One. Two. Three.

Blink.

AFTERWORD

The question I get most often from readers at the close of a book series is, 'Is it really the end?'

Of course Pierce and John and their friends could continue to have many adventures, and perhaps someday we'll hear from them again, but for now it seems best to give them a well-deserved rest.

The inspiration for this series came from Edith Hamilton's fantastic book, *Mythology*. I loved reading this book when I was growing up. The myth of Persephone was always my favourite. I used to wish the Greek god of the Underworld would kidnap me so I could live amongst the dead.

Some of the characters in this series were inspired by myths, and some by real people. Alastor, John's horse, is named after one of the four black horses who pulled the chariot driven by Hades when he kidnapped Persephone (in the Roman version of the tale). Typhon, the tongue-in-cheek name John gives his dog, is also derived from the 'father of all monsters' who attempts to destroy Zeus.

The character of Mr Smith, the dry-witted cemetery sexton, is partly based on an amazing English teacher I had in my freshman year in high school, Mr Kenneth Mann. By giving his students creative writing assignments in addition to the state-mandated curriculum, Mr Mann inspired not only myself but many of my fellow classmates at Bloomington High School South to want to become better writers (and consequently better human beings).

The character of Pierce, whose plight was loosely based on that of Persephone, was inspired by a close friend of mine who had a near-death experience. She filled me in on what it's like to be an 'NDE'. Much like Pierce, my friend says that only by nearly losing her life did she learn to live it to its fullest, and that the only way to fight the darkness is to bring a little light into the lives of those we love.

There are so many people to whom I am indebted for the help they gave me while I was writing this series I could never name them all, but they include Beth Ader, Nancy Bender, Jennifer Brown, Barb Cabot, Bill Contardi, Benjamin Egnatz, Michele Jaffe, Lynn Langdale, Laura Langlie, Ann Larson, Janey Lee, Charisse Meloto, Abigail McAden, Laura Wisen, and of course all my amazing readers. Thank you all. If I were in charge of the Underworld, you would get assigned to the 'good' boat.

MEG CABOT

LIST OF CHARACTERS AND PLACES

Alastor – permanent resident of the Underworld, John's large black stallion; named after one of the horses that pulled Hades's chariot

Alvarez, Mr – principal of Isla Huesos High School

A-Wing – one of the sections into which Isla Huesos High School is divided; allegedly only 'college-bound' academically and athletically gifted students are enrolled in A-Wing

Bryce – a friend of Seth Rector and Farah Endicott; A-Winger

Cabrero, Alexander, aka Alex – Pierce's cousin, her Uncle Chris's son; in New Pathways (D-Wing) programme; dies in the Isla Huesos cemetery in Book 2 but is revived by Pierce and John; now has to live in the Underworld

Cabrero, Christopher, aka Chris – Pierce's uncle, her mom's younger brother; in jail for sixteen years, just back and living with Grandma

Cabrero, Deborah, aka Mrs Oliviera, aka Dr Cabrero, aka Deb or Debbie – Pierce Oliviera's mother

Cabrero, Grandma Angela – mom of Deb, grandma of Pierce and Alex; Chris and Alex Cabrero live with her

Chloe – a girl who died and went to the Underworld and is waiting to pass on

Cody – a friend of Seth Rector and Farah Endicott; A-Wing

Coffin Fest – every year before Coffin Night, a street in Isla Huesos is closed to hold a festival to celebrate those who died but were not given proper burials – John Hayden and others whose coffins were lost in the Great Hurricane of 1846, which destroyed the island's cemetery; some say it also memorializes the people whose bones were found by the Spaniards in the 1500s, causing the island to be named Isla Huesos, or Island of Bones

Coffin Night – an event held only on the island of Isla Huesos during the high school's Homecoming. A coffin is constructed by the senior class and hidden somewhere on the island. The junior class then attempts to find the coffin. If they do so, they are allowed to burn the coffin on the fifty yard line of the school's football field. This means the junior class has 'burned' the seniors. If the juniors fail to the find the coffin, the seniors are said to have 'buried' the juniors

Day, Henry – permanent member of the Underworld, ten years old, blue eyes, former ship's boy on the *Liberty*; dresses in 1840s garb

D-Wing – one of the sections into which Isla Huesos High School is divided; only members of the New Pathways counselling programme for 'troubled' students are enrolled in D-Wing; looked down on by most A-Wingers

Endicott, Farah – Seth Rector's girlfriend; A-Winger and cheerleader

Endicott, Mr – Farah's father; doing spec development on Reef Key with Mr Rector

Engle, Mrs – a woman who died and went to the Underworld and is waiting to pass on

Fates – positive spirits (antitheses of the Furies); not much is known about who/what they are, but the Underworld needs them in order to function properly

Frank – permanent resident of the Underworld, assists John in loading passengers on to boats; attracted to Pierce's friend Kayla Rivera

Furies – evil spirits who've come back to seek revenge on John for where they ended up after passing on

Graves, Mr – permanent resident of the Underworld

Hayden brothers – John's three older half-brothers, lazy spendthrifts, each worse than the last

Hayden, John – the tortured lord of the Underworld, permanent resident; in love with Pierce

Hope – a tame, pale mourning dove that John gives Pierce for company in the Underworld; is able to travel to Earth as well as the afterworld

Isla Huesos – southernmost island off the tip of Florida, where Pierce and her mother moved from Westport, Connecticut, several month earlier; discovered in the 1500s by the Spanish; name means Island of Bones; tourist attraction visited by large number of cruise ships

Liu, Mr – permanent member of the Underworld

Mike – tattooed groundskeeper at IH Cemetery; possessed by the Furies

New Pathways – a programme at Isla Huesos High School for 'troubled' students who are not academically inclined and may need more attention or counselling than average or 'gifted' students; classes are held in the school's D-Wing

Nicole – a friend of Seth Rector and Farah Endicott; A-Winger

Oliviera, Pierce, aka Piercey to Uncle Chris – permanent resident of the Underworld

Oliviera, Zachary, aka Zack – Pierce's father

Ortega, Jade – New Pathways counsellor at IHHS

Ortega, Mrs – Jade's grandmother

Persephone Diamond – large diamond pendant John gives to Pierce when she first arrives in the Underworld in Book 1; it is said to have been forged by Hades and given to his wife Persephone to protect her from the Furies; it turns silver/grey around John, black when a Fury or other threat is nearby, purple around Pierce's friend Kayla Rivera

Rector, Mr – Seth's father, doing spec development on Reef Key with Mr Endicott; was high school boyfriend of Deb Cabrero, and prom king

Rector, Seth – IHHS senior class president, a student leader; he and his friends refer to themselves as the Rector Wreckers; A-Winger

Rector, William – ancestor of current Rectors, involved in intentional 'wrecker' scheme to destroy the *Liberty*

Reed – a boy who died and went to the Underworld and is waiting to pass on

Reynolds, Patrick – Richard Smith's life partner

Rivera, Kayla – best friend of Pierce Oliviera and Alex Cabrero; member of New Pathways programme and a D-Winger

Santos, Chief of Police, aka Chief Santos – chief of police of Isla Huesos

Serena – SerenaSweetie online name; friend of Seth Rector and Farah Endicott; A-Winger

Smith, Richard – Isla Huesos cemetery sexton; only living person on earth besides Pierce who both knows about the Underworld *and* has a relationship with John, and that's because he's an expert on death deities

Typhon – permanent resident of the Underworld, a large, wolf-like dog that is loyal to John